Murder
at the
Washington
Tribune

MURDER
AT THE
WASHINGTON
TRIBUNE

A CAPITAL CRIMES NOVEL

Margaret Truman

Ballantine Books • New York

Murder at The Washington Tribune is a work of fiction. Names, characters, places, and incidents are the products of the author's imagination or are used fictitiously. Any resemblance to actual events, locales, or persons, living or dead, is entirely coincidental.

Published in the United States by Ballantine Books, an imprint of The Random House Publishing Group, a division of Random House, Inc., New York.

BALLANTINE and colophon are registered trademarks of Random House, Inc.

ISBN 0-345-47819-3

Printed in the United States of America on acid-free paper

www.ballantinebooks.com

9 8 7 6 5 4 3 2 1

First Edition

AUTHOR'S NOTE

Readers of other books in my Capital Crimes series know that I always use real Washington places whenever possible. I've never seen a reason to create fictitious restaurants, hotels, parts of the city, or its institutions when so many wonderful real ones exist.

But for this book, I've found a reason to deviate from that practice and to fabricate a newspaper, *The Washington Tribune*.

As everyone knows, there is a real newspaper in Washington, D.C., *The Washington Post*, one of the nation's most influential publications. Politics is Washington's biggest "industry," and what the *Post* publishes each day about our government can have tremendous impact on readers around the country, and at times the world. At the same time, it is a quintessential hometown newspaper, unlike its competitor, *The New York Times*, a national newspaper that simply happens to be published in New York.

There is also *The Washington Times*, an unabashedly right-wing daily paper founded and owned by the Rev. Sun Myung Moon, self-proclaimed ruler of the universe. The *Times* offers no substantial competition for the *Post* despite having some good journalists on its staff.

So, why not *Murder at The Washington Post*, or *Murder at The Washington Times*?

Because certain characters in this book are decidedly unsavory and professionally bankrupt, I'm certain the *Post* or the *Times* would not appreciate having them portrayed as employees of their publications, nor would they countenance the linking of murder with their brand names on the cover of a bestselling novel. More to the point, neither *The Washington Post* nor *The Washington Times*, nor any of the people associated with either paper, in fact played any part in inspiring the characters I've imagined for my book, or the story I've told. And who wants to get letters of complaint instead of letters of praise?

So, *The Washington Tribune* it shall be, and any similarity to the real newspapers in Washington is purely coincidental.

Margaret Truman

New York City

2005

MURDER AT THE WASHINGTON TRIBUNE

ONE

Another speaker came to the podium.

Joe Wilcox leaned close to his wife and muttered just loud enough for her pretty ears only, "Another speaker." He shifted position in his chair and twisted his neck against a growing stiffness and full-blown boredom. With them at a front table were three couples, others from *The Washington Tribune* and their spouses who'd agreed to attend the awards evening with the Wilcoxes out of friendship, or obligation, or maybe a little of both.

The dinner was an annual event for the Washington Media Association, whose members came from the ranks of Washington, D.C.'s, print and broadcast journalists. Like most such groups, its leadership was fond of bestowing awards on deserving members and on their chosen profession, giving that same leadership a reason for taking to the podium to express their views on many things, mostly political. An occasional, usually accidental, bit of humor provided blessed audience relief from those who spoke endlessly, others longer.

At least they're getting to the awards, Wilcox thought as the speaker said "In conclusion" for the third time. Wilcox looked to a table at which his daughter, Roberta, sat. She was the reason Joe and Georgia were there.

The speaker at the podium finally did conclude, and the bestowing of awards commenced, twenty-two in all. Three weeks later—or so it seemed—Roberta was the sixteenth recipient called to the podium to accept the award for Best Local Investigative Reporting—Broadcast, accompanied by the producer and the director of a TV series they'd done on corruption within the Washington MPD.

"Doesn't she look beautiful?" Georgia said.

"Of course she does," Wilcox replied. "Because she is."

Roberta Wilcox did look stunning that evening in a stylish pantsuit the color of ripe peaches. But it was radiance from within that created a virtual aura around her, enhanced by a bright smile that had lit up the nightly news since she'd joined the station three years earlier. "The best-looking newscaster in D.C." was the consensus. She usually wore her auburn hair pulled back when on the air, but this evening she'd let it down, framing an oval face with inquisitive raisin-brown eyes, her skin fair but not pale, her makeup tastefully underapplied. She thanked the station for having given her the freedom and support to pursue the exposé, read helpful names from a slip of paper including the producer and director, and ended by crediting her parents for having instilled in her the natural curiosity necessary to get the job done. "Of course," she added, "I come from good reportorial stock. My father is as good a reporter as there is in this city." She watched him wince, tossed him a kiss off her fingertips, and led her fellow award winners back to their table.

It was announced from the podium that the evening had come to an end, and most of the three hundred men and women left their tables to mingle, gravitating to familiar faces and offering congratulations to the winners, and to their families.

"How'd an ugly guy like you end up with such a knockout of a daughter?" a *Trib* reporter asked Wilcox, accompanied by a laugh and a slap on the back.

"Her mother's genes," Wilcox replied, nodding in the direction of his wife, who'd gone to Roberta's table to talk with her and her celebrating tablemates.

"Must be," Wilcox's friend said. He lowered his voice. "What do you think of Hawthorne getting an award?" Gene Hawthorne, a *Trib* Metro reporter, had been cited for a three-part series he'd done on a local bank's illegal payoffs to a district official.

Wilcox shrugged, which accurately reflected what he was thinking. Hawthorne, in his late twenties, did not rank high on his list of favorite people. Wilcox wasn't alone in his negative view of the abrasive, aggressive young reporter who had a penchant for rubbing colleagues the wrong way, his knife always in search of an unprotected back, it seemed, and there were few toes fast enough to avoid being stepped on. Equally galling was the backing he received from the *Trib*'s ranking editors and management, who obviously viewed the young, smug, sandy-haired, self-possessed reporter as a rising star, which, of course, he was, a bit of news that wasn't lost on anyone at the *Trib*, Joe included.

He saw in the young reporter something of himself years ago when he'd come to *The Washington Tribune*, brimming with ambition and possessing the energy to fuel it. But it had been different at the paper twenty-three years ago. Then, there were still plenty of grizzled veteran reporters from whom to learn, men (almost exclusively) who lived the life of a reporter as portrayed in movies and plays, characters straight out of *The Front Page*, their heads surrounded by blue cigarette and cigar smoke, pints of whiskey in their desk drawers, the rattle and clank of their typewriters testifying to their daily output, spoken words tough and profane, written words sharp and to the point. There weren't many of them left. The younger *Trib* reporters, including Wilcox, had been hired to supplement that veteran staff. But eventually Gene Hawthorne and dozens of men and women like him had been brought in to replace the over-fifty crowd. There had been a flurry of buyouts offered over the past few years, and many newsroom veterans had jumped at the severance package with its generous cash settlement, pension options, and health and life insurance. In came the new blood, working at half the pay of the reporters who'd gone on to their retirement, or in many cases new jobs. One of the *Trib*'s top economics reporters had left on a Friday; his byline appeared over an article in the *Trib* the following Monday, written for a wire service that had eagerly hired him.

It just wasn't the same anymore for Joe Wilcox. He was now a mem-

ber of the dinosaur club himself and was viewed with a certain barely dis-
guised scorn by Hawthorne and his cadre of young hotshots. Joe was two
years from fifty-five, the buyout age, with the lapel pin certifying that
he'd given *The Washington Tribune* the best twenty-five years of his life.

Roberta and Georgia approached and Roberta gave him a hug. She
was taller than her father.

"Thanks for the plug," he said.

"I meant it," she said.

"You look great, honey. Congratulations. That was a hell of a piece
you did."

"I wonder if anyone at MPD will ever congratulate me," she said.

Wilcox laughed. "I'm sure the police are preparing a proclamation
as we speak naming you honorary cop of the year."

"I know it was awkward for you," Roberta said, her expression as serious as her words.

"They'll get over it," he said. "I still have friends over there who
agreed with you. They all suffer when a few foul balls taint the entire
force."

"But if they knew you'd fed me some of the information I used—"

"Which they won't. Don't give it another thought, sweetie."

"Anything new on Kaporis?" she asked.

His response was a shake of his head, and a tiny smile for a thought
that came and went. This daughter-journalist had not asked the question
out of natural curiosity.

⁂

Like her father, Roberta Wilcox had been reporting on the killing of Jean
Kaporis, a young woman who'd joined the *Trib* less than a year ago,
fresh out of the University of Missouri's school of journalism. Kaporis
had been assigned to the paper's "Panache" section, helping cover the
city's vibrant social scene: the weddings of those whose names were
well known enough to justify coverage, fundraisers—a day didn't pass in
Washington when someone wasn't raising funds for something deemed
worthy of their time and effort, important or whimsical—and ideally a
scandal among the rich and famous and thin, a political faux pas, a fatu-
ous misstep that would leave readers tittering. It wasn't the sort of assign-

ment she preferred, but she knew it represented a starting point for many newly hired female reporters, and she threw herself into it, hoping her work would capture the attention of someone in a position to move her into hard news.

That kind of break hadn't happened during her time at the *Trib*. But she had one advantage. She was lovely. Male heads turned and pulse rates sped up whenever she sauntered through the newsroom wearing skirts, sweaters, and blouses that accented her ripe body, donning a linen blazer in summer now and then as a nod to corporate correctness. No doubt about it, Jean Kaporis was a splendid example of young womanhood, every curve and bump properly placed, good genes in ample evidence, and especially a pleasant, willing personality to go with it, all of which attracted many people to her—including whoever had strangled her to death.

A maintenance man found her early one morning a month ago in a secluded second-floor supply closet at the far end of the main newsroom, bruises on her neck, pretty mouth going in the wrong direction as though someone had removed it and carelessly pasted it back on. The autopsy reported that she'd died from manual strangulation, her throat and larynx damaged from pressure exerted by her assailant's hands and fingers. The presence of petechial hemorrhages in the mucous membrane lining the inner surface of her eyelids provided presumptive evidence of strangulation. She'd bitten her tongue, a not-uncommon occurrence with victims of strangulation. The struggle with her attacker had been brief. Although laboratory analysis indicated she'd engaged in sexual intercourse within twenty-four hours of death, there was no outward sign of having been sexually assaulted.

⟨※⟩

"No, nothing new," he told his daughter. "They've been questioning everyone at the paper. Makes sense."

"And?"

"No 'ands,' Roberta. That's all I know. Maybe you know something you'd like to share."

She shook her head.

"Let you know if anything breaks," he said.

She smiled and squeezed his arm. "And I'll do the same."

"Back to the house for a drink?" Georgia asked their daughter.

"Thanks, no, Mom. I promised the guys from the station I'd go out with them."

"Ah, youth," Wilcox said. *Wasted on the young.* To his wife: "What say we call it a night?"

Georgia nodded and kissed her daughter on the cheek. "Not too late," she said. "You need your beauty sleep."

"Mom!"

"I know, I know, but—"

"Not too late," Joe Wilcox echoed, a wide grin crossing his craggy face. "And eat breakfast. You should always start the day with a good breakfast. Diane Sawyer does."

As the Wilcoxes and hundreds of others poured out of the Washington Hilton and Towers on to Connecticut Avenue NW, they were confronted with a chaotic crime scene. A half-dozen marked police cars, lights flashing and radios crackling, had blocked off the wide thoroughfare. Yellow crime scene tape marked an area of the sidewalk almost directly in front of the hotel's main entrance. A body covered by a white cloth lay on the sidewalk inside the taped-off section.

"Hey, Joe!"

A colleague from a competing paper, with whom Joe had covered myriad crime scenes, came up to the couple.

"What happened?" Wilcox asked.

"A drive-by. Middle-aged white guy."

"He's dead?" Georgia asked.

"Very." To Joe: "You covering?"

"No. Night off. This is the same spot where Hinckley shot Reagan back in eighty-one."

"That's right," said the reporter, making a note in his pad. "Forgot about that."

"Let's go," Georgia said.

Wilcox took a final look at the body, shook his head, took his wife's arm, and maneuvered through the crowd in the direction of the parking garage. As they pulled onto the street, Georgia said, "If you want to go back, Joe, I'll drive home. You can take a car service."

"Thanks but no thanks. I'm not missing anything. There'll be another murder to cover tomorrow. There always is. No, this is Roberta's night, and I don't want anything to spoil the memory of her up there getting her award. Damn, she looked good."

It was, he knew, what his wife wanted to hear. She squeezed his thigh and said, "Let's stop for ice cream. I'm in the mood."

"Then ice cream it'll be."

TWO

Joe and Georgia Wilcox had lived in their modest tract home in Rockville since the spring of 1977, having moved to this suburban area of the nation's capital from Detroit. Thirty minutes from downtown, twice that at rush hour, they'd seen their tranquil Maryland suburban haven blossom into an extension of D.C.'s urban sprawl, still leafy and family friendly, but changed from the day they moved in. Home prices had soared, roads and highways were clogged, and malls abounded. Still, it had been a pleasant place in which to live and to raise their daughter, who had been seven when they arrived.

❦

Leaving Detroit hadn't been an easy decision. They'd lived a comfortable, relatively stress-free life in one of the Motor City's suburbs. They were active in the community, their daughter happily attending grammar school, with Joe ensconced as a cityside reporter who'd broken a couple of big crime stories during his time at the *Free Press*. A shot at becoming an assistant Metro editor in a year or two was a distinct possibility.

That changed one day over lunch. Tom Melito, a newly minted friend from *The Washington Tribune*'s recently opened the Detroit bureau, mentioned to Wilcox that the *Trib* was beefing up its Metro staff in Washington, and thought Wilcox should consider applying.

"Damn," Wilcox said as a drop of soup landed on his tie. "I'm not a D.C. kind of guy," he said, dabbing at his tie with a napkin. "Can't take me anywhere. Never get invited to the White House with soup stains on my tie."

"Hey, presidents spill soup, too," said Melito. "Besides, have you ever known reporters who don't have stains on their ties?"

"And on their reputations," Wilcox said.

"Don't play cynic. Doesn't become you. Look, Joe, I'm serious. You're a helluva fine reporter, and the *Trib* is a hell of a paper, big and getting bigger and more influential every day and giving the hallowed *New York Times* a run for its money. The brain trust has decided to really ratchet up local coverage, and they're committing big bucks to it. Metro's already the biggest staff on the paper, and getting bigger. I don't know what you're making here but—"

"No," Wilcox said, shaking his head and inserting his napkin between buttons on his shirt. "I'd never get it past Georgia. She's happy with her job at the library, and Roberta's doing well in school. Besides, my boss winks that he's grooming me for an assistant editor job down the road. But thanks for suggesting it, Tommy."

They spoke about other things during lunch, but Joe's thoughts weren't entirely on those topics. *The New York Times* and *The Washington Tribune* had been in competition for as long as he could remember, vying for the biggest stories with the most impact on the body politic and the nation's conscience. Like every youngster with Yankee pinstripes or Dodger blue in their fanciful futures, *The Times* and the *Trib* represented the big leagues to journalism students across the country, and he was no exception. Sure, there were plenty of jobs in the reporting business that were meaningful and fulfilling. But those two competing newspaper giants in New York and Washington represented "making it," whatever that meant. The *Trib*, he knew, tended to be more sensational than *The Times* in its news coverage, and had its share of critics because of that. But it was no tabloid. It had broadsheet clout, and anyone working for it did, too.

"Joseph Carlton Wilcox at the esteemed *Washington Trib*, huh?" he said to Melito over dessert, laughing at the very notion of it.

"Suit yourself, Joe, but they're looking for Young Turks like you. I don't qualify."

"What are you, over the hill?"

"I am as far as they're concerned back in D.C. They sent me out here to wind down, go peacefully into the night, cover the latest car models, and make it sound like I care. Maybe you're right. It is intense in D.C. Cutthroat, like politics today. Get the story at all costs. Publish or perish ain't only for academics. Used to be fun. No more, and I can't say I'm unhappy being further away from it. But you? You're exactly what they're looking for. You could really make your name there, pal."

Wilcox grunted and dug into his apple pie. The topic didn't come up again until they had split the bill and were standing on the sidewalk.

"Sure you don't at least want to explore the *Trib* thing?" Melito asked. "I can give somebody a call."

"No, I. . . . Sure, Tommy, call somebody. It's not for me. But it'd be interesting to see what golden opportunity I'm passing up."

❧

Wilcox spent the afternoon interviewing two witnesses to a shooting at a downtown public housing complex and filed his story before leaving the office. He'd had trouble pushing aside the conversation with Melito, and thought of little else as he drove to the house he'd called home for the past couple of years. He decided not to even mention it to Georgia. No sense upsetting her with thoughts of another move. The *Detroit Free Press* was his third job since graduating from Northwestern seven years ago with a degree in journalism and marrying his college sweetheart. She'd been a good soldier about it, encouraging him as he moved from a weekly paper to a daily, and then to the larger daily where he now worked, each move advancing his career and bettering his salary. But he knew she considered the *Free Press* the culmination of that career, a major daily in a large city, with room for advancement. For her, this *was* the big time, and he sometimes agreed with her.

Still, there were those youthful visions of one day becoming, say, a foreign correspondent, trench coat and all, his generation's Edward R. Murrow, meeting with shadowy figures in exotic foreign cities while bombs burst around you, scooping others who were after the same story, front-page bylines on a paper like *The New York Times* or *The Washington Tribune* and the resulting notoriety, including prizes—*a Pulitzer for little Joey Wilcox from Kankakee?* Maybe he'd start smoking a pipe.

A pipe *dream*, he knew, like envisioning himself hitting the home run that would lead his favorite baseball team, the Chicago Cubs, into the World Series—finally! He was a beat reporter, covering the city of Detroit the way Hamill and Breslin did in New York, and Kupcinet did in Chicago. *A foreign correspondent?* You've been watching too many movies, he told himself. Be happy with who you are and what you've got.

He eagerly took Melito's call the next day.

"Hey, Joe, just wanted you to know that I got through to my guy in D.C."

"And?"

"Talked to Paul Morehouse. He's assistant managing editor of the Metro section, part of the new regime, a no-nonsense guy but okay. Rough cob. Came over from *The Baltimore Sun*. I told him all about you, in glowing terms, of course, and he said he'd be interested in getting a call."

"I really appreciate it, Tom, but—"

Melito rattled off Morehouse's phone number. "Got it?"

"No, give it to me again."

This time, Wilcox wrote it down.

"It's his private line. Call him." Melito said. "You've got nothing to lose, maybe lots to gain."

Wilcox left the paper that afternoon to make the call from a gas station phone booth. Morehouse answered. He sounded gruff and distracted and squeezed a series of rapid-fire questions into a few minutes. When it was obvious to Wilcox that the conversation was about to end, Morehouse asked, "You as good as Tommy Melito says?"

"I don't know," Wilcox replied. "What did he say?"

"Send me a resume and some clips. If I like what I see, I'll pass it on to Human Resources." He laughed, a bark. "Christ, it used to be Personnel. I'll get back to you."

Wilcox decided to follow through on Morehouse's request without informing Georgia. He'd come to the conclusion that it was a wasted exercise; nothing would come of it. Five days after sending the material by priority mail, he received a call at the *Free Press* from Morehouse. "Can you talk?" the editor asked.

Wilcox looked around the newsroom. "No," he said.

"Call me back."

That night, after dinner had been cleared and Roberta was in her room, Wilcox told his wife of his flirtation with *The Washington Tribune*.

"They want you to go to Washington for an interview?"

"Yes."

"And you want to do it?"

"I think so. It could be a wonderful opportunity for me."

"For *you*. What about us, me and Roberta?"

"I think you'd enjoy living in Washington, Georgia. It's a nice city. Morehouse said the *Trib* is beefing up at every level, in every department. They're willing to pay for the right people."

Georgia turned in her web chair on their small patio and looked out over the garden she'd so tenderly cultivated. A single tear ran down her cheek, and Wilcox moved his chair closer, placing a hand on her shoulder. "Hey," he said, "I don't have the job. Nobody's offered it to me yet. And if you feel that strongly about it, I'll call Morehouse and tell him I've changed my mind, that I'm not interested."

She said nothing for a minute, her attention still on the garden. Then she turned, took his face in her hands, and said, "No, go for the interview, Joe. If you don't, you'll spend the rest of your life wondering what you missed, and that wouldn't be good for us, for our marriage. I just wish you'd included me from the beginning. I fear surprises." She brightened. "Nothing ventured, nothing gained, Joe." He smiled at her use of the cliché. She knew and used more of them than anyone else he knew.

Two days later, Wilcox took a personal day and flew to Washington where he sat with Paul Morehouse in the editor's cubicle on the perimeter of the *Trib*'s Metro newsroom. The air was thick with smoke; the keyboards provided a cacophonous background to their conversation. At first, he was put off by Morehouse's crusty persona that bordered on rudeness. But he soon sensed that behind that exterior was a committed man, someone who had no patience with fools or pretenders. *Like my father,* Wilcox thought as the interview continued, interrupted frequently by phone calls and people sticking their heads into the office with questions. He even got in some questions of his own.

"Say hello to Joe Wilcox," Morehouse told a heavyset reporter who'd walked into the cubicle wearing yellow suspenders with tiny green evergreen trees on them.

"Whaddya say, kid?" the reporter said, shaking Joe's hand.

"He wants a job here," Morehouse said.

The reporter laughed. "Good," he said. "You come to work here, the first person you come see is me. I'll fill you in, show you where the bodies are buried—and tell you who *should* be buried."

"Get out," Morehouse said, waving his hand.

"Nice meeting you, kid. Lotsa luck."

After another twenty minutes had passed, and Morehouse had asked questions ranging from pertinent to impertinent, he stood, yawned, and extended his arms over his head. "Interested?" he asked. He was a relatively short man, tightly packed with a deep chest and hard jaw, prematurely bald—Wilcox judged Morehouse to be only a few years older than he—the beginnings of gray at his temples. Bottle-green eyes seemed always to be asking a question: *Come on, come on, tell me more.*

"Yeah, I think I am," Wilcox said.

"You *think* you are?"

Wilcox smiled. "No, I know I am. Do you guys pay salaries?"

"Let's go to Human Resources. They get testy when we go over their heads about pay."

They went down a long, carpeted hallway lined with photographs from the paper's past, which went back to its founding in 1897. "You're married, huh?" Morehouse commented as they reached a door with the sign HR.

"Yes. Her name's Georgia. We have a daughter, Roberta."

"They okay with you coming to work here?"

"At first—yes, they're fine about it."

"Good. They won't see much of you once you're here," he said, opening the door. "HR'll work out moving expenses, benefits, that sort of stuff. No deep, dark secrets in your past, Joe? A good-looking young guy like you'll have the broads here in D.C. salivating, wife or no wife. HR'll run a background check, fingerprints, the works, like you were going in the army. Or the CIA. Welcome aboard. See you in three weeks."

❧

Three weeks later, Joe Wilcox arrived again in the nation's capital as one of a number of new hires at the powerful *Washington Tribune*. And now, twenty-three years later and forty pounds heavier, he and his wife sat in matching green recliners in the den of their home in Rockville, a tumbler of bourbon in his hand, a finger-pour of Kahlua in her glass, shoes off, feet up, the awards evening behind them.

"Here's to Roberta," Georgia said, raising her glass.

Wilcox lifted his glass and sipped.

"She's off to a good start," Georgia said. "It was sweet what she said about you tonight."

"It was good of her," he said, then added, "but obviously not true."

Georgia started to respond, but held back. The moment had all the trappings of what had lately become a frequent scene in their marriage, her husband lamenting what he considered his failing career, his wife trying to change the subject.

"Did you see what that silly congressman from New Jersey did yesterday on the floor of the House?"

Wilcox nodded and sipped his drink. "Silly is kind," he said.

Joe wasn't a heavy drinker; Georgia had never seen him even slightly tipsy in all the years they'd been together. But unlike some people who became morose after a few drinks, or expansive or even combative, Joe Wilcox tended to become somber and reflective, occasionally about life, especially his own. There were times, but only a few fleeting ones, when Georgia wondered whether her husband could ever become suicidal, so dark were his moods.

"Anything new on the murder at the paper?" she asked.

He shook his head as he went to a small bar, refilled his glass, and returned to the recliner. "Morehouse is on a rampage, wants it solved in-house by staffers, not the police. He wants the story. Edith Vargas-Swayze says he's even stonewalling the cops."

"Is he?"

"Could be. The guy gets more paranoid every day. Somebody comes up with a new rumor and he's ballistic."

She tucked her stocking feet beneath her. "It's scary to think some-one at the paper might have killed her."

"It is, isn't it? I get these pep talks from Morehouse that are supposed to motivate me to crack the story open, come up with some goddamn source within MPD who doesn't exist." His laugh was a snort, and he swirled the ice around in his glass. "Know how I know, Georgia, that the fire's gone from my belly?" She didn't respond. "I know it when I really don't care who killed Jean, except to want to pull the switch on him my-self. God, to see a beautiful young woman like that have her life snuffed out by some sick bastard. I care about that. But getting the story? It just doesn't seem that important to me any more."

"I can understand that," she said. "It's a matter of priorities. But get-ting the story is your job and—"

"Is it, Georgia? Maybe it was. I go to work these days because of the pension. I might as well work for some transit authority, be a toll taker or brakeman on a commuter train." He raised the glass to his lips again, drank, and intoned, "All aboard! Take your personal items with you and watch the closing doors. Toot! Toot!"

She laughed, although she didn't find it amusing. "You wanted to be a journalist, Joe, and you are, with one of the country's most important newspapers. You have every reason to be proud of what you've accom-plished."

"Really?" There was an edge to his voice that wasn't lost on her. "I'm no journalist. I'm a reporter. Proud of what, Georgia? Working the city-side beat for twenty-three years covering cops and robbers? That's hardly what I came to Washington for."

She finished her drink and stood. "I'm beat," she said. "Come on, let's go to bed."

"I'll be up in a while."

She kissed him on the forehead.

After she'd left the room, he got up and went to the wall where the family photos chronicled the past thirty years. Family, *this* family, was important to him. It was the only family he had. His mother and father were dead, as were uncles and aunts, their offspring somewhere in the country. He hadn't kept up with them. His only sibling, a brother, hadn't been heard from in twenty-five years.

Photos of Roberta on the wall at various stages of her life took center stage—graduation ceremonies from junior high, high school, and college, interspersed with candid color shots of birthday celebrations, family vacations, and other passages of a young woman's life. He was immensely proud of his daughter; taking out his handkerchief, he realized he was tearing up, which sometimes happened when he'd had a few drinks and slipped into his introspective self.

He shifted focus from the pictures to the few awards he'd garnered over the years. They amounted to nothing more in the aggregate than pro forma acknowledgments of having been with the *Trib* for twenty-three years, no more meaningful than yearly merit raises. At least the raises bought something tangible.

He was glad Georgia had abandoned him and gone to bed. Had she stayed, he knew what he would have heard from her: "*You have everything to be proud of, Joe. You're a respected reporter. More important, you're a good and decent man, a wonderful husband and father. I hate hearing you degrade yourself and what you've accomplished.*"

Fair enough. He'd feel better about himself—for a minute or two.

But then he'd point out that while he was proud of his family and his place in it, having achieved something greater in his career would not have diminished his role as a husband and father: "*Christ, Georgia, career success and family happiness aren't mutually exclusive.*"

They'd go back and forth a while longer before both realized the issue was beyond resolution. They weren't arguments; they were too predictable to qualify as such. The problem was—and he was quick to acknowledge to himself that this represented only his view—she didn't understand what happens to a man whose dreams are dashed. It can do bad things to you.

He poured what was left of his drink in the kitchen sink and went to the bathroom where his pajama bottoms hung from a hook on the back of the door. He brushed his teeth, rinsed, and took a long, hard look at his mirror image. He hadn't aged any worse than other men. There were jowls where they hadn't been thirty years ago, and his reddish-brown hair had thinned somewhat. His waist had thickened, as one might expect; he'd never been slender, built as he was on the stocky side.

He thought of his wife asleep in their bed, and his depression eased. *You're one lucky guy,* he silently told himself, and carried that thought with him to bed where he kissed her cheek before turning off the bedside lamp.

It took a long time for sleep to come.

THREE

Edith Vargas-Swayze sat at the counter of the Diner, on Eighteenth Street in Washington's Adams Morgan district and tried not to look at the man seated next to her. He was noisily enjoying French toast slathered with maple syrup and a side order of turkey hash. It was seven in the morning, too early to process that. She focused on her cornflakes with sliced banana and black coffee, her usual breakfast fare at this neighborhood institution open 24/7 every day of the year.

She wore a multicolored blouse over a white turtleneck and black slacks, more to conceal the bulge of her standard-issue Glock pistol than to make a fashion statement. She'd been an MPD cop for fifteen years, the past four of them as a detective in the Violent Crimes Branch, which used to be known as Homicide until the MPD brain trust, aided by high-priced consultants, conquered the city's appalling homicide rate with a stroke of the pen.

She'd been starting her day at the Diner for the past two years since she'd left her husband, Peter Swayze, and moved from downtown where they'd lived together to Adams Morgan, the ethnically mixed, lively community north of Dupont Circle named after John Quincy Adams and early settler Thomas Morgan. Their names also became a symbol of racial harmony in 1954 following the Supreme Court's decision in Brown v. The Board of Education. A white school, Adams, and a black school, Morgan, were merged into one, creating the city's only truly integrated community.

Divorce and relocation had been good moves. The marriage had been a mistake from the first. Not that Peter was a bad guy, nor could it be said that Edith hadn't worked at the marriage. But if there had ever been a clash of cultures, it was between the Hispanic Edith and the decidedly WASP Peter. "Good God, Peter, you don't even speak Spanish," his mother had said to him after being introduced to her son's choice of a mate. Edith laughed long and loud. She'd been born in the good ol' USA, thank you, in El Paso, Texas, and her English was every bit as correct as Peter's mother's, albeit decidedly saltier. There was also the divide between how she and Peter spent their days. Each morning, he went to his white-collar job at a local bank where he did something with money, while she spent her days and nights chasing crack dealers down unlit alleys and trying to not get her shoes bloody at grisly murder scenes. Even their skin tones had created a breach. Peter was the palest human being Edith had ever known, constantly changing sides of the street to avoid the sun. Edith couldn't get enough of it, turning her already dusky skin more like copper each summer day. Opposites certainly had attracted, and had repelled as quickly.

Moving to Adams Morgan had reunited her—mother Mexican, father half Spanish and half Irish—joining more than a quarter-million Hispanics living there: Cubans and Dominicans, Brazilians and Mexicans and a token number of Puerto Ricans. Plus, a growing Muslim population, plenty of African Americans, and Asians. Happily renting an apartment with a roof garden, she was free to spend her leisure time up there in a canvas recliner, a tall travel mug of iced Cuban coffee at her side, and ideally never again hearing Peter say, "You'll end up with skin cancer." That he was probably right wasn't the point.

She caught the busy waitress's eye, wrote in the air, and the check was placed before her as the man on the adjacent stool ordered another plate of hash.

"You get the papers yet?" the waitress asked Edith.

"Any day, says my lawyer. He's been saying that for weeks. Can't wait to get it over with and drop the hyphen in my name."

Although she'd been told repeatedly that she never needed to pay for her breakfast at the Diner—"Nice having a cop around," she was told—she always paid full price. She'd seen too many cops get in trouble for less than cornflakes and bananas. She left the Diner and started walking south briskly to catch the nearest Metro at Dupont Circle, a good hike, when her cell phone vibrated, then rang.

"Hello."

"*Buenos dias.*"

She smiled. He always greeted her in Spanish.

"Hello, Joe. *Como está usted?*"

"*Bien, gracias.* You didn't know I was a linguist, did you?"

"I still don't. What's up?"

"Jean Kaporis. What else could be up for me?"

"Nothing new, my friend, but I haven't clocked in yet."

"Morehouse is on the warpath. Or will be soon."

"Until he puts on war paint and starts carrying a spear, I wouldn't worry."

"What about poison arrowheads? He has several."

"Then I suggest you buy yourself a big shield and keep your distance. Look, I can't walk and talk at the same time. Chew gum either. I'll catch up with you later—*if* there's a break in the case."

"Thanks, Edith. Any scrap will do to feed the animals."

As Violent Crime Branch Detective Vargas-Swayze, soon to lose her hyphen, picked up her pace again, she couldn't help but think of the night she and Wilcox had ended up in bed together. Tell someone to not think of pink elephants and . . . A one-night stand, it was called, although they spent little of that night in a standing position. It had just seemed to happen, and it only happened once. Plenty of excuses on her part—the divorce, pressures at work, too much to drink, too long since she'd been in bed with a man. Him? He'd been riddled with guilt, which she'd tried to assuage, successfully, it seemed. "Let's forget about it," she'd said. "It was a one-time thing, Joe. Let's not let it get in the way of the friendship? Okay?"

"Okay," he'd said.

They hadn't mentioned it since.

Wilcox wasn't thinking of that night as he logged on to his computer in the *Trib*'s vast, carpeted, smoke-free, peaceful, and virtually silent newsroom, which had all the ambience of an insurance company. Only the barely audible tap dance of keyboards being stroked intruded on his thoughts.

His meeting earlier that morning with Paul Morehouse had gone poorly.

❧

"Look," Morehouse had yelled once Wilcox and Rick Jillian, a new reporter assigned to the Kaporis story, had settled in chairs across from him, "they're eating our lunch. Jesus Christ, she gets killed right here off our own newsroom and we're last on the MPD food chain. Come on, Joe, you used to be sourced over there, better than anybody on the beat. What's happened? How come all of a sudden they're stonewalling you?"

"They're not," Wilcox responded. He resented a need to go on the defensive. As far as he was concerned, he'd been working the case hard. "Nobody's eating nothing. All the other outlets have is speculation, and they make that sound like inside info. It's all BS."

"Even your daughter?" Morehouse asked.

"What about her?"

"She claimed on the tube that an interview she did with Jean's mother revealed possible suspects and motives. Was she right? What did the mother say?"

Wilcox didn't respond.

"You interviewed the mother. Right?"

"Right, and she didn't say anything that would point to a suspect or motive."

"Maybe you didn't ask the right questions."

"I asked the right questions. Paul, the decision was made upstairs to not turn Jean's murder into a tabloid circus, not here at the highly respected, above-the-fray *Washington Tribune*. Remember?"

The younger reporter turned in his chair to physically look away from Wilcox's sarcasm. Morehouse pretended to take in something interesting in the airshaft outside the office's single window before slowly returning his attention to the reporters. "Rick," he told the younger one, "run another check on visitors who signed in the day Jean died. I know, I know, we've been over it a hundred times but do it again."

Jillian and Wilcox stood.

"Stay a minute, Joe," Morehouse said.

The door closed, Morehouse said, "Come on, come on, Joe, lay it out for me."

"Lay what out?"

"What's eating you."

Wilcox started to respond but Morehouse pressed on.

"You know damn well what I'm talking about. You've been walking around lately with a chip on your shoulder, or looking like you swallowed one. That doesn't do me any good, or the paper. You're the best cops reporter I have, or am I talking past tense?"

Again, he didn't allow Wilcox to reply.

"I met with Mary yesterday. She's greenlighted a task force for the Kaporis story: you, Rick, a couple of researchers, a graphic artist, and that computer whiz, Kahlia, from Research. I want you to spearhead it—but not if you're about to go off the deep end and start seeing a shrink five times a week."

When Wilcox said nothing, Morehouse asked, "Are you?"

"No."

"Good. As long as we're leveling with each other, what's going on at MPD?"

Wilcox shrugged. "They're working the case. That's all I know."

"They're not talking to you?"

"Yeah, they're talking to me, but they don't have a hell of a lot to tell me."

"Because of Roberta? They punishing her old man because of the stuff she did on them?"

"No. That's not happening."

"How do you know?"

"I just—know."

"How far did you get talking to people here?"

"Staffers MPD questioned?"

"Yeah."

"I hit most of them, I think, at least those I know about."

"You think there are others? You think the cops talked to someone we don't know about?"

"It's possible."

"Get the list from MPD."

"They won't release it."

"Jesus, Joe, I don't care about it being *released*. Get it off the record. They spent days here interviewing people."

"And they still think she was killed by one of us."

"If that's true, then everybody upstairs would be very happy if we solved it in-house. Jean's murder is still high profile a month later. Still hot, and will continue to be. There are actually people out there who think the world would be better off if all reporters got whacked. Maybe we can't play Sherlock and bust the case ourselves, but we should at least be out front with coverage. We're it. Come on, Joe, suck it up. Get your team together and pull out all the stops. You'll have your own account number to bill the team's expenses against. This could be the story you've been waiting for your whole goddamn career."

When Wilcox returned to the newsroom, Rick Jillian was there along with Kathleen Lansden, one of two researchers recruited to join the Kaporis task force. Wilcox sat heavily in his chair and looked up at them. "Task force," he said. "Why didn't they come up with a task force a month ago?"

"I guess because—" Jillian started to say.

"Yeah?" Wilcox asked.

"I guess because they figured you were all they needed, Joe. You know, with your sources and—"

"And they were wrong. Is that what you're saying?"

"No, I'm not saying that. Anyway, you want me to get the others together?"

Wilcox smiled to break the tension. "A meeting is a good idea," he said. "How about the end of the day, say six? Nail down a conference room and we'll lay out everything we have. You'd better get on what Morehouse said, check that list again of visitors the day Jean got it: guests up here in editorial, tradespeople, everybody."

"Okay."

Wilcox said to Kathleen, "Pull up that database again, Kathleen, the one listing interviews other media did with Jean's friends and family. Compare it against the interviews I did—*we* did. Let's see who we missed."

"Shall do."

Now alone, Wilcox pulled out notes he'd made. The list was long, more than forty names, many of them editorial coworkers known to have been in the building the night Kaporis was murdered. Interviewing them had brought out overt resentment in some: *"What the hell are you saying, Joe, that I might have killed her?"* Many of them had also been interviewed by a team of MPD detectives headed by Edith Vargas-Swayze, who'd asked tougher questions than Wilcox. He'd placed a red dot next to their names, and a green dot for those individuals claiming to have seen her in the newsroom that night. But even they had little to offer: *"No, I didn't see anything unusual." "No, I didn't see her talking with anyone in particular." "No, I don't know anybody who was getting it on with her."*

Wilcox knew that the list of men and women working that night couldn't be conclusive. It was built upon those names scheduled for the night shift, which didn't, of course, include anyone from the day side who'd decided to work late, or to come back after hours to follow up on a story. There wasn't any record of employees coming and going in and out of the building. All you did was wave your badge at the private security officer on duty in the front lobby and you were in. Had Kaporis's killer been an editorial staffer who'd come in late that night but denied having been there? Unless someone testified to having seen him (or her) there, they were home free, their word the last word. Which was the case with him, Joe Wilcox. After dinner at home with Georgia, he'd returned to the newsroom a little after nine to put the finishing touches on an article about a new MPD initiative to combat gang warfare in the District's southeast quadrant. He'd told the police of his movements and activities on that night, and his own name headed the list on his desk, a tiny red dot next to it.

His questioning of colleagues hadn't produced anything even resembling a lead, any more than MPD's efforts had—unless, of course, their probing had been fruitful.

He studied the list carefully, made checkmarks next to those he wanted to see again, and started calling. Jean's parents, who lived in Delaware, had returned home with their daughter's remains after authorities had released her body. He didn't relish a drive to Delaware and decided to not follow up with them that day. Instead, he called Roberta at the TV station.

"Hey, Dad, I just got in. What's up?"

"Not much. Let me ask you something."

"Hold on."

He heard her shout to someone to arrange for a camera crew at two that afternoon. She came back on the line. "Sorry, Dad. Shoot. You said you had something to ask me."

"Right. Did you say in one of your reports that Jean Kaporis's mother said something that pointed to a suspect or motive?"

There was a telling silence on her end.

"That's right," she finally said.

"Look, I know I'm intruding into your turf, but I'd really appreciate knowing what she told you."

"Dad, I—"

"I know, I know, I'm out of bounds here. But—"

"She told me that her daughter had said she was seeing someone at the *Trib*."

"She said that? I mean, Jean told her mother that?"

"Yes."

"Did you report it? I'm sorry, but I don't catch every one of your newscasts." He laughed. "Some father, huh?"

"About dating somebody at the *Trib*? No, I didn't. She didn't have any names so there wasn't anything to report. The MPD spokesman had already said they were focusing on her coworkers."

Wilcox heard her say to someone, "Hey, get your hands off the cookies."

"Roberta?"

"Sorry. I baked a batch of peanut butter cookies, Mom's recipe, to take to the cop whose mother died from that botched operation last week. You heard about it."

"Yeah, sure. You're baking cookies for him?"

"My secret weapon. Amazing how much information a few cookies will buy."

"I don't wonder," Wilcox said, barely audible.

"Dad? You okay?"

"Oh, sure, Robbie. Just checking in with my daughter, the crack reporter. If anything comes up—I mean, I'm getting a lot of pressure here and—"

"I'll keep you in the loop," she said. "Have to run. Covering an MPD news conference this afternoon, and got to deliver these goodies before the cookie Mafia cleans me out. Love you. Bye."

He hung up, sat back with his arms behind his head, and smiled. Roberta's enthusiasm was palpable, uplifting. There'd been a time when he attacked each day with that same zeal, the world something to be conquered, obstacles no more than minor bumps in the road to be easily vaulted. Age had something to do with it, of course. Roberta, like so many other wide-eyed young professionals, awoke each morning with a sense of immortality and youthful superiority bordering on arrogance. Like the smug, ambitious Gene Hawthorne sitting three cubicles from Wilcox, whose appreciation of experience and history, of the *Trib*'s founders, leaders, and outstanding newsmen whose photos lined the corridor walls, was nonexistent.

Roberta's zest was replaced by the unpleasant realization that Morehouse had been right—he hadn't asked the right questions of Kaporis's mother, actually her stepmother. He'd asked only about young men Jean might have been dating, which elicited a denial by the mother of knowing anything about her daughter's social life. Why hadn't he followed up with specific questions about her life at work, about whether she'd ever mentioned dating a coworker? He would have done that automatically a few years ago. Silently, and emptily, he pledged to get his act together.

He made two other calls that morning, the first to see whether a friend from the Associated Press, John Grant, was free for lunch. He was, and they arranged to meet at noon at the Press Club. His next call was to Mary Jane Pruit, Jean Kaporis's roommate.

"Hello, Mrs. Pruit, it's Joe Wilcox from the *Trib*."

"Hello, Mr. Wilcox."

"I was wondering whether I could grab some of your time later today."

"Why?"

"To go over a few things, some loose ends."

"I have nothing else to say," she said in a sleepy voice. "I told you and the police everything I know."

"I'm sure you did, but there are a few issues I'd like to clarify. I won't take much of your time. Promise."

"What time?"

"Your call. Whatever works for you."

"Three would be okay."

"Three it is. Your place?"

"Uh huh."

"Great. See you then."

He thought about the interview he'd done with Mary Jane Pruit the week following her roommate's murder. He'd asked her about men in Kaporis's life and basically received the same response he'd gotten from the mother. But while he'd accepted the mother's denial of knowing anything, that answer didn't ring true in retrospect coming from a roommate. He was chewing on that thought as he entered the National Press Club at Fourteenth and F Street, NW and went directly to the Reliable Source Bar. Grant was sitting with other members at the bar, a drink already in front of him. Wilcox slid onto a stool next to his AP buddy and ordered a white wine.

"How goes?" Grant asked.

"I've been better," Wilcox said. "You?"

"Good, considering the terrorism Popsicle is now orange flavored. You realize our Muslim friends never have to actually attack us again? All they have to do is keep chattering, as our security experts term it, and we spend another billion protecting targets that aren't going to be hit in the first place. What's new with the Kaporis murder?"

Wilcox sipped his wine. "What's new? Not a thing. You pick up anything around town?"

A shrug and an order for a second drink. "Just the ex-boyfriend," he said to the glass.

"What ex-boyfriend?"

Grant turned to Wilcox. "I was working that real estate scandal—excuse me, *alleged* real estate scandal—involving Congressman Coakely from Maine. Somebody at MPD, who shall remain nameless, told me Kaporis broke up with a boyfriend a month or so before the murder. Hell hath no fury like a spurned boyfriend, especially when the fox you lost in the hunt looked like her. I was looking at pictures the other day. Man, she was gorgeous."

"Yeah, she was. A really nice looking young lady." Although they hadn't worked stories together, he'd gotten to know her a little, casual chats in the halls or cafeteria, a wave when she passed his cubicle. Whenever he thought of her and her brutal murder, he thought of Roberta. How could he not?

"So, tell me about this ex-boyfriend," Wilcox said.

"Nothing there, Joe. The kid split for California right after the breakup. The cops out there interviewed him. From what I'm told, he came up clean. Wasn't even near DC the night she died."

"Thanks," Wilcox said. "Nothing else?"

"Hey, I don't cover the cops beat, Joe. That's your bailiwick."

"Yeah, I know. Sorry. It's just that I need—"

"Need what?"

"A story. An angle, something new on *this* story. You know that old joke about Casey, crime photographer?"

"No."

"They called him Casey, crime photographer, because the way he took pictures, it was a crime."

"Sounds like a line from some old Borscht Belt comic."

"It was. They're looking at me at the *Trib* like Casey."

"No."

"I'm serious."

"Tell 'em to go screw. What've you got, a year, two, to the pension?"

"Two, but that's not the point."

They took a table away from the bar and ordered BLTs.

"You okay, Joe?" Grant asked mid-meal.

"Yeah, sure. Why do you ask?"

"I don't know, you seem down, really down. Everything okay at home?"

"Sure. Fine."

"Your daughter's doing great. I catch her on the news. Ratings up since she went over there, or so I hear."

"That's right. She's terrific. Makes her old man look like an amateur."

They went to the lobby where Wilcox pressed the elevator button.

"You up for some poker?" Grant asked. "Carlos has a game going in the back."

"Thanks, no, John. I've got some interviews this afternoon."

"About the Kaporis case?"

Wilcox nodded as the elevator doors opened.

"If I pick up on anything, I'll call."

"Great. Thanks," Wilcox said as the doors slid closed, leaving him alone with a knot in his stomach for the thirteen-floor descent.

FOUR

Task forces in Washington, D.C., are as ubiquitous as Frisbee tossers on the Mall. When in doubt, and the pressure is on in the military, in government, in corporations—whatever—announce the appointment of a task force by whatever name. Which is what the MPD did that morning for the unsolved Jean Kaporis murder at *The Washington Tribune*. In reality, it consisted only of the two detectives already working the case, Edith Vargas-Swayze, and her partner of the past year, Wade Dungey. They met with their boss, Bernard Evans, over a lunch of hoagies and Diet Cokes in a cramped office at First District headquarters at 415 Fourth Street, SW. On the scarred table were recent clips of stories that had appeared in newspapers and magazines, and transcripts of radio and television news reports.

"See what I mean?" Evans asked.

"Big deal," Dungey said. "Since when do we march to what the media says?"

Evans, whose nickname was "the Professor," was a sixteen-year veteran with a reputation for calmness under fire. He leaned back in his chair and squeezed his eyes shut as though seeking inner calm. Evans re-moved his tortoiseshell-rimmed glasses, rubbed his eyes, replaced the glasses, and opened his eyes. He was a slight man with a chiseled wedge of a face, wisps of gray hair on his bald pate, and a known fondness for tweed jackets and books about the Civil War. He seldom raised his voice, which carried a trace of his North Carolina roots, and was especially adept at resolving personality and professional clashes between his detectives, a valuable, intangible skill in an MPD that sometimes resembled the war he loved to read about.

Dungey had been promoted to detective in the Violent Crimes Branch a year earlier after six years in uniform. Tall—six feet, four inches—and painfully thin—155 pounds—he was a D.C. native who'd spent three years in the army before applying to the MPD. Everything about him was long: his neck with a prominent Adam's apple, fingers, nose, and arms. His nickname, of course, was "Slim."

"The Kaporis murder isn't the only one we're working," said Dungey, uncrossing his legs because one had fallen asleep.

"It is now," Evans said. "I'll give you all the backup I can spare. Look, I don't decide which cases are high profile. The public decides that."

"The media decides it," Dungey offered, his disdain of the press worn on his sleeve like the elbow patches of his sport jacket.

"Whoever," Evans said, not about to get into a debate. "The point is that the Kaporis case isn't about to go away unless we make it go away." Dungey started to say something but Evans held up his hand and sighed wearily. "Beautiful blonde working for one of the nation's most important newspapers is killed right there, on the premises. Chances are good—no, they're better than good—that another member of that Fourth Estate institution did the deed. Unless another murder occurs that involves somebody more interesting than Ms. Kaporis, like a senator or congressman, or cabinet member, she's number one." He pushed the clippings and transcripts around on the tabletop. "This is why the brass wants us to pick up the pace. The brass—our brass—tends to get testy when the press asks why we're not doing our jobs. So starting right now and until the case moves from cold to solved, you two think about nothing else. Any questions?"

"We're it, huh?" Vargas-Swayze said with a laugh. "The task force."

Evans joined her laughter. "What a task. What a force. The mighty duo, Dungey and Vargas-Swayze. Put on your capes and save Gotham." His expression shifted to serious. Okay," he said, "lay out for me everything we've done so far and what we intend to do." He turned to his female detective: "You're well-sourced at the *Trib*, Edith. Somebody inside there must know something about who was cozy with the victim, some reporter she'd been making eyes at and seeing after hours, somebody who got mad enough to squeeze the life out of her."

"I'll talk to them again," she said.

"Good."

"But give me something to offer."

"What do you mean?"

"My sources at the *Trib* are looking for news from us. If I can dribble out some new stuff, it'll go a long way to getting somebody over there to do the same."

"Just don't give away the store." To Dungey: "While Edith works the *Trib*, go back into Kaporis's personal life, friends, roommates, family, anybody and everybody who knew her since she came to D.C."

"I've already interviewed them," Dungey said.

"Wrong, Wade. We're starting from square one. It's a brand-new case. We start today looking outside the box. Toss out everything anyone has said and push harder this time." Evans stood and started to leave. He stopped, returned to the table, picked up his half-eaten hoagie, and disappeared through the door.

Meanwhile, the daily two o'clock editorial meeting at the *Trib* was under way. The assistant managing editor of each section of the paper — National and International; Metro, including the Government Diary and obituaries; the Panache section with its gossipy columns and features, comics, horoscope and crossword puzzles; Sports; and Business — gathered in an eighth-floor conference room to pitch stories they intended to include in the next day's edition. The run-up to the meeting had produced a discernible increase in activity throughout the newsroom. The leisurely pace of the morning had been replaced by a growing sense of urgency, matched in other departments throughout the building. The advertising department coordinated closely with editorial to determine the number of pages that would comprise the paper the following morning. The more ads, the more editorial material would be needed. Simultaneously, a separate editorial staff responsible for the special section that would be inserted the next morning—Health, Food, Home, Weekend, or Real Estate, depending upon the day of the week—put the finishing touches on their product.

"What's new on Kaporis?" Paul Morehouse was asked after he'd gone over the list of stories he intended to include in his Metro section.

"Not enough to lead with. MPD announced a task force this morning, whatever the hell that means."

"What *does* it mean?" asked the deputy managing editor chairing the meeting.

"We're working on it," Morehouse replied. "Mary's greenlighted money for our own task force." Mary Lou Castle, the *Trib*'s comptroller, was the voice of money. "I've got Joe Wilcox heading it."

The deputy managing editor's face went sour. "Is he making any headway?"

"Not yet, but we're ratcheting things up. Joe's been—how do I say it? He's been distracted lately, but that's over. He's well sourced at MPD."

"Well, he'd better get his sources to start saying something. Mail is heavy, asking why we're covering up. You know, protecting one of our own."

"That's nonsense."

"You want to answer the mail, Paul?"

Morehouse didn't reply.

"Jeanette's going to do something on it in her Ombudsman column day after tomorrow."

"Good."

"In the meantime, get something we can run front page this week, some break in the case."

"We're on it," said Morehouse to the man who outranked him in the *Trib*'s hierarchy.

Which sufficed for the moment.

They would meet again at six when final decisions would be made, including which stories would appear on the coveted front page of each section. For reporters writing the stories, being on Page One was like hitting a game-winning home run, grabbing the brass ring, and winning the

Medal of Honor, an Oscar and the America's Cup all at once. They wore their front-page placements like notches on a belt or gunstock. How effectively their bosses lobbied for them at the two and six o'clock meetings went a long way toward determining how many notches they'd end up with — or how many flesh wounds.

Wilcox was on his way out of the newsroom when Morehouse came from the meeting.

"Got a minute?" Morehouse asked.

"No," Wilcox said. "I'm on my way to see Jean's roommate again. Running late."

"Check in when you get back."

You forgot the please, Wilcox thought, and nodded.

❧

Mary Jane Pruit lived in a twelve-story apartment building across the Potomac, in Crystal City, Virginia. The doorman buzzed her and Wilcox was directed to apartment number 8-C on the eighth floor where she stood in the open doorway.

"I appreciate you taking time to see me," Wilcox said.

"It's okay," she said.

Wilcox had been surprised at the apartment's size during his first visit. The living room was larger than his at home, and sliding glass doors opened on to a balcony from which D.C., as well as arriving and departing flights from nearby Reagan National Airport, could be seen. A dining area and kitchen were at one end. A hallway led to what he assumed were the bedrooms, probably a couple of them considering that two single people had lived there.

Mary Jane was a tall, slender young woman with an elongated face framed by blond hair with a bleached coarseness, worn long and straight. She was dressed that day in white shorts, a sleeveless navy blue tank top, and flip-flops. He judged her to be somewhat older than Kaporis, maybe by three or four years. Kaporis had been twenty-two. Her former roommate might by pushing thirty, he thought, but certainly no older than that. She sat in a chair, crossed her legs, and lit a cigarette. An ashtray on a table next to her was almost filled with extinguished butts. Wilcox wasn't sure where to sit. The last time he was there, he'd taken the couch.

But that would place her to his side, an awkward arrangement. Instead, he pulled an ottoman from in front of another chair and positioned it directly in front of her. He pulled a reporter's notepad and pen from his inside jacket pocket and said, "I know we've already gone over things, Ms. Pruit, but I have some additional questions to ask. Okay?"

She drew on the cigarette, snubbed it out in the ashtray, and said, "Go ahead, only you're wasting your time. I don't know anything more than I told you before."

"Fair enough. How long did you and Jean Kaporis live here together?"

"You already asked me that question, Mr. Wilcox. Is this a truth test? Jean moved in here about a month after she came to Washington. That was a year ago, give or take."

"How did she end up living with you? I mean, was this your apartment, or did the two of you find it together?"

"It was mine. Another roommate moved out. A friend of mine met Jean and told her I was looking for someone. That simple."

Wilcox nodded and made notes. He looked up and asked, "Did the two of you get along?"

Pruit laughed and lit another cigarette. "Sure we did."

"I mean," he said, "sometimes roommates have conflicts about— well, about things like noise or friends spending time here or—"

"We got along."

He noted it and said, "The last time we spoke, Ms. Pruit, I asked about Jean's boyfriends. Remember?"

"Yes, I remember."

"You said you didn't know anything about the men in her life."

"I still don't."

"That strikes me as strange," Wilcox said.

"Why?"

"Well, I have a daughter who's had roommates. From what she's told me, the most popular topic of conversation among young female roommates is the men in their lives. Or out of them." He cocked his head, pen poised over the notepad.

"We didn't talk about things like that, Mr. Wilcox."

"What *did* you talk about?"

"Not much. We were on different schedules. I work nights, she worked days at the paper."

"Ships passing in the night."

"Uh-huh."

"Where do you work, Ms. Pruit?"

"I'm a freelancer."

"Oh? Writer? Artist?"

"I'm a freelancer," she repeated. "Let's leave it at that."

Wilcox wrote "freelancer" on his pad, but he was thinking beyond those simple words. What was she, a prostitute, perhaps working for one of the city's many so-called escort services? A freelance *what*?

"Could you be more specific?" he asked.

"Look, I have to be someplace. Could we wrap this up?" Another cigarette.

"Jean's mother said that her daughter was seeing someone who works at the *Trib*. She never mentioned that to you?"

She shook her head, sending her hair into motion.

"Never?" Wilcox said.

"Yeah. Well, she said something about it."

"What did she say?"

A shrug and a stream of exhaled air. "Just that she had a fling with somebody there, some reporter, I guess. That's all I know. We didn't talk much."

She snuffed out her cigarette, stood, and said, "Sorry, but I have to go."

Wilcox replaced the pad and pen in his jacket and followed her to the door, which she opened, standing back to allow him to exit. He was glad to be leaving. He'd begun to sweat despite the apartment's coolness, and felt lightheaded.

"Thanks," he said, stepping into the hallway. The door closed behind him.

He hadn't been there long; it was only three-thirty. He considered calling it a day and going home. Reporters determined how they spent their days, their time pretty much their own when working a story. But Morehouse had asked him to check in, and he'd also scheduled that meeting of his reportorial team at six.

He stopped in a luncheonette where he had a cup of coffee, and checked his voice mail back at the paper. One call piqued his immediate interest. He caught Vargas-Swayze on her cell phone while she and her partner drove to a second interview with a delivery man. He worked for an office supply outlet and had signed in at the *Trib* early on the evening Kaporis was murdered.

"Up for a drink after work?" Wilcox asked.

"After work?" She laughed. "When is that?"

"Whenever you say, Edith. And don't make it sound like you're the only one in town working twenty-four hours a day."

"Oh, I forgot, Joe. You media types work long hours, too. Sure. I've been meaning to catch up with you anyway."

"Something new in the Kaporis case?"

"Maybe. What do you have for me?"

"We have a task force, too, now. I'm in charge," he said.

This time it was more of a giggle. "Where and when?"

"Let's make it dinner. Eight good for you?"

"Sure, as long as it's dark and out of the way. Can't risk my reputation being seen with a reporter." She said it lightly, but he knew there was substance behind the remark.

"Martin's Tavern. As Yogi said, it's so popular nobody goes there any more."

"Are you going to propose to me, Joe?"

"Huh?"

"Propose. Like in marriage proposal. That's where JFK proposed to Jackie."

"I didn't know that. Besides, I'm a married man." The minute he said it, he wished he hadn't.

"And I'm still a married woman, at least legally. Get a corner booth."

Their thoughts were similar, and they didn't involve pink elephants.

☙

"What was that all about?" Dungey asked as Vargas-Swayze pulled up in front of a commercial building.

"My source at the *Trib*, Joe Wilcox."

"Sounded like you're in love."

"Just goofing with him. He's a good guy, a straight-shooter."

"Can't be if he's a media whore."

She ignored him and led the way into the building.

❧

"What did the roommate have to say?" Morehouse asked Wilcox.

"She confirmed to me that Kaporis had told her she'd been seeing someone from here."

"A reporter?"

"She didn't elaborate. She's a tough cookie. I think she might be a hooker of some sort."

Morehouse's thick eyebrows went up. "A hooker?"

"She calls herself a freelancer. When I pressed, she cut me off."

"Do you think there's an angle in this?"

Wilcox shrugged and lifted his hands, palms up. "Like what?"

Morehouse massaged his nose. "Do you think—and I'm only playing what if, Joe—what if Jean was in some way moonlighting? What if she was turning tricks on the side and got one of her Johns mad enough to kill her?"

"Oh, come on, Paul, that's—"

"That's thinking outside the box, Joe."

"Maybe it is, but it does nothing for me."

"Follow up on it."

"How, asking the roommate whether she's a whore?"

"That's not a bad start."

Wilcox knew it was futile to argue the point at that moment and changed the subject. "I'm meeting tonight with a good contact at MPD. She sounded as though she might have something for me."

"Who, the spic cop, Vargas-Swayze?"

Wilcox's frown was one of disapproval.

"All right, the Spanish cop."

"She's the lead detective on the Kaporis case," Wilcox said. "By the way, L.A. police interviewed a former boyfriend of Jean's. He's clean, was nowhere near D.C. the night she got it."

"Where'd you pick that up?"

"A friend at lunch."

"Get somebody out in L.A. to interview him, get a better handle on what she was like out of the office. Or out of her clothes."

Wilcox nodded. "I'm meeting with Rick Jillian and the rest of our group at six. Want to join us?"

"No. I'm tied up tonight."

As Wilcox started to leave the office, Morehouse said, "Why don't you pick Hawthorne's brain. He's really wired in around the District."

"Sure." Wilcox said. "I'll talk to Gene."

He had no intention of asking his least favorite young reporter for anything.

He called Georgia at home to say he'd be late that night.

"You reporters," she said lightly. "Roberta was going to stop by for dinner tonight, but she was given a last-minute assignment."

"A couple more years and I'll be home for breakfast, lunch, and dinner."

"I'd like that."

"No you wouldn't, Georgia. I don't play golf or make pretty wooden furniture. No hobbies. I'll drive you mad."

"Try me," she said. "Take care. Don't be too late."

The six o'clock meeting was no more productive than most meetings, although it did result in a semblance of organization, with Wilcox handing out specific tasks, including assigning someone from the L.A. bureau to track down and interview Kaporis's ex-boyfriend. It ended at 6:45. Wilcox left the building and drove to busy Georgetown where he found, of all things, a parking space only a few feet away from Martin's Tavern, the oldest such establishment in Washington. Management knew him and plopped a RESERVED sign on a corner booth in the most secluded portion of the restaurant. He considered having a drink but decided to wait. He window-shopped up and down Wisconsin Avenue for an hour, stopping in Britches to admire a sport jacket that was too expensive for his budget, and in Olsson's Books and Records where he browsed the classical music section without purchasing anything. Having killed sufficient time, he returned to the tavern, took the booth, and indulged in some serious introspection and reflection, a Scotch, neat, oiling the process.

He was dismayed that Morehouse saw a story potential in the possibility that Jean Kaporis's roommate might be a prostitute, and was sorry he'd even mentioned it. He worked for the prestigious *Washington Tribune*, not some supermarket tabloid. Was it so important for the paper, particularly its Metro section, to have a story every day about Jean Kaporis's murder that it would be content to manufacture "news?" It seemed that way, although he knew Morehouse would have a tough time getting his bosses to run an article based upon speculation and innuendo.

Morehouse's suggestion that he, Joe Wilcox, a twenty-three year veteran reporter, enlist the help of the self-righteous, smug Gene Hawthorne, was especially galling. Morehouse knew of his dislike for the young reporter. Had he made the suggestion in order to humiliate him? If that was his intention, he'd succeeded, at least momentarily.

He finished his drink, checked his watch, and ordered a second. While waiting for it and Edith Vargas-Swayze to arrive, he found himself smiling, and feeling, suddenly, strangely buoyant.

Morehouse had said that the Kaporis story might be the big one Wilcox had been seeking his entire career. Maybe Morehouse was right. Maybe it was time to suck it up and summon new energy to attack the story with the zest he'd demonstrated in the past. He'd recently been going through the motions, he knew, disheartened and dejected, wondering where his career had taken him. He was in the midst of that thought when Edith came through the door, spotted him, and slid on to the bench across from him.

"I was afraid you were standing me up," Wilcox said.

"I'm not that late," she said. "I see you've started without me."

"Just killing time. Drink?"

She shook her head. "Afraid I'll be called back. The natives are restless tonight. Three shootings so far, more to come."

He was glad he wasn't back at the paper. The night reporters assigned to the cops beat would have been dispatched to cover the shootings, and he would have been pressed into service, too. There was always the possibility that he'd receive a call at home or on his cell phone, but that was unlikely now that the Kaporis murder had taken center stage. He'd be left alone to produce something worthy of the Metro section's front page. Hopefully, the attractive woman seated across from him would help.

"So," she said after they'd ordered their meals, Virginia crab cakes for her, lamb chops for him. "Level with me, Joe. Who's the smart money on at the *Trib*?"

"Meaning?"

"Who tops the rumor list in the Kaporis story?"

"Oh," he said, pursing his lips and nodding. "Who done it, you mean?"

"Let me put it another way. Is the paper trying to cover anything up?"

"Protect who killed her? Come on, Edith, be reasonable. The brain trust wants to find the killer itself, clean up its own act, make a splash with it. We've been interviewing everyone who was there that night, or at least those who admit they were."

"And?"

"Nothing, so far. I went over the list of people you interviewed. Obviously, you didn't come up with any more than I did. I was disappointed about the ex-boyfriend."

"Disappointed?"

"Yeah, in you, Edith. I found out through a friend at lunch."

"I wasn't involved, Joe. I knew about it but—"

"I know, I know. It's just that—"

"The LAPD interviewed the kid. Clean."

"Still. You interviewed the roommate, Pruit?"

"Right. Icy lady."

"What do you know about her?"

"The roommate? Nothing. Why?"

He hesitated for a moment. "You should run a background on her. She might be a call girl."

Vargas-Swayze's eyebrows went up. She sat back to allow their food to be placed before them. When the waiter left, she came forward and asked, "Do you know that? I mean, for a fact?"

"No, but it's possible. Worth checking out." It was awkward passing along such a salacious, unsubstantiated rumor, but it was all he had at the moment.

She started to eat, and Wilcox observed her from across the table. He'd always found her appealing, and sometimes lusted for her in a Jimmy Carter sort of way. Passive, carnal thoughts but nothing more than that—the remarkable exception being that one totally unexpected, unplanned, and unlikely night in bed together. He couldn't take credit for having seduced her, which was just as well.

She exuded a fleshy solidness, nothing loose anywhere on her as far as he could see. Coppery skin stretched taut across wide cheekbones beneath large, oval dark brown eyes. Her mouth, of normal size at rest, blossomed into something larger and sensuous when she smiled, a set of very white teeth framed by bloodred lipstick, and rendered whiter against the duskiness of her skin. She was, he estimated, about five feet, four inches tall, with a compact body she probably didn't have to work hard at keeping firm. One thing was certain: there were no rules at MPD against female detectives wearing jewelry. Vargas-Swayze wore lots of it, multiple gold strands dangling down over the front of her white turtleneck, large gold earrings in the shape of fish, and rings of various sizes and design on three fingers of each hand, fingernails nicely manicured and painted to match her lips.

"I interviewed the roommate again this afternoon," Wilcox said, biting into a chop and wishing it had been pinker.

"She said something to indicate she might be in the life?"

"Calls herself a freelancer, but won't elaborate. Who did you talk to today?"

"Aside from my partner and my boss? We interviewed some of the people from outside the *Trib* who'd signed in there that night."

"And?"

"Some possibilities."

"Enough to shift emphasis from somebody at the paper?"

"Could be. We're running background checks on them, which we should have done the first time around."

"Why now?"

"Pressure to solve this thing."

Wilcox smiled. "I'm under pressure, too," he said. "Tell me more about these outside people."

"Off the record?" she said.

"Absolutely."

"Okay. We talked to—"

Her cell phone rang. She fished in her purse, retrieved it, opened the cover and announced, "Vargas-Swayze."

Wilcox watched as she muttered responses to the caller. A few seconds later, she closed the phone and said, "Got to go, Joe. A female down in Franklin Park."

"Not my night," he said, pulling out his wallet.

"Stay," she said, standing. "Finish your chops. Sorry."

"Might as well tag along," he said, also standing and waving for the waiter. "Be there in a few minutes."

FIVE

While waiting for the waiter to return his credit card, Wilcox called the *Trib*'s night Metro editor. "Joe Wilcox, Barry. I've got the Franklin Park call covered."

"We just got it on the radio. What are you doing there?"

"Happened to be on the scene. I'll be back to you."

He signed the charge slip, got in his car, and headed for Franklin Park, or Franklin Square, depending upon which tourist map you trusted. He drove faster than he usually did, and felt his adrenaline flowing faster, too. He hadn't raced to a crime scene in years, having learned over the years to pace himself. Five or ten minutes seldom made any difference; the bodies weren't getting up and going anywhere.

But this was different. Tonight was different. The pervasive blanket of self-pity and self-loathing had lifted, at least for the moment. He felt better than he had in months.

Vargas-Swayze was directing uniformed officers at the K Street entrance to the spacious downtown park when Wilcox pulled up. A half-dozen marked police cars, their red lights flashing, were parked haphazardly along the street. Wilcox started into the park but was stopped by an officer. "He's okay," Vargas-Swayze said, waving him through.

He followed a sloping footpath leading toward the park's central fountain, passing a series of benches beneath tall trees that made it a favorite fair weather brownbag lunch spot for office workers. The cynosure was a bench not far from the fountain. On it was sprawled a woman's body, illuminated by the dancing beams of flashlights wielded by uniformed cops. A handbag that appeared to be made of straw or some other woven material was on the ground in front of the bench.

Wilcox attempted to get closer, displaying the press credential tethered to his neck, but was kept away by another uniform. He looked around for Vargas-Swayze, who was nowhere to be seen. As he squinted to get a better view of the body, additional uniformed police arrived, accompanied by a couple of EMTs. *Save your mouth-to-mouth for someone who can benefit from it*, Wilcox thought.

A young man and woman in white lab coats with EVIDENCE TECHNICIAN emblazoned on their backs and carrying crime-scene investigation kits joined the EMTs. Wilcox knew them from dozens of other homicides he'd covered in the District. Vargas-Swayze walked into the scene and came to Wilcox.

"Know anything yet?" Wilcox asked over the cacophony of walkie-talkie and cell phone chatter. Two cops unrolled yellow crime scene tape and began to cordon off the immediate area.

"No."

"Who discovered the body?"

"Over there." She pointed to a middle-aged man and younger looking woman sitting on a bench a dozen yards from the victim. A uniformed officer stood guard over them, arms folded across his chest.

Vargas-Swayze left Wilcox and went to where the crime scene investigators had begun scouring the ground surrounding the body. They were joined almost immediately by another face familiar to Wilcox, an assistant from the medical examiner's office. Wilcox had forged a friendship of sorts with this doctor, had done him a few favors over the past years, including securing a summer intern slot at the *Trib* for his teenage daughter. The ME waved to Wilcox before approaching the woman's lifeless body. He placed his hand on her neck and cheek, but withdrew it as though it had been hot to the touch. Holding a flashlight of his own, he more closely examined her face and neck. As he did, the techs began photographing the scene using digital still and video cameras.

The ME motioned for Vargas-Swayze to accompany him to a spot outside the roped-off area. Wilcox made his way in that direction, too, but kept a respectful distance until they'd finished their conversation. "Got a minute?" he asked, looking at Vargas-Swayze for a sign that she wouldn't prohibit him from questioning the ME. "Strictly off the record," Wilcox added.

"Looks like a homicide," the ME said, moving to where Wilcox stood, "unless she decided to hang herself from the nearest tree. Of course, she wouldn't have ended up on the bench if she had."

"Hang herself? That's how she died?" Wilcox asked. "Asphyxiation?"

"That's my guess at this juncture," said the ME. "The autopsy will be more specific, but judging from the fingernail marks on her throat, I'd say somebody choked her to death."

"How long do you figure she's been dead?" Wilcox asked.

"Not long. An hour maybe. We'll know more after the autopsy. Speaking of that, I'd better get going."

The ME joined the EMTs as they put the lifeless body into a body bag and removed it from the park.

"Any ID?" Wilcox asked Vargas-Swayze.

"Yeah, but not for you, Joe."

"Forget the name for now," he said. "I know the drill. I saw you talking with the cop who had her purse. Come on, Edith, give me something about her. I'll sit on it until you give the okay."

"She had plenty of cash in her purse," the detective said.

"No robbery."

"Evidently. Twenty-seven years old, according to her driver's license. She's got a press pass."

"A press pass?" he said incredulously. "Who'd she work for?"

Edith shook her head. "I've already said too much, Joe. Try me later."

She turned to leave but he grabbed her arm. "What about the couple over there who discovered her?"

"Older guy, pretty young lady. He lives in the burbs. The way I figure it, he's married and in town for an evening with his young honey. But I don't know that."

"I want to talk to them."

"Be my guest, but you're wasting your time. The guy's panicked that his name will become public. She says he didn't want to get involved, but she insisted they call nine-one-one. Good luck."

She was right. The man and woman refused to give him even their names, the man snarling, "Get the hell away from us!"

Wilcox was on his way back to the crime scene when a voice said, "Hey, Joe." It was a cops reporter from a rival newspaper, who'd just arrived. "What've you got?" he asked.

"Not much," Wilcox replied. "One dead female. That's all I know."

"Homicide?"

"Probably. See you later."

As he retraced his route up the path to K Street, Wilcox saw that two TV remote trucks, their antennas extended, had been positioned at the park's entrance. Coming down the path was Roberta, followed by a cameraman and sound technician.

"Hey," Joe called to her, "fancy meeting you here."

"Hi, Dad. Looks like we missed the action."

"Yeah. It's been buttoned up."

"What's the scoop? Another murder? Must be the full moon."

"Apparent homicide. Female. That's all I know, hon." He was surprised how easily he could lie to his own daughter.

"How come you were here?" she asked, that question suddenly crossing her mind.

"I was in the neighborhood," he said.

She looked at him quizzically.

"Look, I'll give you a call tomorrow. Right now I'd better get back and file."

"Based on what?" she asked.

"I'll make some calls, like you will." He kissed her cheek and was gone.

His guilt kicked in the minute he was back in his car and on his way to the newspaper, but it didn't last long. He was too focused on the events of the evening and his need to write about it. He evaded questions by others in the newsroom as he went to his computer terminal and began the story. When he was finished and had printed it out, he walked into the night Metro editor's office and laid the draft on the desk in front of him.

"This is good stuff, Joe," Barry said after reading it. "You can't nail down who she worked for?"

"I will," Wilcox said.

"What about an MPD statement backing up the possibility that a serial killer is on the loose?"

"I'll get that, too."

"Paul will love it," Barry said, laughing and handing the story back.

"He'd better," Wilcox said.

He was tired as he drove home to Rockville. But once there, he got a second wind. He settled into his den and placed a call to Edith Vargas-Swayze's cell phone. "Sorry to bother you, Edith, but I figured you were still on duty."

"Wrong, Joe. I just got home. You didn't wake me."

"Good. Look, I'm working on a story about tonight's Franklin Park murder and I need something more tangible about where the victim worked."

"I can't give you that, Joe."

"It doesn't have to be specific, Edith. A newspaper? Radio? TV?"

"She was a line producer for a TV station."

"Oh. Which one?"

"Joe, that's it until we decide to release more."

"I understand. You know what I'm thinking?"

"What?"

"I'm thinking that there might be a serial killer loose in D.C."

"A serial killer? Why?"

"Same MO as Jean Kaporis. Young, attractive woman. Works in media. Is strangled to death."

"That's a real stretch, Joe. It takes more than two to add up to serial killings."

"But you can't rule out the possibility."

"No, I guess anything's possible. I'm beat. Sorry about dinner being ruined. The crab cakes were good, at least what I tasted of them."

"We'll do it again soon."

"That's a deal. Good night."

He'd brought with him the CD containing the story he'd written, and inserted it into the den computer. He worked the article over for an hour, adding new lines, cutting others, rearranging paragraphs and changing some key words many times. When he was finished, he went to the bedroom where Georgia slept. His undressing woke her.

"It's real late," she said, glancing at the lighted digital clock-radio. "After three."

"I know," he said. "I was working on a breaking story." He leaned over and kissed her brow. "Go back to sleep, hon."

"Uh-huh. Was it a good night?"

"Yeah, it was. I'll fill you in tomorrow. Have to be in early. No need to get up with me."

"Okay. I'm having lunch with Mimi tomorrow."

"Today. It's today. That's good."

Georgia and Mimi Morehouse, Paul's wife, had become friends over the years, and got together a few times each month for, as Georgia termed it, "Girl-talk. Compare notes on the men in our lives." Joe and Georgia had decided after spending a number of evenings with the Morehouses that only someone with Mimi's glass-half-full personality and ready laugh could put up with someone like her dour, abrasive husband. When the tenor of their relationship came up one day over lunch, Mimi said to Georgia with a chuckle, "Oh, Paul's all right. His bark is worse than his bite." To which Georgia responded, "You take the bitter with the sweet." And they laughed their way through the rest of lunch.

One day, the two ladies at lunch got on the subject of their husbands' fidelity.

"I'd really be shocked if Joe had an affair," Georgia said. "He's—he's just not the type, if you know what I mean."

"What type is that?" Mimi asked.

"You know, the sort who takes off his wedding ring when he goes out of town. A flirt. I'd really be shocked."

"I'd just as soon not know," Mimi offered. "I take the military's approach: Don't ask, don't tell."

"I'm afraid I could never be that worldly," Georgia said.

"Worldly, hell! If I ever found out he was sleeping with some bimbo, I'd take a pair of pinking shears to his manhood."

"Ouch," Georgia said, making a face against that painful vision.

The subject never came up again.

Wilcox set the alarm to go off in three hours and slid into bed next to her. Lying on his back, he waited for sleep to come. But it evaded him for a half hour, during which time he thought of many things, particularly what had happened that evening to shake him out of his lethargy. He felt more alive than he had in months. A vision of a naked Edith Vargas-Swayze filled his thoughts, and he considered reaching for his wife. He fought that urge, and forced Edith from his thoughts, too. As sleep finally did arrive, he smiled at the contemplation of getting up and going to work, something he hadn't experienced in far too long. His final waking thought, displayed in vivid Technicolor, was Roberta's face, her beatific smile filling his screen. Then, whether he wanted it to happen or not, everything went to black.

SIX

No one ever accused Paul Morehouse of having an upbeat personality. But this morning his growls seemed even more frequent and pronounced.

"Good morning," said a young reporter who popped into his office moments after he'd arrived, his takeout coffee still uncapped.

Morehouse nodded and muttered, "How are you?"

"Couldn't be better," she said happily.

"I doubt that," he muttered. "What do you want?"

"I'm pissed about the edit you did on my story yesterday. I—"

"Yeah, I know, I messed with your precious prose. Talk to me later about it, after I've had coffee. Close the door behind you." He watched with an admiring eye as she left, hips and buttocks moving nicely beneath the thin fabric of her skirt.

He'd spent the evening with an assortment of editors from the city's other news outlets at a dinner hosted by D.C.'s mayor, the purpose of which still escaped him. Did the mayor really think that by serving the press small drinks and a lousy big dinner, he'd buy their good graces when it came to covering his missteps? Maybe for some of the mayor's media lapdogs, but not for him, Paul Morehouse. Not only had the evening been a waste of time, the dinner had left him with a sour stomach; a fresh roll of Tums sat next to his Styrofoam coffee cup.

He looked through the glass separating him from the main newsroom and saw Joe Wilcox heading for his office.

"Yeah?" Morehouse said as Wilcox entered.

"I thought you'd want to see this," Wilcox said, laying the article on the desk.

"What is it?"

"Read it."

Morehouse removed the cover from his coffee and took a sip before picking up Wilcox's pages. He leaned back, half-glasses on the tip of his nose, a scowl on his face. "Interesting," he said, dropping the article on the desk. "A serial killer? Based on two murders?"

"Two similar murders, Paul."

"This one worked for a TV station?"

"Right. I'm nailing down which one."

"Same cause of death."

"Right."

"Who's your source at MPD who says it's possibly a serial murder?"

"A good one."

"Your—your Spanish buddy?"

"No. Someone higher up."

"Can't get MPD to go on the record?"

"Not yet. They will. They'll have to when this runs."

"He talked to you on background?"

"Yes."

There was a difference, Wilcox knew, between having a public official speak "off the record" and "on background." In its strictest interpretation, "off the record" meant that whatever was said could not be reported, even without attribution. But speaking "on background" meant the official's words could be reported without naming the source. Those distinctions had become blurred over the years. "Off the record" covered both situations in most journalists' minds, and Wilcox wasn't in the mood to honor such distinctions.

"Get the victim's name and where she worked. The L.A. bureau is interviewing Kaporis's ex out in California. Use what they come up with in the piece."

"Shall do."

As Wilcox turned to leave, Morehouse said, "What about the hooker angle?"

"What about it?"

"I want that run down."

Wilcox nodded, but it didn't represent what he was thinking. He said, "This serial killer angle is front-page stuff, Paul."

"We'll see. Nice work, Joe. By the way, how come you covered Franklin Park last night?"

"I was passing by."

As Wilcox was about to leave, Morehouse said, "Joe, when you get something from MPD, see if you can get them to speculate that if a serial killer is loose, chances are Jean was murdered by somebody from outside the *Trib*."

"That'll be tough. I—"

"Yeah, yeah, I know, but it would help take the spotlight off us, poke a hole in the notion that we might be covering up for one of our own."

"I'll see what I can do."

Wilcox spent the next few hours on the phone working his sources in D.C.'s broadcasting community. He struck oil with a friend at one of the TV stations, who told him the slain woman in the park had worked for a competitor. He called that station and received a reluctant confirmation that the victim had, indeed, worked there. He lied to the person on the phone: "We're going with her name," he said. "MPD has notified her next of kin."

"Really?" the person on the other end said. "The McNamara family must be devastated."

"I'm sure they are," Wilcox said, noting the name on a pad and injecting empathy into his voice. "How old was she? Twenty-six?"

"I don't know," the TV station employee said. "Colleen never said, at least to me."

"Yeah. Well, I'm sure you're all terribly upset losing a colleague in such a brutal way. Thanks for your time."

He inserted the victim's name and the TV station into the story, and ran a computer search on Colleen McNamara. There wasn't much, but there was just enough to help flesh out the piece. She'd come to Washington to take the job at the TV station. That was three years ago. Her name was mentioned in connection with a couple of investigative reports she'd produced for the station. Her address and telephone number were included in the computer-generated bio.

A man answered his call to her residence.

"Joe Wilcox from the *Tribune*. Is there someone I can speak with about Ms. McNamara?"

"You're a reporter?"

"Yes. *The Washington Tribune*. My condolences to the family. I know this is a tough time for you, but I'm working on a story that might help find out who killed her. You're—?"

"Colleen was my fiancée."

"Oh. I'm sorry for your loss, sir. Your name is—?"

"That doesn't matter."

"I just want to be accurate, that's all, and complete. I recognize this is an awkward time for you and the family, but I would really appreciate a chance to get together with you if only for a few minutes. Ms. McNamara, your fiancée, should be portrayed as the wonderful person she was, and should have her professional achievements pointed out."

"Mr. Wilcox, I—" His voice became thick.

Wilcox changed his tone. "Look, there might be a serial killer out there who'll take another victim. I'm sure you want to see that that doesn't happen."

"Of course." Wilcox heard a buzzer in the background. "I have to go. Some other family members have arrived. Give me your number. I'll call you at a better time."

"Sure." He provided his direct line and cell numbers.

He decided to go to the address listed for Colleen McNamara in the hope of catching family members coming and going from the house. As he passed through the newsroom, he stopped to watch Roberta give a report on the Franklin Park killing. She wrapped it into a larger piece regarding the spate of murders that had taken place the night before, and presented no information about the victim other than that she was an apparent homicide, and that the case was in the preliminary stages of investigation: "Stay tuned for more information as we receive it. I'm Roberta Wilcox."

He thought of calling her but didn't. Truth was, he wasn't anxious to have her ask what he knew about the murder in the park. Better to not speak than to lie outright. Once he had his article completed and it was ready to run—hopefully on page one of the Metro section—he'd tell her what he had. Of course, he silently admitted to himself that he had less than the article would indicate. But rationalization was in full gear for Joe at that moment. It was *possible* that the Jean Kaporis and Colleen McNamara murders had been committed by the same person, certainly more possible than some ridiculous connection between Kaporis and her roommate, Mary Jane Pruit. Edith Vargas-Swayze hadn't ruled it out when he'd proffered the notion to her. In addition, the article might prompt MPD to begin considering a serial killer scenario. He'd seen it happen before, the press taking the lead in establishing a working thesis for the police.

He left word that he'd be gone for the rest of the day, exited the building, got in his car, and drove to Colleen McNamara's address, only a few blocks from Franklin Park.

SEVEN

"Hi, Mom."

"Hi, Roberta. How are you?"

"Okay. Busy. I saw Dad last night."

"You did? He didn't mention it. Did you have dinner? He said he was working late."

"No. I mean, he was—working late. I was covering a homicide in Franklin Park and he was there, too."

"Another homicide? It seems that's all you read about these days."

"Dad acted strange."

"Strange? How so?"

"I don't know. He didn't seem happy to see me there, wanted to get away as fast as he could."

Georgia laughed softly. "I doubt that, Robbie. He's always happy to see you. He must have been on deadline."

"I suppose so. He didn't mention being at the park?"

"No. He got home very late, and was gone before I got up this morning."

"Sorry about dinner last night."

"That's okay. With neither of you here, I snacked and took advantage of the quiet. Got some serious reading done."

"Glad to hear it. I'll try to come by in the next few days. I need a Georgia Wilcox fried-chicken fix."

"Anytime. You know that. Take care, sweetheart."

While Georgia Wilcox enjoyed a late lunch and went out to tend her garden, her husband was at Colleen McNamara's home, a taupe town-house on an eclectic street of homes and small businesses. Colleen had shared the downstairs apartment with her fiancé, a serious young man (appropriate, considering what had happened), who'd reluctantly allowed Wilcox to come in — "But only for a few minutes." — "Of course." — "Her mother and sister are here." — "I promise I won't intrude on their sorrow." — "Okay then, but just a few minutes." A tall, albeit pudgy young man, he wore chinos and a red and white striped shirt with an open collar. His glasses were large and black rimmed and had thick lenses.

The kitchen was at the front of the flat. Colleen's fiancé, whose name was Philip Connor, indicated that Wilcox should sit at a small table next to the window. He could see into the apartment's next room where two women, one older, one younger, sat close together on a couch. There were others in that room, but he couldn't see them, only heard their muted voices.

"The police just left," Connor said, joining Wilcox at the table.

"Did they have anything to offer?" Wilcox asked.

Connor shrugged. "They asked a lot of questions. I know they think I did it."

Wilcox's eyebrows went up into question marks.

"I told them I didn't do anything. I loved Colleen. We were going to be married."

"I wouldn't worry about it. They always look first at a spouse or significant other. Statistics say that most murders are committed by . . . when were you planning to be married?"

"Next year. I'm getting my master's degree at Catholic. We wanted to wait until I was settled in a good job."

"That sounds sensible," said Wilcox. "Did you see Colleen last night — before she was murdered?"

"No. She called and said she had to work late and was going to grab a bite with friends from the station."

"Have you spoken with them?"

"No, but the police said they would—after I told them about it."

"What were their names?"

"I don't know. I've met some of her colleagues, but I don't know which ones she was going out with."

Wilcox took a moment to observe the kitchen. It was sunny and cheery and extremely neat, nothing out of place on the counters or in the glass-fronted cabinets. The backsplash was yellow tile, with a paler shade on the floor. Yellow and white curtains fluttered in a breeze through an open window.

He returned his attention to Connor. "Any idea what she was doing in the park?" he asked.

"She probably was walking through it on the way home. I always told her it wasn't a safe place at night, but it didn't seem to bother her." He paused and swallowed hard. "I guess it should have."

As Wilcox made notes in his reporter's pad, Connor said, "You told me on the phone that Colleen might have been killed by a serial killer. Is that true?"

"It's a good possibility. At least the police are considering it. Did they mention it to you?"

"No. That's really scary, that there might be some nut running around killing young women."

"It sure is, Philip. Any thoughts on who might have wanted Colleen dead? Did she have any enemies that you know of?"

"Colleen? Everybody loved her." Tears running down the cheeks now accompanied the hard swallowing. He pulled a handkerchief from his pocket and dabbed at his eyes, apologizing as he did.

"Hey," Wilcox said, placing his hand on the young man's arm, "I understand. I really do." He hesitated before asking, "Do you have a photograph of Colleen? You know, one you really like?"

"Sure. I took a lot of pictures of her. I'm an amateur photographer."

"I'd love to see them—if you wouldn't mind."

"I don't know. I—"

"If you'd rather not."

"No, I guess you can see them. Excuse me."

Connor left the kitchen, and Wilcox moved his chair in an attempt to see the people in the adjoining room. A middle-aged couple sat in chairs to one side of the couch. The man saw Wilcox and glared at him. Wilcox averted his eyes and shifted back to his original position as Connor returned and laid a large photo album on the table. Wilcox opened it, and a large color photograph of Colleen McNamara looked up at him. She was beautiful in an obvious Irish way, fair skinned with a few strategically placed freckles on her nose and cheeks, and large, sparkling, emerald-green eyes filled with life—and love. He looked at a few more pages. *The kid's a pretty good photographer*, he thought. Then again, he had a good, accessible, photogenic subject.

"Did the police ask to see these?" Wilcox asked.

"No. They had a picture from the station, from her personnel files. They said they'd be back to talk to me again."

"Did you get their names?"

He fished two business cards from his shirt pocket and handed them to Wilcox, who recognized the detectives' names.

"I'd like one of these pictures, Philip."

"You would? Why?"

"Let me be candid with you. We'll be running a story about Colleen's murder—in the *Tribune*—and I'd hate to have to use some inferior photograph from her personnel file. It probably wasn't any better than pictures on driver's licenses and passports."

"It wasn't very good," he said.

"I'm sure it wasn't. I think she deserves to have a better picture used, like one of these great shots you took of her. It's only fair. It's only right. I'm sure you agree. You obviously took these pictures with love. It shows."

He thought the young man would cry again, but he didn't. "Sure, go ahead and take one," he said.

"I like this one," Wilcox said, carefully removing the photo from the first page. "It's beautiful," he said. "She's beautiful."

Wilcox stood and extended his hand. "I'd better be going," he said. "You've been very generous with your time, Philip, and I don't want to wear out my welcome. May I call you again if I have further questions?"

"That'll be okay. Do you have any idea when we'll be able to have a funeral for Colleen? Her mom and sister keep asking about that."

"It'll be a while, I'm afraid," Wilcox replied. "When a death is the result of a homicide, the police need to keep the body for a period of time. Here's my card, Philip. Call any time. I'd like to help."

"Thanks. I appreciate that, Mr. Wilcox."

"And please express my condolences to Colleen's mother and sister and other family members. I may try and talk with them in a day or two, once the shock is past."

Wilcox went to his car and dropped down into the driver's seat. While talking with Connor, he'd suffered the same mild lightheadedness and vague nausea he'd experienced when interviewing Jean Kaporis's roommate, Mary Jane Pruit. He rested his head against the seat's back and closed his eyes until the feeling passed, and spent the next few minutes making descriptive notes about the apartment to use in the article.

He knew he'd taken advantage of Connor's vulnerability. The young man was obviously a naïf, his lack of worldliness evident. There had been instances in Wilcox's journalistic career when he'd backed off in deference to the grieving, and had paid the price for that sensitivity by losing some of the emotionally charged aspects of those stories. But he'd operated under his own set of values, and hadn't regretted it.

❧

Tabloid journalism had always been anathema to him, and he'd promised himself that if he couldn't work for a mainstream paper, a newspaper respected for its integrity, he'd find another line of work. He'd held true to that pledge. The problem was, he felt, journalism had violated *his* principles.

He'd seen it happen at the *Tribune*. As circulation dropped off, along with advertising revenues, standards had slipped, too. The almighty bottom line became increasingly powerful; the choice of stories, and the way they were treated, mirrored what had become an almost insatiable drive to return profits to the paper's shareholders. Yes, *The Washington Tribune* had retained respectability through its coverage of national and world events, particularly politics. The *Trib*, along with *The New York*

Times, The Los Angeles Times, Chicago Tribune, Wall Street Journal, Boston Globe, Cleveland *Plain Dealer,* his former employer, the *Detroit Free Press,* and others, had managed to avoid all but a trace of overt capitulation to base public tastes, which seemed to prefer daily doses of dirt from the celebrity murder trial du jour, the sexual escapades of elected officials, and titillating tales of show-business debauchery.

But his level of disdain for tabloid journalism had slowly but surely begun to evaporate—or wasn't there to begin with—along with Underwood typewriters, green eyeshades, and gruff, hard-nosed reporters yelling, "Copy boy!" and "Stop the presses!" New blood at the *Trib,* like the bumptious Hawthorne, carried with them their shallow, one-dimensional view of the world. He knew how they viewed him—an anachronism, a square, over-the-hill hack who'd lost touch with their sadly depleted, morally bankrupt world. Were he writing editorials for the paper, he would write about that reality as he saw it.

He became tense, physically angry, as such thoughts came and went: He'd forgotten more about reporting than they'd ever know.

❧

The ringing of his cell phone startled him.

"Hello?"

"Dad, it's Roberta."

"Oh, hi. I—"

"Where are you?"

"I just came from—I'm in the car."

"I'd thought I'd check in with my best source."

Wilcox forced a laugh. "That's a switch," he said. "I always figure you've got the ins these days."

"I wish. What do you have on the Franklin Park murder, the McNamara woman?"

"You got her name."

"Next of kin has been notified. I'm doing a piece on the six o'clock news tonight."

The immediacy of TV, he thought. She'd have the name out before his article would run. But she didn't have the serial killer slant.

"What've you gotten from MPD besides her name?"

"Hey, I was the one looking for leads."

"Wish I could be more helpful, sweetheart. I, ah—I interviewed the victim's fiancé."

"Damn!" she said. "I called the house but he stiffed me. How did you get him to sit?"

"It wasn't easy. He didn't have much to offer. Nice kid. Broken up, of course."

"Connor. Philip Connor."

"Right. That's his name."

"Dad?"

"Yeah?"

"You wouldn't hold out on me, would you? You wouldn't stonewall your own hardworking daughter?"

"Of course not. Why would you even ask such a question?"

"Because I get a feeling you're onto something with this homicide. Is it linked in some way to the murder at the *Trib*?"

He didn't reply.

"Dad?"

"You can't prove it by me," he said. "They were in the same business, sort of: media. Which reminds me, young lady, you work in it, too. You be careful. There might be some nut out there carrying a hatred of media types."

"Don't worry about me. I talked to mom. How about getting together for dinner at the house? I told her I needed an injection of her fried chicken. Besides, there's someone I'd like you to meet."

"Oh? Who's that?"

"A fellow I've been seeing. You'll like him. He's a lot like you."

"Really? Is that good?"

"You know it is. I'll let you guys know a good night for me."

"Looking forward to it, Robbie. Got to run." He pursed his lips and sent her a kiss, ending the call.

EIGHT

MPD detectives Edith Vargas-Swayze and Wade Dungey spent most of the day conducting follow-up interviews with people personally involved with Jean Kaporis. Like others questioned for a second time, Mary Jane Pruit offered nothing beyond her original answers. But because Wilcox had raised the possibility at dinner with Vargas-Swayze that Pruit might be involved in prostitution, the detective did what she hadn't done the first time around, probed into how the dead girl made a living.

"I'm a freelancer," May Jane replied to the question of how *she* made a living.

"A freelance what?" Dungey asked.

"I don't think I have to answer questions like that," Mary Jane said, lighting a cigarette. "What does that have to do with Jean's murder?"

"You mind not smoking?" Dungey said, waving his hand in front of his face.

"It's my apartment," Pruit said.

"That's true," Dungey said, "but I'm allergic to smoke." He stared at her until she snuffed out the cigarette.

"Maybe what you do for a living has nothing to do with Jean's murder," Vargas-Swayze said, "but we'll be the judge of that. Now, what kind of freelance work do you do, Ms. Pruit?"

A huffy sigh preceded, "I work for an escort service."

"Which one?"

"It's not what you think. It doesn't involve sex. There are wealthy men who come in from out of town and like to have an attractive, intelligent woman on their arm."

"Yeah, yeah, we know how it works," Dungey said. "What's the name of the service you work for?" In contrast to his partner, who sat ramrod straight in a chair, the gangling Dungey enveloped his, arms and legs draped around the chair like a skinny octopus.

"I think I want a lawyer," Mary Jane said.

"Why?" Vargas-Swayze said. "If your escort duties don't involve sex, there's nothing you've done that's illegal. Which agency?"

"Starlight," she said in a barely audible voice.

Vargas-Swayze noted it in her pad. She asked without looking up, "Did Ms. Kaporis know what you do for a living?"

"Sure she did."

"Did she approve?"

Mary Jane guffawed and lit up, caught Dungey's harsh look, and put it out. "Why should she approve or disapprove? Like I said, it doesn't involve sex or anything else illegal."

"Did Jean ever express an interest in working for the Starlight agency, maybe part time?"

"No, but she would have made more money than at the newspaper."

Or as a cop, Dungey thought.

"Did you suggest she make some extra money by working as an escort?" Vargas-Swayze asked.

"We talked about it."

"You tried to recruit her?" Dungey asked.

"No," she said emphatically. "I don't recruit people. I told her that she could make good money, that's all. She said she wasn't interested."

"Never even gave it a try?" Dungey said, his tone incredulous.

"Never."

"We'll check with the agency," Dungey said.

Vargas-Swayze picked up the questioning again, asking about boy-friends about whom Kaporis might have confided in her roommate. And again, Mary Jane's reply did no more than hint at a mention of some-one at the *Trib* having had some sort of fling with Kaporis. They asked a few more questions before announcing they were leaving. When they reached the door, Dungey turned. "You go to college?"

The expression on her face indicated surprise. "Yes," she said.

"You graduate?" Dungey asked.

"Yes, I did."

"What kind of degree?"

"What is this?" she asked.

"Just curious," he said.

"If it's any of your business, I have a degree in education."

"That's nice," Dungey said. "You should get yourself a teaching job and get out of the escort biz. The next time we see you, it's liable to be on a slab down at the morgue, either because one of your fat-cat johns didn't like the service you gave him, or because of those coffin nails you suck on."

When they were in their car, Vargas-Swayze asked Dungey, "Why did you get into her education?"

"Because broads like that bug me. Here she is a teacher and all, and she ends up selling her bod to a bunch of sleazy rich guys, probably Arab potentates and fat politicians, all for a buck. She's a great-looking chick, but she's dumb. I hate dumb women."

"I didn't realize that," Vargas-Swayze said, smiling.

"Well, now you do."

She didn't intrude on his unexpected mood all the way back to head-quarters where they were scheduled to meet with other detectives and their boss, Bernie Evans. Dungey was not usually forthcoming about his personal thoughts and feelings, as though to reveal such things might render him vulnerable. She knew little about how he spent his off-duty hours except that he was a bachelor who, as far as she knew, dated occa-sionally when he wasn't playing basketball in amateur leagues around the city. Basketball seemed his consuming passion, and she'd been told he was a good player. But even that aspect of his life was mentioned to her only in passing, usually when asked by a male detective how a game had turned out the night before. Okay, she thought, he doesn't like dumb women. She didn't like dumb anybody, male or female. There was obviously more to learn about her spindly partner.

℥

Roberta Wilcox sat in an editing room with the producer of the six o'clock news and the male anchor. They were editing a piece about the recent increase in murders in the District, leading with the most recent killing of Colleen McNamara in Franklin Park.

"It's weak," the anchor said as the partially edited report played on a large computer screen. "Murder isn't news in D.C."

"I agree," Roberta said, leaning closer to the screen to better see a piece of video tape.

"Roberta says it might be a serial killer," said the producer.

"No I didn't," Roberta responded, swiveling in her chair and facing the anchor. "All I did was speculate whether it could be. Jean Kaporis at the *Trib*, and this latest victim, both worked in media. Both good-looking. Both strangled."

The anchor's laugh was dismissive and degrading. "Come on, Roberta," he said, "that's ridiculous. Kaporis was killed by somebody at the *Trib*, pure and simple."

"Oh? Maybe the person at the *Trib* is a serial killer," Roberta said. She was tempted to repeat what her father had said, but didn't. But she had called MPD's public information officer earlier that afternoon to raise the possibility.

℥

"Jesus," the IO had replied, "we don't need the press creating a soap opera, Roberta. The Kaporis and McNamara murders are two separate cases, with two separate assailants. Please, don't start a rumor like this."

"I'm not intending to," she'd said. "Just thought I'd ask whether you people are considering the possibility."

"Well, we're not."

"Gotcha."

༄

"I raised the question with the IO over at headquarters," she told the anchor. "He responded the way you have."

"Of course . . ." the producer said.

"Of course what?" the anchor asked.

"Maybe we could raise the possibility. Maybe we could—"

"Not on my newscast," he said in his familiar stentorian voice. "Let's not sink to speculation. I have to get to makeup. *Ciao!*"

With the anchor out of the room, Roberta told her producer about what her father had hinted at.

"Your dad thinks it could be the same killer?"

"He didn't say that, but it's obviously on his mind."

"Your father's one of the best crime reporters in the city. If he thinks it's a possibility, I—"

"He's just blue-skying," Roberta said, returning her attention to the editing screen. "He does it all the time. Let's get this piece finished. I'm tired of looking at it."

༄

Bernie Evans sat in the First District's squad room with eight detectives from the Violent Crimes Unit, all of whom reported to him. Four others were missing: two had called in sick; the remaining pair were in the field working the initial investigation of a domestic homicide that had occurred only hours earlier when a woman, who walked in on her husband in bed with a neighbor, knifed the neighbor to death.

"She should have done the husband," a detective said after Evans had explained the absence of the two detectives.

"He'd better keep his jock strap on," said another. "Right, Edith?"

She ignored him and suggested to her boss that they get on with the meeting.

Evans had initiated these regular get-togethers in an attempt to ensure an exchange of information. The intelligence debacle that had consumed Washington since the September 11, 2001, terrorist attacks wasn't lost on him, and he was determined that a failure to share information among his detectives wouldn't happen on his watch. While it was rare that findings from one homicide investigation proved useful in another, there had been times when it had.

"Okay, what do we have?" Evans asked the detective seated to his right.

"Not much at this stage," he said, consulting a pad. "Deceased was McNamara, Colleen, white female, age twenty-six, employed as a TV producer. Death occurred in Franklin Park, approximate time of death between eight and nine P.M. Manner of death strangulation, although not firm yet. Crime scene search revealed nothing so far, except for footprints in dirt surrounding the bench on which she was found. Prints might be the assailant, but maybe not. That's about it, Bernie."

"Edith?"

Vargas-Swayze, one of two female detectives in the room, flipped open her notebook and gave a rundown on the interviews they'd done that day, including the admission by Mary Jane Pruit that she worked as a paid escort.

"What's she look like?" a male detective asked.

"Dynamite," Dungey said. "But dumb."

"Since when do brains matter with a hooker?" the male detective said, laughing.

"Let's stay on topic," Evans said. "The IO told me he's gotten queries about whether the Kaporis and McNamara murders might be linked in some way."

"Doesn't compute," said another detective. "What's the press looking for, a sensational peg to hang their hat on?"

Evans looked to Vargas-Swayze for a response. She said, "Until proved otherwise, I'm still working on the assumption that Kaporis was killed by somebody at the *Tribune*. Nothing else makes sense to me."

"But what if that killer at the *Trib* decided to go outside the paper and take another victim?" Evans asked.

Vargas-Swayze shrugged. "That's always a possibility," she said. To the detectives working the McNamara case: "That play for you?"

"Who knows?" one of them replied. "The McNamara hit only happened last night. But we'll keep it in mind."

After other unsolved cases were discussed, Evans implored everyone to not make public statements about any of them, especially the Kaporis murder. "And let's put the McNamara case in that same category," he added, "in case some linkage does emerge. Talk to your dog or cat if you have to talk to anybody."

Vargas-Swayze and Dungey spent a half hour after the meeting going over plans for the next day.

"Feel like a quick dinner?" she asked.

"Thanks, no. I've got a game tonight. Another time. But I'll give you a lift home. It's on my way."

He said little during the drive to Adams Morgan. As she was about to get out of his green Ford Escort, he said, "You know what's bothering me?"

"That Mary Jane Pruit is dumb?"

"Besides that. You know that delivery man we interviewed, the one who was hauling office supplies to the *Trib* the night Kaporis got it?"

"Yeah. Michael—what's his last name?—Michael La Rue."

"Right. La Rue."

"What bothers you about him?"

"I don't know. Something is sending a signal up my spine."

"Maybe you wrenched your back," she said, lightly.

"Very funny. Let's talk to him again tomorrow."

"Sure. Whatever you say. Hope you win tonight."

"Thanks. I hope so, too. Good night, Edith."

She put on the lights in her apartment, changed into white running shorts, an aquamarine Celia Cruz T-shirt, and sneakers, her standard-issue Glock nestled in a custom-made pouch in the front of the shorts, and went for a two-mile jog. Back in the apartment, showered and dressed in shorty pajamas and a robe, she heated leftover takeout in the microwave and ate without enthusiasm in front of the TV. She watched the ten o'clock news, on which Roberta Wilcox's six o'clock report was repeated, and thought of Joe Wilcox. How proud he must be to see his only child achieve success in his chosen profession. She was in the midst of that thought when the phone rang.

"Hello, Edith. It's Joe Wilcox."

"I was just thinking of you," she said.

"Positively, I hope."

"Definitely positive. I was watching your kid on TV. She's good, to say nothing of lovely."

She didn't say that she found the report to be lacking substance. Murders were not big news in D.C. those days. The only new thing Roberta had to report that night was that the latest victim was Colleen McNamara, who worked for a competing station.

"Yeah," Joe said. "She's a winner. Look, Edith, I'm putting a story to bed about the Franklin Park thing, and thought I'd touch base with you one more time before I wrap it up."

"Sorry, Joe, but there's nothing new on the case. Even if there were, I still couldn't talk about it. Bernie Evans came down hard on us today about leaks. The gag over the mouth is tight and secure."

"I'm sure it is," he said. "But I keep hearing stirrings about the possibility that Kaporis's and McNamara's murderers might be the same person."

"Nothing to that, Joe. Hot air. Empty rumors, plain and simple. No evidence."

"So, you've heard them, too?"

"What would a police force be without rumors, Joe? Evans said the IO received calls about a possible serial killer connection."

"From the press?"

"Who else? Drop it, Joe. That's my advice."

"I can't," he said. "We're going with that slant tomorrow."

She sighed and shifted in the recliner. "I wish you wouldn't," she said. "Bernie Evans knows you and I are close. He'll accuse me of feeding you the rumor."

"And I'll deny you did."

"Because I didn't."

"Exactly. I'm just giving you a heads-up."

"Thanks—for nothing."

"Edith?"

"Yes?"

"*Muchas gracias.*"

"*De nada, amigo. Buenos noche.*"

Her cordless phone went dead. She went to the kitchen, poured a glass of orange juice, and returned to the chair. Her thoughts wandered to the night she'd made love with Wilcox. Had she compromised her professional relationship with him when she stripped off her clothing in a fit of passion and sexually indulged herself? It wasn't the first time she'd wondered that, although it had never impacted how they dealt with each other on the job as cop and reporter. Was that about to change? She hoped not.

She flipped through channels and settled on a Spanish-language movie on the local Hispanic outlet. She lasted a half hour, her head drooping to her chest during commercial breaks. The set was snapped off and she headed for the bedroom. The ringing phone stopped her.

"Hello?"

"Edith. It's Peter. I hope I didn't wake you."

"Hello, Peter," she said to her estranged husband. "No, but I was on my way to bed."

"Good. I'm glad I didn't wake you. How are things?"

"Great, but they'd be better if your damn lawyer would send my damn lawyer the papers."

"Can we get together and talk?"

"About what? You're not about to renege on what we decided, are you?"

"I wouldn't do that," he said.

"The hell you wouldn't. When it comes to a buck, Peter, you'd kill to save one."

"You know that's not true."

"What do you want to talk about, Peter?"

"Us."

"Forget it."

"Please, Edith. All I want is the chance to tell you what's on my mind—and in my heart."

She plopped in a chair and pulled her bare feet beneath her. "Peter," she said softly, "there is nothing to talk about. Our marriage is over."

She didn't want to believe what she now heard on the other end of the line. Was he weeping?

"Jesus," she mumbled to herself. "Peter, stop it," she said into the phone.

"I'll kill myself, Edith."

She kicked her feet out from under her and sat up straight. "Stop talking nonsense!"

"I will, Edith. I swear I will. All I'm asking for is a few minutes with you. Please. I'm begging you."

She tried to sort out her thoughts. She didn't believe his threat. It was a call for attention, that's all, a pathetic, stupid attention getter.

On the other hand . . .

"All right," she said with a sigh. "When?"

"I can come there right now."

"To my apartment? Absolutely not. A public place, somewhere quiet. Can you pull yourself together and behave?"

"Oh, yes, Edith. I promise. The Fairfax Bar, in the Westin Fairfax?"

"Oh, God," she said. "How romantic." They'd spent their wedding night at that hotel.

"It has those private little alcoves in the bar. Remember? A half hour?"

"Yes, I remember, Peter. But keep one thing in mind. I'm a cop. I have a gun. And if you try to play games with our financial settlement, try to weasel out of it, I'm liable to use it."

NINE

PARK MURDER RAISES MPD CONCERN
Newspaper and Park Murders Linked?

That was the headline and subhead on the lead story of the *Trib*'s Metro section front page the following morning. Accompanying the story were side-by-side headshots of Jean Kaporis and Colleen McNamara. The interview a reporter from the LA bureau had done with Kaporis's former boyfriend ran as a sidebar: "Jean was a really nice girl. I'm real upset about what happened to her." He said they'd dated for only a few months shortly after she'd arrived in Washington, but decided to sever the relationship soon after: "It was an amicable breakup. We had different ambitions," he said. "I'm an actor now, a movie actor."

Joe and Georgia Wilcox sat at the kitchen table in their Rockville home, the paper open to his bylined article.

"Gives me the creeps," she said.

"I know," he said.

"Seems like the boyfriend in L.A. is more interested in plugging his acting career than grieving for his former girlfriend."

"Oh. I wasn't thinking of that," Joe said.

"I hope they don't just accept what he's said. Boyfriends are the first suspects in every murder. Aren't they?"

"What? Sure, that's right."

"Do they really think there might be a serial killer loose?" she asked.

"They have to be open to any possibilities," Joe said. "Nothing gets ruled out."

"Joe, do you think Roberta is in danger if this madman is preying on young women who work in media?"

"No, but she should take precautions, like any young woman in the city. She's smart and can take care of herself. But nothing's lost by reminding her now and then—which you've been doing with regularity anyway."

His words failed to comfort, judging from worry lines etched into her brow.

"More coffee?" she asked, picking up the carafe and pouring a second cup for herself.

"Thanks, no," he said. "I've got to get downtown."

"I'm glad you decided to sleep in this morning," she said. "You looked exhausted when you came home last night."

"Yeah, I guess I was dragging. Feeling better now though." He got up, came around behind, leaned over and wrapped his arms around her. "Aside from what the story says, what do you think of the writing?" As many years as he'd been writing for a living, her opinion always mattered.

"Terrific," she said. "You put your heart and soul into it, and it reads that way."

"Maybe I haven't lost the touch altogether," he said, smiling and going to the window that overlooked the garden, including his small vegetable patch relegated to a corner.

"Of course, you haven't," she said, joining him.

"Happens to the best of us," he said. "You lose energy and drive. Lots of guys I know have. I see them down at the Press Club. The spirit is certainly willing but the flesh is weak, along with the mind." He turned and placed his hand on her shoulders. "I was beginning to think I was losing it, Georgia."

"And now you know you're not," she said, perkily. "Who called when I was in the shower?"

"Paul."

"I imagine he's happy that his best reporter came through."

"Yeah, he's pleased. At least I think he is. You never really know with him. He wants a follow-up tomorrow. I don't have much to go on unless somebody at MPD decides to open up."

"What about your sources? Edith?"

"She's under a gag order about the Kaporis murder. But I'll give her a try. Got to run." He kissed her lightly on the lips, pulled back, then kissed her again, harder and longer this time.

"My," she said when they'd disengaged. "What did I do to deserve that?"

"There's more where that came from, baby," he said in his best Humphrey Bogart voice, lisp and all.

He was on his way out the door when she stopped him. "I forgot to tell you. Roberta wants to come by for dinner tomorrow night. She has a new beau and wants us to meet him."

"Yeah, she mentioned him to me the other day—says he's like me."

"Then you should approve of him."

"Why? Lots of days I don't like myself."

"Oh, stop it. You'll like him. Take my word for it. Our daughter has good common sense when it comes to the men in her life."

"Really? What about that foul ball, Bobby whatever his name was?"

"That was an exception. Just be sure you're here tomorrow night."

"I'll do my best." She looked angrily at him. "I'll be here," he said.

"Go on, go to work," she said. "We need the money."

Her comment about needing money resulted from an experience Joe had had years earlier. He'd nurtured a relationship with an enforcer for organized crime as a source for a story. The hit man, with the unlikely name of Maurice, had invited Wilcox to dinner at his house, which Wilcox reluctantly accepted. During dinner, Maurice went into the kitchen where his wife confronted him, screaming, "Goddamn it, Morrie, go out and kill somebody. We need the money." Ever since, Wilcox went off to work with that order from Georgia to bring home the bacon. On a slab. A private little joke between them.

Although it was past normal morning rush, traffic was clotted. He tuned to all-news station WTOP where the news reader turned to the D.C. area; speculation about a serial killer on the prowl was the second story in the segment: "According to this morning's *Washington Tribune* . . ."

He turned the radio louder and took pleasure in hearing his article cited. That he'd manufactured the anonymous police source bothered him less this morning than it had the previous day and night. The possibility of there being a serial killer was not far-fetched. Besides, without it, the article would never have run. Reporting that someone at MPD had floated the theory gave the story credence, enough to have satisfied Paul Morehouse. It hadn't been easy sailing. Morehouse's boss had been reluctant to run the piece without attributing the MPD source, and it took a heated half-hour meeting before the piece was given the green light. Wilcox was aware that his reputation had helped the cause, and he was gratified that Morehouse had gone to bat for him in a way he'd not done recently. He was also pleased that his suggestion to run the pictures of the two female victims side-by-side was accepted. The visual impact was strong: two attractive, talented young women possibly the victims of a depraved killer, their promising lives and careers snuffed out prematurely. He'd recounted in the article his interview with Colleen McNamara's fiancé, Philip Connor, describing the apartment, and the young man's tears as he spoke of his beloved fiancée. And he'd played heavily on the similarities in the murders: both lively young women, each working in media, and both strangled to death.

It wasn't as though he'd fabricated the entire story, the way others had done in recent memory at other newspapers, plunging them and their employers into ignominy. He'd never stoop to that, he assured himself. The continuing story needed a slant, a provocative underpinning to give it wings. Morehouse hadn't balked, in fact had championed his cause with higher-ups. If the article caused young women in the city to be more alert and self-protective, it would have served a positive purpose.

And if it turned out that there was no serial killer, so be it. Who'd been hurt? No one. It was merely a theory.

He switched off the newscast along with his stream of rationalizations, parked the car, and waved his employee badge at the private security guard in the *Trib*'s lobby. As he walked through the newsroom on his way to his desk, a colleague looked up from his computer and said, "Hey, congrats, Joe. Nice piece."

"Thanks."

"I'm lockin' up my daughter," said another coworker with a laugh.

"Not a bad idea," Wilcox said.

He felt buoyant, more alive than he'd felt in months. There were a dozen message slips on his desk, and he quickly rifled through them. He was about to return the more important ones when Morehouse came up behind him.

"Calls from your adoring fans?" Morehouse asked.

"I didn't know I had any, Paul."

"You sure as hell don't over at MPD. Come on, I want to talk to you."

Morehouse shut the door to his office, perched on the edge of his desk, and smiled. "You've got the boys and girls in blue up in arms, buddy."

"Really?"

"Yeah. I got a call this morning from an assistant commissioner. He started moaning about your article causing undue panic with the city's citizenry. You should be ashamed of yourself."

Wilcox thought for a moment that Morehouse was serious. When he realized he wasn't, he grinned and relaxed in his chair.

"What do you need, Joe?"

"For what?"

"Follow-ups. This is big, and it'll get bigger. The commissioner told me he wanted the name of your MPD source. They'll string him up if they find out who he is. Or *she*." He gave Wilcox a knowing look. "Your Hispanic buddy?"

"No comment, Paul, except it wasn't her. But they'll be looking at her."

"What else can you get from your source?"

"I don't know."

"Get everything you can for tomorrow. I want to go page one again. You won't argue with that, right? What about the roommate, the hooker angle?"

"There's nothing there, Paul. Let's say she does work for an escort service. That's not illegal."

"Who's she work for?"

"I don't know."

"Find out. See what they have to say. I liked the interview you did with McNamara's fiancé. Her mother and sister are here?"

"Yeah. They were at the apartment but looked like they were in shock. I was uncomfortable talking to them."

"Joe." He said it like a teacher chiding a child. "They should be over their shock by now. Get a statement from the ME supporting the same manner of death in both cases. And it wouldn't hurt to corral a half dozen or so pretty single women and get their reaction to a serial killer roaming the streets."

Wilcox stood and made a move for the door.

"And Joe," Morehouse said, "contact one of your shrink sources and get a profile of how a serial killer thinks, the kind of guy he might be, a loner probably who pulled wings off butterflies when he was a kid, the usual. Maybe a shrink at one of the hospitals to give it weight."

Wilcox was glad to be out of Morehouse's office and in the semi-sanctity of his own cubicle. He couldn't seriously argue with the editor's thinking. His suggestions made sense for follow-ups to a story about a serial killer, whether it was a figment of the reporter's imagination or not. Actually, Morehouse's instructions made things easier. Wilcox hadn't been sure how to proceed with a second article, particularly whether or not to draw upon another fictitious quote from his alleged MPD source. He was glad he didn't have to, at least for that day.

Obtaining a quote from a mental health professional was easy. A clinical psychologist at Howard University Hospital had been only too happy to offer quotable insight for him to use in many of his articles over the years. She dropped what she was doing at the hospital to take his call.

"Read my piece this morning?" he asked.

"Sure I did. Let me guess. You want a profile of what kind of guy goes around killing pretty young women."

"Something like that," he said. "I know you'll be generalizing but—"

"Not a problem. First tell me, were either of the two victims sexually assaulted?"

"No report yet on the most recent. The autopsy on Jean Kaporis here at the *Trib* indicated she'd had intercourse within twenty-four hours of being murdered, but there didn't seem to be any sign of assault."

"It would be unusual if sex wasn't involved. I've never known a serial killer who wasn't after sexual gratification, as perverse as it might be. Let me ask you something else. Why are the police considering this a serial killing? According to my textbook, it takes three related murders before that scenario comes up."

Her question took him aback. She'd never challenged him before, probably, he'd surmised, because she didn't want to risk losing media exposure. She was a true media hound, always showing up on TV talk shows as the expert on myriad topics, most particularly sexual dysfunction. Her popular Sunday evening radio show was often devoted to that gritty subject.

"I don't have the answers for you," he said. "Maybe the police know more than they're letting on."

"There might be other murders with similar MOs?"

"Maybe. How about a brief overview of the typical serial killer, nothing too deep, a thumbnail sketch. If this isn't a good time for you, I can—"

"No problem, Joe. Always happy to help."

Wilcox smiled. Of course she was willing to help, provided he spelled her name right.

"Okay, here's Serial Killer 101," she said. "A nerd? No. Our fellow is probably intelligent, charismatic, charming, and/or good-looking. Of course, I'm, talking about serial killers who entice female victims with smooth talk. They're almost always good talkers. If this guy you're writing about isn't a sexual deviant, then the profile might not apply. Often, some form of childhood abuse is in their background."

"Psychotic?"

"I doubt it. Serial killers are usually psychopaths. There's a difference. A psychotic killer would be out of touch with reality and have trouble eluding the police as a result. Chances are he's keenly aware of what he's doing, that it's criminal. Ultimately, it's a power thing. Determining life and death with the vulnerable gives him an inflated sense of power, something he needs because inside, he's pathetically insecure, maybe impotent. Chances are he's proud of what he's accomplished and keeps every newspaper account of the murders as trophies."

"Likely he's from the D.C. area?"

"As opposed to a vagrant passing through? I'd put my money on his living here."

"You said he's probably smart. What kind of job would he have?"

"That's always interesting, Joe. Very often, these people hold jobs below their intellectual level. Menial jobs. In some ways it fuels their sense of anger against what they perceive to be a world that doesn't appreciate them. A lot of them have had jobs with law enforcement: police forces, security guards, things like that." She paused. "Joe, you said in your piece that both victims worked in journalism. Are you saying whoever killed them is motivated by that?"

"I wasn't saying anything specific, just pointing out that similarity. What do you say?"

"That's a stretch, I say. Do you know how many serial killers are estimated to be running loose in America these days?"

"No, tell me."

"Forty, maybe fifty. That's a Department of Justice figure. You can't prove it by me."

"This has been great," Wilcox said, aware that members of his "task force" in the Kaporis murder had gathered and were standing around, waiting for him to get off the phone. "As usual, you're the best."

"My pleasure, Joe. You ought to come on my radio show some night."

"And talk about sexual dysfunction?"

"Sure, if you're interestingly dysfunctional. Keep in touch."

"Got a minute?" Rick Jillian asked after Wilcox had ended the call.

"Yeah, sure. Hi, Kathleen."

Kathleen Lansden, the researcher assigned to Wilcox, and Jillian pulled up chairs.

"Great piece this morning, Joe," Kathleen said.

"Yeah," said Jillian. "How'd you get a cop to admit they're looking into the serial killer angle?"

"You do this long enough and develop enough sources," Wilcox replied, "things break your way sometimes. What do you two have?"

Jillian ran over the list of *Trib* staffers he'd talked to, all of them having been interviewed by the police.

"And?" Wilcox asked. "I'm sorry to rush things along, but I've got a busy day ahead of me."

"Well—" Jillian said, glancing around the newsroom.

"Well *what?*"

Jillian, a foppish young man with a penchant for bow ties, leaned close and spoke sotto voce. "There's some talk, Joe, that Hawthorne might have been seeing Jean out of the office."

"Is that so? Who says?"

"A couple of guys mentioned it. Actually, one was a woman. Nobody said they know it for certain, I mean, nobody says they saw them together. It's more like an undercurrent."

"Hawthorne, huh?" Wilcox mused. "Makes sense, I suppose. Nice looking young guy, not married. And she was a knockout."

"Very," Kathleen said. "But not quite the word I'd use."

"Think you can find out more?" Wilcox asked Jillian.

"I don't want to ask him," Jillian said. "Based on just a rumor."

Wilcox looked at Kathleen. "Are you close to Hawthorne?"

She shook her head. "Talk to him now and then, but with his ego, it's hard to have a conversation."

Wilcox smiled at her characterization of Gene Hawthorne, which matched his evaluation. *Wouldn't that be something?* he thought.

"I'll talk to him," Wilcox said. To Jillian: "What about the visitors Morehouse wanted you to follow up on?"

"I'm working on it. Nothing so far."

"Who'd we miss on the interview list?" he asked Kathleen.

She handed him a list containing a dozen names.

"Good. I'll follow up. Rick, I need short interviews with a half dozen pretty women living in the District. Pretty and single."

"Why?"

"To see what they think about a serial killer possibly working D.C. Morehouse wants it for my next article."

Jillian laughed. "Great," he said, smiling broadly. "Nice way to meet single women."

"Don't you want me to interview single men living in D.C?" Kathleen asked, playfully.

"Sorry, Scarlett, not this time, unless a woman starts knocking off single men. If so—"

"I can't wait."

"Good. In the meantime, I want you to contact escort services in the D.C. area."

"Why? I'm being fired?"

"Only if you say no to me. Start with the biggest. See if a Mary Jane Pruit works for any of them."

"The roommate?"

"Yup. I need something by end of the day."

"If you say so."

"But Kathleen, whatever you come up with is for my ears and eyes only. Just me. Morehouse doesn't see it."

"Gotcha."

"Get going, both of you. I'll be out of the office most of the day. We'll meet here at six."

He was about to call Jean Kaporis's parents in Delaware when an incoming call took precedence.

"Dad, it's Roberta."

She had something serious on her mind, he knew, from her tone, and from using her full first name. Happy calls came from Robbie.

"Hi, hon. I understand we're getting together for dinner tomorrow night."

"Right, but—"

"So tell me about this new boyfriend. Will I like him?"

"I hope so. Dad, I read the article this morning. Big space—nice placement. Congratulations."

"Thanks."

"Who gave you the serial killer quote at MPD?"

"Oh, come on, Robbie, you know I can't reveal that, even to my favorite daughter. And don't say it. You're my only daughter."

"Was it Edith?"

"No, it was not."

"I'm disappointed, Dad. You promised you'd never stonewall me."

"I haven't."

"Knowing the cops are working a serial killer angle is pretty big stuff. It got you page one."

He held his anger in check. Although she was his daughter, someone for whom he'd throw himself in front of a truck, he didn't appreciate being chastised by her.

"Look," he said, "I'm sorry you think I stonewalled you. I was working against a hell of a deadline Paul Morehouse imposed. I—"

"What about the boyfriend in L.A.?"

"Him? I knew nothing about him. They inserted that sidebar without telling me. Besides, he had nothing to say except that he's an aspiring Brad Pitt."

"Anything else you haven't told me?" she asked, her tone cold.

"No. How about you? Anything to pass on to me?"

"No."

"See you tomorrow night at dinner," he said. "Let's find some time and talk about this. Now's not a good time."

"Fine. Have a good day."

Click.

Philip Connor answered Wilcox's call.

"Mr. Connor, it's Joe Wilcox at the *Tribune*."

"Hello, Mr. Wilcox. I read your story in the paper this morning. Colleen's picture looked nice, really nice."

"Yes, it did. Mr. Connor, I—"

"Will they find the bastard who killed Colleen and the other girl?"

"I'm sure they will, as long as people like you continue to speak out. Are Ms. McNamara's mother and sister still there?"

"Yes."

"I was hoping they could find time for me today."

"They're still pretty upset, Mr. Wilcox."

"Of course they are, but I'm sure the police interviewed them."

"They did."

"It's important that their voices be heard. If the citizens of this city become outraged enough, that puts the pressure on the police to add additional resources and manpower to the hunt for the killer."

"I see."

"Would you be good enough to ask them if they'll spare me a few minutes? I'll make myself available any time that's convenient for them."

"Hold on."

He came back on the line. "They said they would, Mr. Wilcox. Her mom's not that keen on it, but she agreed. Her sister, too. They said it would be best for them later in the afternoon."

"Four?"

"That will be fine, I guess."

"Good. I'd like to talk to you again. See you at four."

Wilcox enjoyed interviewing people, and knew he was good at it, as good as any cop. Of course, they had the advantage of being authority figures capable of tossing you in jail, and could play out the good cop–bad cop scenario. But he had power, too. He could take what you said and slant it any way he wished, turning the most innocuous statement into a damaging one. He didn't do that like bottom-feeder reporters often did, but men and women on the other end of his pen knew he could, and perhaps would.

He especially liked second interviews because he had the advantage of what had been said during the initial one. Amazing, he thought, how versions of an event could vary from one interview to another, details altered, new recollections surfacing, attempts to correct or change the record.

He made some notes in preparation for the interviews and was about to call Jean Kaporis's parents in Delaware when Gene Hawthorne stopped by the cubicle.

"Good morning, Gene," Wilcox said, pleasantly.

"Hey, Joe. Nice play on the serial killer story. Really nice."

"Thanks."

"Joe, Paul suggested I pop by and spend some time with you. He thought I might be helpful in the pieces you're working on. I know you're well sourced, but I've got a few contacts that could be helpful."

"Do you? I appreciate the offer, Gene, but—"

He was about to blow him off, but thought of what Jillian had said. Was there the possibility that Hawthorne had a personal relationship with Jean Kaporis?

"That would be great," Wilcox said. "How about lunch?"

"Today?"

"Yeah. I'm free. I'll take you to the Press Club."

He knew what Hawthorne was thinking. He'd once heard Hawthorne comment that he wouldn't be found dead being a member there. "Bunch of over-the-hill hacks," he said, "has-beens drowning in martinis and rehashing the past."

The young reporter's mischaracterization hadn't surprised Wilcox. Typical of him and others like him, shallow young people lacking any understanding and appreciation of institutions like the Press Club. President Calvin Coolidge had laid the cornerstone for the club in 1926, making it the oldest professional and social media organization in the country, and the largest with more than four thousand members. Its Speakers Luncheon series was the most prestigious and influential news lecture series in America; more heads of state had appeared at the club than at any forum in the world outside the Oval Office. Its membership included the most important names in journalism, men and women of distinction who'd defined responsible journalism.

Over-the-hill hacks and has-beens? Wilcox had thought after hearing Hawthorne pontificate to young colleagues.

"Okay," Hawthorne said. "What time?"

"Twelve-thirty. I'll meet you in the lobby. You know where it is, I assume."

"Sure I do. But one thing, Joe."

"What's that?"

"No pitches over lunch, okay? I'm not the club type." A big grin accompanied this statement.

"Oh, no fear of that, Gene," Wilcox said. "You've got nothing to worry about."

He watched Hawthorne swagger off. Joe wondered whether the heat of his anger showed in his reddened face and the pulsating veins in his neck.

Jean's father was warm and cooperative on the phone, and said he and the Mrs. would be happy to talk to him any time. To Wilcox's relief, he said they would be happy to drive to Washington to meet. The only caveat was that they not have to come to the *Tribune* Building where their daughter had died. They agreed to meet for breakfast at nine the following morning at the Old Ebbitt Grill on Fifteenth, NW.

With that interview nailed down, he called the office of the District of Columbia's medical examiner. His doctor friend was one for whom he'd done favors over the years.

"Hello, Joe," the assistant ME said, his voice sounding like it was being squeezed through a very narrow opening. "Nice piece this morning."

"Thanks."

"But what's this serial killer nonsense? It takes two to tango, Joe, but three or more to qualify as serial murder."

"So I've been told. But it wasn't my idea. MPD's floating that theory."

"They should know better. What can I do for you?"

"I need a confirmation that both Jean Kaporis and Colleen McNamara were murdered in the same way, by asphyxiation. Strangulation."

"You have it."

"Have what?"

"Confirmation. That's the way both young women were killed."

"I can quote you on that?"

"No. You'd better quote the boss. He's signed off on manner of death in both cases. I'll tell you this. If a third young woman, who happens to work in the media, ends up being killed in a similar fashion, I'd say then there might well be a serial killer in our midst."

"Let's hope that doesn't happen," Wilcox said.

"Yes. Let's hope. Stay in touch."

He spent the remainder of the morning starting work on a follow-up story for the next day's edition. As he walked through the newsroom on his way to lunch, he looked up and stopped to watch Roberta deliver a report on the noon news.

"I've been told by a reliable source in MPD that emphasis in the Jean Kaporis murder case—the young reporter at *The Washington Tribune* who was strangled to death a month ago in a storeroom at the paper—is now focusing on individuals who had been on the premises the night of her death, but not necessarily someone employed by the *Tribune*. I have also been assured by MPD sources that speculation that a serial killer might be involved in both the Kaporis case and the more recent murder in Franklin Park, is without merit. The police are treating the two killings as separate and unrelated incidents, perpetrated by two different individuals."

Her statement that someone within MPD was denying that there was a serial killer on the loose was to be expected.

But the claim, "by an unnamed source within MPD," that they were now looking at someone from outside the *Trib* in the Kaporis case, was worth following up. Who was his daughter's source? Did she really have a source? It would have seemed inconceivable to him, until now, that she, or any other responsible journalist, would fabricate a source.

He paused, pushed that thought from his mind, and geared up for lunch with Hawthorne.

TEN

"Maybe you're talking to the wrong people, Roberta."

The comment was made by the managing editor of the six o'clock news, Roberta Wilcox's boss. He'd called her into his office to discuss coverage of the murders.

"I'm working every source I have," she said, her voice mirroring her defensiveness.

"I know you are," he said, "but somebody over at MPD seems to be working the other side of the street from you." He'd come to television from editorial positions with print media, including the *National Enquirer*, where he'd earned a reputation as a tough, inventive reporter. There were those who said that *inventive* reporters were akin to *creative* accountants, many of whom ended up in jail. No matter. Roberta's boss was good at sensing what enticed viewers to tune in, and the ratings proved it.

"I'm not sure I understand," she said.

"Somebody at MPD is floating the serial killer theory. Your father's article confirms that."

"I don't know who he spoke with."

"Can you ask?"

"I did. He's not about to divulge his sources." She smiled and answered his next question before he asked it. "Even to his daughter."

He slid a sheet of paper across the desk. On it was a long list of typed names. She scanned it and gave him a quizzical look.

"People who've called in asking about the serial killer. They're concerned, of course."

"We don't know if there is a serial killer," she said. "I can't get anyone at MPD to even proffer the possibility. The official line is that the two murders were committed by two different people."

" 'Official line,' " he repeated, scornfully. "Since when do we adhere to the official line? Look, Roberta, the *Trib*, thanks to your father, is ahead of us on this. If it ends up that there isn't a nut running around killing people, so be it. But we can't ignore the possibility." She started to say something, but a wave of his hand silenced her. "Let's at least cover the story on the basis that there *could* be a serial killer in D.C."

"All right," she said. "Any suggestions on how to go about that?"

"Sure," he said. "Start by interviewing single women in the District. You're a single woman, Roberta. You'll be able to empathize with them and get them to empathize with you. Also, dig into the history of serial killings in the area, do a profile on serial killers from the past. I'll clear airtime for you tonight and in the future. We'll run it as an investigative series, a five- or six-parter, and buy print ads supporting it. Questions?"

"I can't do the interviews and do the research at the same time."

"Use freelancers for the research. Pull out all the stops." He pointed to the list of callers on his desk. "This is going to mushroom. I want it to mushroom and I want to stay ahead of it." He sat back in his chair, hands behind his head, and smiled. "Should make you feel good, getting the jump on your father, huh?" he said.

❧

Gene Hawthorne was reading National Press Club literature in the club's lobby when Wilcox arrived.

"Drink?" Wilcox asked.

"I don't drink," the younger man said.

"I'll bet you're a vegetarian, too," Wilcox said, without an edge.

Hawthorne shook his head. "Not completely, Joe. I skip red meat, but chicken's okay."

"Then chicken it'll be," Wilcox said, leading them into the dining room where they were seated by a window. Hawthorne had a Diet Coke, Wilcox a Virgin Mary.

"Know what they call Virgin Marys in England?" Wilcox asked.

"No."

"Bloody Shames. Catholic waiters took offense at having to ask bartenders for Virgin Marys, so they changed the name."

"Oh yeah? Interesting?" Hawthorne said, not looking up from the menu.

Wilcox said, "So, Paul thinks you can help me with the serial murder articles. Go ahead. Shoot. I'm all ears."

"What are you having?" Hawthorne asked, nodding at the waiter who'd suddenly appeared at tableside, order pad and pencil at the ready.

"A hamburger, rare," Wilcox said.

"I'll have the chicken salad," said Hawthorne, "and easy on the mayonnaise." He looked at Wilcox. "You were saying, Joe?"

"The help you can give me. I'm looking forward to what you can offer."

Hawthorne shrugged. "I have a few contacts that might be useful, that's all," he said. "I'm pretty well wired in at City Hall."

"City Hall? Sounds good. Think you can get me a statement from the mayor about serial killers running loose in his city?"

"I don't know about the mayor. Maybe one of his aides."

"I know aides over there, too," Wilcox said. "If you can't get the mayor, I—"

"I'll see what I can do for you," Hawthorne said. "About the mayor."

"Good. What other sources do you have, Gene? Are you wired in, as you put it, with MPD?"

"I know some people there, but you're the cops reporter."

"That's right, I am."

Hawthorne looked around the room before leaning closer to the table and saying, "Look, Joe, I know you don't like me, and I understand. I—"

The arrival of their lunches broke the tension, and they focused on eating. Hawthorne was the first to break their silence.

"Let's be honest with each other, Joe," he said. "I know what you think of me. I've heard the comments from others, ones you've bad-mouthed me to. Like I said, I can understand it. Guys like you, older guys at the end of their careers, resent young guys like me coming in and taking over. That's natural, I guess, sort of built into the scheme of things." He gave a boyish grin. "But that shouldn't be a reason to dislike me. I mean, I like you, Joe."

"That's nice to hear," Wilcox said, popping a final French fry into his mouth.

"No, I mean it, Joe. You've paid your dues and deserve a nice retire-ment, time to play golf or work in the garden or things like that. Some day I'll enjoy the same things."

"I'm not close to retiring," Wilcox said, his jaw working against rising anger. He felt a little woozy, and the burger sat heavily in his stomach.

"I know," Hawthorne said. "I didn't mean you were."

Wilcox wiped his mouth with his napkin, shifted in his chair, drew some breaths, and asked, "How well did you know Jean Kaporis?"

"Huh?"

"Jean Kaporis? How well did you know her?"

Hawthorne, too, shifted in his seat and appeared to be processing what Wilcox had asked. Wilcox waited.

"Why do you ask?"

"Just curious, Gene. Rumors are that you might have had a close re-lationship with her."

Hawthorne guffawed and found another posture. "A close relation-ship? That's ridiculous."

"But you knew her."

"Of course I did. So did you. So did anybody working there. What are you doing, Joe, trying to manufacture some sort of story about us so you can point to me as the guy who killed her?"

"I just asked, Gene. I'm not trying to do anything."

The young reporter appeared to have been shaken during the ex-change. Now, he adopted a confidence bordering on arrogance. "You should be working for some tabloid, Joe," he said. "You have a tabloid mentality."

His comment further angered Wilcox, who had to fight an urge to strike out physically across the table. Hawthorne, sensing he'd struck a nerve, continued. "Tell you what, Joe," he said, "I'll feed your need for gossip journalism. Yes, Jean Kaporis and I got it on. Coffee together, drinks after work." His smile was cruel. "I bet you want to know what it was like in the sack with her, huh, Joe? Guys your age forget what it's like. Am I right, Joe?"

Wilcox stood abruptly and walked to the bar. He ordered a Scotch, neat, signaled for the waiter to bring him the check there, and watched Hawthorne strut from the room.

"Damn!" he muttered to himself as the drink was placed in front of him, dismayed at how he'd handled the encounter. He'd intended to calmly put this annoying bugbear in his place, to show him up not by confrontation, but by encouraging him to self-destruct. It hadn't happened. He'd allowed his emotional dislike to trump his intellect, even to the extent that he'd invited Hawthorne's mocking claim of having slept with Jean Kaporis.

"Everything okay, Mr. Wilcox?" the barman asked.

"What? Yeah, everything's okay."

"Fill 'er up again?"

"No, no, thank you. I have to get back to work."

The bartender must have noticed that he'd become unraveled. Embarrassed, Wilcox signed the checks, returned greetings from others at the bar, and left the club, intending to go back to the office to further prepare for his four o'clock interview with Colleen McNamara's mother and sister. Instead, he walked without purpose, stopping in at a bookstore. Maybe I should retire and write a book, he thought, but realized that he had nothing to write about. He sat at an outdoor table in front of a luncheonette and sipped a coffee and watched the world pass by. There was a moment when he considered skipping the interview with the McNamaras, going home and going to bed. What had the TV talk show star Jack Paar once said? "They can't hurt you under the covers."

But that spasm of defeatism passed. He decided to not bother getting his car. Instead he took a taxi to the apartment shared by Colleen McNamara and her fiancé, Philip Connor. By the time he arrived, his depression had lifted, replaced by a renewed burst of enthusiasm. *You're damn good,* he told himself. *Get in there and prove it!*

ELEVEN

While Joe Wilcox suffered the aftermath of an acidic lunch with young master Hawthorne, detectives Vargas-Swayze and Dungey stood on the loading dock of an office supply company warehouse in an industrial area of Southwest. With them was Michael LaRue, one of the company's many deliverymen. He was a tall, trim man with a coppery tan, and black hair pulled into a small ponytail.

"And you delivered the supplies that night and left the building?" Vargas-Swayze said.

"That's right," LaRue said through an engaging smile. "The *Tribune* is part of my regular route. I've been there often since I came to work here." His voice was deep and well modulated; Dungey quietly observed that LaRue spoke well, like a teacher or some other educated person. Detective Dungey also decided that he dyed his hair.

"And you took the supplies up to the newsroom? Why didn't you leave them downstairs in the receiving area?"

His laugh was meant to reassure. "When I have a large delivery to make, that's where I take it, to receiving. But that night, as I remember, we'd gotten an emergency call for some supply or other—I don't know what it was exactly—and I was dispatched to run it over there. You can check inside. They'll have a record of what I delivered."

"But why were you allowed by the security guards to bring it upstairs?" Dungey asked.

"You'll have to ask them," LaRue replied, meaning the *Trib*'s private security force. "It's not the first time they've waved me through. I think the people up in the newsroom leave word with the guards when they know that something they really need is on its way. I don't know that for a fact, but I believe that's the way it works."

Dungey pulled out a photograph of Jean Kaporis and showed it to LaRue.

"That's the same photo you showed me the last time," LaRue said. "What a tragedy. She looks like such a lovely young woman."

"Do you remember seeing her when you made your delivery that night?"

Another cheery, gentle laugh. "I'm sure I didn't, Detective. I think I would have remembered such a beautiful woman. No, I didn't see her."

"You took the supplies you were delivering to a storeroom, away from the main newsroom?"

"Correct. That's where I was told to take the boxes."

"How many boxes?"

"Two, I recall. Two small ones. Oh, I do remember that before I took them to the storeroom, someone, a reporter I assume, asked me to open a box. I did, and she removed one of whatever was in it and took it to her desk."

"That wasn't Jean Kaporis?" said Dungey.

"No, no, it wasn't. I can assure you of that."

"How long have you been working here?" Dungey asked.

"Four or five months."

"You gave us your address the last time we spoke," Vargas-Swayze said. "How long have you lived there?"

He frowned in thought. "Six months?" he said. "Give or take."

"You're not from here," she said.

"No. I'm from the Midwest."

"Where in the Midwest?"

"Illinois, mostly."

"What brought you to the D.C. area?" Dungey asked.

LaRue's smile disappeared. "A bad divorce," he said. "My second. I'm a two-time loser, I'm afraid. I learned after my first divorce that the only smart thing is to give her everything and walk away, start over. That's what I did. I packed up and headed east."

"Why Washington?" Vargas-Swayze asked.

He shrugged. "I visited here a few times when I was married, you know, played tourist, saw the sights. I really liked it, so once the divorce— the second one—was final, I got in my car—she didn't get that—and drove here. I'm glad I did. I like it a lot."

He looked around the loading dock. "I really have to get back to work. It's a good job and I'd hate to lose it. Can we talk again? I'll be happy to come to your office any time you want."

"We'll get back to you if we have more questions," Dungey said, snapping closed his notebook. "Thanks for your time."

"Sure. I read there might be a serial killer in Washington. I sure hope that's not true."

"So do we," Vargas-Swayze said. "Have a good day."

Back in their car, Vargas-Swayze said, "So, are you still uneasy about him? He computes for me."

"Yeah, only let's run a check on him. He was there the night she got it. Can't hurt."

"Right."

He said as they drove back into midtown, "You were telling me about getting together with your husband last night."

"That's right, I was."

The Westin Fairfax Hotel, on Massachusetts Avenue NW, had gone through various name changes and ownership over the years, but had never lost its opulence. Former Vice President Al Gore had lived there in the 1950s when his father was a United States senator. Having the tony Jockey Club within its walls only added to its élan.

Peter Swayze had arrived before Edith and secured one of the cozy booths in the bar. He stood when Edith entered the room and attempted to give her a welcoming hug, but she avoided his arms and quickly slid into the booth. He sat next to her.

"Drink?" he asked. "The usual?"

"What is the usual, Peter?" she asked.

His laugh was strained. "You don't think I'd forget something as important as that, do you?" he said. "A margarita with a splash of Alizé, no salt."

She looked up at the waiter who'd suddenly and silently appeared and said, "Beer. Corona, if you have it, a Bud if you don't. In a bottle."

"Sir?" the waiter asked Swayze.

"I, ah . . . gin and tonic, please."

"So Peter," she said, "here we are."

"When did you start drinking beer?"

"The day we split. Why are we here?"

"Do you have to be nasty?" he asked.

"I'm not being nasty," she said. "I just don't want to spend any more time here than I have to. I go to work early."

She took him in as he sat back in the booth. He looked haggard, somewhat unkempt, which was surprising, almost shocking. Her soon-to-be former husband had always been a clotheshorse and was scrupulous about his grooming. And he was hypochondriacal, further accentuating his fastidiousness. But tonight there was stubble on his pale face, and his hair wasn't carefully arranged as it usually was. He wore a wrinkled blue denim sport jacket, white button-down shirt with one collar point unbuttoned, and baggy chino pants.

She squinted in the dim light and took a closer look. "What's with the new look, Peter?" she asked.

He glanced down at his shirtfront, back up at her and said, "I lost my job, Edith."

"Oh. I'm sorry to hear that. A downsizing?"

"Something like that. They brought in a new management team, including a guy who ended up my new boss. An idiot. We didn't see eye-to-eye from day one."

A series of thoughts ran through her mind as their drinks were served. Peter made a lot of money working for the bank, and had received substantial bonuses during the time they were married. He had a 401K plan into which he invested the maximum amount allowed, and it was matched dollar for dollar by the bank. He was also tightfisted, she knew, someone who agonized over how much to tip in a restaurant, and who would go far out of his way to save a few cents on an item, often spending more in transportation to a bargain than what he saved. He wasn't about to miss any meals.

"Enough about me," he said. "I worry about you."

"Why?"

"The way you spend your days and nights. There's a killer out there preying on beautiful young women like you."

"I don't think I have anything to worry about Peter. In the first place, I'm not a beautiful young woman. In the second place, anybody tries to mess with me and he's past tense. And third, there is no serial killer."

"I read the paper," he said.

"And you know you shouldn't believe everything you read."

He raised his glass. "It's great seeing you again, Edith, here in this place that's special for us. Remember?"

She picked up her bottle of beer, ignored the glass the waiter had brought with it, and took a swig. As she placed the bottle back on the table, he placed a hand over one of hers. "I really miss you, Edith."

She pulled it back. "Peter," she said, "are you actually suggesting that we drop the divorce and get back together?"

"I think so," he said.

It crossed her mind that now that he was out of work, he might be looking for her to support him until he found another job. But she didn't express that callous thought. Instead, she said, "That's out of the question. It didn't work, Peter. We both know that. We're better off not being with each other."

He didn't reply.

"I thought you were serious about the woman you were seeing," she said.

"There wasn't anything there," he said. "It was purely physical."

On whose part? she wondered.

"Are you seeing anyone?" he asked. "Anyone you're serious about?"

"No, I—I really don't think that's any of your concern."

"Then you aren't even willing to give it a try?" he said. "Even for a period of time, say a few months?"

She shook her head. "Afraid not, Peter."

This time, her hand touched his. "It's just better this way," she said, withdrawing her hand and checking her watch. "Look," she said, "I have to be up early, and I have a very busy day ahead of me. I'm glad we talked, Peter. I don't mind staying in touch, but—"

"I talked to my lawyer today," he said, motioning for the waiter.

"I meant to ask about that. When are the papers coming through? It's been forever since we settled on the terms of the divorce and—"

"We have to talk about that," he said.

"Talk about *what*?"

"The terms. My attorney feels they should be changed in light of my current financial situation."

"Your current financial situation?" It came out in a burst of incredulity.

"I don't have a job. The market is tight, especially in this economic climate. My unemployment benefits will run out. Besides, my attorney says that because you have a steady job and no one to support besides yourself, it's only fair that you contribute money to me—or, at least, not expect me to pay alimony to someone like you who has a good job and obviously doesn't need the money."

"Your attorney is a scumbag!" she said, loud enough to cause the waiter, who'd brought the check, to frown and quickly walk away.

"Hey, hey," he said, trying for her hand again, but it had joined the other one on her lap.

"This is why you got me to come here tonight, to try and get me to agree to change the terms of the divorce?"

"Keep your voice down," he whispered.

"I'll talk as loud as I please, damn it," she said. "Is this why you dressed up like some down-and-out bum? I was wrong. *You're* a scumbag, Peter, you *and* your goddamn attorney. You tell him he's a *tacaño*. For your information, and in case your mother wonders, that's Spanish for 'blood-sucking leech.' And you, Peter are—"

"You don't have to make a scene," he said. "And don't say bad things about my mother."

She had a fleeting, satisfying vision of pulling out her Glock and shooting him in the head. She glanced at the check and said, "The total is sixteen dollars and forty-five cents, Peter. Twenty percent is three-twenty-five. Don't stiff the guy. Unlike you, he makes an honest living."

It took her a few hours to unwind at home, aided by a glass of dark Jamaican rum and Tito Puente on the stereo. Her anger eventually dissipated enough so that she was able to get into bed and to fall asleep. One of her final thoughts before drifting off was that if there had ever been any doubts about ending the marriage to Peter Swayze, tonight put them to their final rest. The last thing she remembered before blacking out was chuckling.

∾

"He sounds like a real jerk," Dungey said.

"He's a type, that's all. I almost shot him in the bar."

"Nah."

"Well, it did cross my mind. Did you win your game last night?"

"We lost, but not by much."

"Where to next?"

"Lunch. I'm hungry. How about a slice?"

"Sounds good to me."

∾

Wilcox's interview with Colleen McNamara's mother and sister didn't produce much in the way of material for the next article, although he did lead the sister into saying that Colleen had expressed fears of walking alone at night in downtown D.C.

"Did she ever discuss the murder that happened at the *Tribune,* my paper?" he asked.

"Yes, she did," replied the sister. "She said she'd been at the newspaper a few times and thought security wasn't good. In fact, she told her boss at the station that they should make their security better."

"Interesting," Wilcox said. "What about men she was seeing? Did she talk about them with you?"

"There was only Philip. They met right after she came here. There was no one else in her life."

The mother, who'd been mostly silent, chimed in. "She never should have been out walking alone with killers loose on the streets."

Wilcox noted the comment in his pad.

"And why didn't Philip walk her home?" the mother added in a low voice. "I never have trusted him."

"Mom, please," the sister said. To Wilcox: "Anything else?"

"No. You've been generous with your time at what must be a very painful moment. I appreciate it."

"I hope he rots in hell."

"Who?" Wilcox asked.

"The serial killer."

"I'm sure he will," Wilcox said.

Colleen's fiancé was arriving at the apartment as Wilcox went down the steps to the sidewalk.

"Sorry I couldn't be here," Connor said.

"That's okay," Wilcox said. "They're nice ladies."

Philip nodded. Wilcox thanked him for his cooperation, and said he'd be back in touch if anything new developed.

Rick Jillian and Kathleen Lansden were waiting for him in the newsroom when he returned to the *Trib*.

"How did you do getting quotes from single women?" he asked Jillian.

"Great," he replied, laying a computer printout in front of Wilcox. "I got seven good quotes, names, et cetera. One of 'em gave me her phone number."

Kathleen laughed. "You must not look like the serial killer type."

"I guess not," Jillian said. "Hey, check out this one." He pointed to one of the quotes. "She's a stripper in that club, Archibald's, on K Street. I figured a serial killer might hang out in a place like that, so I popped in and talked to one of the girls."

"For research purposes only," Kathleen said, rolling her eyes.

"That's right," Jillian said. "Read what this stripper—her name is Coco—said."

Wilcox read the quote: " 'Most of the men who come in here are nice guys, businessmen, tourists, decent guys. But sometimes there's a creep, you know, a weirdo who looks like a serial killer.' "

"Serial killers don't usually look like creeps," Wilcox said.

"I know," Jillian said, "but I thought it was worth a shot."

Wilcox nodded as he read the rest of the quotes. "Good job," he said.

"I struck out," Kathleen said. "Every escort service I talked to refused to give the names of the women who work there. Can't blame them, I guess."

"Did you specifically ask about Mary Jane Pruit?" Wilcox asked.

"Sure. One guy who works at the Starlight agency—he ended up asking whether I'd be interested in working for him—he seemed surprised when I mentioned her name. It's in my notes."

Wilcox was pleased that Kathleen had been unable to ascertain whether Kaporis's roommate worked as a paid escort. It was an avenue he wasn't interested in following, and he hoped Morehouse would drop it. It was more than just his discomfort with the scenario. His boss seemed unreasonably anxious to pursue avenues other than those involving *Trib* employees. As hardnosed as Morehouse could be about generating news stories that resonated with the public, he seemed to be leaning even more these days toward tabloid journalism.

Wilcox spent the next three hours writing his follow-up article for the next day's paper, ending it with the quote from Colleen McNamara's mother: "I hope he (the serial killer) rots in hell!" Morehouse had cleared front-page space, and Wilcox wrote to fill the length that had been set aside. He worked uninterrupted until nine, when he sent the finished piece to Morehouse over the internal computer network, and ten minutes later went to his boss's office.

"Nice," Morehouse said. "But where's the history slant I suggested?"

"I didn't have time, Paul. I have Rick and Kathleen working on it for the next piece."

"Okay. It's good to see you back among the living. I was getting worried about you."

"I never left it," Wilcox said. "See you tomorrow."

"Yeah. Oh, by the way, Joe. Hawthorne came in this afternoon. He said you had lunch together at the press club."

"Right."

"He says you've got a bug up your rear end about him."

"Me? Why would he say that?"

"Ask him. If he's right, get rid of it. I don't need discord."

"Sure, Paul."

"Good work, Joe. I see why I hired you twenty years ago."

"Twenty-three," Wilcox corrected.

He'd packed up things to bring home with him and had taken a few steps in the direction of the elevators when his ringing phone stopped him. It might be Georgia or Roberta, he reasoned, and picked up.

"Joe Wilcox here," he said.

"Hello, Joe," the male caller said.

"Can I help you?"

"I don't think so, but I would love to get together—for old time's sake."

"Who is this?"

"It's Michael, Joe."

"Michael?"

"Your brother, Michael. I don't blame you for being shocked, Joe. It's been a very long time."

"Where are you calling from, Michael?"

"My apartment here in Washington."

"Washington? You're here?"

"Yes. I thought we might have a drink together. My treat."

"Now? I can't. I—"

"Tomorrow?"

"I, ah—I'll call you. Let me have your number."

"I hope you won't disappoint me, Joe, after all these years," Michael said after giving Wilcox his phone number. "I won't be here during the day, but I expect to be home by five."

"I have dinner plans tomorrow night," Wilcox said.

"I understand, Joe, I truly do. But let's not allow too much time to pass. After all, we are family."

"I'll call," Wilcox said.

"I know you will, Joe. You always were responsible, a man of his word. I look forward to hearing from you. Good night, Joe. Best to your lovely wife and daughter."

TWELVE

Michael LaRue did as he often did at the end of a workday. He drove to the apartment house in which he lived on Connecticut Avenue NW, found a parking space on the street, and walked two blocks to a small, Italian storefront pizzeria and restaurant on a side street, where he'd become a regular since moving to the neighborhood five months earlier. The mom of the mom-and-pop operation greeted him as he came through the door. Her husband, a bulky man wearing whites, and sporting a long, drooping handlebar moustache, tossed a greeting from behind the counter where he slathered a piecrust with tomato sauce, and sprinkled mozzarella cheese and slices of pepperoni over it.

"Ah, Mrs. Tomaso," LaRue said, kissing her on both cheeks. "You're looking lovely this evening."

"Go on," she said. "There was a time when I was beautiful, back in Italy. Too many years ago to remember."

"You're like fine wine," he said, "getting better with age."

"Come, sit," she said, leading him to what had become his regular table, a small one with two green vinyl-covered chairs beneath a fading mural of an Italian seaside town, identity unknown.

"Vino?" she asked.

"Yes, a glass of house red. And some breadsticks, if you don't mind."

Breadsticks and wine in front of him, he opened that day's *Washington Tribune* to the Metro section and read Joe Wilcox's article—for the second time. When Mrs. Tomaso reappeared to take his order, she noticed what he was reading and said, "Animals! Serial killers! No such thing ever happen in *Italia*. Only here in America. Washington is the worst. Murders every night, two, three, sometimes four."

His laugh came out soft and comforting, as it was meant to be. "This is a lovely city," he said, "no worse than others."

"In the daytime maybe," she said. Then, she leaned closer to him. "At night, everything changes. Am I right?"

"I suppose it does," he said, folding the newspaper and setting it on the green linoleum floor next to his chair. "Do you know what I've always thought?" he asked.

"What?"

"I've always thought that if you're looking for a serial killer, you should first look at those men who drive the ice cream trucks through neighborhoods."

"Why?"

"They have to spend all day listening to those dreadful tunes that play, over and over—'London Bridges Falling Down,' 'Happy Birthday'—." He sang: "With a knick-knack, paddy-whack, give the dog a bone, this old man came rolling home."

A schoolgirl giggle came from her.

"Even I would become a serial killer if I had to listen to that all day, every day," he said, waving off the menu she held. "I'm hungry," he said.

"Of course you are," she said, "and I stand here talking too much."

"And I sit here singing silly songs," he said. "Lasagna?"

"Joey made it fresh today."

He smiled at her calling her sixty-year-old overweight husband "Joey." The name might have fit forty years ago when he was a swarthy young Italian stud seducing his bride-to-be, but those days were long gone, for both of them.

"Lasagna it will be," he said, "and a simple green salad with your wonderful house dressing."

"Garlic bread?"

"Not tonight."

"You see a young lady tonight, huh?"

"You never know," he replied with a mischievous grin.

Besides that day's newspaper, he'd brought a book with him, which he read while eating. He finished his meal with a cup of cappuccino, paid in cash, kissed Mrs. Tomaso on both cheeks, bade her husband a pleasant night, and went to his apartment on the ground floor of an elegant, six-story brick building that had once been someone's stately home.

His apartment was at the rear of the building; windows in the small bedroom overlooked a compact brick patio and a garden that needed tending. There was an old-fashioned look to the apartment; it was slightly tattered and in need of fresh paint, but impressively neat. The furniture was nondescript but useful, function trumping form. A corner of the living room, with windows facing the street that ran along the side of the building, was devoted to a work area consisting of a hollow core door supported by two short, putty-colored metal file cabinets, a large cork bulletin board, and a small folding table providing an additional work surface. A portable electric typewriter sat on the desk, along with a desk calendar, pens, pencils, and scissors in matching coffee cups, a telephone, halogen desk lamp, and a stack of books neatly piled with the larger ones on the bottom, creating a pyramid. The room's white walls were virtually void of art or photographs, with the exception of three replicas of old theater posters displayed side-by-side, but not benefiting from having been hung with care. A relatively new TV set and VCR sat on a cabinet on which its previous owner had painted what passed for an oriental design in reds and yellows. Next to it an electric guitar leaned against a small amplifier.

Maggie, a Maine coon cat that LaRue had adopted from the local SPCA shortly after moving in, greeted him the moment he stepped through the door. Michael LaRue liked dogs and cats, and might have opted for a dog, were he not away from the apartment so often, working double shifts at the office supply company for the overtime. He'd changed out of his deliveryman's uniform before leaving work, placing it in his employee locker, and put on a tight black T-shirt that followed the contours of his sculpted torso, and jeans that enhanced his lower half. After checking the cat's food and litter, he went to the bedroom where he stripped off his clothing, slipped into a pair of gym shorts, and inserted a workout video into the VCR. At the end of the half-hour video, he showered away the sweat, changed back into what he'd worn home, and stood before the bulletin board that was covered with articles carefully clipped from *The Washington Tribune*. They all carried Joe Wilcox's byline.

He sat at the desk, turned on the lamp, and withdrew a thick folder from one of the file cabinet drawers. Although he'd already read everything in the folder dozens of times, he began reading each piece of paper as though never having seen it before. There were photographs, too, many of them old and faded, others much newer. Some were shots he'd taken recently with a small, inexpensive digital camera; others had been snipped from local newspapers and magazines.

He dwelled on what was in the file folder and on the bulletin board, his mood vacillating from pleasurable memories to profound sadness, and anger, too. Maggie had climbed up on to the back of his chair and draped herself over his shoulders and around his neck, which the cat often did, much to Michael's satisfaction. He had no concept of the passage of time until the cat suddenly leapt to the floor, her front claws digging into his neck. He touched the skin and examined his fingertips to see whether she'd drawn blood. She hadn't. "You devil," he said playfully, shaking his finger at her.

He looked at his watch. It was time to do what he'd decided he would do that night. He picked up the phone and dialed Joe Wilcox's direct line at *The Washington Tribune*.

✍

He sat in silence after the call to his brother. Hearing Joe's voice seemed surreal, and he tried to hear it again in his mind. He'd been planning that phone call for months, always putting it off for one reason or another, finding excuses to delay another day, trying to script what he would say, and how he would respond to what Joe might say. Hearing Joe answer the phone provided a momentary shock. He'd deliberately called his work number at night, hoping to be connected to voice mail. The conversation had gone by so fast that he wondered whether it had ever taken place. But he knew it had, and he was glad.

He picked up the phone again and dialed another number. A woman answered.

"Carla, it's Michael."

"Hello there," she said. "What are you up to?"

"Thought I'd go over to Kramerbooks for some coffee and conversation. Join me?"

"I don't know, I—"

"Oh, come on, Carla. The night is young. Besides, I wanted to talk to you about a concept I have for a novel based on Homer's Elysian Fields. I've been reading the *Odyssey* again and want to discuss my idea with you."

Carla, whom LaRue had met at Washington's venerable Kramerbooks and Afterwords Café, in Dupont Circle, agreed. She was an editor at a small publisher of regional guides, and they'd hit it off almost immediately, their love of literature, and an even greater fondness for discussing it, cementing the friendship. She was a good-looking woman in her mid-thirties, a few pounds away from being overweight and always assiduously working to avoid that happening. Her glasses were extremely large and round, with black frames and thick lenses. Her hair was dark, touched with premature gray, and she wore it loose so that it reached halfway down her back. Although they spent considerable time together, their relationship had never advanced beyond friendship, which did not necessarily reflect her feelings. She found Michael LaRue to be an appealing man, both physically and intellectually. Once, after he'd told her he'd been a professor of literature at the University of Illinois, she'd asked the obvious question: "Why are you working as a deliveryman?"

To which he'd replied, "Because I've had enough of academia and all its pretensions. I made a decision to pursue a simpler life after a divorce left me shaken and unsure of who I was, or what I wanted to be—when I grew up." That lovely smile emerged. "I don't want to teach literature. I want to enjoy it as a reader. I want to read every book ever published, and become really good on my guitar, maybe write songs for my own enjoyment."

After hearing him play his guitar for her one night at his apartment, and being extremely impressed, she'd tried to persuade him to appear at open mike nights in local coffee houses.

"That would defeat the whole purpose," he said. "I play for me, and only for me." He quickly added, "And for you, of course."

She never brought it up again.

&

"Besides," he announced on the phone this night, "I have something to celebrate."

"What's that?" she asked. "I love celebrations."

"Can't tell you," he said. "Be content to celebrate with me without knowing why."

"Ah, my mysterious friend Michael," she said with a laugh. "A half hour?"

"A half hour."

THIRTEEN

Y ou had trouble sleeping?" Georgia asked Joe the next morning as they sat in their kitchen. It was 6:30 A.M.; he'd been up, showered, and dressed for more than an hour.

"Yeah. It must have been the fast food I ate last night at the paper."

That morning's edition of the *Trib* was open on the table.

"HE SHOULD ROT IN HELL"
Grieving Mom Speaks Out About Serial Killer

"I wouldn't trade places with you for the world," she said with an admiring smile.

"What do you mean?"

"Having to speak with the families of victims after a tragedy."

"At least I don't do what the TV types do, shove a microphone in people's faces an hour after a family is wiped out in a fire and ask how they're feeling. I'd better get going. I'm meeting Jean Kaporis's mother and father at nine."

"Watch it—your daughter's a TV type. You still believe the serial killer angle?"

"Yeah. But I never said I believe it, only that the cops are romancing the possibility among themselves." He took his sport jacket from where he'd draped it over the back of his chair, put it on, kissed her, and headed for the front door.

"Joe," she said, following him.

"Yeah?"

"Are you okay?"

"Yeah, sure."

"You seem—oh , I don't know. You seem preoccupied."

"I guess I am. Must be the lousy sleep and another full day. I'll be late."

"No, you won't. Roberta and her new boyfriend are coming tonight for dinner. Remember?"

He slapped the side of his head. "I absolutely forgot. Don't worry, I'll be here."

Clouds that had rolled in overnight opened as he drove to the District, and his wipers had trouble keeping up with the deluge, as well as with the torrent of thoughts that had consumed him since receiving the call from his brother.

It had kept him awake for much of the night, and dominated his every thought that morning. He'd considered telling Georgia about it but couldn't bring himself to do it. Michael's sudden injection into his life represented for Joe Wilcox a monumental and unwelcome intrusion, a Category Five hurricane, a nuclear bomb.

It had been almost forty years since they'd had any contact, enough time for Joe to have virtually forgotten that Michael even existed, although mental snapshots of him occasionally came and went, each causing a jolt to the nervous system, a jab in the stomach. Michael's name hadn't been mentioned in Joe's house since early in his marriage to Georgia; Roberta didn't know that she had an Uncle Michael.

"Damn him!" Joe fairly shouted within the confines of his car. "Goddamn it!"

Anger represented only one of his emotions since receiving the call. There was guilt, too, forty years of it. When guilt gripped him, as it irregularly did, he went through a mental exercise of absolution. Cognitively, he could rationalize his behavior toward his brother, excuse it, chalk it up to the circumstances surrounding their forty-year estrangement. But then the emotional quotient butted heads with reasoning, leaving him as confused as ever about what he felt, or more important, what he should feel.

Georgia had suggested early on that he seek counseling to help rid himself of any conflicts he might be harboring. He never followed through. He didn't need to bring to life on some shrink's couch what he'd decreed as dead, his only brother.

He dreaded going to his cubicle and checking voice messages. To his relief, Michael had not called again. Of course he hadn't. Joe had said that *he* would call. The number left by Michael was still on his desk. He crumpled the paper into a ball and held it above the wastebasket but didn't drop it. Better that he should dial the number rather than receive another call from Michael there at the office, or, God forbid, at home.

Michael said he would be away during the day. Did he have a job in Washington? Where did he live? He'd said he was calling from his apartment, not a hotel. That meant he intended to stay. The possibility was chilling.

Why had he come to Washington? Of all the places in the United States to which he could have relocated, why did it have to be here?

The answer was obvious. He'd chosen Washington because that was where his brother and his brother's family lived. Another chill, another flip-flop of his stomach.

He dialed the number Michael had given him. A taped voice on a machine answered:

"Hello. You've reached Michael. I can't take your call at the moment, but leave a message and your phone number after the beep—leave it v-e-r-y slowly, please, or repeat it—and I'll get back to you in short order."

The beep sounded as Joe lowered the receiver into its cradle. Michael had an answering machine, another indication that he wasn't just passing through. As he stared at the phone, a comforting thought occurred. Maybe it had been a prank call by someone who'd learned that he had a brother he hadn't seen in years, and decided to torment him, a crazy person with a grudge against him for something he'd written. Lord knows he'd had his share of nuts over the course of his career.

The voice on the answering machine echoed in his mind. Was it really Michael's voice? He had no way of knowing. Michael was sixteen the last time Joe had seen him, or heard him speak.

The phone rang, causing him to flex in his chair. He picked up the receiver with trepidation.

"Joe, it's Jeanette." Jeanette Roos was the *Trib*'s ombudsman, gender aside. "I need to talk to you."

"About what?"

"About the serial killer series you're doing."

"What about it?"

"The unattributed MPD source you quoted."

Wilcox's stomach tightened.

"I'm doing my next column about how reporters use unattributed or anonymous sources at times for their stories. I have to cite our rules about it, Joe, and therefore explain why you were allowed to fall back on one."

"Why me?" he said. "They do it all the time around here."

"I know, I know, but there isn't a choice lots of times, especially with politicians. I'll level with you. Our leaders in the executive suite are evidently getting steam from MPD about the serial killer claim. MPD brass claims that no one in the department is floating that scenario. The pols are coming down hard on the cops to catch this so-called serial killer before he kills again. Our leaders, especially Harris and Wright, want me to defend our decision to go with your stories based upon an anonymous source. What can you give me?"

"Nothing, Jeanette. I do have a very good source over at MPD who says they're working with the serial killer concept. I believe him." She started to say something, but he interrupted. "And don't ask whether I'd be willing to share my source with anyone here. Morehouse gave the piece the green flag, and so did *his* boss. End of story."

"Hey, Joe," she said, "don't snarl at me. I just work here, like you."

"Yeah, sorry. I'm a little edgy this morning."

"Problem?"

He forced a laugh. "My daughter is bringing a new boyfriend for dinner tonight. That's enough to make anyone uptight."

She laughed along with him and ended the conversation.

He checked the clock. Almost 8:30. Morehouse buzzed him: "Need to see you, Joe."

"I only have a few minutes," Wilcox said as he entered Morehouse's office. "I'm meeting with Jean's mother and father."

"Good. Look at this." He handed Wilcox a message slip.

"What does someone at Fox TV want with me?"

"They want the famous Joseph Wilcox on one of their talk shows tomorrow night."

"What talk show?"

"D.C. Digest. They're doing a half hour on the serial killer. Give 'em a call."

"I don't want to go on a talk show, Paul."

"Yes, you do, Joe. It's good for the paper. You, too. I've cleared it with PR. Call 'em back and tell 'em you'll be there."

Wilcox shoved the message slip into his jacket pocket and left for his breakfast at Old Ebbitt Grill with Jean Kaporis's parents. He entered the Washington landmark restaurant and bar and asked the young woman at the podium if anyone had come in looking for Joe Wilcox. She pointed to an older man with a cane, and a considerably younger woman.

"Mr. and Mrs. Kaporis," he said, extending his hand. "I'm Joe Wilcox."

"A pleasure, sir," replied the father. "I'm Marshall Kaporis. This is my wife, Victoria."

"Thanks for making the trip," Wilcox said, leading them to the podium where they were immediately assigned a table in the bustling restaurant.

"Is there any progress in the investigation?" Marshall Kaporis asked the moment they were seated. Although he was probably in his early to mid-seventies, there was a youthful glow to him. *Maybe being married to a younger woman does that for you,* Wilcox mused. On second and closer inspection, Victoria Kaporis was not as young as she'd appeared to be in the lobby, nor as he'd envisioned when interviewing her by phone. He pegged her as early fifties, with skin that had enjoyed, then suffered too many hours baking in the sun. She had strong facial features and surprisingly pale blue eyes, considering her coloring. He had noticed in the lobby that she had a hell of a figure for someone on the Social Security side of fifty. Marshall Kaporis had done okay for himself.

"I should let you know, Mr. Wilcox," Victoria said, "that Jean was not my daughter. She was my stepdaughter."

"Yes, I'm aware of that," Wilcox said.

"They had a wonderful relationship," Marshall said, his eyes moistening.

Wilcox said, "Speaking of daughters, I understand you were interviewed by my daughter, Roberta."

"Yes," Marshall replied. "A lovely young woman. She was extremely courteous and sensitive to what we'd just been through."

Wilcox grinned. "She's a good reporter—better, a good person. You mentioned to Roberta that Jean had confided in you about some of the men she'd been seeing since coming to Washington."

Marshall and Victoria looked at each other.

"I don't remember us saying that," Victoria said.

"Well," Wilcox said, "maybe you weren't that specific. But I did hear that you might have some information that could help in the investigation."

Marshall's cane slipped off the back of his chair and hit the floor with a loud crack. A waiter picked it up and rehooked it over the chair. "Sorry," Marshall said.

"Bad back?" Wilcox asked.

"Knees. I've had two replaced."

"At the same time," Victoria clarified.

"Ouch," Wilcox said. "Jean never mentioned who she was dating? She was a beautiful young woman. I'm sure there were plenty of men pursuing her."

Marshall beamed. "Jean was always popular," he said, not attempting to mitigate his pride. "Class president in her junior year, and won a few local beauty contests. I'll bet your daughter did, too."

"No, Roberta never pursued that. Breakfast?"

Marshall and Victoria Kaporis spent the next forty-five minutes talking about Jean with expected parental pride. Wilcox listened attentively and responded appropriately, but his mind wandered to the only name consuming him.

"Was Jean an only child?" he asked after their plates had been cleared.

"Yes," Marshall said. "I'm afraid she was spoiled because of that. My wife and I doted on her." He smiled and patted Victoria's hand. "Of course, once Jean's mother died—cancer, a long battle, bless her—Victoria stepped right in and doted on Jean, too."

"I understand," Wilcox said, looking for their waiter. As much as he liked these two people, he was anxious to leave, to get back to the paper and work on the next day's article—and to see if Michael had called. As they waited for the check, he asked, "Did you know the young man Jean had been dating here in D.C., the one who went back to California after they broke up?"

Marshall shook his head. "No," he said, "that was after—"

Wilcox waited for him to finish. When he didn't he said, "After what?"

Marshall sat back, his pleasant face turning serious. "Jean had gotten involved with a married man," he said. "I shouldn't be telling you this, or anyone for that matter."

Wilcox waited silently.

"But you seem to be a trustworthy man."

A reporter's most valuable asset, being trusted.

"You wouldn't print this, would you?"

"Not if you don't want me to."

"Please don't."

"You have my word. But I don't know what it is you don't want me to print," Wilcox said.

"Jean was involved—but only briefly—with a married man," Marshall said. "She didn't know he was married when she started seeing him. When she found out that he was, she was devastated."

"She talked to you about this?"

"Yes. She came home over a weekend and told us about it."

"I felt so sorry for her," added Victoria. "Poor thing, she'd been duped by this man, lied to, taken advantage of."

"Who was he?" Wilcox asked.

They looked at each other before Marshall said, "We never knew his last name. I think his first name was Paul."

"Paul?" Wilcox said. "No last name?"

"No," Marshall said, slowly shaking his head.

"What did this Paul do?" Wilcox asked.

"It didn't last long," Victoria offered. "Their affair, I mean. Only a few weeks, according to Jean."

"What did Paul do for a living?" Wilcox repeated.

"She never said," Marshall answered, "and we didn't ask questions. We just let her talk, which is what she needed."

"She didn't need us probing," Victoria said. "She needed to vent, that's all. She felt much better when she left."

"Have you met Jean's roommate, Ms. Pruit?" Wilcox asked.

"Yes, once," the father answered. "We'd come to visit Jean and went to her apartment. A nice young woman—"

"If only she didn't smoke those ghastly cigarettes," Victoria Kaporis said. "It wasn't a healthy environment for Jean to be living in."

But it didn't kill her, Wilcox thought.

"They had an arrangement," Marshall said. "Mary Jane was never to smoke in Jean's bedroom. She kept the door closed all the time to keep out the smoke."

"Sounds like a sensible arrangement," Wilcox said.

"I suppose it was," Victoria said, not meaning it.

They parted on the street in front of the restaurant.

"Thank you for the breakfast, sir," Marshall said, shaking Wilcox's hand. "And thank you for caring about Jean. I hope you find who killed her."

"That's for the police," Wilcox said, "but sometimes we get to help. Thanks again. Safe home."

Back at the *Trib*, he called Roberta at the TV station and was told she was out on assignment. He had started writing the next article when he remembered the note from Fox TV. His call was answered by *D.C. Digest*'s producer.

"This is Joe Wilcox from the *Trib*. I understand you'd like me to appear on your show tomorrow night."

"Yes, we would. Thanks for getting back to us. We plan to have you, one of our correspondents, and an MPD representative."

"I really don't know what I can offer," Wilcox said. "Everything I know is in my articles."

"That's okay, Joe," said the producer. "Looking forward to having you." He gave Wilcox where and when he was expected to show up, and ended the call.

A call to Georgia found her busy in the kitchen preparing chicken for frying.

"I'm going to be on TV tomorrow night," he said.

"You are? That's wonderful. What show?"

He gave her the particulars, which she dutifully wrote down on a magnetic pad affixed to the refrigerator.

"Any calls?" he asked.

"Some," she said. "There was—"

"Any for me?"

"No, I don't think so. Are you expecting someone to call you here?"

"No, no one in particular. I'd better get back to work if I'm going to get out of here in time for dinner. Heard from Roberta?"

"No. She's probably running around town taping her reports. Go on, Mr. TV Star, get your story written. And don't be late!"

Kathleen Lansden and Rick Jillian had prepared a history of serial killers in the Washington area over the years and left it on Wilcox's desk that morning in his absence. There hadn't been many such criminals in D.C., at least not according to official police records, or accounts written in the press, the most recent exception the two snipers who'd gone on a killing rampage, choosing their victims at random. But the two young staffers had supplemented their research with stories from other cities, enough for Wilcox to more than flesh out his story.

As he wrote, he realized he needed something official from the police, or City Hall, to give the article more immediate substance. He called, and reached Edith Vargas-Swayze on her cell phone.

"*Buenas tardes*," he said.

"Hello, Joe."

"How goes it?"

"I've been better."

"Ooh, doesn't sound very good. Anything I can do?"

"Add my former husband to the list of the serial killer's victims."

"He doesn't kill men."

"Maybe he'd be willing to make an exception," she said. Wilcox was pleased that she so easily referred to a serial killer. "What's up?" she asked.

"I'm working on tomorrow's piece. Anything new? Off the record, of course."

"No."

"You're not alone."

"Right."

"Will you be alone in the next hour?"

"I, ah—probably. I'll call you."

"Fair enough."

Wilcox ate lunch at his desk, worked on the story, and waited for her to call. Each time his phone rang, he jumped and hesitated picking up the receiver. None of the calls fulfilled his fear that it might be Michael, and as the afternoon wore on, his concerns lessened, faded like a bad dream that's forgotten in the morning.

"Hi Joe, it's Edith."

"Hello. I just got a notice that you're holding a press conference at four."

"So I hear. We're further debunking the serial killer angle."

"Uh huh. Has anyone queried you about being my source?"

"No. What are you saying in tomorrow's article?"

"Nothing new. I was hoping you could give me something. Will you be at the press conference?"

"I'll be as far away as I can get. We talked to Jean Kaporis's roommate again."

"Mary Jane Pruit."

"You were right, Joe. She works as a paid escort for the Starlight Escort Service."

Wilcox wrote it down. "Did you come up with any connection to Kaporis?"

"That she worked as an escort, too? No. Pruit admits she tried to convince Kaporis to try her hand at it for the money, but Kaporis refused."

"I'm glad to hear that," he said.

"Why?"

"I don't know, I'd hate to think that one of our staffers was involved in that kind of extracurricular activity. Are you still focusing on people who might have been a visitor here the night she died?"

"We're reinterviewing everyone, but no progress. I'd tell you if there was."

"I appreciate that. I owe you a dinner. The last one was a washout."

"How about tonight? I'm free."

"Love to, but Roberta's coming for dinner with a new beau. If I don't show, you'll have *my* homicide to investigate. Tomorrow?"

"Looks good to me."

"It'll have to be after I do my TV thing."

"What TV thing?"

"I'm going to be on *D.C. Digest* discussing the serial killer. One of your people will be on, too."

"You may launch a whole new career, Joe. A serial success."

"Never happen. I don't have a good side. The show's from six-thirty till seven. Meet you at seven-thirty?"

"You got it. I'll check in tomorrow."

He'd no sooner ended the call than Morehouse summoned him to his office.

"What've you got for tomorrow?" Morehouse asked.

"History, mostly. I'll plug in whatever comes out of the MPD press conference this afternoon."

"Get somebody to counter what they say."

Wilcox's expression was quizzical.

"Get one of the young women you interviewed. No, better yet, get back to somebody in Jean's family, or the McNamara girl's. MPD will debunk the serial killer idea, get somebody to answer that, say something like it's okay for the cops to claim everybody's safe, but 'that doesn't do my little girl any good.' Something along those lines. I don't want to lose the momentum on this. Newsstand sales were up yesterday. You're striking a nerve, Joe. Don't lose it."

As Wilcox started to leave, Morehouse asked, "Anything new on the escort service connection?"

Wilcox hesitated. "No. I had Kathleen check every escort service in the city. She came up with a cropper."

He didn't enjoy lying to his boss, but felt justified in this case. It was bad enough that he'd fabricated an MPD source to give the story a necessary peg, but he wasn't about to sully the reputation of Jean Kaporis. It would be easy to link her to prostitution by innuendo through her roommate's way of making a living. It wouldn't matter that the roommate denied Jean had taken her up on her suggestion that she become a paid escort. The simple fact that they lived together would be enough to plant that unsavory seed.

He sat at his desk and pondered what to do with Morehouse's suggestion—no, order—that he come up with someone to counteract what the MPD was likely to say at their press conference, that no serial killer was being sought in D.C. He decided his best source would be Colleen McNamara's fiancé, Philip Connor.

"Hello, Mr. Wilcox," Connor said.

"Hello, Philip." Wilcox said. "How is everyone holding up?"

"Pretty good. Colleen's mother really liked your story this morning."

"I'm happy to hear that. Tell you why I'm calling. The police are holding a press conference this afternoon to debunk the theory that a serial killer might be loose in the city, and might have killed your fiancé."

"I didn't know that," Connor said. "I thought they told you they believed it."

"One of my sources did. You see, Philip, the problem is that the police and the politicians in this city don't want to look as though they're not doing their job in keeping citizens safe. They way they figure it, the less the citizens know, the better. But think of the ramifications of that. People let their guard down and it creates a much better opportunity for the killer to strike again, to kill another young woman like Colleen. Pretty scary, huh?"

"It sure is."

"I just thought you'd want to know about this, and give you a chance to make a comment."

"Gee, I—"

"Having the police take this unsubstantiated stand sure doesn't do you or Colleen's family any good, does it?"

"No."

"And it certainly doesn't do Colleen any good. The point, Philip, is that it would provide a valuable public service for you to let the citizens know of the pain you and Colleen's family have suffered. That way, maybe Colleen's death won't be in vain if you point out how important it is for the city's young women to be vigilant, to look over their shoulder, take some extra precautions. I admire the police as much as anyone, maybe more. I work with them every day. But they aren't always right. Does what I've said make sense?"

"Sure it does. If people don't stand up for what's right, then—"

"Exactly. I knew you'd see it that way. What statement do you want to make?"

"I don't know, I—"

"You said that even though the police aren't calling it a serial killing, you feel every young woman in the city should be aware and concerned until the killer is caught."

"I—"

"Which is so true, Philip. So true."

"That's the way I feel."

"And so do I. I appreciate the chance to speak with you again. I'll stay in touch."

Wilcox plugged in the quote he'd created for Connor, and added additional information on the American history of serial killers. At a few minutes before four, he went to a small lunchroom off the newsroom, turned on the TV, and waited for the press conference to begin. He probably should have been there, he knew, but he didn't have any questions to ask, the only reason for showing up in person. The DC cable news channel carried the conference live and in its entirety. The official statement delivered by the assistant police commissioner lasted less than ten minutes, and Wilcox jotted a few notes. The assistant commissioner took only a handful of questions from reporters before leaving the podium. A press conference to announce a negative was not exactly prime-time material. Wilcox switched to Roberta's station where his daughter had just begun a live report from the scene of the conference.

". . . and the assistant commissioner stated that based upon what evidence MPD currently has in the two murders, there is no reason to suspect that the same killer is behind the deaths. He went on to caution against panic and asked that citizens go about their daily lives as they normally would. But this reporter has learned from interviews with a number of men and women that while the official MPD stance dismisses the existence of one killer, tension is running high, particularly among the city's vulnerable young women. As one told me, 'I don't care what the police say. I'm putting extra locks on my apartment and staying out of parks at night.' Until the deaths of these two young women are solved, the city will undoubtedly remain on edge. I'll be hosting a special series on the vulnerability of single women, especially careerists, of which this area has many. Stay tuned for times and dates. I'm Roberta Wilcox reporting from MPD headquarters."

Wilcox winced as he turned off the TV and returned to his desk. Until hearing the comments from the press conference, and Roberta's report, the potential ramifications of having launched the serial killer scenario seemed harmless enough. But it had developed legs almost overnight, and perhaps had led his daughter down a precarious path. Two phone calls reinforced that fear.

"Joe, it's Ken Marsolais." Marsolais was the *Tribune*'s editorial page editor. "We're going with an editorial Sunday on the serial killer and how he's paralyzing the city."

" 'Paralyzing the city?' That's a little strong, isn't it?"

"I think so, but it comes down from on high. Got a minute to get together? We'd like your input."

"I can't do it now," Wilcox said. "I'm up against a deadline."

"Sure. Give me a call whenever you get some breathing room. Nice work, by the way."

"Thanks."

The second call was from the paper's public relations VP. "Hello there, media star," she said.

"Not by choice," he said.

"Well, Joe, you'd better get your tonsils in shape and get your best suit out of hock."

"You make it sound like I'm choosing something to be buried in."

"You don't have my permission to die until this is over," she said. "I've got three more requests from talk shows in addition to *D.C. Digest*: two radio, one TV."

"Ah, come on," he said. "I'm a writer, not a talking head."

"I know you don't have to make appearances, Joe. It's not in your contract. But—"

Wilcox looked up as Hawthorne walked by, a smirk on his face.

"No, it's okay," Wilcox told the PR lady. "Set up whatever you want. I'll do what I can."

"Thanks, Joe. You're a trouper."

He finished the next day's article and delivered it to Morehouse.

"Nice," Morehouse said, "but there's not a hell of a lot of meat."

"It's the best I can do, Paul," Wilcox said, annoyed.

"Nice the way you handled what came out of the press conference," Morehouse said.

"Thanks. Well, good night. I have to get home. A family dinner."

As Wilcox went to the door, Morehouse's wife appeared. Mimi Morehouse was a petite, bubbly woman with short blonde hair and an almost perpetual smile.

"Hey, Joe," she said, accepting his kiss on the cheek. "Paul says you guys are really onto a big story with the serial killer."

"Looks that way," Wilcox said. "How've you been?"

"Great, if I can ever get the old man here to take some time off. I'm determined to take an Alaskan cruise before I die."

"It's cold in Alaska," Morehouse said, coming around his desk.

"Not in the summer," she said.

"Big mosquitoes in the summer," he said. "They carry tourists away."

"Well, hope you get to take your cruise," Wilcox said. "Got to be going. Roberta is bringing her latest boy toy to the house for dinner tonight."

"I watch her all the time," Mimi said. "You must be a very proud poppa."

"I certainly am," Wilcox said. "Have a good evening."

"You, too. Now to collect Paul."

The phone on his desk rang as he was about to leave. Pick it up? He did. It was Georgia, calling to remind him about their plans that evening.

"On my way out the door," he said.

He'd no sooner set the receiver down, relieved, when the phone sounded again.

"Joe? It's Michael."

"Oh, hello, Michael. You caught me on my way out the door."

"A nice evening at home with the family?"

"That's right, I—look, Michael, I told you I'd call when I got a chance. I will, but right now I—"

"Family is so important, Joseph, more important than anything in life. You're my family. You, and your wonderful wife and beautiful daughter, too, of course."

Joe couldn't keep the anger out of his voice. "I told you I'd call, Michael. Let's leave it at that."

Michael's voice was smooth and even, deep and without any overt hint of emotion. "When will you call, Joseph?"

"Tomorrow. I have to leave."

"I'm off tomorrow," Michael said.

He's off, Joe thought. *He has a job in Washington, which means he intends to stay.*

"I'd like to see you tomorrow. Can we arrange that?"

"I don't think so. I have a busy day, and—"

"Maybe I should set up something through Georgia. You know how women are, more social than men. Perhaps we could get together at your house and—"

"I'll try to free up some time tomorrow, Michael."

"Four o'clock? At my apartment? I'll put out some goodies and—"

"Yeah, fine. Four o'clock at your apartment. Where is it?"

He wrote down the address Michael gave him.

"I'm looking forward so to seeing you, Joseph," Michael said. "I can't tell you how much it means to me to reestablish ties with my family. You go on, Joseph, and enjoy your evening. Good night now."

FOURTEEN

Tom Curtis was first to arrive at the Wilcox home. Roberta had called to say she was running late, and that Tom would drive himself. Joe Wilcox called from the highway. There had been an accident involving a tractor trailer and a minivan that had blocked traffic for miles. Altogether an average night on roads leading in and out of D.C.

Curtis was in his thirties. He worked as a bartender and had an ambition, he told Georgia, to one day open his own restaurant and bar. He was tall, good-looking, and personable, cast in the bartender role. He offered to help Georgia in the kitchen, but she told him he was a guest, not hired to work the party, but invited him to make the drinks: "I'm sure you can make a better drink than I can."

"What's your pleasure?" he asked.

"Nothing for me—yet. Take care of yourself."

He poured two fingers of Scotch over ice and wandered out on to the patio. It was a pristine early fall night. The recent inclement weather had blown to the east, leaving clear skies and a cool breeze from the north-west.

Joe arrived next.

"Sorry I'm late," he told Georgia, kissing her on the cheek and look-ing through the window at where Curtis stood at the edge of the garden. "That's him?"

"Yes. His name is Tom. He's a bartender."

"Great."

"And very nice."

"That's good to hear. Back in a minute."

He ran upstairs and changed into more casual clothing, returned to the kitchen, poured himself a drink, and joined Curtis on the patio.

"Joe Wilcox, Tom, happy you could make it tonight."

"I'm glad I could, too, Mr. Wilcox," he said, his handshake firm.

"Please, it's Joe. I understand you tend bar. Night off?"

"Yeah. I don't get many."

"Where do you work?" Wilcox asked.

"McCormick and Schmick's, on K Street."

"Nice place. Great fish. I go there often."

"Great happy hour, too. Tip time."

"Yes. Sorry Robbie is running late. You never can tell in the TV news business."

"So I've learned," he said pleasantly. "Yours, too. I've been reading your articles."

"People talk about it at the bar?"

"Sure. We get a lot of single women during happy hour and they're uptight." He laughed. "Later? Just tight."

"Tension affect tips?" Wilcox asked.

"I'll have to do an analysis."

Their conversation had just turned to the baseball season when Roberta bounded onto the patio.

"I am so sorry I'm late," she said, kissing her father, then Curtis, on their cheeks.

Wilcox couldn't suppress a wide smile. His daughter, that impish toddler who'd blessed their lives, had grown into a stunning, effervescent woman. He silently reminded himself to not be too judgmental about Tom Curtis. No man would be good enough for Roberta, an attitude, which if played out, would doom her to a lifetime of spinsterhood.

"How's things in the glamorous TV biz?" Wilcox asked.

"Daddy, nobody says glamorous anymore. Crazy, crazy," she said. "Insane! They keep wanting more but insist on cutting our news budget."

"The competition must be intense," Curtis offered, "with all the cable news channels."

"Exactly," Roberta said.

"I don't have to worry about competition," Curtis said with a boyish grin. "As long as I make the martinis dry and the Cosmopolitans sweet, I'm golden."

Wilcox smiled and realized Georgia had emerged from the kitchen and stood at his side. "How's the chicken coming, Chicken?" he asked.

"Just fine."

"Mom makes the best fried chicken in North America."

"Oh, stop it," Georgia said. "Maybe in Rockville."

Wilcox realized Roberta hadn't been served a drink, and asked what she wanted.

"I'll make it for her," Curtis offered.

"He's a pro," Roberta said, slipping her arm in his and heading for the house.

"How'd it go today?" Georgia asked her husband.

"Okay. I finished the piece for tomorrow's edition."

"I saw the police press conference this afternoon," she said. "They say there is no serial killer."

"The official line, that's all. To be expected."

"I saw Robbie's coverage of it, too," said Georgia. "It sounds as though you two think alike about it."

"I saw her," Joe said. "The problem with the police approach is that it lulls everybody into complacency. Until it's proved to me that there's no serial killer out there, I'm all for prudence and commonsense security. Nice fellow, Mr. Curtis."

"Yes, he is."

He finished his drink and chuckled.

"What's funny?"

"This thing has even got me a little uptight. You read my interview with the shrink. Serial killers are usually good-looking, intelligent, good talkers—" He leaned close to her. "Hell, maybe Curtis is one."

"That's not funny, Joe," she said, meaning it.

"I know, I know. Sorry. I need a refill."

Curtis's frequent verbal reviews of Georgia's fried chicken and the gusto with which he ate affirmed her reputation. Conversation at the table was spirited, with a lot of kidding between Roberta and Tom. Joe contributed to the banter, but his mind eventually was elsewhere. The phone rang in the middle of dinner. Joe started to get up, but Georgia was quicker.

"Wrong number?" Joe asked when she returned in seconds.

"A hang up."

"Inconsiderate," Joe said.

Had it been Michael who'd called? Joe felt like a cheating husband, flinching whenever the phone rang at home. There were many reasons he'd been faithful to Georgia all these years—with one notable exception—among them not wanting to live with such fears. *Fatal Attraction. Spare me that sort of tension.*

But here he was, suffering the very fear he'd determined to not experience. Had Tom Curtis not been there, he might have told Georgia and Roberta about Michael's sudden and unwelcome intrusion into his life. No, that would take some thinking on his part. As upset as Georgia might be at the news, she'd handle it. But Roberta was a different story. She'd been deprived of the knowledge that she had an uncle all these years because her father had insisted she not be told. Georgia had fought him on that decision when Roberta was a small girl but eventually acquiesced, realizing how strongly he felt about it. The subject had seldom come up again during the ensuing years. Occasionally, Georgia would casually mention Michael during a conversation, tossing out a throwaway line intended to draw Joe into a discussion. "Will we never tell her about him?" she'd ask if he allowed the conversation to continue.

"Maybe someday," he'd reply. "Maybe someday."

Had that "someday" arrived? he wondered as the two women in his life cleared the table, with Curtis pitching in. Usually, Joe would be carrying things along with them into the kitchen. But this night he remained at the table, wondering what to do and dreading another ringing of the phone.

They had dessert in the living room, gigantic homemade cookies and coffee, with everyone declining after-dinner drinks. To Roberta's feigned horror, her mother dragged out photo albums and started showing family pictures to Curtis. Joe wandered outside to the patio, and Roberta soon followed.

"Your guy's okay," he said, "pretending to be interested in those photos."

"You like him?"

"Sure."

"Dad?"

"Huh?"

"They're pressuring me at the station to do a series on the serial killer angle, a five- or six-parter."

"I heard you say that in your report this afternoon. Congratulations!"

"I'm not sure I want to do it."

"Why?"

"Oh, I don't know, pride, I suppose. Your series of articles is what's spurred them to come up with it."

He looked at her, brow furrowed. "You said it was a matter of pride, Robbie. How so?"

She hesitated, her eyes on the garden, and kept them there as she said, "I don't want to build my career based upon you, Dad."

"I never thought you were," he said, a tinge of hurt in his voice.

She turned to him. "No," she said, "there's more than that. Yes, I feel a little as though your series will end up being the basis for my reports." He started to respond but she cut him off. "There's also a gut feeling I have that maybe this serial killer obsession isn't justified."

"Why do I have the feeling I'm being accused of being obsessed?"

She placed her hand on his arm. "Well," she said, "aren't you?"

"No." He didn't want his anger to show. "Paul Morehouse, my boss, is obsessed. Me? No. I'm just doing my job."

"And enjoying it," she said flatly.

"Not really."

"Please, Dad, no offense, but the pieces you've been writing seem—well, they seem so *tabloidy*. Is there such a word?"

"I don't think so. Or there should be. Is there tabloid TV?"

"Yes, but some of the writing is so unlike you. It's so unlike the *Trib* for that matter. Anyway, I just wanted to mention it and get it off my chest. I hope you're not mad."

"Not at all." But he was, mad and embarrassed, and was thankful when Georgia and Curtis joined them.

"I really have to be running," Curtis said. "This was great, getting to meet you both, and enjoying an incredible meal. The fried chicken at Georgia Brown's is great, but yours tops it, Mrs. Wilcox."

Roberta left a few minutes after him, and both Joe and Georgia were sure the young couple intended to meet up somewhere in town and enjoy being alone, out from under her parents' microscope.

The parents went to the kitchen where he helped scrape plates and load the dishwasher.

They were close to finishing when the phone rang. Joe grabbed it off the kitchen wall. "Hello?"

He heard someone cough, a male cough.

"Hello!" he said, as though speaking to a deaf person.

The phone went dead.

"Another hang up?" she said.

"Yeah. Annoying."

Georgia announced she was going to bed to read. She kissed him and said, "Don't stay up too late."

"I won't."

He went to the den, poured himself a short drink, neat, removed his shoes and sat in a recliner. His eyes scanned the photos on the wall and mantel, resting on a montage of Roberta at various ages. Seeing her display warmth and closeness to Tom Curtis—was it love?—depressed him, and he swallowed against a lump that was forming in his throat. He knew he would lose her one day. That's the way it was supposed to be, nurturing and guiding your children into productive, responsible, happy lives until they were out of the nest and flying successfully on their own. He could accept that; one had to accept it or go mad.

But her comments to him that night about the articles he'd been writing represented a different sort of loss. She was criticizing the very thing that defined him: his professional life. He knew many men who referred to their children when describing themselves and what they'd accomplished in life. Describing yourself by describing your offspring? Not for him. True, bringing up kids was tough, and succeeding at it was an achievement of which to be immensely proud. But for a man—and he readily acknowledged, at least to himself, that his feelings were sexist— there was more than parenting to define who you were and what you'd gotten done during your precious time on earth.

Those thoughts, and soon so many others, swirled uncontrollably about him as he sipped his drink and tried to bring order to them.

The phone calls that night. It had to have been Michael. How dare he inject himself that way? He was now glad that he would see Michael face to face the next day. He would confront him directly about whether he'd made those two nuisance calls. But his next thought was that the calls were irrelevant in the greater scheme of things, only serving to give credence to Michael's very existence, which he'd been fighting since the first contact with his brother. He didn't want him to exist, and had actually, inexplicably, tried to will him dead.

Georgia interrupted his introspection. "Come to bed," she said from the doorway.

"Yeah," he replied, getting up and carrying his empty glass to the kitchen. "You think they're serious?" he asked absently.

"Robbie and Tom? No, I don't. Not yet. But if they are, we'll hear about it soon enough. Come on, tomorrow's another day."

FIFTEEN

Washington, D.C., is not prime territory for single women seeking a mate. There are a lot more single females than eligible single males there than in most cities. Bright, healthy women gravitate to the nation's capital in search of the sort of adventure that the intriguing world of government and politics can provide. Working in the city's major industry may not rival mountain climbing or skydiving for sheer thrills, but the pervasive pull of power, and rubbing elbows with it, can be intoxicating, stimulating, as well as on more than one occasion, an aphrodisiac.

The news business, too, exerts a grip on ambitious young people looking for challenge and public recognition. Like other so-called magnetic professions, journalism jobs generally pay less than other professional pursuits and the hours are long. But that's a small price to pay for escaping the more mundane pursuits of, say, banking, accounting, or teaching. Are most single young women in Washington biding time until the elusive "Mr. Right" comes along? Hardly. That was *then*. Many of today's well-educated, savvy, and sexually aware women, using their smarts, education, and ideas in every corner of the former swamp now known as the nation's capital, have relegated Mr. Right to the era when flight attendants were called stewardesses, a steno pad was a primary career asset, and only men dared rent porn videos. It isn't that should a real Mr. Right come along, they wouldn't sign on to becoming Mrs. Right. But rather than waste time with the Mr. Wrongs—of which there are plenty in D.C.—they prefer their own company, thank you, marching to the beat of their own drummers and enjoying the rhythm.

Roberta Wilcox was a good example.

She and Tom Curtis had, as her parents suspected, met up again after dinner at the Eighteenth Street Lounge (known to regulars as ESL) above a mattress shop south of Dupont Circle. The restored mansion was once the home of Teddy Roosevelt, who robust as he was, might not have enjoyed the mix of acid rock, hip-hop, and reggae emanating from the elaborate deejay's booth. After passing muster by a burly, dour bouncer, the couple entered the club, one of the hottest venues in the city. They skirted the dance floor and made their way to an outdoor deck at the rear of the club where they found the last two vacant chairs at a tiny table. They ordered drinks—a Cosmopolitan for her, Scotch and soda for him—and smiled at each other.

"Your folks are nice," he said over the din.

"I know," she said. "I'm lucky to have them, to have been brought up by them."

"Did you plan to follow in your dad's footsteps, getting into journalism?"

"I guess so. He likes to think I did."

"I was talking to him about the stories he's been writing. He's funny. He asked me whether tips have fallen off from single women at the bar because they're uptight."

"He asked you *that*?"

Was he going to quote what Tom had said in his next article? she wondered. She hoped not.

They hadn't been dating long and spent the next half hour getting to know each other a little better, telling tales about their lives, their growing up, school experiences, especially mortifying ones, and discussing what they currently did for a living.

"You're an only child, huh?" he said. "No brothers or sisters?"

"None that I know of," she replied with a chuckle. "We have a very small family, a couple of cousins somewhere in the country, but just the three of us here. Actually, I'm happy it's this way. All attention is focused on me—ta da!"

He laughed. "I come from a big family," he said, "three brothers and two sisters. All attention definitely wasn't focused on me. Dance?"

"Sure."

After fifteen minutes of sweaty gyrating on the hardwood dance floor with less space in which to maneuver than a Tokyo subway car, they headed for the club's exit, knowing that they would continue the evening in bed. The only decision left to be made was whether it would be her bed or his. They chose Roberta's because she had to be up early, while he didn't go on duty until four in the afternoon. It was the third time they'd slept together. As on the previous two occasions, their lovemaking was unsure but generally satisfying. As they sat up in bed leaning against the headboard, she realized she was conflicted. It would be nice to wake up next to him in the morning. On the other hand, she wanted him to leave. He solved her dilemma when he said, "I think I'd better be going, Robbie. I'd love to stay, but you've got an early start tomorrow. Frankly, if I stay, I'll want to repeat this and spend the morning doing it. Or the week. Okay?"

Her expression of disappointment was genuine, if not slightly exaggerated. She kissed him good-bye at the door, latched it behind him, and sat at her window overlooking the quiet street. She couldn't put her finger on it and was unable to codify her feelings at that moment, but they weren't about Tom Curtis. She was thinking of her father.

He'd changed, no doubt about that. Was it simply a matter of growing older, of facing mortality, of losing physical strength and mental acumen? That would be normal. She'd seen it in many senior citizens, their gait less steady than in their youth, their minds not quite as sharp. If so, she could readily accept it.

But there was another dimension to the change in her father, one less predictable and easily explained. She knew he was disappointed in his career now that it was winding down. Her mother had spoken to her about it, mentioning more frequent bouts of depression over the past year, and outright expressions of failure. He was wrong to feel this way, of course. He'd had a good career. How many reporters got to work for such a newspaper as *The Washington Tribune*? He'd been there how many years, twenty-four, twenty-five? He'd covered many of the city's most infamous criminal cases, murder, rape, arson, crimes involving elected officials, the whole spectrum of society's underbelly. He'd done it with aplomb, his interviews skillfully conducted, his research meticulously mounted, the pieces written with style and concision, not a word wasted, everything tracking so that the reader was never left in the dark. He was the consummate pro. On top of that, he'd been a wonderful father and husband, always there for her and her mother, even-tempered, witty, a joking but caring man who truly honored the human condition.

A failure? Hardly.

But there was more, she knew, and it was that intangible something that eluded her. She shouldn't have criticized his writing, calling it "tabloidy," correct word or not. But it was. She'd read everything he'd written since she was deemed old enough to be exposed to the dark side of the city. He didn't keep copies of his stories, a testament to his basic humility. But she remembered many of the articles, especially the more recent ones leading up to the serial killer series. His tone and approach was markedly different from everything else she recalled reading.

He'd said his boss, Paul Morehouse, had pressured him into taking the tack he had. She'd met Morehouse on many occasions; he and his wife, Mimi, had been dinner guests at the house on a number of occasions. She liked him and his gruff, no-nonsense demeanor, and knew he ran a tight ship. If he had pressed her dad to take a more sensational approach, she understood. Her boss at the TV station was somewhat like Morehouse, under pressure from above to do whatever it took to boost ratings, and by extension increase advertising revenues. Sure, the basic rules of credible journalism were bandied about, and there were attempts to honor them. But things had changed dramatically in even the short time she'd been at the station. The 24/7 cable news channels were setting the pace and agenda, recycling the day's most startling stories over and over, the most titillating murder trials, the bloodiest family slayings, the most salacious scandals, and the juciest sexual escapades, preferably involving a politician or movie star.

That editorial philosophy had been driven home to her during her first year on the job. She'd had the makings of a provocative story in which a city official might be accused of sexual harassment. Her boss told her to run with it. She replied that she thought it needed additional checking, a second corroboration, perhaps even a third.

"Hey, sweetheart," she was told by the producer, "this story is too good to check. Run with it."

Before now, her father had often expressed scorn at what he considered to be the demise of responsible journalism. He'd been decidedly old school and she'd admired him for that, even though he failed, in her estimation, to take into account the realities of the situation. Times had changed; journalism had changed. Whether its evolution was good or bad seemed irrelevant to her. Technology had transformed the news business. There had long been competition to get the story, then to get it first, and the advent of the telegraph, and telephone, the radio, and now TV and the Internet had made it a race to get and spread the news in real time, preferably while it was happening—car chases, robberies caught on surveillance cameras, fires, and, of course, trials. You had to move fast or be trampled by the competition.

She had little patience for those who labeled the media left-leaning. Right-wingers owned the nation's media. What was more important, the decisions behind what stories to cover and how to cover them had little to do with politics. Ratings and ad revenue weren't Democratic or Republican. You ran with what would pull in the most viewers. That simple. End of story. Case closed.

She decided before returning to her rumpled bed that she would raise her concerns directly with her father at the first opportune moment. In the meantime, she needed sleep to be ready for what the next day would bring. Whether journalism had lost some of its honor and luster or not, she was a journalist and would do what was expected of her.

❧

Joe Wilcox needed sleep, too, but didn't get much that night. He lay in bed and felt his heart race and could feel the throb of his pulse. He dozed off a few times, but each time he looked at the glow of a digital clock at bedside, time had advanced only a few minutes. He gave it up at five, quietly slipped out of bed, and showered. Dressed in his robe and slippers, he went downstairs and, despite knowing it was too early for delivery, looked down the driveway for that morning's *Tribune*. He went to the foot of the stairs and listened to hear if Georgia was awake. Confident she wasn't, he walked into the den, opened one of three closets, got down on his knees and rummaged through a series of square boxes until finding the one he wanted. He withdrew it, took it to a game table covered with green felt, switched on a lamp hanging over the table, pulled up a chair, and removed the box's cover. Layers of white tissue paper were neatly layered on top. He removed the paper and dug down deeper, his fingers coming to rest on a manila envelope whose flap was secured with a strand of red string wrapped around a plastic button. He laid the envelope on the table, undid the string, folded back the flap, withdrew the envelope's contents, and placed them in the harsh, direct light from above. There were yellowed newspaper clippings in which photos were embedded, and a half dozen faded snapshots of Michael as a teenager. Wilcox went to his desk, took a magnifying glass from a drawer, returned to the table, and closely examined what was in the envelope, spending more time on the pictures than the clippings. Finished, he sat back, closed his eyes, and exhaled a sustained, loud breath. He was drained; it was the first time that night he felt sleep would come easily. He cocked his head. Georgia was stirring upstairs. He reversed his procedure, returning the box to the closet, and went into the kitchen to turn on the coffee that had been set up the previous night.

"Good morning," Georgia said through a yawn.

"Good morning, hon. Sleep well?"

"Yes. You?"

"Afraid not."

"I've never known you to be an insomniac," she said pleasantly, pulling a package of English muffins from the refrigerator.

"Yeah, it is new for me. Too much on my mind, I guess," he said, sitting at the table.

"Want to talk about it?"

"About *it*? What's *it*?"

"What's keeping you awake these nights."

"Nothing specific, Georgia. Just a lot of pressure at work and—"

"Joe," she said, joining him at the table, "you've been under pressure at work hundreds of times and you never lost a minute's sleep. I don't want to probe into your personal life, but if there's something you want to get off your chest, I'd love to hear it."

He forced lightness into his voice: "My personal life? Like what, confessing I've been having an affair?"

"I sometimes think that," she said. "I wondered whether the hang ups last night were from a girlfriend."

"Oh, come on, Georgia, that's—"

"Just a fleeting fancy," she said, taking one of his hands in hers. "I know you don't have a girlfriend on the side, Joe. I told Mimi that."

"Told her what?"

"That I'd be shocked if you had an affair."

"Thanks for the testimonial."

"I didn't mean it that way."

"I know you didn't."

"Do you think Paul cheats on her?"

"No. I mean, how would I know? Maybe he does. Maybe he's got a harem stashed away in Georgetown. This is not a subject I really feel like getting into this morning."

"Case closed," she said. "But I do know that something is bothering you. I care, that's all. I love you."

It struck Joe that this was a good time to tell her about Michael, and he might have had she not gotten up from the table and exited the house to retrieve the morning paper. He went upstairs to their bedroom, dressed for the day, and returned to the kitchen.

"Muffin?" she asked.

"Thanks, no. I'll grab something downtown." He kissed her.

"You look nice," she said, accompanying him to the door. "All ready for your TV show."

"Thanks," he said, having forgotten about the show. Had he remembered, he might have dressed differently. He hadn't bothered to look at the paper before leaving, but heard his article mentioned on his car radio. The news reader was in the middle of the story when Wilcox's cell phone sounded.

"Wilcox."

"Joe, it's Edith."

"Hi," he said. "I'm in the car on my way downtown. What's up?"

"I need to talk to you, Joe. Off the record, of course."

"Of course."

"Can we meet?"

"When?"

"This morning?"

"Give me an hour? Where?"

"The Bread Line on Pennsylvania?"

"You've got it."

SIXTEEN

Michael LaRue had gone to dinner the previous night with another tenant of the apartment house, a pugnacious, divorced former career army man who'd sustained wounds in the first Gulf War and was on full disability. The day Michael moved in, they met and found themselves getting together now and then, playing chess or checkers, going out for an occasional inexpensive meal, and discussing world affairs, or more often arguing about them. Although Michael was neither a registered voter nor had he demonstrated an affiliation with a political party, he billed himself to Rudy and others as a born-again conservative Republican. That melded nicely with his new friend's political philosophy but represented perhaps the only thing they shared aside from being single men who happened to live in the same building.

Rudy, who walked with a distinct limp and who often spoke of the plate in his hip, did not like Michael's favorite neighborhood eating spot, Tomaso's Pizza Parlor and Restaurant. "Cheap guinea food," he said when Michael first suggested going there for dinner, and they avoided it.

But on this night, Michael insisted, and Rudy reluctantly went along, grumbling all the way.

Mrs. Tomaso had given Michael her usual demonstrative welcome and seated the men in a booth near the front window. Michael ordered a glass of house red while Rudy, who drank heavily and consumed a number of pain pills each day, asked for Skyy vodka over ice.

"I am sorry," Mrs. Tomaso said, "but we do not have that." She pointed to two small shelves behind the counter on which a few bottles of hard liquor were displayed.

"What kind of a joint is this?" Rudy mumbled. He downed the vodka she brought him and ordered another. By the time their food was served, Rudy was well on his way to drunk and had become verbally abusive to the restaurant's proprietress.

"Shut up, Rudy," Michael said a few times after his dinner companion had hurled insults at the woman. That caused Rudy to turn on Michael, calling him a "fairy" and a "weak-kneed fag." Mr. Tomaso responded to the raised voices and came around the counter from where he had been preparing pizzas for a takeout order. Michael waved him off and called for a check. Rudy got up from the table unsteadily and staggered out the door, followed a minute later by Michael, who'd paid the bill and apologized profusely to the Tomasos.

They walked back to the apartment building. When they reached the front door, Michael grabbed Rudy by the throat and rammed him against a wall. "You ever do that again and you'll need dentures to go with that plate in your hip," he snarled. "Those are my friends, you bastard, and nobody talks to my friends like that, especially to a woman. You understand?"

Rudy tried to loosen Michael's grip on his throat. Michael, his face twisted with rage, let go and stepped back. He unlocked the door, grabbed Rudy by the back of his shirt, and propelled him inside and to his apartment door. "The keys," Michael demanded. "Give me the keys." He physically ushered the burly ex-GI into the apartment, across the living room and into the bedroom where he threw him on the bed.

"Sober up," Michael said, and left.

Now, the morning after, Michael was up early. After a vigorous hour of exercise, including lifting a set of weights he kept in a corner behind a chair, he showered, dressed in black jeans and a black T-shirt, and left the apartment, stopping for that morning's edition of *The Washington Tribune* and reading it over a breakfast of fresh fruit, a hard roll, and coffee at a local bakery. Joe's byline was on page one of the Metro section as it had been all week. Reading Joe's article twice before tearing it from the paper, he carefully placed it in a small leather bag he carried over his shoulder.

His next step was Dean & Deluca in Georgetown where he purchased small portions of hors d'oeuvres—charcuterie, smoked salmon mousse, and tapenade. The attractive middle-aged woman who served him was flirtatious, which he enjoyed, and it enhanced an already good mood.

He took a leisurely stroll through the Watergate complex before entering its liquor store and buying a fifth of each of the shop's own Watergate brand of Scotch and bourbon, which he found amusing, and a bottle each of a mid-priced red and white wine. Small sourdough rolls from the Watergate Bakery completed his shopping. He seldom took cabs in the city but decided to do so this morning and was back in his apartment before noon. He spent an hour arranging his purchases on a large serving platter, which he put in the refrigerator along with the white wine, and tidied up the apartment. He knew of a florist a few blocks away and went there, returning with a simple bouquet of colorful flowers in a vase purchased from the shop.

He answered a knock on the door. It was Rudy. "Busy?" he asked.

"Yeah, I am, Rudy."

"What's with last night?" Rudy asked.

"I don't have time, Rudy. But I suggest you get your act together, at least if you want me as a friend." He closed the door in his neighbor's face and smiled. He was glad Rudy had come to ask about what had occurred the previous evening. If nothing else, he provided decent chess and checkers competition.

After a light lunch, he practiced the guitar until two, napped until three, and passed the hour before his brother was to arrive by reading a recently published book about Islam and its emerging role in world affairs.

The Bread Line was doing its usual frenetic business when Wilcox walked in. Vargas-Swayze had secured a table, and he joined her. She looked as though she hadn't had much sleep; there were dark, puffy circles beneath her large, dark brown eyes. She'd applied her makeup more heavily than usual that morning, he noted, and was wearing even more jewelry than was her custom.

"How are you?" he asked.

"I've been better."

"Hubby problems?"

"Yup. Would you believe the bastard is trying to get *me* to pay *him* alimony?"

Wilcox couldn't help but chuckle. "Looks like fem lib has gotten expensive. Coffee?"

With coffee, and cinnamon buns in front of them, he said, "What is it you want to ask me, Edith? I don't have a lot of time."

"Okay," she said, "I know you're following the serial killer trail, Joe. I think you're wrong—there've only been two killings, not a half-dozen—but that's your call. I'm sure it's selling papers. I'm operating on the theory that the murders are unrelated."

He started to respond, but she said, "Hear me out."

"Okay," he said, and sat back in listening mode.

"Let's say the same guy did both murders. If so, I'm convinced that he works for the *Trib*."

"Why?"

"Because it doesn't make sense to me that an outside sicko would find his way into the paper and kill Kaporis there. Offing somebody in a park is easy. Pulling it off at the *Trib* is too hard. Why would he take the chance?"

"Have you taken a close look at our security lately?" Wilcox asked. "It's even worse than at the airport."

She came forward. "But why would he do it, Joe? If both homicides had taken place inside a news organization, I'd think differently. But there's one at the *Trib*, and one in the park. No, Joe, either the murders are unrelated, or you've got a whackjob working at the paper."

Wilcox thought a moment before saying, "Let's say you're right. Let's say—and I'm still going with the serial killer scenario—let's say there's someone working at the *Trib* who killed both Jean Kaporis and Colleen McNamara. That squashes the personal motive. Right? You've been running with the theory that Jean was killed by someone who'd had a relationship with her, got rebuffed or something, and became mad enough to strangle her. But why the McNamara girl? He was rebuffed by her, too? What is he, some ugly guy with terminal bad breath? We've got a couple of strange-os working at the paper, but nobody fitting that description."

She smiled. "I interviewed everybody who was in the newsroom the night Kaporis died, and I'd say there are a couple of guys who fit that description."

"I hope you're not including me," he said.

"Present company excepted," she said. "You know every one of the men I interviewed, Joe. You're a reporter. You pick up on things others wouldn't. Give me a name or two I can zero in on."

It just came out. "There's a young reporter named Hawthorne."

"I remember him. Nice looking young guy, personable."

"That's a matter of opinion. All I know is that rumor has it that he might have been having some sort of a personal relationship with Kaporis."

"Anything to substantiate that rumor?"

"I asked him point blank about it."

"You did?"

"Yeah. He admitted he'd had coffee with her and drinks after work."

"Hmmm," she said. "Anybody else?"

"No. When I spoke with Kaporis's father and stepmother, they said Kaporis had been having an affair with a married guy here in D.C."

"Someone from the *Trib*?"

"They didn't know what he did for a living. Name is Paul, they seem to remember her saying."

"Could have been somebody at the *Trib*," she said. "Right?"

"I suppose. My boss's name is Paul. Paul Morehouse."

"The murdering type?"

"No. There are a few Pauls in News. But hell, the *Trib*'s got twenty-five hundred employees, Edith. Could have been anybody, and not necessarily someone from the News division. There's advertising, production, business, circulation—everyone has the same employee ID. Those other types are in and out of the newsroom all the time. What about visitors to the newsroom that night? Outsiders?"

"We're still following up on them," she said.

He paid the bill and they left the bustling restaurant.

"We still on for dinner tonight?" she asked.

"Yeah. Seven-thirty. Where?"

"Feel like slumming? Come on up to my neighborhood."

"I'd hardly call Adams Morgan slumming these days," he said.

"Then make it Felix, on Eighteenth, between Belmont and Columbia Roads. They serve comfort food—and I need some comfort." She smiled. "Have a good TV show tonight. I'll watch you."

He'd managed to suppress an urge to tell her about his brother's sudden and unwelcome arrival in Washington, and his dread of going to meet him at four that afternoon. Maybe he should have seen a shrink and talked out his feelings. He felt terribly alone at that moment, like someone about to undergo cancer surgery without anyone who cared at his side. He tried to adopt a more positive attitude as he drove to his office at the *Tribune*. Perhaps he was overreacting and was being unfair to Michael. After all, he was his only sibling, a blood brother who'd gone through hard times and now looked to him, his brother, Joe, to help forge a new life in a new place. By the time he'd parked his car and was heading through the *Tribune* Building's lobby, he'd given himself a lecture: Be positive and upbeat when you go to Michael's apartment. Give him the benefit of the doubt. Welcome him into your life, and hear what he has to say about his ambitions and plans. Be supportive. Open your heart. Reach out. Express pleasure at seeing him after so many years.

But when he was about to leave his office at 3:45, that positive spirit had dissolved like sugar in hot water, and he left the building with a tight jaw and knotted stomach.

SEVENTEEN

Wilcox had trouble finding parking on the street and circled the block a few times until a space opened up across from the address Michael had given him. It was a few minutes after four when he completed his parallel parking and shut off the engine. He sat quietly and stared at the building for a few minutes before slowly leaving the car and crossing the street. He paused at the door, drew a breath, entered the foyer, and read the names on the tenant panel on the wall. Listed next to the apartment number was the name MICHAEL LARUE. Strange, he thought as he pushed the button opposite the apartment number.

"Joseph?" the voice came through a tiny speaker.

The tinny sound startled Wilcox. "Hello?" he said, leaning closer to the panel.

A buzzer and the metallic sound of the door lock disengaging filled the confined space. "Joseph, come in."

Wilcox pushed open the door and stepped into the hallway that ran from the front to the back of the building. A door opened at the far end and Michael stepped into the hall. "Down here, Joseph," he said.

Wilcox approached this man, his brother, who was silhouetted in light from inside the apartment. Joe's initial reaction was to Michael's height. He hadn't remembered him being so tall.

"Well, well," Michael said, smiling. "You *are* here. How wonderful."

Joe tentatively extended his hand, which Michael shook enthusiastically.

"Hello, Michael. I—"

"Come in, come in," Michael said, turning and entering the apartment. Joe followed.

He stopped a few feet inside and took in his surroundings; soothing recorded classical music came from unseen speakers.

"Like it, Joseph?" Michael asked, indicating the apartment with outstretched arms. "It isn't especially large, but it's perfectly adequate for one person. Come in, come in and sit, make yourself at home. Take that chair over there. It's the most comfortable one."

Joe ignored the invitation and instead went to the window and looked out on to the side street. A passage in the music caught his attention, and he cocked his head.

Michael noticed. "Like classical music, Joseph?"

"Debussy," Joe replied. *"La Mer."*

"Ah ha," said Michael. "You obviously do like classical music. And some of the most familiar. Jazz, too?"

Joe turned and for the first time since entering the apartment took a close look at his brother. While he'd been struck at Michael's height, he now was aware that this man he hadn't seen for decades was also physically fit. His black T-shirt was molded to his slender yet muscular torso. He hadn't begun to bald as Joe had, nor had gray appeared. His hair was very black—dyed? Joe wondered—and neatly trimmed on the sides, but featuring a ponytail. What was especially evident was his tan. His face and arms were bronzed; piercing green eyes seemed to reflect inner bemusement.

"Jazz?" Joe said. "No. I've never gotten into that. Some Dixieland maybe." He noticed the guitar and amplifier. "You play, Michael?"

Michael stood by the instrument. "I play at it," he said. "All those

years in the hospital gave me nothing but time to learn. I tried art but realized that wasn't for me, so I turned to music, for which I seem to have
a greater affinity. People say I've become quite proficient. I certainly love
it. Do you play an instrument?"

"Afraid not. Michael, I—"

A cat appeared through the open bedroom door.

"This is Maggie," Michael said as the animal came to Joe and rubbed
against his leg. "A Maine coon cat, a lovely breed. They sell for more
than a thousand dollars from breeders. I rescued this poor thing from the
SPCA. Cost me a hundred-dollar donation. Well worth it. Drink? I have
wine, Scotch, or vodka. I believe you're a Scotch drinker, but maybe you
enjoy variety."

"Nothing, thank you. Oh, some Scotch on the rocks, a small one.
I'm doing a television show this evening."

"How exciting. Back in a jiffy."

How did he know I drink Scotch? Joe wondered as Michael came
from the kitchen carrying the platter of hors d' oeuvres. He set it on a
small table and said, "Drinks on the way," and disappeared again.

Joe found himself relaxing. The music was nice, and the initial shock
of finally confronting Michael had worn off. He went to the platter of
food and tasted some. Michael returned carrying a glass of Scotch on the
rocks and a half-filled glass of white wine. He handed Joe his drink and
raised his glass. "To brothers, Joseph, and to being close again. Cheers!"

After clinking, they sat on the small couch.

"I suppose there are many questions I should be asking," Joe said, sipping his drink.

"And I have questions, too," Michael said in a low baritone. "Where
shall we begin? I know. You're the reporter. Asking questions is your business. Go ahead, Joseph, interview me as though . . . as though . . . as
though I'm a movie star who's been out of the public eye for a while and
am making a comeback." He laughed. "No," he said, "I'll ask the first
question. How did you become a journalist? As I remember, the only
thing you thought about was football and baseball."

Joe couldn't help but smile. "Yeah, I suppose I was a jock back in
high school."

"And chased all the pretty girls," Michael added. "Maybe I should have pursued sports and pretty girls back then. Maybe I wouldn't have—" His words trailed off.

"Hey, Michael, you don't have to talk about it if you don't want to. I'd understand."

"Oh, no, Joseph. There was a time when I was too embarrassed to speak of what I'd done. It was too painful to ever mention it. But I learned how important it is to be open and candid, to face one's life squarely, the good and the bad, the high and the low points. Oh, no, Joseph, I don't have any problem being honest about myself and who I was. Notice I put that in the past tense? Who I was and who I am now, are two very different people."

Thank God, Joe thought. "How did you know I drank Scotch?" he asked. "I was thirteen when you last saw me."

"Aha," Michael said, standing and going to the center of the room. "Caught in the act. Well, Joseph, it took a significant amount of time for me to get up the courage to call you. During that time I decided to get to know you from afar, gain a sense of who my brother was before seeing him face to face. I've been spying on you." He said it with dramatic flair, an actor supplying the curtain line in a British murder mystery.

"Spying on me? You've been following me?"

"Sometimes. I've taken the public tour at your newspaper a few times and saw you working at your desk, in your cubicle. As a matter of fact, I've seen you at work other times."

"How so?" Joe asked, feeling uneasy again.

"I work for an office supply company, Joseph. I deliver supplies to businesses, including *The Washington Tribune*. I saw you once when I brought something to your newsroom."

"That's interesting, Michael," Joe said, finishing what was in his glass.

"A refill?" Michael asked.

"Thanks, no. Tell me more about spying."

"Oh, I waited outside your building one day and followed you to lunch. You met a very handsome woman. Hispanic, I surmised. That's when I noticed you drank Scotch. I was at the next table. It took every ounce of restraint on my part to not reach over, pat your hand, and announce who I was. But I didn't want to interrupt your conversation."

He didn't mention that he'd seen Edith Vargas-Swayze again, when she and her cop partner interviewed him at work.

The idea that he'd been spied upon as he went about his daily routines caused Joe to squirm. "When else did you spy on me, Michael?"

"Oh, my goodness, Joseph, I sense you're offended at what I did. If so, I apologize. It's just that after so many years, and the circumstances that kept us apart, I was reluctant to simply pop up like a jack-in-the-box and announce, 'Here I am, brother.' Do you understand?"

"Yes, I understand," Joe said. "I see that you've changed your name. LaRue, is it?"

"Yes. I decided that if I was going to get a fresh start in my life, I needed to wipe away everything from the past."

It would have been better if you had, including me, Joe thought, not pleased with that uncharitable view.

"LaRue has a nice ring to it, don't you think?" Michael asked.

"Yes. A nice ring." Joe fell silent, his attention on the cat, who had climbed up on a windowsill and was playing with the blind's cord.

"Joseph," Michael said, aware his brother's attention was elsewhere.

Joe turned and faced him. "What?"

"I realize how shocking it must be for you to be sitting next to me after so many years. Frankly, I never thought I'd have this opportunity again, that I would die in the hospital. Forty years is a very long time to be put away. At first, I kept track of the days on a calendar, crossing each one off, filled with anger that my life had been taken away from me."

"It was your anger that put you there, Michael," Joe said, not sure he should have.

"Yes, it was. I couldn't accept that at first. Everyone else was wrong except me. The world conspired against me—and I admit, Joseph, that that included you and mother and father."

Joe winced.

"Did you ever read *I'm Okay, You're Okay?*"

"Yes, I did."

"I thought it was a brilliant book. I saw myself in it. I was okay, the world was not."

Joe recalled the groundbreaking book in which the Freudian concepts of ego, superego and id were redefined as adult, parent, and child, and one's way of viewing others helped define how successful they would be in establishing relationships. His interest stemmed from his job as a cops reporter writing about society's criminal element. Criminals, the book pointed out, tended to function with the attitude that they were okay but others weren't. Emotionally healthy people were the I'm okay, you're okay individuals, whose positive outlook applied not only to them but to the rest of society.

"With the help of the good men and women at the hospital, I eventually shed my anger and was able to see that not only was I okay, but that my fellow men were, too. And women, of course." Michael laughed. "Women! I envy you, Joseph, having a beautiful, loving wife and splendid daughter."

"You don't know Georgia," Joe said.

"True. Oh, well, I might as well admit it. I've taken the liberty of enjoying an advance peek at your Georgia, too, and Roberta. Of course, I see Roberta all the time on TV. But—"

"How dare you?" Joe said forcefully.

"How dare I *what?*"

"Sneak around spying on my wife and daughter. What did you do, stalk them?"

"That would be criminal," Michael said with a modicum of indignation. "I wanted to feel that I at least knew what they looked like before actually meeting them. Is that so terrible?" He didn't give Joe a chance to respond. "You're forgetting, Joseph, that I've not been as fortunate as you in life. You went on to become a respectable journalist. You married the girl of your dreams and fathered a loving daughter. I've had none of that, but I intend to make up for lost time. Won't you help me achieve that, Joseph? I've paid my debt to society, paid it in full. I came to Washington because my only living relative was here—*my brother!*"

Joe stood and went to where the cat was now sleeping on the sill. He ran his hand over its head and back, waking it and eliciting a rumble of a purr. He liked four-legged animals. He and Michael had had dogs and cats growing up, and he and Georgia had brought strays into the house and raised them with love. Their last pet, a mixed breed rescued from the local pound, had been put to sleep at the advanced age of sixteen. That was two years ago, and they'd never pursued having another animal in the house.

He leaned closer to Maggie to better hear her contented sounds, and wasn't aware that Michael had come up behind him. When he realized it, he straightened with a start.

"I didn't mean to frighten you," Michael said.

"You didn't," Joe said, moving toward the door. "I'd better be going."

"Your TV appearance," Michael said. "You'll be talking about the serial killer?"

"Yes."

"I'll be watching, Joseph."

"Good."

"Joseph."

"Yeah?"

"This won't be the last time we spend time together. Don't tell me that it is. Don't destroy me again."

"What the hell are you saying, that I played a part in what you did and what happened to you?"

"No, no, no, no, no. I learned, among many things, that it's important that I take full responsibility for that. What I am saying, Joseph, what I'm begging—and I hate to beg—is that you bring me into your life. I desperately need that, Joseph. I was told it's vitally important for me to reestablish contact with family. Please."

"Michael, I—" Joe managed a smile. "Welcome to the family, Michael. But let's take it slow. Okay?"

"Absolutely."

"Give me some time to adjust to this and to bring Georgia into it."

"Take all the time you need, Joseph. But in the meantime, we can meet now and then, can't we?"

"Sure. Now and then."

There was an awkward moment when Joe was afraid Michael would hug him, embrace him physically. He stepped away to avoid it and said, "Take care, Michael."

EIGHTEEN

Wilcox had an hour and a half to kill before appearing on *D.C. Digest*. Had he not planned to have dinner with Edith Vargas-Swayze after the TV show, he would have grabbed a bite before it. He considered going back to his office at the *Trib* but decided against it. Because there was no breaking news upon which to base another article in the series, he was off the hook for a day—but only a day. Morehouse had said that he expected the story to pick up again, and had urged Wilcox to pull out all the stops to make that happen. Newsstand sales since the articles had begun to appear were up by 8 percent, and subscriptions had increased, too.

He found a coffee shop near the TV studio and wiled away the time sipping an iced coffee and nibbling on a piece of lemon pound cake to take the edge off his appetite. But nothing could take the edge off his thoughts about having gone to Michael's apartment.

Cognitively, he was happy that his brother was no longer confined to the Illinois hospital where he'd been a patient for so many years. That Michael had come out of that experience looking as good as he did and with a relatively positive view of his future, was admirable. His desire to reintegrate with Joe and his family wasn't unreasonable. As he'd said, his doctors urged him to reestablish contact with his family as part of his post-hospital recovery.

But as those good thoughts came to him, they were accompanied by a visceral dread. The way Michael had begun the process of reintroducing himself to Joe and the family was upsetting at best. To think that he, Georgia, and Roberta had been spied upon, followed, their movements deliberately observed by someone with an agenda, sent a shiver up Joe's spine. And there was Michael's threatening tone during his phone calls, and at the apartment. When Joe had demonstrated initial shock and reservation at hearing from a brother he hadn't seen in four decades, Michael had hinted he would go through Georgia: "You know how women are, more social than men."

As he sat in the coffee shop, these thoughts caused new anger to bubble up and to sour the taste of cake in his mouth. The truth was—and he had to admit it to himself—he did not want Michael Wilcox, or LaRue if he preferred—back in his life.

❧

He'd been twelve years old when the murder had taken place. Michael, his taller, handsome, all-knowing big brother, was sixteen at the time. The victim had been a neighbor, Marjorie Jones; blond, flirtatious, and physically developed beyond her fourteen years. She had a habit of not always drawing the shade when undressing in her small second-floor bedroom, which Michael had discovered one evening. After keeping his find to himself for a week, he eventually shared it with his younger brother.

One night after dinner, when it had become dark, Michael allowed Joe to huddle with him behind an elm in the side yard and wait for Marjorie to put on her show.

"She wants us to see her naked," Michael said in his worldly wisdom. Joe didn't understand why any girl would want boys to see her without clothes, but he never challenged Michael's analysis of what became an almost nightly event.

"Look, look," Michael said when the light came on and Marjorie appeared. Joe giggled. "Shut up!" Michael said.

If she wanted them to see her, Joe reasoned, why would it matter if she knew they were there? But he didn't say that to Michael. He kept silent as Marjorie began to take off her clothes, slowly, looking as though she might be posing, disappearing from view, then coming back into the frame created by the window.

"Look," Michael said, "she's gonna take off her bra. Oh, man!"

"Did you ever see hair?" Joe asked.

"Shut up. Yeah, of course I did. Look."

Marjorie faced the window as she unhooked her brassiere and allowed it to drop to her feet.

Joe squealed.

Marjorie came to the window, leaned over to look outside, straightened and pulled down the shade.

"You little jerk," Michael said, slapping Joe across the face. "See what you did?"

Joe whimpered and walked away, his hand to his stinging cheek. It was the last time Joe would see Marjorie Jones alive. She was discovered the next morning choked to death in a thick clump of wild raspberry bushes at the far reaches of the Jones property. Thorns from the bushes had torn into the flesh of her partially nude body. Her skirt had been lifted, and her sweater and bra were up around her neck. Her panties had been torn, exposing her genital area. Her mother, a stern, overweight woman with a crooked mouth, found her daughter's lifeless body when she went out early in the morning to pick raspberries for canning. She told the local sheriff that she'd assumed Marjorie had gone to bed the night before and was sleeping late. "You know how these teenage girls are," she told the sheriff. "All they want to do is sleep late." She was at a loss to explain how Marjorie had ended up outside in the dead of night.

Joe looked out his window that morning and was excited at seeing so many police cars in front of the Jones house, lights flashing, the sound of voices over two-way radios crackling in the already hot, humid air. He went into Michael's bedroom where his brother was in bed, the covers pulled over his head.

"Michael, Michael," he said, shaking him. "Wake up. The police are over at the Jones house. Something must have happened."

Michael told him to get away, but Joe kept shaking his brother until he angrily sat up.

"What happened to you?" Joe asked. Michael's face and hands were covered with deep, bloody scratches.

"Nothing happened," Michael said. "Now let me sleep."

"But the police are here and—"

Michael pulled the covers back over his head, and Joe left the room to continue observing the scene from his bedroom. Mr. and Mrs. Jones were talking with the sheriff and other officers. At one point, Mrs. Jones turned and pointed at Joe's house, causing him to duck down out of sight. What was going on?

Still in his pajamas, he ran downstairs where his mother was in the kitchen preparing breakfast.

"Mama, did you see next door? The police are there and—"

"None of our business, Joseph," she said, looking briefly at him before returning to her chores at the old gas stove. "You get yourself upstairs and dressed proper, and tell your brother to do the same. There's work to be done around here."

Joe put on the clothes he'd worn the day before and went into Michael's room again. "Michael, you have to get up," Joe said. "Mama says she wants us downstairs 'cause there's work she wants done and—"

Michael bolted upright as the sound of someone knocking on the downstairs door reached the bedroom. "Who is it?" he asked.

"I don't know," Joe said. "Let's go down and see."

Michael shook his head. "Look," he said, "I'm not here. Okay? You go down and say I must have left here early."

"Why?"

"Just do what I say, Joey. It's important."

"Okay."

Joe left the room and descended the stairs. His mother stood at the front door talking through the screen to the sheriff and two uniformed officers. She turned and said to Joe, "Where's Michael? I told you to get him up and—"

"He's not here," Joe said, afraid to look directly at his mother or the men on the other side of the door.

"Where is he?" she demanded.

"I don't know. Honest, I don't know. Maybe be left early to go some-place."

"We'll have to take a look for ourselves, Mrs. Wilcox," the sheriff said. "If you don't mind."

She stepped back to allow them to enter. Joe watched wide-eyed as the sheriff led the other officers up the narrow staircase. "His room's to the right," Mrs. Wilcox yelled after them.

She looked at Joe, whose expression mirrored the confusion and fright he felt. "You go outside," she said. "No reason for you to be here." With that she went up the stairs, slowly, tentatively, head cocked to allow her to better hear what was occurring on the second floor.

Joe didn't follow his mother's order. He came to the foot of the steps and listened to the men's voices: "Check in there," he heard the sheriff say. A moment later, his mother wailed, "Oh, my God!"

"Get him outta there," the sheriff commanded.

"I didn't do nothing!" Michael shouted.

Joe went up the stairs two at a time and came to Michael's open bed-room door. It was hard to see beyond the bulk of the three lawmen, but when one of them moved aside, he saw that Michael was huddled at the rear of his shallow closet, his knees drawn up to his chin. His brother was crying and saying over and over, "I didn't do nothing, I didn't do nothing bad."

Mrs. Wilcox turned and saw that Joseph was taking it all in. She grabbed his ear and said angrily, "You obey me now, Joseph, and go downstairs. We've got big trouble here. Go on. Git!"

He did as he was told this time. He went outside to the elm tree where he'd joined his brother the night before and sat on the ground, his eyes on the door from the kitchen. As he waited, he heard the sound of his father's car as it turned off the road and came up the dirt driveway. Michael Wilcox senior had left for work early that morning at a wood-working mill twenty minutes down the road from the house. He'd been employed at the mill for almost twenty years and had recently been pro-moted to foreman on the day shift. The family had celebrated that night with a fudge cake, Mr. Wilcox's favorite, baked by Mrs. Wilcox, and a glass of nonalcoholic wine for the adults, soda for Michael and Joseph.

Drinking alcoholic beverages was forbidden in the Wilcox home; mother and father were staunch churchgoers and active in church affairs and events.

Joseph ran to his father as he exited the car. "Something bad's happening, Papa," he said breathlessly.

"They inside?" his father asked. He was a tall, gaunt man with unruly gray hair, and wore coveralls over a white T-shirt with JESUS SAVES emblazoned on the front.

"Michael's hidin' in the closet," Joseph said.

"Mama's in there with them?"

"Yes, sir."

"The Jones girl's dead?"

His father's words shocked Joseph. "Marjorie's dead?" he said weakly.

"You stay here and don't talk to nobody. You got that?" his father said.

"Yes, sir."

The senior Wilcox, who'd received a call from his wife the moment things had erupted next door, walked purposefully toward the house. Joseph felt a wave of relief sweep over him. His father would make everything right. He always did. Every time Michael had gotten into trouble at school, which was often, his father would go to the school and return bearing the news that Michael would not be expelled and would be given another chance.

Marjorie was dead?

What did that have to do with Michael?

He remembered the cuts and scratches on his brother, and his relief evaporated.

What had Michael done now?

Marjorie was dead?

Did Michael hurt her?

Sounds from the kitchen shut off his thinking. He watched as the kitchen door opened and the two uniformed officers brought Michael through it, one on each side of him. Michael was bent over, and Joseph saw that his hands were tied behind him. He stopped walking and dropped to his knees. The officers jerked him to his feet and continued toward their cars, which were still in front of the Jones house. Mrs. Wilcox stood at the kitchen door and cried. Joseph's father was nowhere to be seen.

He watched them put Michael in the rear seat of one of the marked patrol cars. The door was slammed shut, and the officers got in the car and drove away, kicking up dust.

"Joseph!" his mother yelled.

He ran to the house and burst into the kitchen. His father was on his knees praying in front of a statue of the Virgin Mary that occupied a corner of the kitchen, beneath a picture of Christ on the cross. His mother took his hand, led him to his father, and the three of them said disparate prayers; Joseph didn't know what to pray for but silently asked that whatever had happened that morning and the night before would go away. "Let Michael be okay, God. I love you, God. I love Michael."

⚬

Michael Wilcox was charged in the murder of Marjorie Jones. The elected county prosecutor added rape to the initial charge, but an autopsy indicated intercourse had not taken place. Her hymen was intact. Attempted rape was a possibility, but it was decided that adding that charge would only muddle the case for murder in the first degree. A public defender was assigned to represent Michael, who'd confessed to the crime his first night in custody. His attorney came to the house shortly after being assigned and met with Mr. and Mrs. Wilcox. Joseph had been told to stay in his room, but he sneaked out and lay at the top of the stairs while they conferred downstairs.

"I'm afraid there's not a lot I can do for Michael," the attorney said. He was an older man who attended the same church as Michael's parents. "He's confessed to the murder, and all the evidence supports that confession."

"Do they want to kill him?" Mrs. Wilcox asked.

"Yes, ma'am. The prosecutor is calling for the death penalty."

She closed her eyes and prayed silently.

"The crooked shall be made straight, and the rough places plain," her husband said aloud, citing Isaiah's prophecy about the coming of the Messiah. "My firstborn has brought a plague to this Christian house."

"I understand," the attorney said, "but we have a legal problem here. I know the two of you well. You are hard-working, decent people who follow the word of the Lord and practice His moral teachings. But the law doesn't always recognize such truths. What we must do—what I must do—is to try and spare Michael's life. He was obviously not of his right mind when he committed this act. The young Jones woman evidently had questionable moral principles. Michael has told me of seeing her undressing in the window of her own bedroom, enticing and corrupting impressionable young men like your son."

"A harlot!" Mr. Wilcox said with finality.

"Perhaps not that," said the attorney, "but someone who must be, at least, partially culpable in this unfortunate incident. I know that your fine son has had many troubles in his young life, at school, in the community. His anger and aggressiveness is well known in Kankakee."

"He's been a bad seed," the father offered. "I pray, most merciful Father, to be forgiving of me for bringing such a soul into Your world." He said it to the ceiling.

It became silent downstairs, and Joseph crawled to the very edge of the stairs to better hear. Finally, the attorney spoke.

"The important thing," he said, "is to spare Michael's life."

"But you said—" the mother said.

"I said the prosecutor is asking for the death penalty. But I believe I might be successful in pleading insanity for Michael. If so, he would be found not guilty by reason of insanity and would be remanded to a hospital for the criminally insane."

"Insanity," the mother wailed, and began to cry.

"He must be that," said the father. "Only an insane person would do such a terrible thing."

"Exactly," the attorney agreed. "I believe that based upon Michael's past behavior, and the behavior of the young lady next door, I stand at least a decent chance of defending Michael on that basis. There's also the possibility that a plea bargain can be struck with that as the outcome. Citizens around here aren't keen on laying out thousands of dollars for trials. The prosecutor's comin' up for reelection soon. He might see the wisdom of sparing the county that expense."

"I see," the father said.

"Do I have your permission to pursue that course of action?"

"Michael has taken a life," the father said. "It is written in Exodus that there shall be eye for eye, tooth for tooth, hand for hand, foot for foot."

"But our God is forgiving," the mother said. "If Michael's life can be spared, it will be God's will."

And the will of twelve jurors, the attorney thought.

"Please," Joseph heard his mother say. "I don't want my firstborn to die."

After a long pause, the father said to the attorney, "I hereby give my permission."

"I will have to discuss it with Michael," the attorney said.

"I will tell him what to do," said the father. "How long will he remain in the institution?"

"Until he is judged fit to rejoin society. It will be years. But I stress to you that I may not succeed in achieving a not guilty verdict, or be able to arrange a plea bargain with the prosecutor. But I assure you I will try."

"That is all we can ask," the mother said.

"Let us pray," the father said.

The muffled words of prayers drifted up the stairs. Joseph returned to his room, flung himself on his bed, and sobbed, his body heaving until there were no more tears to shed.

Michael was held without bail until his trial, which commenced seven months later. Joseph asked his parents if he could join them when they visited Michael in jail, but was rebuked each time. Going to school was torture for him. Classmates taunted him about having a pervert, a sex fiend, and a killer for a brother. Marjorie Jones's mother and father shunned any contact with the Wilcox family. Two of her older brothers attacked Joseph on a few occasions, sending him home with a bloody nose and violet circles around his eyes. He never cried in school, or when suffering the brothers' pummeling, but when in the sanctity of his bedroom, he would weep so hard that nausea would result. He considered running away but could not muster the courage to do it. His parents came down hard on him to do well in school despite "the plague your brother has cast over this family," and he did, spending many hours alone with his schoolbooks—and his dreams of one day escaping to a better, gentler life.

Michael's attorney was unsuccessful in brokering a plea deal with the prosecutor, and the murder trial of Michael Wilcox went forward. It was the talk of the county and of the state of Illinois. Each courtroom day was played out on the front pages of newspapers across the state, with a picture of Michael frequently accompanying the articles. The press accounts were the only conduit Joseph had to what was happening to his brother. His mother and father refused to discuss anything with him, or to allow him to attend the trial. Nor did his father make an appearance in the courtroom. He went to work at the mill each day, leaving visits to the courthouse to his wife, who was faithful in her attendance.

The trial lasted six days. After closing arguments, during which Michael's attorney frequently invoked God and the Bible in pleading that his client's life be saved, the jury deliberated for only four hours before announcing its verdict: Not guilty by reason of insanity.

The judge imposed sentence a week later. Michael Jeremiah Wilcox was to be confined to a state mental hospital until such time that medical authorities deemed him sufficiently cured to once again take his place in society.

During Michael's early years in the institution, Joseph frequently asked his mother to allow him to accompany her when she traveled to see his brother on visitation days. Her answer was always negative, which only fueled his speculation and fantasies about what it must be like for Michael in such a place. His father refused to visit even once, and retreated into his own inner world, going to work, returning to the house at four, and secluding himself in a corner of the living room where he read the Bible until dinner. Michael's name was never mentioned, and Joseph eventually accepted this prohibition.

Church remained an important part of the family's weekly activities, and Joseph was expected to fully involve himself. That meant attending services on Sunday mornings, a Bible class one night a week, and a youth prayer group every other Saturday. He grew to dread attending church. Not only did he find the experience boring and uninspiring, he sensed the change in attitude of the other parishioners toward him and his family. They were friendly and courteous enough, but looked at him in a way that made him uncomfortable. Once, he overheard a woman tell another, "That other Wilcox boy's the one I'd be worried about. Insanity is in the blood and genes, runs right through a family like any other disease."

His father died during Joseph's senior year in high school, keeling over at church one Sunday morning as he passed the collection plate, a chore in which he took great pride and pleasure. The funeral was sparsely attended, some men from the mill, a few neighbors, and those members of the congregation who attended all funerals as a godly social obligation. The reverend praised the father for his love of God and love of the church. Mrs. Wilcox asked Michael's lawyer if there was any possibility that Michael might be allowed to attend, but was told that was out of the question.

Joseph graduated among the top of his class and went off to college on a partial scholarship, which supplemented a small amount of money left by his father. He'd edited his high school's small newspaper; the scholarship was based upon that and his stated intention to pursue a career in journalism. He came home on breaks during his first two years and wanted to visit Michael. But his mother forbade it, and he never pressed her to change her mind. She died during the summer between his sophomore and junior years. He sold the house, which had been left to him in her will, and never again stepped foot in that house, on that land, at the cemetery where both parents were buried, or in a church. Nor did he attempt to see Michael. As far as he was concerned Michael was dead, too, and he decided it was better that way. He forged his life as a reporter, met and married Georgia, and fathered Roberta. He'd succeeded in escaping and had freed himself from the family into which he'd been born, and vowed to never look back. He'd kept that vow for more than forty years.

Until now.

Knowing how difficult parking was in Adams Morgan, he took a taxi there, telling his turbaned driver to take him to the busy corner of Eighteenth Street and Columbia Road, the heart of this section of the city. He was glad Edith had suggested having dinner there. While Washington was no longer considered a culinary wasteland—it now had as many good restaurants as any other major city—the city's eateries tended to reflect the pretentiousness of the city itself and its political heavyweights, the food not always matching up to the promise. But Adams Morgan's eclectic array of restaurants served authentic ethnic cooking, one of the reasons tourists and native Washingtonians alike flocked to this gentrified conclave north of Dupont Circle, which had become Washington's Latin Quarter and Greenwich Village rolled into one.

The intersection was chockablock with people. Aromas from the kitchens of ethnic restaurants and sidewalk food vendors hung heavy in the air. Salsa and Afro-Cuban music poured from speakers outside nightclubs and open-air cafés, causing some on the streets to move to their rhythms. He stopped to admire an Andean band of pan-pipers playing their native music. After dropping a few dollars in a case at the feet of the band's leader, he moved down the block to where two African stiltwalkers perched precariously high atop their slender stilts, their colorful costumes and hats blowing in the breeze, wide smiles on their coal-black faces. The energy on the street was contagious and uplifting, and he forgot about his visit with Michael and what it might mean to his life. But by the time he'd navigated the crowds to the restaurant, his elevated spirit had sunk back to its previous level.

Edith Vargas-Swayze stood outside beneath the restaurant's large chrome and neon sign talking with a well-dressed black couple when Wilcox arrived. She introduced him to them, promised they'd be in touch, and the couple walked away.

"What's he do?" Wilcox asked.

"Lawyer, securities, and a good one. Or so I'm told. She owns a dress shop downtown."

"I should have been a lawyer," Wilcox said. "Or owned a dress shop."

She laughed. "You'd look funny in basic black with pearls, Joe. Hungry?"

"No, but a drink would be welcome."

"They make the best martinis in town," she said, leading him inside. She stopped suddenly. "Hey, I caught you on TV. You were great."

"Thanks, but being a talking head isn't my thing. I've got some more lined up. Good PR for the paper—or so I'm told."

"Ever been here before?" she asked about the restaurant.

"Yeah. A couple of times, but not recently. It's like a throwback to the eighties."

"I love it here, especially on Friday nights."

"Why Friday?"

"The chef serves up matzoh-ball soup, challah bread, and brisket."

"This place goes kosher?" he said, laughing.

"On Friday nights."

"I thought you were Hispanic."

"Orthodox Hispanic."

"Oh."

They were led to a table away from the lively bar.

"Glad we could do this," he said. "We didn't get much of a chance to talk last time."

"Duty called."

After ordering drinks and a platter of crisply fried calamari to go with them, she asked how he'd felt about his TV appearance.

He shrugged. "Went okay, I guess. Your MPD spokesman was smooth in debunking the serial killer theory."

"Yeah, he was good. He always is. The commish puts him out in front of the cameras whenever he wants a point to be made. You held your ground."

"All I did was say that it's possible that a serial killer is prowling the streets."

"And you said someone from MPD told you we were considering it."

"That's right," he said, shifting position in his chair. "Hell, Edith, how can you *not* consider it?"

"Considering it is one thing, Joe. Telling the public is another."

"The public has a right to know."

"Not if it panics them and causes them to change their daily lives."

"That's not the point, Edith. You have to understand that—"

He was glad their drinks and calamari arrived to interrupt the conversation. He didn't want to get into an argument with her. He and Edith had been friends for a long time; she'd been at his house for dinner and celebrations a number of times, including a surprise birthday party Georgia had thrown for him a month earlier. And, of course, there was that

sweaty night in a tangle of sheets that threatened to redefine their otherwise platonic relationship.

He lifted his glass. "Here's to your conversion to Judaism," he said.
"*L'chaim!*"

"*Salud!*" she said, touching the rim of her glass to his and laughing.

They slipped into a conversation about her current woes with her estranged husband. The more she discussed it, the angrier she became
until, at one point, Wilcox thought she might tip over the table. "Hey,"
he said, "you'll get through this. You married a jerk, that's all. No judge
is going to buy his story about being out of work and broke and needing
financial support from you."

"You sound like some naïve kid, Joe. There are plenty of judges who
are jerks, too, black robes and alleged wisdom or not. Believe me, I've
seen plenty of them."

"I was trying to make you feel better," he said.

"I know, I know. Maybe I can make you feel good."

"Oh? I can't wait."

She thought he'd taken her comment as sexual innuendo. "Let's not
go there, Joe."

"What?"

"Let's order."

She waited until they were on dessert to make him feel good. She
leaned across the table as far as she could and said, "The pen truly is
more powerful than the sword, Joe. You've proved that."

"How?"

"Based upon your articles about a serial killer, my guys are about to
go public and acknowledge the possibility and announce the formation
of a special task force."

"Why?" Wilcox asked.

"Heat from the city pols. Because of your articles, lots of pretty young
women are calling to say they're scared, and asking what the police are
doing to catch the guy." Wilcox started to say something but she continued. "Now, Joe, I'm telling you this off the record. Right?"

"Right. When are they going public?"

"Not sure, A day or two. I still don't buy it, Joe. Don't get me wrong.
I'm not doubting that you got somebody at MPD to give you the

serial killer scenario, and I understand how the similarities between the two murders—good-looking young women working in the media, both strangled—adds some support." She shook her head. "The tail really *can* wag the dog, huh?"

"I suppose so."

The news that MPD would now give credence to his reports did not please him. It was all based upon a lie, albeit a small one, that was now growing in importance. The tail wagging the dog, indeed!

But he didn't dwell on that, any more than he was able to focus on much of the conversation at the table that night.

Michael!

It was always Michael invading his thoughts.

"This was nice," Vargas-Swayze said over coffee.

"Yes, it was," Wilcox said. "Aside from MPD deciding to sign on to the serial killer possibility, what else is new in the investigations?"

"Unfortunately, not much. Everybody's got a theory. One killer or two? Thanks to you, Joe. Crimes of passion or premeditation? Targets of opportunity or carefully planned? Somebody who works at the *Trib?* Some homeless guy? My partner, Dungey, who's no fan of the press, tends to agree with your serial killer angle."

"That's nice to hear," Wilcox said.

"He's looking into the young reporter you mentioned, Gene Hawthorne."

"Probably nothing there, but it was worth mentioning."

"Of course it was."

"You were going back to question people who were at the paper the night Jean Kaporis was killed. Anything worthwhile there?"

"No. Still, Dungey has latched on to a few," Edith said.

"Based on what?"

"His gut. Nothing more than that. He's like that, Joe. He trusts his instincts more than most cops I've worked with. We all think our instincts are the best, but they usually don't pan out."

"You can't convict anyone on instincts," Wilcox said.

"How true," she said. "The only thing I've learned from questioning those who were in the building the night of the murder is that you guys at the *Trib* eat a hell of a lot of pizza."

He laughed.

"And use a lot of office supplies."

He frowned. "I wasn't aware of that," he said.

This time she laughed. "We spoke with a couple of deliverymen for office supply companies who made deliveries that night."

He thought of Michael, who'd said he was delivering supplies for an office supply company, and had made a delivery to the newspaper.

"Any names?" he asked.

"Pizza deliverymen?"

"Yeah, and office supply guys."

She shook her head. "There's nothing worth pursuing with them," she said. "Dungey latched on to one guy, didn't feel comfortable with him, but he's not pursuing it, at least for the moment."

"Who was the guy?" Wilcox asked, sounding as casual as he possibly could.

She scrunched up her face. "French name. LaGlue. LaBrew. I think Dungey is uncomfortable with anybody with a foreign sounding name. He's a real Smith and Jones kind of guy. Good basketball player by the way. He's . . . Joe?"

"What? Or. Sorry. My mind wandered there for a minute. Happening more and more these days. Come on, let's go. It's past your bedtime and—"

"*My* bedtime?" she said, punching his arm.

"All right," he said, "*my* bedtime." He kissed her on the cheek and hailed a passing empty cab. Another kiss on the cheek and he was gone, his thoughts as murky as the dark backseat of the cab.

NINETEEN

W hat've you got on the murders?" Paul Morehouse asked when his senior reporter arrived the next morning.

Wilcox had been asking himself that same question. Because Morehouse wanted more from him, he was determined to oblige. At least this time they would be based upon truth.

"MPD's close to announcing that they've set up a special task force to hunt down the serial killer."

"Where'd you get that, Joe?"

"A source."

"How close are they to making the announcement?"

"A day, maybe two."

"They've been debunking the serial killer angle from the beginning," Morehouse said. "What changed their mind?"

Wilcox shrugged.

"Can you get it on the record?"

"No," Wilcox said with a shake of the head. "Not until they go public with it. A few days at the most."

"Go with it tomorrow," Morehouse said. "Anonymous MPD source."

"Okay."

"What else?"

"At the moment? Not much. I'm working some leads today. Hopefully, they'll pan out."

Wilcox was almost out Morehouse's door when his boss stopped him. "Hey, Joe, don't miss this."

Wilcox returned to the desk and accepted the memo Morehouse handed him. He read it, scowled, and said, "A little premature, isn't it?"

"Hey," Morehouse said, extending his hands palms out in a defensive posture. "I don't make policy around here. I just follow it. Be sure to go, huh? They're serious about it upstairs."

Wilcox retreated to his cubicle. Gene Hawthorne walked by and glanced in at Wilcox, who muttered to himself and read the memo again.

It was addressed to Wilcox, and had come from the *Tribune*'s vice president of human resources. In it, the veep pointed out that because Wilcox was within two years of retirement, he was eligible for the buyout program that had been initiated a year earlier. He was instructed to report to a conference room on the executive floor at three that afternoon for a briefing on his options.

He tossed the memo on his desk and looked at his watch. Eight o'clock. What time did Michael go to work? He picked up the phone and dialed his brother's number, intending to leave a message on the machine. Instead, Michael answered. "Joseph," he said, as though getting the call was akin to winning a lottery. "I'm so glad you called. I was afraid you might let too much time pass. I loved seeing you yesterday, both in person and on the telly. You were wonderful, really showed up the others on the show with you."

"Thank you, Michael. I appreciate that. Look, I started thinking after leaving your apartment yesterday that you're right about how important it is for us to reestablish a relationship after all these years. I'm sure you understand how shocked I was to hear from you and to know you were no longer at the hospital."

"Of course I understand, Joseph, and I told you that. I am willing to go at whatever pace is comfortable for you and your family." His exaggerated diction annoyed Joe.

"The family. Well, I do want to go slowly there, Michael. Let's spend whatever time together is necessary for us to forge a new bond. Once that happens, I would love to introduce you to Georgia and Roberta. Tell you what. I know you're working but—"

"Wrong, Joseph," Michael said in a scolding way, a teacher chiding a student who'd given the wrong answer to a quiz question. "I've been doing some serious thinking, too."

Joe filled the ensuing pause with, "And?"

"I called in this morning and gave them my resignation, effective today."

This time, Joe initiated the pause. His immediate reaction was fear that Michael would seek financial support from him. "How are you going to support yourself, Michael?"

"You sound worried, Joseph."

"Worried? About what?"

"About money. Was I looking for money from you?"

"Michael, I—"

"I wouldn't blame you for worrying about that. After all, you're not a Bob Woodward or some other reporter who's gone on to write bestselling books. I'm sure you've made a decent living and all that. Does Georgia work?"

"No. Not any more. I'd like to get together again today, Michael."

"That sounds splendid. Dinner?"

"I'll have to play that by ear."

"Come to the apartment first. Drinks are so expensive in restaurants. We can have one here and then decide whether to go on to dinner."

"That would be fine, Michael. Fiveish?"

"I have an appointment at five, but—"

"We'll make it later," Joe said.

"No, come at five," said Michael. "I will leave a small envelope containing a key to the building's front door, and one to my apartment, beneath the faux planter to the right of the front door."

"Michael, I really don't—"

"Joseph, we are brothers. Aha! I'll have duplicate keys made for you and they will be in the envelope. Yours to keep."

"All right," Joe said. "What time will you be back from your appointment?"

"Six, six-thirty at the latest."

After hanging up, Wilcox made a routine call to MPD's office of public affairs and spoke with a deputy there. "Hear that you're setting up a task force to focus on the serial killer possibility."

The cop on the other end of the phone laughed. "No comment," he said.

"I'll take that to mean I'm right," Wilcox said.

"Jesus, Joe, now that you're a talking head, don't let it swell up."

"No fear of that," Joe said. "I'll dutifully report your lack of comment."

He read comments made by single women to Rick Jillian, one of which caused him to laugh out loud: "I had a dream last night and saw the serial killer in it," one woman told Jillian." She went on to describe him as being unusually tall—"at least six-six," she'd said—with a greenish complexion and a patch over one eye. "He spoke in tongues," she added.

Armed with more rational quotes generated by Jillian's interviews, and with some additional psychological material from researcher Kathleen Lansden, Wilcox spent the rest of the morning writing the next edition's feature piece.

Georgia called at eleven: "Joe, Roberta wants to talk with us about something."

"Talk about what? Is she all right?"

"I don't know. She sounded serious. She's working tonight, but she's coming to the house tomorrow night for dinner. I want you here."

"Sure. She wouldn't give even a hint of what this is about?"

"No."

"She's not planning to marry that Curtis guy, is she?"

"Joe, stop asking questions. I don't know what she's doing. You will be here."

"Of course I will. I'll be late tonight though. Don't hold dinner."

He decided to have lunch at the press club, and went there a little after noon. It was a pleasant day in D.C., sunny and warm but not hot.

He rode the elevator to the club's floor and took a seat at the Reliable Source Bar.

"Mr. Wilcox, sir," the barman said. "How are you on this fine day?"

"Okay, thank you. A bloody, extra horseradish."

The drink had no sooner been placed before him when John Grant, his friend from the Associated Press, sidled up, slapped him on the back, and took the adjacent stool. "How goes it, Joe?"

"Pretty good. You?"

"Could be worse. I got up this morning, took a breath, and it worked. That puts me ahead of the game. What's new on the crime beat?"

"Not a hell of a lot. I'm working some leads on the young girl-killer story."

"Oh, speaking of that—" The bartender stood waiting for Grant to order.

"—martooni, up, with two olives." Grant resumed his conversation with Wilcox. "What's with this hooker angle?"

Wilcox, who'd just taken a sip of his drink, coughed, and swallowed hard. "What hooker angle?" he asked, knowing the answer.

"I was talking this morning to someone in the shop who covers D.C. She said something about Jean Kaporis's roommate working for an escort service. That true?"

Wilcox didn't want to admit he knew nothing about it. At the same time, he didn't want to acknowledge that he *did* know but had decided not to use it.

"I've heard the rumor," he said, taking another drink. "I don't see any relevance to the murder."

Grant leaned close. "Is it possible, Joe? I mean, could Kaporis have been turning tricks after hours and pissed off some client?"

"I doubt it, John. I really doubt it. Where did your friend get it?"

"She didn't say."

"Are you moving it on the wire?"

"This morning."

They enjoyed their drinks in silence until Grant said, "What's with your buddy Hawthorne?"

Wilcox turned to him. "My buddy?"

Grant laughed and ordered a second drink. Wilcox declined.

"Yeah, your buddy, the hotshot reporter with the attitude. I heard you and he got into it up here."

"I'll be damned," Wilcox said, reconsidering and asking for a second drink. "What's this place become, a little old ladies' club? Yeah, I brought the bastard here for lunch and got into it with him. He left in a huff, which was fine with me."

"That's not the way he tells it," Grant said.

"You talked to him?"

"No, but I heard him talk about it."

"How did that happen?" Wilcox asked, feeling increasingly agitated.

"I was in the Trib Bar, that little joint up the street from you," Grant said. "Hawthorne was there with a half-dozen yuppie friends, pontificating and shooting off his mouth after a snootful of booze, trying to impress the gals who were with him—who, by the way, were knockouts. Anyway, our young Mr. Hawthorne is giving a lecture on how journalism has changed, and how people who've been in it for a while can't keep up with the changes."

"Changes for the worse," Wilcox muttered.

"That's not the point, Joe. Hawthorne starts telling a story about this over-the-hill reporter who took him to lunch here at the club. God, he went on about how the club is nothing but a haven for hacks and losers. Tickled his audience, who were all about his age. I was tempted to take a shot at him, but my pugilistic days are long gone."

"He mentioned me by name?" Wilcox asked.

"Yeah, once. At some point in the story, one of the gals asked who the reporter was who took him to lunch. He said it was Joe Wilcox, which was not an unfamiliar name to one of the nubile young ladies because she associated you with the serial killer stories. That triggered recognition from the other, who said she'd seen you on TV. So did I, Joe. You've got a new career ahead of you. Let's have lunch. I'm starved."

"I'm not staying," Wilcox said, draining his second drink. "No, I, ah, I have an appointment somewhere. I have to be somewhere. I have to— I'm sorry. Good seeing you. I have to go."

"Okay," Grant said. "Hey, Joe, about Hawthorne. Don't let it get to you. I just thought you'd enjoy hearing the story."

"Sure. Yeah, I did."

Wilcox stood and asked for his bill.

"I've got it," said Grant. "Go on, go to your appointment."

Grant watched his friend leave the room. "You notice anything strange about Joe?" he asked the bartender, who'd been serving drinks at the National Press Club for more than twenty years.

"He looks a little uptight, Mr. Grant."

"That's an understatement," Grant said, shaking his head. Unstated: *The guy's cracking up.*

Wilcox walked to the *Tribune* Building but didn't enter. He went past the entrance and wandered aimlessly along nearby streets. There were times when he thought he might pass out and took refuge against a building wall, trying to be as subtle as possible so as to not draw attention to himself. Mild nausea came and went. *What's wrong with me?* he wondered. He felt like an old man, feeble and easily victimized, taking careful steps to avoid falling, crossing intersections with great care, starting across when the light changed but hesitating because he wasn't sure whether it was safe to go to the other side.

After forty-five minutes of this drifting, he felt sufficiently composed to return to the newspaper and his cubicle. He'd no sooner settled in his chair and started to check e-mails and voice mail messages than Morehouse summoned him.

"What's up?" Joe asked, taking a seat across the desk from the editor.

"What've you got for tomorrow?"

"Just what I sent you before lunch."

"What's the problem, Joe?"

"There is no problem, Paul. I'm working my sources. Hopefully, I'll have more tomorrow." It seemed insufferably hot in Morehouse's office, and Wilcox dabbed at his brow and upper lip with a handkerchief.

"You sick?" Morehouse asked.

"Sick? No. It's hot in here."

"Well, Joe, it'll get a lot hotter if we don't come up soon with a different slant on the murders. We took the lead in packaging the serial killer idea, thanks to you. Now that we have, we can't just drop it. Everybody else in town is running with our story, Joe. I'm not running a journalistic charity here."

"I'm doing all I can," Wilcox said, weakly.

"I doubt that."

Wilcox stiffened. "Now wait a minute, Paul," he said. "Don't tell me whether I'm giving it my all. I resent that!"

Morehouse came from behind his desk and stood at the window overlooking the main newsroom. Wilcox started to get up to leave but Morehouse motioned for him to remain seated. The editor said, without looking at Wilcox, "You know I like you, Joe."

Joe didn't respond.

"I always have," Morehouse said, his attention still on the scene through the window. "Times have changed, though. You aware of that?"

It was more of a snort than a laugh from Wilcox. "I've noticed," he said.

Morehouse propped himself on the edge of a two-drawer file cabinet. "You've been a hell of a good cops reporter, Joe. I mean that. There's nobody in this city who could top you."

" 'Could?' " Wilcox said. "That sounds past tense."

"The way things are going," Morehouse said, "we're all about to become past tense—but only if we let it happen."

"Meaning?"

"When I hired you, Joe, I was the boy wonder around here, the youngest editor of a major section in the paper's history. I have to admit that it was awkward at first bossing around grizzled veterans, guys who'd forgotten more than I knew. And it was all guys, the old-boy fraternity at work, women need not apply." He paused and glanced through the glass again. "I was a lot like Hawthorne and the other Young Turks out there, Joe, full of myself and looking down at the old-timers." He laughed. "Funny how fast you become an old-timer, too." He snapped his fingers. "Like that! One day the wunderkind, the next day the guy with the bad back and molded shoes."

Wilcox didn't know how to respond. In all the years he'd worked for Morehouse, he'd never heard him slip into retrospection like this, even after their professional relationship had morphed into a friendship of sorts. Morehouse's asperity was well known, his temper on a hair-trigger. But quiet soul-searching wasn't incorporated into his psychological map.

What are you getting at? Wilcox wondered.

Morehouse addressed Wilcox directly now, his index finger poised to lend weight to his words. "Now, you listen to me, Joe Wilcox. You may not like what's happened to this business over the years any more than I do. You don't like Hawthorne and his ilk and neither do I. But times have changed big time. We don't as much report the news any more as we turn it into a story that has marketability. Sales, Joe, the bottom line, ad revenue, increased circulation, dollars and cents, that's where it's at these days, and like it or not, we either embrace that reality, or we get out of the way before the Hawthornes of the world run us over."

"I know you're right, Paul," Wilcox said. "The news business isn't what it was when I saw myself as the next Ed Murrow or Ernie Pyle. But I won't take a backseat to anyone, including guys like Hawthorne. *Especially* guys like Hawthorne."

Morehouse grunted and resumed his chair behind the desk. "We're in a fight to survive, Joe, like the airlines. People no longer automatically open their daily newspaper every morning and catch up on the news. There's cable and the networks, the bloggers on the Internet, the radio talk shows and the Matt Drudges of the world. We're losing ground every day. That's why we have to give readers what they want, in this case a reason to buy the *Trib*."

Wilcox said nothing, and an awkward silence settled over the office.

"I'm putting Hawthorne on the serial killer story, Joe."

Wilcox fairly came out of his chair. "You're *what?*"

"Putting Hawthorne on the story. I know you two don't get along, so I'm not suggesting you work together. You go ahead and continue to work your sources, and do the writing. He can't hold a candle to you when it comes to that. But he'll be working his contacts, too." He slid a sheet of paper across the desk. Wilcox picked it up and read a statement from the mayor, in which he called upon the city's women to go about their daily lives as usual, but to also exercise prudence and caution until the killer is brought to justice.

Wilcox threw the paper down on the desk. "Why didn't he give this to me?" he demanded.

"For the same reason you won't have anything to do with him, Joe. You guys act like you hate each other." Wilcox tried to say something but Morehouse said, "I don't give a goddamn whether you and Hawthorne ever say a word to each other. What I do care about is following through on the serial killer story we initiated. You catch your daughter on the noon news, Joe?"

"Roberta? No. Why?"

"She reported that AP is investigating the possibility that there may be a connection between Jean's murder and what her roommate does for a living."

"That's unconscionable," Wilcox said.

Morehouse came forward. He'd been calm until this moment. Now, his face reddened and his voice mirrored his anger. "I asked you, Joe, about that connection with Kaporis's roommate, and you told me nothing panned out. You lied. I called Jillian and Lansden in and asked them about it. Lansden said she'd told you that the roommate—what's her name? Pruit?—worked for the Starlight agency. Did she?"

"No. She said the guy at the agency hesitated or something when she mentioned Pruit's name. That was it."

"So, where did AP come up with it?"

"Ask somebody at AP."

"Ask your daughter."

"Yeah, I will. Is that it?"

"I could say don't let me down, Joe. Take what Hawthorne gives you, work your own side of the street, and keep this serial killer story on the front page. Better yet, Joe, don't let yourself down. Make me a hero upstairs and we'll both go out in a blaze of glory."

Morehouse watched his veteran reporter slowly get out of the chair and go to the door. His hand was on the knob when Morehouse said, "Believe me, Joe, I don't like this any more than you do."

Wilcox turned, smiled, nodded, and left, wishing his boss hadn't felt compelled to add that final disingenuous comment.

TWENTY

Wilcox went to his cubicle and placed a call to the detectives' room at First District headquarters.

"Edith," Wilcox said, "I just heard about the AP story on the Kaporis murder and that her roommate, Pruit, worked for an escort agency."

"Right."

"I talked to my daughter who used it on the noon news today. She says it came from MPD."

"It might have, Joe. I don't know."

"But you knew about the possible link," he said. "I was the one who told you."

"I remember. Sure. My partner and I followed up on it. Ms. Pruit said she worked for the Starlight agency."

"Why didn't you tell *me?*" Wilcox asked, audibly exasperated.

"Because—because it didn't occur to me to tell you, Joe." She lowered her voice. "There's nothing to it. It's a red herring. Look, I can't talk now. I'll get back to you."

He pulled up the AP story and added portions of it to his article: "MPD is investigating a possible link between the murder of *Washington Tribune* staffer Jean Kaporis and a Washington escort service for which the victim's roommate is alleged to have worked."

Next, he wove the mayor's statement into the story, using it as the new lead. And he added Jean Kaporis's father's comment that his daughter had indicated she was dating a married man in Washington named Paul. *No*, he thought, *I promised I wouldn't use that*, and struck the line.

Satisfied that the article read right, but not feeling especially good about having written it, he filed it electronically with Paul Morehouse. As he prepared to leave, Gene Hawthorne sent him a computer instant message, asking whether Wilcox had gotten the mayor's statement.

"Yes," Wilcox wrote back.

"I'll see what else I can come up with," Hawthorne wrote.

Wilcox didn't bother responding.

He called Roberta at the TV station.

"Hi," he said. "It's Dad."

"Hi," she said. "Only have a second. What's up?"

"You're coming to dinner tomorrow night?"

"Yes."

"What's this thing you want to speak to your mother and me about?"

"I'll tell you tomorrow, Dad."

"Okay. Hey, I just learned that you went with an AP story about Jean Kaporis's roommate working for an escort service."

"Dad, I really have to run."

"I had that information, Robbie, but decided to not use it."

She said nothing.

"Where did you get it?"

"MPD."

"Oh? Who?"

"I'll see you tomorrow night," she said.

"Using the escort service slant is real tabloid journalism, Roberta, and I—"

A click in his ear ended his speech.

Rick Jillian, who'd been told to develop a short chronological feature on the Son of Sam serial killer case in New York for possible inclusion as a sidebar to Wilcox's article, tapped Wilcox on the shoulder, causing him to jerk to attention.

"I wake you?" Jillian asked.

"Wake me? Of course not. I'm just leaving."

"Here's the Son of Sam piece, Joe."

"Great. File it with Paul. I'm out of here."

The phone rang. It was the VP of human resources asking why Wilcox hadn't kept his three o'clock appointment.

"Sorry," Wilcox said, "but I got busy. The serial killer story, you know."

"You're doing a great job with that," the VP said. "When can we meet?"

"Tomorrow."

"Three?"

"Sure."

Wilcox beat a hasty retreat to the elevators, not because he was running late, but because he wanted out of the newsroom and building, to be as far away from it as possible. He got in his car and headed for Michael's apartment building on Connecticut Avenue NW, arriving a little after four-thirty. A parking space across the street and a few buildings up from Michael's opened up and Wilcox maneuvered into it. He was about to get out of the car but reconsidered, remaining instead inside and watching the door to the apartment building. Minutes later, Michael appeared carrying an envelope, which he slid beneath a large flowerpot near the front entrance. Michael came to the sidewalk and looked around before heading on foot in a direction opposite from where Wilcox was parked.

Wilcox waited long enough to be sure his brother wouldn't be returning to get something he'd forgotten and went to the flowerpot. The envelope contained two keys on a simple key ring. Wilcox tried one in the front door. It worked, and he entered the building's interior, went down the long hallway, and stopped in front of Michael's apartment. He was in the process of inserting the second key into that door when a man's voice said, "Who are you?"

Wilcox turned to face a burly man leaning on a cane.

"Who are you?" the man repeated.

"Mr. Wilcox's—Mr. LaRue's friend," Wilcox answered. "Who are *you?*"

"Rudy. I'm his friend, too. He ain't here."

"I know. He gave me his key."

Wilcox turned his head to avoid the alcoholic fumes coming from this man named Rudy. "Excuse me," he said, opening the door and stepping into the apartment, aware of Rudy's eyes boring into his back. He closed the door and drew a deep breath. Maggie came from the kitchen, looked up at him, meowed, and preceded him into the living room.

Wilcox stood in the center of the room. It was quiet; only an occasional honk of a car horn on Connecticut Avenue violated the silence. He went to each window and looked out, his thoughts as jumbled as the apartment was neat. In the narrow, old-fashioned kitchen, the day's dishes had been washed, rinsed, and left to dry in a blue dish drainer. A vase of wilting flowers sat next to the drainer.

Back in the living room, Joe sat in a chair next to where Michael's guitar and amplifier stood. He picked up the instrument and ran his fingers over the strings, the sound barely audible without amplification. He considered turning on the amp but was afraid he'd do something destructive, push the wrong button or turn the wrong knob.

The hollow core door on file cabinets on the opposite side of the room was as tidy as everything else in the apartment. The only items on its surface were the old electric typewriter, a desk calendar, and a halogen lamp. He sat at the desk, opened the file cabinets' drawers, and perused their contents, barely disturbing papers as he went through them. He withdrew an envelope from a photo processing shop and rifled through the small color snapshots, most of them of Michael at an undetermined outdoor social event. He removed one from the pack that showed Michael alone, smiling into the camera, and placed it in his inside jacket pocket. A recurring chorus of ideas accompanied his seemingly aimless search. Were he pressed, he would have denied the thoughts he was having at that moment. But they were present, coming and going like mental dust bunnies.

Michael had murdered a young woman when he was a teenager and been found legally insane.

Michael had moved to Washington prior to the first of the two murders having taken place.

Michael worked for an office supply company and had made deliveries to the newspaper, including the night Jean Kaporis was killed.

Michael was in excellent physical condition, certainly strong enough to have strangled Kaporis and Colleen McNamara.

Michael was using a false name.

Edith Vargas-Swayze and her detective partner had questioned Michael; the partner found something troublesome about the deliveryman with the funny, French-sounding name.

None of which meant Michael had had anything to do with the murder of Jean Kaporis or McNamara. Still, it was a provocative notion, albeit unlikely, to ponder, and he continued to do that as he finished rifling through papers in his brother's desk.

He went to the small bedroom. The bed was made, the corners of the sheet tight and precise, military style. He looked in the room's only closet. The few clothes were hung carefully, the fronts of shirts and two suits facing in the same direction, slacks and jeans folded over hangers and occupying their own space. Three pairs of shoes on the floor were polished and lined up heel-to-heel, toe-to-toe.

A round table covered by a black cloth served as a night table. On it was a digital alarm clock, a lamp, and a five-by-seven color photo in an easel frame. Wilcox picked it up and examined the woman more closely. She appeared to be in her thirties. She wore large, round glasses with black frames; her hair was long and dark, with streaks of silver. She had a nice smile.

He checked his watch. It was five-fifteen. Michael said he wouldn't be back until six or six thirty. He returned to the living room and again sat at the desk, Maggie occupying one corner of the table, where she licked her paws clean. He'd carried with him into the apartment a file folder in which he'd collected hardcopy clips of the *Trib*'s stories about the Kaporis and McNamara murders, including the articles he'd written, and placed it on the small table next to the desk, arranging papers so that they partially obscured it.

The cover was off the typewriter. He turned on the power, pulled open one of the file drawers, removed a sheet of blank paper and rolled it in behind the platen. Five minutes later he pulled the page from the typewriter, folded it carefully, and put it in the inside pocket of his sport jacket. Next, he found a blank Number Ten envelope, placed it in the typewriter, and typed an address on it. He turned off the typewriter, made sure everything on the desk looked the way it had earlier, sat on the couch and browsed magazines until Michael walked through the door.

"Ah, Joseph," Michael said, extending his arms as though expecting Joe to run into them. Joe didn't leave the chair. "You obviously found the keys. Good. They're yours to keep, and I hope you make frequent use of them. Drink? I need a glass of wine. You?"

"Wine will be fine, Michael."

"Stay right where you are, Joseph. The service in this establishment is first-rate."

Michael returned with the wine, handed a glass to Joe, and opened a yellow director's chair that had been folded in a corner of the room. He raised his glass: "To brothers," he said.

Joe tilted his glass in Michael's direction before sipping. "You say you've quit your job," he said, deliberately sounding nonchalant.

"That's right. It was a good job, and they treated me decently. But I felt it was time to look for something else, perhaps something more in line with my interests and abilities. I've decided to explore nonprofit opportunities."

"Oh? Why?"

"To pay something back to society, Joseph. I feel a need for that. You probably don't understand, but—"

"Have you had any success finding such a job?"

"I've just started looking."

"How long will you be able to go without an income?" Joe asked, not caring whether it represented an inappropriate intrusion into his brother's financial life.

"Oh, for a while," Michael replied. "You'd be surprised how much I was able to save during those forty years in the hospital. They didn't pay patients much for the menial tasks we performed, but with nothing to spend it on, it mounted up. That, and the trust fund mother left, will tide me over for quite a long spell."

"Trust fund? Mother left you a trust fund?"

"You didn't know?"

"No, Michael, I didn't know."

He pressed his fingertips to his lips. "And she probably never wanted you to know," he said. "Me and my big mouth." He leaned forward and placed his hand on Joe's knee. "I'm sure she meant well, Joseph. She knew she didn't ever have to worry about you, not with the bright future that lay ahead for you, college, a career, family, all those things that money can't buy. But I suppose she reasoned that if I was ever released from the hospital, I'd have nothing on which to fall back, no education, no career, no income." He sat back and smiled. "It is absolutely amazing how much interest builds up over forty years, even on a meager investment."

"I imagine it does," Joe said.

"At any rate, Joseph, you didn't come here to discuss my career aspirations. Are we going to dinner?"

"Not tonight, Michael. I can't stay long."

"Pity. Oh, well, you will let me play one song for you. I'm anxious that you know my time in the hospital wasn't entirely wasted."

Joe protested but Michael ignored him and went to the guitar, switched on the amplifier, and played random, rich chords until sliding into a bouncy version of what Joe eventually recognized as "Bye Bye Blackbird." Although Joe was not musically trained, nor did he possess a sophisticated musical ear, it was obvious to him that his brother had become a talented guitarist. The fingers of his left hand moved quickly and effortlessly over the instrument's frets, while his right fingers plucked at the strings, singularly and in bunches, an adventuresome improvisation that threatened to stray from the familiar melody, but never did, anchored by it instead, Michael's creativity demonstrated within its framework. When he finished and the final chord had faded, Joe applauded. Michael bowed his head and turned off the amp.

"That was very good, Michael," Joe said. "Impressive."

"Thank you. Of course, it's just an example of something good coming out of something bad. Had I not been incarcerated in that hospital for so many years, I never would have had the inclination or time to practice the guitar. I was inspired by Joe Pass."

"Who?"

Michael laughed as he sat in the director's chair. "You obviously are not a jazz lover. Joe Pass spent many years in prison because of his involvement with drugs. He had nothing to do but practice his guitar playing. When he came out of prison, he was the best jazz guitarist in the world."

While Joe had been impressed by Michael's playing, he found himself gripped by resentment, particularly about being given a lecture on music and some obscure jazz guitar player. He felt at once a feeling of inadequacy sitting there with this older brother, who'd spent virtually his entire adult life committed to a hospital for the criminally insane, a sick, depraved murderer who'd sexually assaulted and brutally killed a young girl, a neighbor, an innocent being. He was grappling with these thoughts when Michael asked, "More wine?"

"Sure," Joe said, not knowing why he'd elected to prolong his discomfort.

"So, Joseph, tell me about yourself," Michael said after delivering the second glass and again taking the director's chair. "I know what you've *become* since we were teenagers, but not what you think and feel. What are your views, your perspective on life?"

"I hadn't thought about such things recently," Joe said.

"Politically?" Michael said. "Is it true that all journalists are left-leaning liberals?" He said it with a laugh.

"No, it's not true," Joe said.

"I hope not," Michael said. "I've had all these years to think about politics and how it influences our lives." He slowly shook his head; his face formed a serious mask. "So much of society has been destroyed by liberals who've turned us into soft, weak citizens, always looking for the next handout, forever wanting the government to take care of us rather than being expected to take care of ourselves." He lowered his chin and assessed Joe's reaction to what he'd said. "You don't agree, Joseph."

"It isn't a matter of agreeing or disagreeing, Michael. It's just that—"

"I know, I know. What is this former madman doing pontificating about how we should live our lives? Here I am, suddenly thrust upon society after forty years of dutifully taking my medications and sitting through thousands—yes, literally thousands of hours of banal group therapy, in addition to thousands of hours sitting one-on-one with my personal therapist who asked stupid, moronic questions over and over until I learned the answers he expected and regurgitated them on cue, never failing to smile or to assume a deep sense of seriousness of purpose where and when suitable to the moment."

He'd said it in a monotone. Now, he rose in the chair to a ramrod position and spoke in a louder, more authoritative voice. "I challenge anyone to survive what I've survived, Joseph—to face more than fourteen thousand hours of that form of degradation—and not end up feeling somewhat superior to those who make up this sad world."

Joe didn't know what to say in response, so said nothing.

Michael's tone suddenly softened, as though a switch had been activated. A wide smile crossed his tanned face, accompanied by a low, self-effacing chuckle. "What am I doing?" he said, "mouthing off to my one and only brother. What is wrong with me? I suppose having my thoughts and beliefs suppressed for so long has left me in need of a soapbox. Forgive me, Joseph."

"It's okay, Michael. I think I understand."

"Actually," Michael said, "there are advantages to being held in an institution for forty years. I've found it difficult since being released."

"Really? How so?"

"Little things that become big things. I never had to even think twice about what to wear each day. Like being in the army, I suppose. Two uniforms, summer and winter. I wore hospital pajamas most of the time. Not terribly stylish, but functional. I ate what they served me, except for those special nights when we were allowed to cook our own meals. Even then, we were told what ingredients to use." He sighed deeply. "No decisions to be made, Joseph. I'm having trouble making them now that I'm a so-called free man."

Joe placed his empty glass on the floor. "I'd really better be going."

"If you must," Michael said, standing. "I have a suggestion, Joseph."
"Which is?"

"I suggest that the next time we meet, it be at your house."

"No, Michael, I don't think so. As I've said before, I—"

"If I didn't know better, Joseph, I'd almost say you're ashamed of me."

"That's not it and you know it," Joe said. "Getting you together with Georgia and Roberta will be on my timetable, not yours."

"You sound angry."

"I'm under a lot of pressure at work."

"Ah, yes. Of course. The serial killer. Anything new in that regard? Is my kid brother about to solve the case?"

"Thanks for the wine, Michael, and the concert. I'll be in touch."

"Joseph, if I've offended you, I—"

Joe went to the door, stopped, and turned. "You've done nicely, Michael. You've obviously put your life together and I commend you for that. But forty years is a lot of time, and I'm not sure it can ever be made up. Why don't we stand back, take a deep breath, and maybe try it again some time in the future. This is not a good time. I wish you well."

He wasn't sure whether the expression on his brother's face was anger or hurt. He didn't care. He left the apartment and almost bumped into the man with the cane whom he'd met upon arriving.

"Is he in there?" the man asked.

"Yes, he's in there," Joe replied, and walked quickly out of the building, went to his car, started the engine, swore loudly, tuned the radio to a classical station, cranked up the music, and pulled away from the curb, almost sideswiping oncoming traffic.

TWENTY-ONE

When Wilcox arrived at the *Trib* the following morning, there was an e-mail message from Morehouse on his computer: *Follow up on the escort service link. Check the agency to see whether Jean Kaporis had ever taken assignments from them.*

Wilcox walked into his boss's office. "I disagree," he said flatly.

"With what?"

"Following up on the escort service. What are we trying to do, Paul, paint Jean as a hooker? She's dead, for Christ's sake. She was young but she was one of us. She was no hooker."

"I'm not saying she was. Do you have a better angle to pursue for tomorrow's edition?"

"As of this moment? No."

"So develop the escort agency slant. It doesn't have to focus on Jean. Check MPD and see whether women working for escort services have ever been murdered in the line of duty. Get Jillian and Lansden to interview some of those gals, find out how dangerous the work is. Get their views on the possibility that the serial killer might have met his victims through escort agencies. While you're at it, see if the McNamara girl didn't turn a few tricks in her spare time, too."

Wilcox knew it was futile to argue. He returned to his cubicle and pretended to work the phone, looking busy, calling friends at other media outlets to ask what they planned to do as follow-ups to the serial killer story. At eleven, he called home and confirmed with Georgia that Roberta was coming for dinner, and that he would be home in time to join them. He'd just completed that call when one of the mailroom's young employees arrived with the first of two mail deliveries for that day.

"Morning, Mr. Wilcox," he said, handing Joe his bundle of mail.

"Good morning. All well with you?"

"Doin' okay. You have yourself a good day, Mr. Wilcox."

He started opening his mail. There were letters from readers of the newspaper either chastising him for unduly frightening the public with his articles (he silently agreed), or praising his courage, insight, and dedication to keeping the public informed. He saved one envelope for last. After taking pains to satisfy himself that his actions were unobserved, he used a letter opener made by Roberta in grade school in the shape of a bird's head and beak to slit open the envelope. He removed the single sheet of paper, unfolded it, and stared at the typewritten words.

"Jesus!" he said, loud enough for a reporter in the next cubicle to hear.

"What's up, Joe?" the reporter asked.

Wilcox handed over the page from the envelope to his colleague.

"Wow!" was the reaction.

The reporter stepped into Wilcox's cubicle and handed back the letter. "What are you going to do?" he asked.

"I don't know. It could be a joke, some clown playing games. Then again—"

"You have to treat it as legit, Joe."

"I know, I know. I'll run it by Paul."

"What's the postmark on the envelope?" the reporter asked.

Wilcox picked up the envelope and examined the printing surrounding the thirty-seven-cent stamp. "The post office right down the block," he said.

"He's a real nutcase," said the reporter.

"Looks like it. Excuse me."

Morehouse was in conference with a couple of *Tribune* executives when Wilcox approached his door. The Metro editor waved him away. Wilcox held up the letter and fluttered it in front of the glass. Morehouse, annoyed at the intrusion, got up from behind his desk and came to the door. "I'm in a meeting," he said.

"I know. Sorry to interrupt, but I thought you should see this right away. It arrived in today's first mail."

Morehouse took the letter, put on half-glasses tethered by a multicolored ribbon, and read. When he was finished, he handed it back to Wilcox and chewed his cheek. "It just arrived?"

"Yes."

"All right. Let me finish up in here. Don't show it to anybody. Got that?"

"Of course."

"We'll meet in a half hour." He started to return to his office, stopped, looked at Wilcox, and said, "This is good, Joe. This is really good."

Wilcox bided his time in his cubicle. The reporter in the adjacent space asked what Morehouse had said, but Wilcox deflected his questions. Ten minutes later, Morehouse called him to return to his office.

"You think this is legit?" Morehouse asked after Wilcox had settled in a chair behind the closed door.

"I have no idea," he replied. "But I think we have to treat it as though it is."

"What does the guy want?"

"What he says in the letter. Don't give it to the police, he says. Don't try to trace it. He says he'll be in contact with me again."

Morehouse thought for a moment before saying, "He doesn't say we can't publish it in the paper."

"Not specifically, but I'm not sure how he'll react if it does appear. He might break off contact if we run it."

"Not likely," proclaimed the editor. "This fruitcake wants the attention and notoriety. He'll be disappointed if we *don't* run it. "

"I don't know, Paul."

"Yeah, well, you know how these guys think. Make the accompanying article personal, Joe. Play on how the serial killer has chosen you as his conduit to the world. Respond to him in the piece. Encourage him to stay in touch. Promise you'll respect his needs and wishes. Set up a running dialogue. You're his buddy, his confidant. This is big stuff, Joe, not only for the paper, but for you, too."

"I'll get on it right away, Paul. We'll drop the escort angle?"

"For now. Good work, Joe. Very good work."

Wilcox ordered in Chinese and spent the rest of the day writing the article to accompany the letter. Another meeting took place later that afternoon between him, Morehouse, and the *Trib*'s chief legal counsel, who'd been brought into the situation by Morehouse. The debate involved whether the paper should show the letter to the police prior to publishing it. The consensus: The article would run, along with the letter. The police would be brought in once the paper was on newsstands. To tip law enforcement prior to that would risk a leak, allowing other media to scoop the *Trib*.

At five, Wilcox informed Morehouse that he was leaving.

"It's a great piece, Joe, but it needs some sharpening."

"You'll have to get somebody else for rewrite," Wilcox said. "I've got a command performance at home tonight."

"Okay. Nice work, buddy. Let me ask you something. How does it feel to have a maniac out there sending you love notes?"

"Not good," Wilcox said.

"Well, get used to it, my friend. This won't be the last letter you get from him. Count on it."

"I know," Wilcox said. "I know."

He retrieved his car from the parking lot and headed home. He'd wondered all afternoon whether he could go through with this scheme that had been hatched on the spot at his brother's apartment. He'd assumed he would have trouble doing it. But somehow, for some reason, it all seemed reasonable now. No debilitating bout of conscience, no second thoughts.

Roberta's silver Toyota was in the driveway when Wilcox pulled up, and he parked beside her. *What's on her mind that she's called for a meeting?* he wondered as he turned off the ignition and got out of the car. As he approached the front door, the sound of music stopped him. He cocked his head and tried to identify it. Georgia seldom played music while working in the kitchen, preferring talk radio to keep her company. When she did opt for music, it invariably was from their collection of classical CDs. This wasn't classical music coming through the open front windows. It was guitar jazz.

Strange, Wilcox thought as he opened the door and stepped into the foyer. He dropped his briefcase on the floor, opened the foyer's second door, and walked into the living room. The music was louder now, a song written by somebody like Cole Porter or another composer of popular show music. As he approached the kitchen, Georgia came from it.

"Hi," he said, about to kiss her.

"Why didn't you tell me?" she asked.

"Tell you what?"

"About Michael. Your *brother*, Michael."

"I—"

"He's here," she said.

Wilcox walked past her to the kitchen and looked out to the patio where Michael and Roberta sat at a green wrought-iron table, glasses in front of them.

"Why didn't you tell me?" Georgia repeated.

"I was going to," he said, "but it all happened so fast and—" His face turned hard. "How dare he just show up here?"

"I didn't know what to do when I answered the door," she said. "I didn't know who he was. When he said he was your brother, Michael, I almost passed out."

"I'll get rid of him."

She grabbed his arm. "Please, Joe, don't make a scene," she said. "I'm not angry that he's here. I just wish you had—"

Wilcox entered the kitchen, crossed it, pulled open the sliding glass door to the patio, and stepped outside.

Michael, who faced the door, jumped up and said, "Joseph. You're home."

Roberta turned in her chair. "You didn't tell us," she said, not sounding very angry.

"I decided to take the bull by the horns and just show up," Michael said. "I'm glad I did. How wonderful to finally get to meet your lovely wife and daughter." He indicated his outfit—a tan sport jacket worn over a black T-shirt and jeans. "I hope you don't mind my informal attire," he said. "I was confident you good folks didn't stand on ceremony."

"You look fine," Roberta said.

Joe stood rigidly, glaring at his brother, who sported a wide, white smile.

Georgia came up behind her husband and said, "Michael brought some wonderful wine, Joe, and the CD I put on. It's by a famous guitar player."

"Joe Pass," Joe said. "He spent many years in prison for drug offenses where he practiced playing his guitar every day and—" He returned to the kitchen and poured himself a large drink.

"I know you're upset, Joe," Georgia said in a hushed voice, "but try not to be. Let's just enjoy the evening. We can talk about it after he's gone."

"Damn him!" Joe said.

"Joe, please, for my sake. He's your brother. Please."

"I don't like him with Roberta."

"Why? Oh, because of—"

"Yeah, because of *that*! What does Roberta want to talk to us about?"

"I'll fill you in later. It's nothing serious. She came early and we talked. Everything is fine." She went to the stove and picked up where she'd left off preparing dinner.

Joe went to the living room and snapped the stereo into silence. The sudden hush was louder than the music had been. He returned to the kitchen and again looked out to the patio, where Roberta was laughing loudly at something Michael had said.

"Enough!" Georgia said. "Either tell him to go, or pull yourself together and welcome him." Her tone said she meant it.

"All right," Joe said. "We'll get through the evening, but after that—"

"Yes, Joe, after that we'll talk. Now go out and join them and make him feel at home."

Her acceptance of Michael's presence astounded Joe. It had been late into their courtship that he told her about his brother and what had happened to him. He'd done it with trepidation, certain that knowing he had a brother who'd murdered, and who'd been judged to be criminally insane, might sour her on the relationship with him. It didn't, although she had, at times, demonstrated concern.

&

It was early in their marriage. They'd gone out for a pizza and saw a movie. After the show let out, they'd stopped in a coffee shop for dessert; Georgia loved ice cream, especially coffee ice cream, and Joe was always happy to indulge her frequent yen for it. They'd recently begun discussing a family. He knew she wanted children, and like her yearning for coffee ice cream, he was happy to oblige. It wasn't a deep-seated need for him. He simply assumed that children came with marriage, and he was willing to assume the responsibilities of fatherhood.

"Want to start tonight?" he asked in the coffee shop, his hands on hers.

"Start what tonight?"

"Having a kid." He gave his best leer, and winked.

"Oh." She blushed, and looked around to see whether others had overheard his proposition. She slid her hands from beneath his and resumed eating her ice cream.

He tried to read her mood. Usually, she was ebullient, a glass-half-full person who seemed always to be smiling and never morose, never scowling. But it was a scowl on her pretty face that night.

"What's the matter?" he asked.

"Nothing."

"Come on, Georgia," he said. "I know when something's bothering you. What is it?"

"Not here."

They drove home in silence. After they'd changed into pajamas and were ready to go to bed, she said, "I'm sorry, Joe. I know I'm not being fair. Something *is* bothering me."

"So, tell me. Have I done something wrong? Did I say something that upset you?"

She slowly shook her head. They were in the bedroom, sitting side-by-side on the bed. A full moon visible through the room's skylight cast uncertain light over the room. She turned, gripped his hands, and said, "Joe, I'm afraid."

"Afraid? Of what?"

"Of having a child."

He laughed. "I think I know what you mean," he said. "I'm not the one who'll have to waddle around for nine months and give birth. But women do it every day and—"

"It isn't that, Joe. It's—it's Michael."

"My brother?"

"Yes."

"What does he have to do with us having a child?"

She didn't respond, nor did she have to. He knew what she was thinking, that it was possible that madness was in the Wilcox genes, that any child they had might carry those genes.

"That other Wilcox boy's the one I'd be worried about. Insanity is in the blood and genes, runs right through a family like any other disease."

Those words overheard from the churchgoing neighborhood woman were etched in his mind, and had been since she uttered them so many years ago.

"Look," he said, trying to mitigate the anger he felt, not at what she thought, but because he resented having been put in this position by a brother, "things like Michael's problem aren't carried in anyone's genes."

"How do you know that?" she said.

"I just know it, that's all."

"You can't be sure, Joe. My mother—"

"What about your mother? Did you talk to *her* about this?"

"Yes. She says—"

"It's none of your mother's business, damn it!"

"It isn't? Our child will be her grandchild."

"What does she know about genes and heredity, Georgia?"

"I'm not saying she *knows* anything about it, Joe. But she does have concerns, just as I do."

"Let's talk about this another time," he said.

"All right."

A few minutes later, the lights out, everything silent and peaceful, she said, "Would you agree to talk to a doctor about it?"

"What doctor?"

"Someone with medical knowledge about such things. A pediatrician maybe, a psychiatrist?"

His deep sigh said to her that he wouldn't consider what she'd suggested. But to her surprise, he said, "Sure. You pick a doctor and we'll go talk to him."

She kissed him lightly on the lips and turned over, her tears absorbed by her pillowcase. She desperately wanted a child.

After considerable research, she found a female pediatrician who also boasted a doctorate in psychology, and they made an appointment for a consultation. It pained Wilcox to talk with a stranger about his family, particularly his brother's past, but the doctor was a kindly older woman with gray hair pulled back into a tight bun, and whose glasses were large, round, and framed in red. She listened carefully and exuded warmth and nonjudgmental concern. After she'd heard Wilcox's thumbnail sketch of his family and Michael's incarceration as a mental patient, the doctor smiled, sat back in her chair and said, "You understand, of course, that it's impossible for me to comment with any assuredness about your brother's mental condition without having had the opportunity to examine him and review his records. Is it possible that he suffered a brain abnormality that was eventually overridden by therapy and counseling? Yes, that's possible. And if that brain abnormality had a genetic component, is it likely that it would have been passed along to you, Mr. Wilcox? That's highly unlikely—unless, of course, either of your parents suffered the same abnormal genetic makeup. You say your mother and father were very religious."

"My father especially," Wilcox said, "although my mother was deeply religious, too. Is that significant?"

"It could be. Your brother might have been deathly afraid of your father's reaction if the young lady next door had accused him of sexually accosting her. He might have killed out of that fear. I find it interesting that your brother was declared not guilty by reason of insanity based almost entirely on his attorney's pleading to the jury to find him insane."

"Are you saying that Michael might not have been insane?" Georgia asked.

"No, I'm not saying that. I'm simply raising the possibility that legal considerations overrode medical ones. Your parents wanted his life spared, and his attorney achieved that. Again, as I said earlier, I'm in no position to judge Michael's level of sanity or insanity. But I will say this."

Joe and Georgia leaned forward in their chairs.

"My instincts tell me that for you to forgo the joy of having children because of a vague fear that your child might—and I emphasize *might*— inherit Michael's mental problem would be a shame, in my opinion. My advice? Go home, screw your brains out, get pregnant, and enjoy your lives. Michael isn't a part of it, literally and figuratively. He's past tense. This is your life together in the here and now, and I remind you that this isn't a dress rehearsal for life. This is it!"

They giggled on the way home over the older therapist's use of the vernacular but took her advice, spent that afternoon making love, and nine months and three days later, Georgia gave birth to a healthy baby girl they named Roberta.

❧

Joe rejoined Michael and Roberta on the patio.

"Dad, Michael emulated the fellow playing the guitar, Joe—?"

"Joe Pass."

"He learned to play the guitar while he was—while he was away, and—"

"I must interrupt," Michael said. "I know how much you want to spare my feelings by using euphemisms for the past forty years of my life. I was not 'away.' That sounds too much like an extended holiday. I was remanded to a mental institution because I killed an innocent young woman and was judged to be insane by a jury of my peers. If I don't accept the reality of that, I'll be violating a crucial tenet of my release and recovery. Facing it head-on is important to me, and I hope it will be for you, too." He'd said it in a serious tone. Now, he brightened and added, "I believe I am now as sane as anyone else in this world, which maybe isn't saying a great deal, but—"

"I think it's wonderful the way you acknowledge what you did, Michael, and how you face that reality in your new life," Roberta said, looking to her father for confirmation.

Joe nodded and left it at that.

"Enough about me," Michael said. He turned to Roberta, "I have been watching you on TV ever since I arrived in Washington," he said, "and I am so impressed that I have such a talented niece. You're better than Barbara Walters and Diane Sawyer and that lady on 60 *Minutes*, Leslie—?"

"Leslie Stahl," Roberta said. "And I'm not better than them, but thank you for the compliment."

"Don't be modest, Robbie," Michael said. "Allow me to be the proud, long-lost uncle."

His use of the familiar version of Roberta's name pricked Joe.

Georgia came from the kitchen and joined them at the table. "Dinner's almost ready," she said. "I'm afraid it's not much, last minute and all, but—"

"I have a feeling," said Michael, "that even last-minute meals at the Wilcox house are gourmet."

"Michael's writing a novel," Roberta said.

"Are you?" replied Georgia. "That's wonderful. Joe has always intended to write a novel but—"

"Writing for a newspaper is enough writing for me," Joe said. "From what I've noticed, there are too many bad novels being published as it is."

Roberta frowned, and checked Michael for his reaction to her father's pointed comment. He didn't seem to be offended. His smile was as wide as always as he said, "Joe is right. Too many books, half of them not worthy of publication."

"What is your novel about?" Georgia asked.

"Oh, it would take all night for me to explain that," Michael said.

"Publishers and novelists I know say that if you can't sum up a novel in a few sentences, chances are no one will ever understand it," Joe said.

"How right they are," Michael said.

Georgia asked her husband to select a wine to go with dinner.

"Anything I can do to help?" Michael asked, standing.

"Not a thing," Georgia said.

Michael was a gregarious guest at the dinner table, telling tales from his years in the mental institution, many of them amusing, some heart-wrenching. Georgia and Roberta seemed to hang on his every word, which annoyed Joe. He said little during the meal, his responses to questions terse and sometimes tinged with sarcasm. They'd almost finished when Michael asked, "Anything new on the killer, Joe? By the way, your articles are wonderful."

"As a matter of fact, there is something new."

"What is it?" Georgia asked. "Has there been a break in the case?"

"In a sense," Joe responded, looking at Roberta, whose expression said she was waiting for her father to elucidate.

"Don't keep us in suspense," Michael said.

"I received a letter today from the serial killer," Joe said.

"A letter?" Georgia and Roberta said in unison.

"Yes. A short letter addressed to me arrived at the paper. Today."

Roberta's interest was palpable. "What did it say?" she asked.

Joe replied, "It said he was contacting me because of what I've been writing about him, and that he intends to stay in touch with me."

"Why didn't you call me?" Roberta asked, exasperation in her voice.

"I was too busy writing the story. It'll run tomorrow."

"With the letter's contents?" Roberta asked.

"Right."

"Did you contact the police?" Georgia asked. Her tone was decidedly gloomy.

"Not yet. We'll bring them in on it tomorrow, as the story runs."

"Excuse me," Roberta said, getting up from the table and going to the patio where she dialed a number on her cell phone. Georgia, too, left the table and went to the kitchen.

"That's quite some news," Michael said to his brother.

"Yeah. Excuse me."

Joe joined his wife in the kitchen. "You okay?" he asked.

"I don't like it, Joe," she said.

"Don't like what?"

"That the killer is corresponding with you. I don't like it at all that a madman who kills young women knows who you are and is writing to you."

"I'm not worried about it," he said, placing his hands on her shoulders. "They'll catch him and it'll be over."

"If he knows you, he knows who Robbie is, too."

"Of course he knows who she is. She's on TV every night."

"This is different."

"I suppose it is, hon, but there's not a lot I can do about it."

"You could stop writing about him."

"I don't think Paul would appreciate that. Besides, I've finally latched on to a story that I can call my own. Look, let's talk about this another time." He lowered his voice. "I'm trying to do what you wanted, play the gracious host to Michael." He gave her shoulders a squeeze and returned to the dining room where Roberta was preparing to leave.

"I have to run," she said. "Something's come up at the station and—"

"Whoa," Joe said. "You aren't going to try and scoop me, are you?"

"Not if you have anything to say about it," she replied tartly. "I can't believe you didn't share this with me before tonight."

"I told you, Robbie, I was busy all afternoon writing the story and trying to free myself up to be here tonight."

Michael and Roberta faced each other. She extended her hand and said, "I have to admit, Uncle Michael, that meeting you has been one of the biggest shocks of my life. I never even knew you existed. But now that I do, I hope we see lots of you, and I mean lots." She planted a kiss on Michael's cheek, gave her father a cursory peck on his, was more demonstrative with her mother in the kitchen, and was gone.

"I suppose I should be on my way, too," Michael said.

"You drove?" Joe asked.

"I don't have a car. I took a cab. It cost a fortune from downtown."

"I'll drive you," Joe said.

"I don't want to put you out, Joseph."

"You won't be. Give me a few minutes."

"I'm driving Michael home," he told Georgia, who came from the kitchen and extended her hand to Michael.

He kissed it and said, "To a wonderful chef, hostess, and sister-in-law. I am in your debt."

She couldn't suppress a small smile. "Come back soon," she told Michael. "I mean that."

"Oh, I shall," he said. "Wild horses won't be able to keep me away."

Michael prattled on during the ride back into the District, and Joe silently wished he would shut up, say nothing, not remind him that he was even in the car. When they pulled up in front of the apartment building, Michael said, "I know you're angry with me, Joseph, for showing up at the house as I did, but I felt compelled to do it."

"You act on everything you feel compelled to do?" Joe asked, not attempting to disguise his anger.

"Your meaning isn't lost on me, Joseph. No, I learned to control my urges during my years in the hospital. Tell me the truth, Joe. Do you view me as a potential threat to your wife and daughter?"

Joe guffawed. "Threat? Why would I think that?"

"Because of who I am, a sex-crazed murderer who was judged to have been insane."

"Are you, Michael? Are you a threat to anyone?"

"Am I a serial killer, you mean? Did I write you, my brother, the journalist, in that capacity?"

"Don't be ridiculous."

"I try not to be, Joseph. I'm sorry my unannounced presence caused you such grief. I'll call ahead in the future. Thank you for the evening, the dinner, the conversation, and for the ride home. Please stay in touch. Don't let your preconceived notions about me ruin what can be a joyous reunion between blood brothers. We are that, you know, whether you like it or not. Good night, Joseph. Thank you again."

Joe watched his brother enter the building and shut the door behind him. He pulled away from the curb with uncharacteristic abandon, and drove too fast back to Rockville, desperately trying to sort out his feelings. It wasn't until he'd pulled into the driveway that the unpleasant, hurtful truth struck him with the force of an exploding airbag.

Michael Wilcox, aka Michael LaRue, had come farther in his life, despite forty years behind bars, than he, Joe Wilcox had. Michael was free, truly free from the sort of bars behind which he, Joe, had ended up. His brother was self-assured, musically talented, erudite, charming, well-read, and socially clever. His freedom hadn't been taken from him when he was incarcerated in that hospital. To the contrary, it had liberated him from the confines of the modern outside world, wrapped him in a protective blanket under which he could learn to play his guitar, read his books, indulge his fantasies, and think, thumbing his nose all the while at those on the other side of the locked gates.

His anger and sadness drained from him as he left the car and entered the house.

"Want to talk about it?" Georgia asked.

"No. I want to go to bed. I'm very tired."

"Roberta and Tom Curtis are talking about becoming engaged."

"I'm sorry to hear that. Good night."

TWENTY-TWO

Wilcox rolled out of bed at six the next morning. His mood had improved considerably. He turned on the mixture of regular and decaf coffee and went to the driveway for that day's *Tribune*. Back in the kitchen, he opened to the Metro section. A reproduction of the letter ran big in the center of the story.

Dear Mr. Wilcox:

I feel like we know each other. You've been writing about me in your newspaper even though we've never met. I want you to know that the young women who were killed were not worthy of being alive. They, and newspapers like the one you work for, corrupt everything decent and good. This is not the last time I will write to you, Mr. Wilcox. And don't let the police interfere with our communication. That would be unfortunate.

To his astonishment, a smaller photo of himself was included in the article, taken a few years ago by the paper's PR department while establishing a speakers' bureau. *Did I ever look that young?*

Georgia joined him, and he showed her the piece.

"It gives me the chills," she said, filling two coffee cups.

"I didn't know they'd run a picture," he said.

"I almost wish they hadn't," she said. "What do you think about Robbie's announcement that she and Tom are considering becoming engaged?"

"Oh, right. I'm sorry. I'm afraid I wasn't in a very good mood last night. They're serious? I mean, really serious?"

"Semiserious," she said. "They're discussing it. She wanted us to know before they went any further."

He said nothing, continuing to read his article, mindlessly unhappy over some editorial changes that had been made to his original copy. "No passion in the world is equal to the passion to alter someone else's draft." H.G. Wells's comment came and went.

"Joe?"

"Huh?"

"Robbie and Tom, what do you think?"

"I think it's too soon for them to be talking about engagement and marriage. They haven't known each other long enough."

"I suggested that, too, and she assured me they would take their time. It's important that she has our approval, Joe, particularly yours."

"Sure. He seems like a nice enough fellow, but time will tell. I do think that—"

The ringing phone interrupted.

"Joe Wilcox," he said into the mouthpiece.

"It's Edith, Joe."

"Hi. I have a feeling I know why you're calling."

"I'm sure you do. This letter, Joe. You should have reported it the minute you received it."

"It wasn't my call, Edith. A corporate decision."

"I'm on my way to the paper to pick it up. I need to talk with you."

"Of course. I'll be there within the hour."

"No," she said. "Let's meet somewhere else first."

"If you say so."

"I say so. That coffee shop across the street from the *Trib*."

"See you there."

He left Georgia in the kitchen and took his cup with him to the bathroom where he showered and shaved. She was still reading the paper when he reappeared.

"I'm sure he knows where you live," she said.

"Who? The nutjob? Probably." He kissed her on the top of her head and headed for the front door. The phone rang. Georgia answered. "Joe, it's for you. The Fox news channel."

He took the cordless phone from her and walked into the dining room. When he returned, he replaced the phone in its wall mount and said, "They want me on one of their news shows. I'll have to clear it with public affairs. Got to run, sweetie. I'll call you later."

Edith was seated at an outdoor table when he arrived. Two Styrofoam cups sat on the table.

"Half-and-half, one sugar, right?" she said.

"Right. So, what do you think?"

"I think I don't know you, Joe."

"Why do you say that?"

"You get a letter from the serial killer—and I have to admit I was wrong and you were right about there even being one—and instead of turning it over to the police, you use it to generate a big story in the paper. That could be considered suppressing evidence."

"Oh, come on, Edith. It isn't *that* serious. I only received it yesterday. You'll have it this morning. Less than twenty-four hours."

"Enough time for the public to know it exists and for *The Washington Tribune* to have a major scoop. And for MPD to have to run from behind and maybe miss a shot at the killer. Local boy makes good, entices serial killer out of his lair, creates a splash with big newsstand sales, and advertisers clamor to buy space. The market economy at work—except that two women are dead, Joe—out of the market. Sorry, but that's a different world from what this humble civil servant knows."

"You're overreacting."

"Drink your coffee before it gets cold."

He obeyed.

"Has he called you?" she asked.

"The killer? No."

"He might."

"He might."

"I want a tap on your phones at the office and at home."

"At home? Georgia won't like that."

"I'm sure she doesn't like that her hubby is on a first name basis with a whacko killer, either."

"She said something to that effect."

The detective pointed an index finger at him. "Joe," she said, "don't play games with me. Okay? This is no longer just a story that sells newspapers. The letter is now a police matter."

"Sure. I understand," he said. "I'll cooperate with you in any way I can."

"Good. You saw your daughter's piece on the letter, I assume."

"No, I didn't," he said, finishing his coffee, which left a metallic taste in his mouth.

"This morning. She obviously got it from you."

"She was at the house for dinner last night. I mentioned it."

Edith sat back and smiled. "She was cute the way she couched it. She said that in the interest of full disclosure, the recipient of the letter was her father, a *Trib* cops reporter."

"She's okay," he said, joining her in the smile. "You coming to the office?"

"Yup."

The meeting was held in a conference room off the newsroom. Present were Vargas-Swayze, Wilcox, Morehouse, the paper's legal counsel, the VP of public affairs, and the *Trib*'s executive vice president for administrative affairs.

"I'm outnumbered," Edith said after she'd been introduced to everyone.

"But you carry the gun," the public affairs head said.

"Shall I lay it on the table?" she asked.

"Please don't," the executive VP said, sounding as though he took her seriously.

"Let's get down to why we're here," Morehouse said. He slid a manila envelope across the table to her. She slipped on a pair of latex gloves, opened the envelope, and removed a plastic baggie.

"Nice it's in the plastic bag," she said, "but I assume it's been handled."

"Sure," Morehouse said. "Joe, me, others. Our prints are all over it. Sorry."

"Our lab people will compare whatever's on there with anyone who handled it here. Where's the envelope it came in?'

"Oh, right," Morehouse said, pushing a second envelope to her.

"Okay," she said. "Now, let's talk about how we cooperate in getting this guy off the street."

The meeting lasted slightly less than an hour. Wilcox walked Edith to the elevators.

"You comfortable with what we came up with?" she asked.

"Do I have a choice?"

"Sure you do. But it'll be easier if you aren't fighting it."

"No fear of that," he said. "You'll let me know what steps you take next, preliminary lab reports, all that good stuff."

"To the extent I can, Joe. I'll be back to you."

He went to his cubicle where dozens of phone and e-mail messages awaited him, some from media outlets wanting interviews, others from colleagues around the city congratulating him, asking questions, or joking about his newfound role as father confessor to a serial killer.

"Nice catch, Joe," Gene Hawthorne said.

Wilcox swung around in his chair. "Thanks."

"If there's anything I can do, I'm—"

"Yeah, sure. I'll let you know," Wilcox said, showing his back to the young reporter again.

He let his voice mail take his calls for the rest of the morning, choosing the few he wished to return. But he picked up a call that came a few minutes before noon.

"Joseph? It's Michael."

"Oh, hello."

"Joe, about last night, I realize how impetuous it was of me to simply show up at your home like that, especially after you'd asked that we go slow in melding me into your family's life."

"I was surprised, that was all," Joe said. "No apology necessary."

"You forgive me?"

"Look, Michael, I'm up to my neck here today."

"I imagine you are, Joseph. That was a powerful piece in today's paper. Georgia seemed unhappy that the killer has chosen you as his conduit."

"She'll be fine. It's natural that she'd be uneasy about it."

"Of course. What a wonderful family, Joseph. Exemplary. I owe you a dinner. I owe everyone a dinner. Can we make a date?"

"Not at the moment, but I'll get back to you. What's your schedule the next few days?"

"Busy actually. Two job interviews tomorrow, morning and afternoon."

"Nonprofits?"

"One is. The other isn't what I aspire to—it's more like the job I just left. But one has to be realistic, doesn't one? The money mother left me won't last forever."

Joe had forgotten about that money; Michael's mention of it stabbed him in the stomach. He understood why their mother had taken steps to provide for Michael should he ever come out of the mental hospital. But the funds had sat there earning interest for almost forty years. His early years with Georgia and a baby had been lean ones. Having a nest egg would have helped, would have taken the strain off them. In a word, he resented what his mother had done, no matter how he might rationalize it. A victory for his brother, a slap in his face.

"Let's talk in a few days," Joe said. "Good luck with your interviews."

"Thank you, Joseph. I'll let you know how they go. Love to Georgia and Robbie."

He got to Morehouse before leaving for lunch.

"I can't handle all the media calls, Paul, and write tomorrow's piece."

"Let public affairs handle the media stuff, Joe. But make yourself as available as you can. What've you got for tomorrow?"

"A think piece," he replied. "How it feels to be in contact with a serial killer."

"You can't mention the phone taps, or the surveillance on the post office."

"I know. I thought I'd call Jimmy Breslin in New York. The Son of Sam kept writing to Breslin. I've met Jimmy a few times. He's not doing his regular column any more, but he's still active. I can probably get some good quotes from him."

"Good move. When do you think the killer will contact you again?"

"I don't know if he will."

"Of course he will, Joe. He can't read your piece today and not write another letter, maybe call. By the way, your cop buddy is a knockout."

"Edith? Yeah, she's an okay lady."

"You, uh—?"

"No. I'm heading out for lunch. I'll get on tomorrow's piece when I get back."

"You're tearin' 'em up, Joe. Hey. Human Resources called. How come you haven't talked to them about the buyout package?"

"Because I'm not interested in any buyout, at least not until this thing is over. I'll check back in later."

A new call on his voice mail intrigued him enough to return it. The caller was an editor at a large book publisher in New York.

"Thanks so much, Mr. Wilcox, for getting back to me so soon," she said "Do you have a book agent?"

"Book agent? No, I don't."

"Good. I'd rather deal directly with you anyway. We might be interested in signing up a book by you about this serial killer series you're doing. He wrote you, I read this morning."

"That's right."

"True-crime books can be bestsellers. May I call you Joe?"

"Sure."

"Good. I'm Melanie. Can you come up to New York?"

"When?"

"As soon as you can. I believe we can offer a contract that will make it worth your while."

"Impossible now. I'm really busy."

"I'll come to Washington. What's a good day for you? Tomorrow? The next day?"

"Ah, I'll have to get back to you."

"Fine, but don't let too much time pass. I've already discussed this with our editorial and marketing people. We're serious."

He took her number and left the building, stopping in at a florist on his way to the Press Club to arrange for flowers to be sent to Georgia. He'd paid and was leaving the shop when he had another thought. "I'd like to have flowers sent to my daughter, too," he told the clerk. "At the TV station where she works. They go to Roberta Wilcox."

"Roberta Wilcox?" the clerk said. "I watch her all the time. I knew the name was familiar. And you're the one who's been writing about the serial killer."

"That's me," he said.

"You've got me scared to death," she said. "I keep the door locked most of the day."

"I noticed I had to knock," he said.

"You can't be too careful," she said, "not with a fiend loose on our streets."

"I couldn't agree more," he said, signing the credit card slip and wishing her a pleasant day.

He was greeted when he entered the Press Club by a number of the guys, all of whom had something to say about his involvement with the serial killer. The attention was not unwelcome, and he found himself eagerly answering their questions, parrying their jibes, and enjoying the drink to which he was treated. Some well-wishers wanted to continue their conversation over lunch, and they settled at a large, round table where the drinks kept coming, and the conversation became more rambunctious.

"So, Joe," someone asked, "how many calls have you gotten from the coast this morning?"

"The coast?"

"Hollywood, pal. They make a movie about almost anything these days."

"Who'll play Joe?" another asked, which set off a flurry of suggestions from around the table, many of which generated loud laughter. "Tom Cruise? Nah, he's too young."

"I was thinking of Robert Redford," Joe offered.

"Come on, he's older than you are, Joey."

"I know. How about Julia Roberts?"

"Julia Roberts! She's a—woman."

"So what? They do whatever they want out in Hollywood. Hell, they might make you black in the film, turn it into a story from the 'hood."

"I might write a book about it," Wilcox interrupted, "depending, of course, on how the whole thing turns out."

"We knew you when," someone said.

"Yeah. I got a call this morning from a New York book publisher."

"Get an agent" was suggested.

"The hell with an agent," someone else counseled. "Do the deal yourself."

If he didn't have a story to write for tomorrow's edition, Wilcox would have been content to stay there for the rest of the day, maybe even get drunk the way he had a few times earlier in his career when surrounded by other journalists. Those were happy, carefree times, long before a sense of his own mortality increasingly entered his consciousness. He felt a measure of that youthful abandon while enjoying lunch that day with his friends, but knew it was just a fleeting reincarnation.

"I really have to go," he said after finishing lunch. He reached for his wallet, but someone clamped a hand on his arm. "Hey, Joe Wilcox, your money's no good today. Just remember us when they're casting extras for the newsroom scenes."

"I will, I will," Wilcox said, getting up from the table and shaking hands. "Thanks for the lunch and drinks," he said. "You're the best."

The final comment he heard as he walked away was from the only woman in the group: "Lock that daughter of yours up, Joe, until the nut is put away."

Her words dampened the exuberance he was feeling, and stayed with him as he rode the elevator down to the lobby and headed back to the *Tribune* Building. *The danger to Roberta.*

By the time he got there, however, his mind was focused on what he had to write, and he hunkered down in his cubicle, the words filling his computer screen as though coming from some automatic compartment inside his brain. On many days, it was a struggle to finish an article, even though much of what he'd written over the years was boilerplate—"The police have reported that another homicide took place last night . . ."

This story was different. This story flowed from him. He'd created it.

It was like writing fiction, a novel, a creative act with him as the center-piece. He was free to vent his feelings, to pull from his inner core and express himself as he'd never been able to do before as a who-what-why-when-where journalist.

He took a break and called Jimmy Breslin in New York, who was gracious in sharing his feelings about being on the receiving end of letters from New York's infamous Son of Sam. He wove those comments into the piece, rewrote the lead, plugged in a comment by an MPD spokesperson who pledged an all-out campaign to bring the serial killer to justice, polished the ending, and dispatched it to Paul Morehouse.

The editor came to the cubicle ten minutes later. "Great piece, Joe," he said. "Beautiful, especially the way you handled the turning over of the letter to the cops. Makes us sound like public citizen number one."

"Thanks," Wilcox said. "I think I'll pack it in, make it an early night."

"Everything going smoothly with the media requests?"

"I'll check in with public affairs before I leave. I got a note from them that *The National Enquirer* wants to interview me."

"Well . . . Do it, Joe. Clear everything first."

"I got a call from a book publisher in New York."

Morehouse's eyebrows went up, and he whistled. "That could be big stuff, Joe. Congratulations."

"Thanks. Nothing concrete, just a feeler."

"Say hello to Georgia and Robbie," Morehouse said. "Make sure they know that I won't let all of this go to your head."

"They'll appreciate that, I'm sure."

Georgia called before he left work to thank him for the flowers, clearly touched.

"Glad you like them," he said. "Let's go out for dinner tonight. I'll be home in an hour."

"I've already started dinner," she said.

"So, stop it. I'm really in the mood to go out. Pick a place and make a reservation, a steak house maybe, or lobster."

"It sounds like we're celebrating something," she said.

"Maybe we are, Georgia," he said. "Maybe at last we are."

TWENTY-THREE

Roberta was getting ready to run out to meet Tom for a fast lunch at a Chinese restaurant. But before heading out, and despite already being late, she placed a call she'd been considering all morning.

"Uncle Michael?"

Michael laughed loudly. "Ah, it must be Roberta," he said. "I love it, being called Uncle Michael. How are you, my dear?"

"Fine. I just called to say that last evening was many things, shocking to be sure, and—how can I put it?—it was wonderful. It's amazing to me that Mom and Dad were able to keep you a secret for so many years."

"I'm sure they had their reasons," he said, his tone more rueful.

"I'm dying to know more about you, Michael, about the novel you're writing, your music career, your—"

"No, no, no, no, no," he said. "There's no musical career as such, Robbie. I'm strictly a closet guitar player, playing for my own amusement."

"You never play in public?"

"Absolutely not, although an occasional friend has heard me strum away here at my apartment."

"I would love to hear you play," she said. "Would you consider allowing a family member to join that inner circle?"

"Of course. Your father has heard me."

"He has?"

"Yes. The first time he visited me here."

"That devil, not telling me."

"What are you doing this evening?" he asked.

"The usual. I have a report on the six o'clock news, and back to do another at eleven. In between, I'm pretty much free, until nine anyway."

"Splendid," he said, "I don't claim to be a gourmet chef, but I did spend quite a few years working in the hospital's kitchen and learning my way around a stove. My fellow patients said they preferred my cooking above all others."

"I'm sure whatever you come up with will be special. I'll come at seven."

"Good. I look forward to it."

"There's one condition, though, Michael."

"And what is that?"

"That you play a tune or two for me."

"It will be my pleasure." He gave her his address.

Roberta's tendency to run late was a bone of contention with Tom, albeit a minor one. He believed that people who were chronically late were seeking attention, keeping everyone waiting for their arrival, but hadn't expressed his harsh analysis to her.

"Sorry," she said, sliding in next to him in a booth. "I was on a call."

"You're always on a call," he said, not unpleasantly. "Your ear is starting to look like a phone."

"I happen to think I have pretty ears," she said with mock indignation.

"And I happen to agree." He kissed her ear. "Let's order. I'm on at two."

Their order in, she said, "You'll never believe what happened last night."

"At work?"

"No, at the house. I had dinner with Mom and Dad. I told them that we're considering getting engaged."

"You *what*? That's a little premature, isn't it?"

She gave him her best pout. "You aren't backing out, are you?"

"I mean telling your folks. What did they say?"

"Actually, I only told my mother and didn't get to discuss it with dad. I'm sure she did after I left. Anyway, there was a surprise guest at dinner."

"Who's that?"

"My uncle Michael."

He didn't respond as the waiter brought their communal dishes and set them on the table.

"It was incredible," she said.

"What was?"

"Meeting my uncle Michael."

"Meeting him?" he said, spooning portions on to their plates. "You never met him before?"

"No. In fact, I never even knew he existed."

Tom's hand and spoon stopped in midair. "You didn't know you had an uncle?"

"Right. I do now."

He finished serving and took a bite of steamed dumpling before asking, "How could you not know you had an uncle? Where's he been, in a foreign country? In jail?"

"Close."

She filled him in on Michael's background and he listened intently, eating as he did. When she was finished, he said, "That is some story, Robbie. He murdered somebody, a young woman?"

"Yes."

"And they decided he was insane?"

"Uh-huh."

"I'm not sure I'd want somebody like that in my family," he said.

"You don't," she said. "It's my family, not yours."

"It'll become mine if we get married."

"He's fascinating," she said. "He used his time in the mental hospital to learn to play jazz guitar, and he's writing a novel. He's very well-read, Tom, and utterly charming."

"Is he?"

"Are you angry with me?"

"Of course not. It's just that—"

"Just that what?"

"Just that sometimes you can be unbelievably naïve."

"About Michael?"

"Yeah. I mean, people like that don't just get better, Robbie, because they get some kind of treatment. People like that are—"

"Stop saying 'people like that,' " she said.

"I'm talking about people who kill other people," he said, motioning for a check. "It's in their genes. They don't just get over it like the flu or a broken bone."

"I have to get back," she said, not attempting to hide her pique.

He paid the check and they left the restaurant.

"I'm having dinner with Michael tonight," she said as they stood on the sidewalk. "At his apartment. He's cooking dinner, something else he mastered while hospitalized."

"Good," he said. "I'll call." A kiss on her check and he was quickly gone.

She spent the afternoon preparing her report for the six o'clock news, and debating whether to tell her parents of her plans for the evening. She decided not to, remembering how angry her father seemed at seeing Michael at the house. She'd tell them tomorrow.

❧

For MPD detective Edith Vargas-Swayze, lunch didn't include egg rolls or sweet-and-sour chicken. She ate at the station house, a pie with sausage and mushrooms delivered from a neighborhood pizzeria, and a Diet Coke from a machine in the lobby. Sharing the table was her partner, Wade Dungey, and their boss, Bernard Evans.

"There was no problem with putting a tap on Wilcox's line at the paper?" Evans asked. He lunched on an egg salad sandwich brought from home.

"No," Vargas-Swayze replied. "They were perfectly willing. His home phone is another matter."

"We'll get a court order," Evans said.

"I'd rather Joe approve it voluntarily. His wife's the problem. He'll speak with her. I know her. She'll say okay."

"What's the lab say?" Evans asked, folding the piece of wax paper and his napkin into tiny, precise squares and dropping them into an over-flowing wastebasket.

"They'll run prints on it." she said, "and do an analysis of the type-face. Looks like it was written on a typewriter, not a computer printer, that's for sure."

"The paper?"

"Nothing fancy we could trace. Plain white, hard surface, high gloss."

"Good for prints," Dungey said.

"Why do you figure he mailed it from the post office down the block from the *Trib*?" Evans asked.

"Makes sense to me," Dungey said.

"I don't mean whether it makes sense, Wade," Evans said. "It just seems to me that whoever this guy is probably lives close by. He lives in the District, not a suburb." To Dungey: "Are you finished running those backgrounds on people who were at the *Trib* the night the Kaporis girl was killed?"

"Close."

Before ending the meeting, Evans said, "Put a tail on Wilcox. This nut is liable to want a face-to-face."

"Not enough cheese," Dungey groused to his partner as they sat at their desks filling out reports. "We should have ordered it with extra cheese." They left the precinct at three and went to the car assigned them for that day. He slid behind the wheel.

"Where to?" Edith asked.

"Let's swing by the address the Frenchman gave us." He consulted notes he'd retrieved from his locker. "LaRue. Michael."

"Why?"

"No good reason. You have a better suggestion?"

They pulled up in front of the apartment building.

"Nice older structure," he said.

She knew he was interested in the city's architecture and had taken tours of various neighborhoods sponsored by historical societies, a side of him that surprised her. Somehow, Wade Dungey didn't seem the type to appreciate architecture, art, or other staid, static things. But she'd learned over the years from dealing with a variety of people, good and bad, that you couldn't always tell a book by its cover.

For her, buildings and their spaces couldn't be modern enough. Form meant little to her; function was everything. As she sometimes said to friends after separating from Peter, "What I really want out of life is a one-room apartment where everything is Formica, there's a drain hole in the floor, and all I have to do is hose it down every once in a while."

"Let's stop in and see if he's home," Dungey said. "Make a social call."

Michael's intercom interrupted his dinner preparations. "Yes?" he asked.

"Detectives Dungey and Vargas-Swayze, Mr. LaRue," Dungey announced.

"Oh? I wasn't expecting anyone. I'll ring you in."

He stood outside his apartment door to greet them as they came down the hall.

"Sorry to barge in on you like this," Dungey said, "but we were in the neighborhood."

"Is something wrong?" Michael asked.

"No, nothing's wrong," Dungey said. "Just a couple of follow-up questions."

"Of course. Come in."

"You play the guitar?" Dungey asked, spotting the instrument the moment they entered.

"Just a little," Michael said.

"I always wanted to play the guitar," Dungey said. "Never got around to it." He did a three-sixty. "Nice little place you have here."

"Thank you. I'm quite comfortable. You're obviously here because of the murder of the young lady at the newspaper. I'm afraid I've already told you everything I know. I delivered supplies there that night but don't recall ever seeing her. I wish I had more to offer. All this talk of a serial killer being responsible for that murder and the murder of the girl in the park is most upsetting. What sort of animal could do such a thing?"

"A two-legged animal," Dungey said. "Four-legged animals don't kill anybody unless they're in the jungle and haven't had a meal in a while."

"Yes," Michael said. "An important differentiation. Have you developed any leads?"

Vargas-Swayze said, "You said you're from the Midwest. Illinois, was it?"

"That's right."

"Mind if we look around?" Dungey asked as he went into the kitchen.

"I suppose I should object," Michael said, following him. "I think I'm supposed to ask to see a warrant or something like that." He said it with a noncombative laugh. "Or have I been watching too many cop movies?"

"You could ask for a warrant," Dungey said. "We don't have one. Looks like you're getting ready for a dinner party."

"I am having a guest for dinner," Michael said. "A young lady, as a matter of fact."

"That's nice," Dungey said. "What's on the menu?"

Vargas-Swayze stood in the living room. She was uneasy at her partner's approach. This Michael LaRue wasn't a suspect, simply one name on a long list of people who happened to be at the *Tribune* the night Jean Kaporis was killed, or who had had some sort of relationship with her. This constituted harassment in her mind, and she decided to end the visit.

"Thank you for your time, Mr. LaRue," she announced. "We appreciate being allowed to come in without notice."

Michael emerged from the kitchen, followed by Dungey. "I am willing and happy to help in any way I can," he said. "Just as long as you don't view me as a suspect. I've never killed a thing in my life, in or out of the woods. I capture spiders and other insects with a paper cup and sheet of paper and release them outside. Every living thing deserves respect."

"Ants and wasps, too?" Dungey asked.

Michael laughed heartily. "No, you're right, detective. There are exceptions."

They left the apartment, and Michael watched through a window as they went to their car and drove away. He'd begun to perspire and hoped they hadn't noticed. He closed the blinds, fell to the floor, and did push-ups until a rap on his door stopped him. "Who's there?" he yelled.

"Rudy."

"Go away. I'm busy."

"Who were they?"

"Who?"

"The guy and woman who were just here. They look like cops to me."

"They're old friends, Rudy. Now go away."

"Everything okay with you?"

"Yes, everything is fine. Good-bye, Rudy."

The sound of Rudy's cane hitting the floor faded as he walked away. Michael returned to the kitchen and finished the prep work for dinner, carefully wrapping prosciutto and cheese in lightly breaded chicken breasts, and adding delicate flavoring to white rice. Showered and dressed in gray slacks, a flowing white shirt worn loose, and sandals, he sat at his desk, removed the first ten pages of the novel he'd started writing a few days ago, and placed them on the bare surface so that they would be clearly noticed by Roberta. He was about to get up and practice the guitar when his eyes noticed the edge of an unfamiliar file folder beneath papers on the side table. He pulled it out, opened it, and saw that it contained his brother's articles along with other written materials about serial killings. *How did this get here?* he wondered. *Joe must have left it by mistake.* He browsed the papers in the file, closed it, and returned it to where he'd found it. He checked his watch; still hours before Roberta's arrival. After placing a bottle of chardonnay in the refrigerator, he turned on his guitar and amplifier and ran through songs contained in a thick fake book of a thousand popular tunes, the sweet sounds blanketing the small room and relieving the tension he'd felt earlier. Music does, indeed, soothe a savage breast, he thought as every other aspect of his life, every hurtful, cruel, unfair, and degrading element of it was lost in the rich chords created by his fingers on the strings.

⁓

The last of their wine was poured, and dessert menus were placed in front of them.

"The steak was wonderful," Wilcox said. "How was your stuffed shrimp?"

"Excellent," Georgia said. She shook her head, a smile on her face.

"So, what's that about?" he asked.

"You, Joe. Here you are receiving letters from a serial killer and you're in the best mood I've seen you in months. Maybe years."

"One letter," he said. "But why is that strange? I've been looking for a major story for years, something I can get my teeth in and call my own. I've got that with this one, Georgia, and I'm happy about it."

"I'm seeing a new side of my husband, and I thought I knew every one of them. You're obviously enjoying the notoriety, and that's different. You've always been critical of writers who succumb to the media spotlight."

"Don't worry," he said. "Paul told me to assure you that he wouldn't let any of this go to my head."

"I don't care if it does—go to your head," she said. "Just as long as the happiness lasts."

He said nothing.

"Will it?" she asked. "Last?"

"I think so," he replied. "When I suggested we go out for dinner tonight, you asked whether we were celebrating something."

"Are we?"

"Possibly. I got a call today from a publisher in New York. They want to discuss my doing a book about the serial killer and my role as his conduit. The editor, a nice gal, said she'd even come down to Washington to talk to me about it."

She reached across the table and grasped his hands. "Joe, that's wonderful. You've always said you'd like to write a book but didn't have anything worthwhile to write about. Now you do."

"Well," he said, "I don't want to count chickens before they're hatched—I can't believe I used that cliché; it's one of your favorites—but I don't want to jump the gun. I mean, I don't have a book deal yet, and it will all depend, I'm sure, how this thing with the killer plays out, whether he'll continue to contact me and whether I'll play some role in bringing him to justice. We'll just have to wait and see about that. But if things go right, I'd say we really will have something to celebrate."

"Have you told Roberta?"

"No, and I'd just as soon keep it between us until there's something more concrete. Deal?"

"Deal!" She squeezed his hands. "But promise me one thing."

"Whatever you want."

"Promise me that you'll do everything possible to keep this away from us, from the family. I don't need a serial killer arriving at the door like—"

"Like Michael?"

"I didn't want to say it."

"But you thought it. Interesting."

"What is?"

"That you link the serial killer and Michael in your mind."

"I didn't do that, Joe. It's just that—"

"It's just that it's perfectly natural to have done it. After all, he has killed in the past, a young woman, and was judged to be insane. Now, he shows up in Washington, and two young women are strangled to death since his arrival."

"Please, Joe, don't. You don't really think that Michael could be the murderer." She paused. "Do you?"

"Of course not. Just letting my creative juices run wild. Maybe there's a novel in me after all. Make a hell of a story, wouldn't it?"

She picked up the dessert menu. "Nothing for me," she said. "Just coffee, decaf."

Joe waved the waiter over. "One rice pudding," he said, "two decaf coffees, and two spoons." As the waiter turned to leave, Joe added, "And two cognacs, please. We're celebrating."

⁂

"Dinner was superb," Roberta told Michael. He'd set a small, folding table in the living room, and had included a vase of fresh flowers and two candles. The chardonnay bottle was empty.

"Let me help you clean up," she said, reaching for her plate and silverware.

"Absolutely not," he said. "Guests are forbidden from cleaning up anything when in my home. Go make yourself at home. I'll just be a jiffy. Coffee is ready to go, and I have a lovely lemon flan for dessert, provided you aren't watching your waistline. From what I can see, you have no need of that."

She left the table and sat at his desk. He'd put a Joe Pass CD on the compact stereo unit during dinner.

"Joe Pass," she called to him.

"Yes, my idol," he said from the kitchen.

"He's wonderful."

"The best."

Her eyes went to the manuscript.

"I've never gotten into jazz," she said as she picked up the first page and started to read. "Not my generation's thing."

"I understand," he said from the kitchen. "Coffee's almost made. Just be a minute."

"Take your time," she said, reading the second page. She didn't realize he'd come up behind until she felt his weight against the back of her chair. "Oh," she said. You startled me."

"I certainly didn't mean to do that," he said. "I see you're reading my literary output."

"I hope you don't mind."

"Not at all. I'm flattered that you'd even be interested."

"The flan was like floating," she said twenty minutes later. "Everything was." She glanced at her watch. "I'd better think about leaving."

"Oh, not so soon," he said. "I haven't played for you."

"That's right," she said, "and you promised. Will you? I have time for a song or two."

"My pleasure."

She sat at the desk as he pulled up a chair next to the amplifier, turned it on along with the guitar, and spent a few minutes tuning the strings to his liking, and adjusting the volume. "Anything special you'd like to hear?"

She shook her head. "Whatever you choose."

He opened the fake book, hunched over the guitar as though trying to incorporate his body into its very frame, examined the music for a moment, and started playing. Roberta didn't recognize the tune; a bossa nova, "Wave." She focused on Michael as he moved through the changes to the song, totally absorbed in what he was doing, in a different place, his body subtly moving with the rhythm he'd established. She found herself moving, too, but her thoughts weren't exclusively on the music. She kept thinking about the pages of his novel she'd read. Not what they said, but the way the pages *looked*. It was almost as though she'd seen them before. Was her mind playing tricks? Why would they look so familiar? Silly. She forced her attention to what Michael was doing as he finished the song.

"Bravo!" she said, applauding.

"Thank you," he said, bowing from his sitting position. "Another?"

She consulted her watch again. "I have time," she said, "but only one more."

As he hunted through the book for a different selection, she again looked at the pages on the desk. *What is it?* she wondered.

I've seen this before. She considered taking a page, but was at a loss as to how she'd explain it to him. He struck a series of inviting introductory chords before launching into another tune she didn't know, "You Go to My Head." The rich chords and lovely melody drew her in and she forgot about the pages.

He'd reached the bridge of the song when a loud, incessant knocking at his door caused him to stop playing and to look angrily across the room. The knocking got louder; it was now a banging with something other than knuckles.

"Damn it!" he growled, putting down the guitar. He opened the door. "What the hell do you want?" he shouted at Rudy, whose cane was poised to deliver another blow.

"I gotta talk to you," Rudy said loudly, his words slurred.

"Get away," Michael commanded.

Rudy poked his head into the apartment and saw Roberta. He tried to push past Michael, but was held in check by the bigger man. "I told you to get away," Michael said, his threatening tone underlining what he was saying. He shoved Rudy away from the door and slammed it in his face, which prompted more rapping with the cane, and muttered curses.

Michael walked away from the door and stood a few feet from Roberta, who'd stood and grabbed her purse from where she'd left it on a small table. His rage was palpable. His body shook, and his face was twisted with fury.

"I am so sorry," he managed in a quavering voice.

"Who was that?" Roberta asked.

"A neighbor. A neighbor from hell. A drunk. How dare he intrude on our lovely evening together?"

"I'm just sorry you're so upset," she said. "I loved tonight. Everything was perfect, the meal, the conversation, and your performance. Thank you, Michael, for playing for me. You're even better than Joe Pass."

"You're very kind," he said. "You drove?"

"Yes. I parked right up the street."

"I'll walk you to your car."

"That's not necessary. I'll—"

"I insist. With this madman running around killing beautiful young women, I'd never forgive myself if anything happened to my only niece, nor would your mother and father."

As they exited the building, Rudy was there leaning against a tree. He took a few wobbly steps toward Michael and Roberta. As he did, Michael grabbed him by the collar of his jacket and threw him to the ground. He landed hard, causing Roberta to wince and to turn away. Michael stood over him. He placed his foot on Rudy's chest. "You drunken bum. You'll never bother me or my guests again."

Roberta and Michael walked to her car. The tension in Michael's body was transmitted to her through the hand he'd placed on her arm.

"I'm so sorry you have to put up with someone like that," she said. "You never know what your neighbors will be like until you move in."

"He's scum, that's all," Michael said, attempting to control the tremor in his voice and his rapid, shallow breathing. "I might have made a mistake when I was young—a very big mistake—but people like him make me look like a saint."

She wasn't sure she agreed with his thesis, but didn't express her reservation. Instead, she said, "Thank you again, Michael, for a lovely time. I'd like to do it again soon."

"Any time you say."

He placed his hands on her upper arms, looked into her eyes, and planted kisses on her cheeks, one on each, then a second.

"Good night," she said as she climbed into the car, started it, looked back at him, and drove away.

It wasn't until she was home and preparing for bed that it came to her, one possible reason for thinking she'd recognized the pages of his manuscript. They looked as though they'd been typed on the same type-writer as the note from the serial killer to her father. She rummaged through a pile of newspapers until coming up with the edition in which the letter had been reproduced as part of the article.

"Wow" was what she said. And to herself: Oh, wow!

TWENTY-FOUR

Vargas-Swayze was happy to work late that night. Not so for Dungey. He'd pulled a hamstring during a basketball game and had asked for time off, but was pressed into an extra shift because the full moon seemed to bring out the homicidal urges of some. For her, working an extra shift would keep her mind off the divorce and the nasty turn it had taken. For both, the overtime pay was welcome.

A woman stabbed her boyfriend to death after she found he'd been seeing their voluptuous female neighbor. A sixteen-year-old boy had been beaten to death by a gang whose members coveted his jacket and sneakers. While these incidents occurred in the city's less affluent neighborhoods, the evening's homicides weren't restricted to those areas. A German industrialist, in Washington on company business, was mugged and shot to death not far from the State Department in relatively upscale Foggy Bottom. So much for diplomacy on the streets. And another man had been found bleeding to death in Franklin Park, the scene of Colleen McNamara's murder not many nights before. He died en route to the hospital without having identified his assailant.

"How's your leg?" Vargas-Swayze asked Dungey as they left the building at three in the morning and headed for his car.

"Hurts," he replied with a crooked grin. "They say you're supposed to play through the pain, but that's BS. I hurt, I don't play."

She laughed. "Did you want to play in the NBA when you were a little kid?" she asked.

"Nah. I wanted to be a major-league baseball player, but it wasn't for me. I'm built more for basketball. Want something to eat?"

"I'm hungry," she said.

She told him over platters of eggs and bacon at the Diner, her favorite haunt in Adams Morgan, the latest details of her ongoing financial hassle with Peter Swayze.

"The guy is slime," Dungey said as they pulled up in front of her apartment building. "You're a lot better off without him."

"You don't have to tell me that," she said. "I'm more aware of it every day. By the way, you never said what you thought of our visit with LaRue."

"I was wrong about him I guess," he said. "I don't get the same bad vibes I did the first time around. You?"

"He seems okay. When are you going to run an ID on him?"

"Maybe I'll get around to it if I work twenty-four seven. See you tomorrow."

"Today. It's today."

"Yeah, it is, isn't? Good night, Edith."

"Good night."

She'd almost reached the front door to the building and was fishing in her purse for her keys when a honking horn caused her to turn. Dungey had switched on the lights in the car and was waving for her to rejoin him. She leaned in the open window on the passenger side. "What's up?" she asked.

"This," he said, handing her a computer printout of details, pointing to the section dealing with the DOA from Franklin Park.

"What about it?" she asked.

"The address," he said.

She squinted in the dim light. "Oh," she said.

"Yeah," he said. "This Rudolph Grau lived at the same address as our French friend."

"He had to live somewhere," she said.

"I know. Just thought it was interesting."

"We'll be back there later to canvas the building."

"Right. Well, anyway, I thought it was worth mentioning."

"It was, Wade. Grab some sleep. See you in a few hours."

TWENTY-FIVE

When they got home from the restaurant, Joe and Georgia Wilcox, one hunger sated, made love, an infrequent event of late. Both slept soundly. Joe was first up, feeling refreshed. After showering and dressing in his favorite gray suit for a TV interview later in the day, he donned an apron and made scrambled eggs and toast, another infrequent event, and had it ready and piping hot when Georgia appeared in a freshly pressed robe.

"Still celebrating?" she asked playfully.

"Right you are," he replied, "but not about the book. I thought I'd forgotten how to do it—and don't give me that 'it's like falling off a bicycle' routine."

"You haven't forgotten a thing," she said. "Not even your bicycle. What's up today?"

"The same. I've got to come up with a new slant for the series."

"I wish they'd catch him."

"So do I, but not too soon."

"Joe!"

"I didn't mean it the way it sounds, Georgia. I hope they catch the guy before he kills anyone else. At the same time, I'd like to be able to play out the story a while longer. Morehouse sure as hell would like that."

He finished breakfast, kissed her, and said, "We should do it again soon."

"I'm here," she answered, walking him to the door. "You look great."

"Thanks. Be sure to watch."

"I will. I'll tape it and run it over and over."

He drove his usual route into the District, but instead of going to the *Tribune* Building, he drove to Michael's apartment house. He parked a block away and called his brother's number. The machine answered. He hung up without leaving a message, got out of the car, and went to the door. The duplicate keys Michael had provided allowed him to enter the building and the apartment. Maggie meowed as she came from the kitchen where she'd been eating from her bowl, and rubbed against his leg. He bent and ruffled the fur behind the cat's ears, went to the desk, pulled a piece of blank paper from where it was neatly stored in a drawer, inserted it in the typewriter, and began to type. Ten minutes later, and after assuring himself that everything was as it had been when he entered, he bade Maggie a farewell, locked the apartment behind him, and emerged from the building. An older woman, pulling a collapsible shopping cart, came up the walkway. She stopped, blocking his way. "Terrible, isn't it?" she said.

"Hello," he said and tried to go around her.

"Poor man, being killed like that."

His first thought was Michael.

"Who was killed?" he asked.

"Mr. Grau, from One-E. Do you live here?"

"No, ma'am."

"He had a drinking problem, you know, but one can't be harsh in judging him, with his war injuries protecting us and the country. Poor man. He was in such pain and—"

"Excuse me," Wilcox said, using the grass to circumvent her and walk quickly to his car to drive off.

Not long after he left, Edith and Dungey arrived to go through the motions of questioning others in the building about the deceased's habits, known enemies, close friends, and whether anyone heard or knew anything about the killing. Knocks on Michael LaRue's door went unanswered. Talks with residents revealed that Rudy Grau was a hard drinker, a difficult man at times, but considering the wounds he incurred defending the country—and that he always walked with a cane—"Why didn't he use it to ward off his attacker?"—and that he always helped the other tenants of the building with heavy grocery bags and the like—and that he sometimes went out to dinner with Mr. LaRue, the nice gentleman in 1C—but little else. The interviews completed, the detectives returned to the park where they sought someone who might provide information or have seen something to help in the investigation. A wasted exercise, one of hundreds they'd walked through in the course of their careers.

～

Morehouse called an editorial meeting soon after Wilcox arrived at the *Trib*. Lacking anything new on the killer, it was decided not to try and force another article on the subject, which was fine with Wilcox. He had other stories to write that day, including an article about the previous night's spate of murders; the media appearance would take time, too.

He called MPD's public affairs office to get a quote about the most recent killings in the District, dutifully took down what the officer said, which was not much, and began to work on the piece, which was not much, either. Once he had the details written, he would attempt to contact family members of the victims in the hope they would give him some quotable comments, the more anguished the better. It wasn't long ago that the tabloid and TV practice of wringing quotes from grieving relatives of murder victims was anathema to him. He ran through imaginary dialogues. *"What are you feeling at this moment?" "Oh, I'm just tickled to death that my son and husband were killed during the holdup." "How did you feel . . . ?"* But readers liked hearing about others' pain. That's what his chosen life's work had come to, and it was either get with the program or take early retirement.

The last report he reviewed was on the knifing of one Mr. Rudolph Grau, found barely alive in Franklin Park, who'd expired in the rear of an ambulance between the park and the hospital. According to MPD, no immediate family members were known to exist, nor had the wielder of the knife been identified.

Wait a minute, Wilcox mused. Franklin Park. Two murders there within days of each other. He tried to recall other homicides in that particular park and came up empty. The victim's name was Grau. Rudolph Grau. The shopping cart lady at Michael's apartment building asked whether he knew that a resident named Grau had been killed. The inquisitive neighbor he'd bumped into at the apartment building during his second visit there said his name was Rudy. And there was Grau's address on the police report—Michael's address.

What kind of coincidences are these?

He put aside his jumbled thoughts about the Grau stabbing long enough to make calls to the homes of the other murder victims from last night. With any luck, he'd reach people willing to talk on the phone.

The mother of the teen slaughtered over a pair of sneakers and a jacket was so inconsolable that Wilcox could barely make out what she said, but he did decipher that her son was a good boy who never hurt anyone, and that if they weren't forced to live in such a lousy neighborhood he would be alive today. No argument from Wilcox.

The sister of the man knifed to death over his alleged fling with the buxom neighbor said in a calm, steady voice that her brother was a fine, God-fearing man who suffered from a weakness of the flesh—didn't everyone?—and did he deserve to die for his indiscretion?—and he was now in the hands of the good Lord, who would make the final judgment and forgive him his sins and—"

A spokesman for the Washington office of the German conglomerate referred Wilcox to its Munich headquarters. *"Danke,"* Wilcox said, the only German word he knew, and decided to not bother making the overseas call.

He ate lunch in the employee cafeteria, caught up on two months' worth of expense accounts, was interviewed for three minutes on the local CNN channel, and headed home. He left the highway and wended his way into his subdivision. He'd lived there for so long that he seldom took note of what was going on, people walking their dogs or trimming shrubbery, or the stages of bloom on trees and bushes. But this day his antenna was up, and he took in his surroundings as though there for the first time, a potential homebuyer scouting the neighborhood.

He turned onto his street and drove slowly, eyes glancing right and left. He passed a Verizon repair truck parked six houses from his; someone must be having phone trouble he reasoned—hopefully not the whole block.

He slowly crossed the street's center line, pulling up in front of his curbside mailbox so that it was within his arm's reach from the driver's side. The mailman had flipped up the red metal flag. That it remained up meant that Georgia hadn't fetched the mail, which was what he'd hoped. She seldom did, seeming to never remember that it would be there, and it was his habit to grab it before pulling into the driveway. He pulled a clutch of mail from the box, almost allowing some catalogues and magazines to slip from his hand and fall to the ground. Another look around preceded his next move, which was to remove the letter he'd written at Michael's apartment from his inside jacket pocket and slip it in with the day's mail. It didn't matter that his fingerprints would be on it. Of course they would be. He'd handled it along with the other mail.

"Hey, anybody home?" he yelled on his way to the kitchen where he dropped the mail on the countertop in the same spot he always did.

"What are you doing home so early?" Georgia asked as she came from the basement where she'd been folding laundry.

"I finished up early," he said, hugging her. "Nice to be home at a decent hour for a change."

She returned to the basement to complete her chore. He hung his jacket over the back of a chair, stripped off his tie, poured a small Scotch, and took it to the patio. It was a lovely day, warm but not uncomfortable. He drew a deep breath, sipped from his drink, sat at the table and extended his legs in front of him. She joined him a few minutes later.

"Drink?" he asked.

"Too early, thanks. What's new? You were great on TV."

"Thanks. I felt comfortable. Not much new at the paper. We decided that since there's nothing new, we'd skip tomorrow's edition."

"Good," she said. "Have you heard from Michael?"

"No. Robbie?"

"Not today."

She turned in her chair and saw through the window the pile of mail on the kitchen counter. "Mailman bring anything interesting?" she asked.

"I didn't look."

She fetched the mail, brought it to the patio table, and started going through it. A home-decorating catalogue caught her attention, and she browsed it, pointing out items that appealed to her, including a set of vivid red silk sheets and pillowcases. "Like it?" she asked.

"Very sexy. We should have had them on the bed last night."

"Our old sheets did just fine, don't you think?"

He laughed. "Sorry, but I wasn't thinking about the sheets last night."

She squeezed his hand and continued perusing the catalogue. Finished, she went back to seeing what other mail was there. Joe watched out of the corner of his eye.

"What's this?" she said, pulling the sheet of paper, sans envelope, from the pile and unfolding it.

"What is it?" he asked. "Some contractor drop off a flyer? That's against the law."

She handed it to him without a word. Her face went ashen, and she wrapped her arms around herself.

He pulled half-glasses from his shirt pocket and read. "Jesus," he said. "He must have put it in our mailbox himself."

"Call the police," she said.

"Right. I'll call Edith. This is hitting too close to home."

Before placing the call, he made a copy of the letter on their fax machine that doubled as a photocopier and slipped it under other papers on the desk in the library.

Georgia stayed on the patio, her fist pressed against her lips. When he returned, she asked, "Did you reach her?"

"On her cell. She and her partner are heading here now."

"I hate this, Joe."

"I know, I know, but it'll be okay. I'll ask the police to provide security. If they won't, we'll hire our own. Don't worry, Georgia, we'll be fine." He patted her hand to reassure, knowing it wouldn't.

Vargas-Swayze and Dungey arrived forty-five minutes later and Wilcox handed them the letter.

"He's ratcheting it up now, isn't he?" Vargas-Swayze said, her reaction raising Georgia's already elevated anxiety level.

"You listed in the phone book?" Dungey asked.

"No," Wilcox replied. "We've been unlisted for years. Too many nuts out there read something you write and decide to challenge you up close and personal. But it's not tough to find out where anybody lives. I've done it plenty of times chasing down stories."

"Can we have police protection?" Georgia asked.

"I'll see what I can do," Vargas-Swayze said. "Did you notice any strangers in the neighborhood today, Georgia?"

"No. I've been in the house all day. Those hedges out front block the view of the street. I can't even see the mailbox from here."

"I wonder why he didn't mail it," Dungey mused, "like the last one."

"He's delivering a message beyond what he wrote, Joe," Vargas-Swayze said. "He's making a point that he knows where you live."

"What I find interesting," Wilcox said, "is that the first letter didn't attack me personally. This one does. He's angry that my articles paint what he calls a 'warped picture' of him. Warped picture! What other view can you have?"

"But he isn't cutting off contact with you. He says he'll be in touch again, maybe by phone. This line here: 'We should discuss my feelings, Joe. Perhaps I'll call and we can have a long chat about that and other things.' "

"He called me Mr. Wilcox in the first letter," Wilcox said. "Now it's Joe."

"Looks like the same typewriter," Dungey said, holding the letter by its corner and slipping it into a plastic sleeve he'd carried from the car.

"How about some coffee, hon," Wilcox suggested to Georgia.

"Not for us," Vargas-Swayze said. "We have to get back."

Wilcox walked them to their car.

"Did you talk to Georgia about a tap on your home phone?" Vargas-Swayze asked.

"No, but go ahead and do it. Do you think you can arrange for some sort of security here at the house?" he asked.

"At least for a few days."

"A suggestion?"

"What?"

"Keep the fact that my phones are tapped and that there'll be security here under wraps. I don't want to scare him away. Keeping a channel open between him and me might lull him into making a dumb move."

"Makes for a good story, huh?" Dungey said as he opened the driver's door.

Wilcox frowned at him. "Meaning?" he said.

"Nothing."

Wilcox turned to Vargas-Swayze. "Thanks for coming personally. Georgia's really upset over this. Knowing some of your people are around will make all the difference."

"Mind a suggestion from *me*?" she asked.

"Of course not."

"Don't take this guy lightly, Joe. His tone in the letter is angry."

"Don't worry, I won't. Thanks again."

He watched them pull away and thought of Dungey's comment about it making for a good story. Had the detective sensed something? Did he know something? Impossible. Edith had said a few times before that her partner was a downbeat, cynical sort of person. Typical cop, Wilcox thought as he returned to the house, wondering whether he should tell Georgia about the murder of Michael's neighbor. He decided not to. He'd follow up on that tomorrow and see how things fell.

"I'd better call Paul and tell him there's something new to report," Wilcox told his wife.

His editor wasn't at home, but he reached him on his cell phone. Blaring rock and roll music in the background made it difficult for Wilcox to hear, and he wasn't sure Morehouse would hear, either, but he spoke loudly and filled him in.

"Can you put something together for tomorrow?" Morehouse shouted.

"I'd rather wait a day," Wilcox responded. "Georgia is upset over the letter. I'd just like to spend the rest of the evening with her."

"Come on, Joe, give me something. She'll go to sleep at some point, right?"

Wilcox hesitated, then: "I'll come up with something."

"Good man."

"What's that music? Where are you, Paul?"

"See you in the A.M.," Morehouse said, and signed off.

Joe and Georgia ordered Chinese food that evening. The delivery-man's ringing of the doorbell caused Georgia to shudder; she uttered an involuntary moan. After dinner, they settled in the den and aim-lessly watched television, including one of that season's stupid reality shows.

"I feel like *we're* in a reality show," she commented when he changed the channel to public television. It was broadcasting a chapter of a British crime series. "Please, Joe, no murder mysteries tonight."

He forced a laugh and found a silly sitcom where the laughs were also forced—on a recorded track. Georgia's patience ran out after a few minutes and she again tried to reach Roberta, first her apartment, then her mobile phone.

"She must have turned off her cell," she said. "No answer on either phone. I left messages."

"She's probably doing some recording. She'll call back. We'll catch her on the news at eleven. Sit and relax. I'll turn off the TV and we'll put on some music."

Georgia fell asleep in her chair. After a while, Joe gently woke her and urged her to go to bed.

"Are you coming?" she asked sleepily.

"I'll be up in a bit." He kissed her. "Sleep tight. This will all be over soon."

He went to bed three hours later after writing a story about the sec-ond killer letter, and e-mailing it to the paper.

≈

"I can't tell you how upset I am."

Michael and Roberta Wilcox sat side by side in his apartment.

"It wasn't as though I really liked the man. He was abrasive, espe-cially when he drank, which was most of the time. You experienced his drunkenness yourself. But there was something I respected about him. I believe I might have been his only friend."

"It must have been a shock," Roberta said, "to hear that someone you knew well had been stabbed. How did you find out?"

"When I came home from job interviews I had today, there was a card on my door from the police. I called them immediately, of course, not having a clue as to why they wanted to speak with me. I'd already been interviewed twice about the murder of the young woman at the *Tribune*."

"They interviewed *you*?" she said. She held a glass of wine that she hadn't touched. "Why?"

"I'd made a delivery to the newspaper the night she was killed. I was working for an office supply company at the time. Someone in the newsroom needed what I had right away, so I was sent directly to the paper. The police, I'm sure, interviewed everyone who'd been there that night. At least I hope they did. They wouldn't be doing their job if they didn't. I expected the same detectives I'd spoken with earlier to show up this evening, but a different team arrived, very nice, very polite. I told them what I knew about Rudy, that I hadn't seen him all night, and was here practicing my guitar. They took my statement and left." He rolled his eyes and drank. "I'm evidently the poster boy for being at the wrong place at the wrong time."

"I didn't know you'd been at the *Tribune* the night Jean Kaporis was killed," she said.

He sighed deeply. "I believe I'll have a second glass of wine. It's been that sort of day, one surprise after another, including your call and being here. You haven't touched yours, my dear. The vintage not to your liking?"

"Oh, no, it's fine," she said, sipping as he went to the kitchen.

When he returned to the couch, he offered his glass in a toast, and said, "Here's to better days ahead."

She followed the ritual of touching rims but didn't drink. "Michael," she said, "I feel terrible for what you've gone through, not only here in Washington, but early in your life. Frankly, that's why I called and asked to see you tonight."

"Oh?"

She started to continue but he cut her off. "I sense a modicum of pity in your voice, Robbie. I don't deserve pity, nor do I want it."

"It's not pity I'm feeling, Michael, it's admiration."

"For me? There's nothing to admire in me, Robbie. I'm a murderer who spent forty years in a hospital for the criminally insane. Admiration? That should be reserved for astronauts and missionaries."

"I disagree," she said. She tasted her wine, placed the glass on the coffee table, turned, and spoke with animation. "I've always felt that anyone who overcomes great adversity is to be admired. I have tremendous respect for alcoholics who get sober and drug addicts who get straight. There are people born into poverty who rise above it through sheer will and determination to become successful citizens. People conquer illness, including mental illness, to live healthy, productive lives. That sounds like you, Michael, doesn't it?"

A melancholic expression crossed his handsome face; she wondered whether he might shed tears.

"I'll get right to the point," she said. "I'd like to do a documentary about you."

His plaintive expression broke, and he smiled. "I don't know what to say," he said. "Am I flattered that you would view me in that light? Of course. Am I somewhat shocked that you would even consider such a thing? Very much so. But my initial reaction aside, I want to hear more. I *need* to hear more."

She spent the next fifteen minutes outlining her proposal for him—that she would write, produce, and direct a multipart documentary about how he rose above his childhood and subsequent incarceration to become a productive, law-abiding citizen. It would focus on the positive use to which he had put his forty years in the institution—becoming a skilled musician, a first-rate cook, a man whose intellectual curiosity led him to become a voracious reader, and who was working on a novel of his own.

He said nothing. He leaned back, flipping his ponytail over the back of the couch, and closed his eyes, the wineglass cupped in both hands. She took the moment to take note of his lean, conditioned body beneath his tight black T-shirt, the tan face, the serene expression on his chiseled face. Her eyes strayed across the room to where the initial pages of his novel sat on the desk.

The sudden feel of his hand on hers was startling, but she didn't remove it. He squeezed harder, opened his eyes, turned to her and said, "I am extremely touched, Robbie, that you perceive me in such a positive way. I would be honored to be the subject of your documentary."

She stood, went to the center of the room, and said, "Then let's get started. I have an hour before I have to be back at the station. We can begin the interviewing process now. Game?"

He leaped from the couch, put his right hand on her waist, took her right hand in his left, and waltzed her around the room, humming "All The Things You Are" in her ear in three-quarter time. Their dance lasted a minute. He released her and said, "I hope my favorite and only niece isn't offended at my impetuousness."

She shook her head and smiled. "Not at all," she said. "Now, can we begin?"

"By all means. Consider me yours."

She left the apartment an hour later, a yellow legal pad filled with notes. And in the black vinyl folder containing the pad was a page from his novel, which she'd taken during his bathroom break.

✿

Vargas-Swayze and Dungey returned to the precinct after their visit to the Wilcox home, and handed the letter they'd been given by Wilcox to an evidence technician on duty.

"The report came back on the first letter," the tech told them. "It's on your desk, Edith."

There were no surprises. The letter had been filled with fingerprints, many of them smudged. But the final item piqued her curiosity, and she called the lab. "What does this note on the bottom of the report mean?" she asked a senior lab manager, who was working late that night. He was one of the least favorite people with whom she had to deal on a regular basis, a genetically nasty little man with a wicked eye twitch and a perpetual curl to his mouth.

"Well, what does it say?" he asked in a nasal, condescending voice.

"It says," she said, successfully stifling her annoyance, "that one print, which matches others on the letter, seems to have been placed on the paper before the letter was typed. *Before* is underlined."

"Yessss?"

"I don't have time to play games," she said. "I'm just a cop, you're the expert. Just tell me what it means."

His sigh was long and loud. "It means, detective, that somebody touched the paper when it was blank. The print is beneath the typed letters."

"I see," she said. "Which further means that this particular print could belong to the person who actually wrote the letter."

"Very good, detective. Anything else I can do for you?"

Drop dead, she thought. "No, but thanks for the explanation. Have you matched that set of prints through the Bureau with other known prints?"

"Yes. They'll fax you the results in the morning."

"Well, great," she said. "Have a nice night."

"Jerk," she muttered as she handed Dungey the report. As they discussed the lab's findings, the surveillance team assigned to keep an eye on Wilcox and his house walked in after having parked the borrowed Verizon truck in the vehicle pen.

"Hey," Edith called after them, "did either of you see anybody approach the Wilcox mailbox?"

"The mailman," one of them answered.

"That's it?"

"That's it. Nobody went near that mailbox except the mailman. Oh, and the subject. He pulled up to it in his vehicle and took the mail from the box. Never got out of his car."

"You guys were awake the whole time?" Dungey asked.

"Stuff it," one of the surveillance team told the long, lanky detective, and walked away with his partner.

"Touchy," Dungey muttered to Vargas-Swayze. "Let's call it a night," he said, stretching, yawning and wincing at the pain in his hamstring. "My leg's killing me. Maybe I ought to go on disability."

"Maybe you should," she said, "but not now. I don't need a new partner at this point. Besides, you got hurt playing basketball, not while you were on duty."

"Yeah, but—"

"Suck it up, Wade. Play hurt. I have a feeling something's about to pop."

"Like what?"

"I don't know exactly. Maybe we'll get an answer when they match the print that's underneath the typing. In the meantime, there's that murder in Franklin Park, the neighbor of our friend with the French name. I've got your vibes now about him, two murders and he's close to both. Come to think of it, he doesn't live far from Franklin Park and was at the *Trib*, which puts him in proximity to three killings."

"Millius and Warrick were going back to check him out and requestion others," Dungey said. "Let's see what they got from him."

"Right, and run that background check you keep putting off."

"Shall do, boss."

"Don't be a wise guy," she said. "I'll be a little late tomorrow, probably nine-thirty. A meeting with my lawyer."

"Ride home?"

"No, thanks. I'm going to hang here for a while, catch up on some things. Go on, get some sleep."

She spent the next hour going over the Kaporis and McNamara files, not knowing what she was looking for but hoping something would shout out at her. Her thoughts drifted to Joe Wilcox and the letters he'd received from the serial killer and eventually wandered back to the first article he'd written alleging that someone at MPD had confirmed to him that the serial killer scenario was being seriously considered. He'd raised that possibility with her shortly before the article appeared. What had she said? Something vague, along the lines that it took more than two killings for them to be considered the work of the same person. But she'd also agreed with him that anything was possible. Had he used that conversation with her to justify his article? Had he lied about there being an unnamed MPD source who advanced that theory to him? Couldn't be, she decided. Joe Wilcox was an experienced newsman who often decried the slippage of standards in his profession. As far as she was concerned, Wilcox would be the last reporter to fall into the trap of fabricating a story. That was for young hotshots impatient with the pace of their careers and yearning for instant recognition and gratification. Not old pros like Joe Wilcox.

She was about to call it a night when detectives Jack Millius and Ron Warwick entered the detectives' room.

"How goes it, Edith?" Millius asked, slumping in his chair and rubbing his eyes.

"I'm packing," she said. "Hey, did you two get back to the place on Connecticut to interview neighbors of the guy found in Franklin Park?"

"Yeah," Warwick said. "Like we needed to catch another case. I might as well give up my apartment and move in here."

"Did you talk to Mr. LaRue?"

"Yeah, we did," Millius said. "Nice enough guy, although I have a certain distrust of men his age wearing a ponytail."

"What did he have to say?" she asked.

"Was home all night—"

"Practicing his guitar," Warwick added. "I don't trust guys his age with ponytails who also play the guitar. Nothing sadder than an old rockstar wannabe."

"A neighbor confirms he was there," Millius said. "An older woman who says Mr. LaRue and his guitar sometimes keep her awake at night. Says she heard him playing until midnight."

Vargas-Swayze nodded.

"What's your interest in him?"

"Just curious. Wade and I spoke with him a couple of times earlier about the Kaporis murder. He delivered office supplies to the paper the night she got it."

"Any breaks?" Millius asked.

"*Nada*," she said. "*Mañana.*"

෴

Joe and Georgia Wilcox watched their daughter on the eleven o'clock news. The phone rang minutes after she'd gone off the air. Joe answered.

"Hi sweetheart," he said. "Mom and I watched. Nice job."

"Thanks. Everybody good there?"

"I think so. How about you? Got anything earth-shattering on my favorite story?"

"As a matter of fact, there are some things brewing, Dad."

"Oh? Like what?"

"I can't get into it," she said. "You understand. I'm working a source, a good one. Once I break it, I'll lay it all out for you."

"That'll be a little late, won't it?" he said, the edge to his voice not lost on her.

"Can't help it, Dad. Anything new on your end?"

He considered telling her about the letter.

"Not a thing, sweetheart. I'll put Mom on."

TWENTY-SIX

L et's get out of here," he shouted at the young woman next to him at the bar. "I can't hear myself think."

"One more dance?"

"Hell, no. Come on. The music's rattling my teeth."

She was an inch taller than he was. She had very white skin, very red hair, very large, round, powder-blue eyes, and a figure that confirmed that she was one of the two major sexes. She wore a white and brown scoop-neck peasant blouse that exposed freckled cleavage, and a tight pair of tan slacks. Her name was Kelly. Last name, Ames.

Morehouse paid cash at the bar and propelled her toward the door, aware as he'd been all evening that he was the oldest human being in the dance club. He'd felt acutely uncomfortable during the one time he'd ventured onto the dance floor with her, attempting to appear at home but knowing he looked like an elephant plopped into the middle of a ballet.

They left Club Heaven and Hell on Eighteenth Street in Adams

Morgan and stood on the sidewalk where he mopped his brow with a handkerchief and sucked in fresh air.

"The night is young," she said happily.

"Yeah, well, I've got a bitch of a day tomorrow. Where's your roommate?"

"Home visiting her folks in West Virginia. What are you suggesting, sir?"

She knew precisely what he was suggesting because he'd suggested it two or three times before since they'd started seeing each other. Her answer was always to lead him back to her apartment in Crystal City, on the Virginia side of the Potomac. She and her roommate had an understanding. If either of them were about to bring a man to the apartment, the other would vacate unless the notice was too short, or there was a compelling reason for the homebound roommate to stay put. No problem this night.

꿍

They'd met at Georgetown University when he'd given a lecture to graduate journalism students on the changing role of local news coverage. She'd asked a couple of intelligent questions following his talk, and approached him at the lectern as he gathered up his notes. He realized she was being flirtatious, and happily played the game.

"I had another question to ask," she said, "but it would have been awkward in front of everyone."

"What is it?" he asked.

She looked around before saying, "Can I buy you a drink or a cup of coffee, Mr. Morehouse? It would be my pleasure."

He checked his watch. "Sure," he said, not sure where this was leading but willing to find out. She wasn't the first young and attractive aspiring female journalist who'd made such an approach over the years. He didn't have any illusions as to why they did. He was on the wrong side of fifty; it wasn't his body they coveted. It was his position at the paper that drew certain outgoing young women looking for a mentor—and a break—to him. So be it.

The question she'd said she wanted to ask was more a statement of her goals in life, including, of course, the sort of journalism job she sought. In a sense, she'd managed to choreograph a job interview when none had been offered. *Good for you*, he thought. Good reporters weren't shy, nor were they necessarily honest when going after a story. He liked her spunk and directness. He also liked the smell of her when they sat next to each other in a booth in a dark bar not far from campus, and the press of her thigh against his.

"Where are you going now?" he'd asked, feeling the two bourbons he'd consumed. She'd nursed a frozen peach margarita. It was four in the afternoon; he'd promised Mimi he would take her to the movies that night.

"Home, I guess, unless you have a better suggestion."

"I'd suggest we have dinner together but I've already made other plans."

"Maybe another time," she said.

"Yeah. That would be great. Let me have your number."

He drove her to Crystal City. They pulled into the circular driveway in front of the building. He put the car in park. "I've really enjoyed meeting you," he said, "and—"

She interrupted with a long, wet, open-mouthed kiss, her tongue finding his. His hand found a breast through her blouse.

"Please call me," she said, moving his hand away. "You're a very nice man, and I really feel we have something in common."

With that she exited the car and trotted to the building's entrance, where the doorman opened the door for her. She paused, turned, threw Paul a kiss, and was gone.

෨

They'd begun this particular evening with dinner at the tony Citronelle, in the Latham Hotel in Georgetown. Kelly had commented on how expensive every item on the menu was, which he dismissed with a cavalier sweep of his hand. Truth was, he wasn't happy at how much the evening was costing but chalked it up to the cost of doing business—monkey business to be sure. A *Tribune* colleague from the international desk was having dinner there with his wife, and stopped by Morehouse's table.

His slightly raised eyebrows and sly smile told Morehouse what he was thinking.

"Meet Kelly Ames," Morehouse said casually, "soon to join my staff."

"A pleasure," the foreign editor said, shaking her hand. "Good luck. He'll work you to death."

When he'd gone to rejoin his wife at a table on the other side of the room, Kelly said to Morehouse, "Were you serious?"

He shrugged, picked up the menu, and said, "Let's order."

Morehouse enjoyed not having to keep track of time this particular evening. Mimi was away visiting her aged mother in Des Moines and wouldn't be back for another two days.

"You're amazing," Kelly said after they'd gone to her apartment. She propped herself on an elbow and looked down at him in bed.

"How so?"

"You're such a wonderful lover, like you were a lot younger."

"You're just saying that."

"No, I wouldn't do that. Some of the younger guys I've been with aren't nearly as good as you. You're—well, you're experienced, I guess."

"Got anything to drink?" he asked, sitting up. Uncomfortable with his nakedness, he reached down, grabbed his boxer shorts where he'd dropped them next to the bed, and put them on.

"There's some beer in the fridge, I think," she said, not at all self-conscious about her nudity as she went with him to the kitchen where he pulled two bottles from the refrigerator. He sat at a small table wedged into a corner. "Put something on," he said.

She giggled. "Getting all hot and bothered again?" she asked.

"Go on," he said, "get a robe or something."

She returned wearing an aqua sweatsuit and joined him at the table.

"Did you mean what you said to the man in the restaurant, about me being on the Metro staff?" she asked.

"I don't have any openings at the moment," he said.

"Did you talk to anyone else at the paper about me?" she asked after taking a swill of beer from the bottle.

"Yeah, I did."

"What did they say?"

"I talked to an editor with the Panache section. She said she'd be happy to read your resumé and interview you. But you have to finish school first."

"I'm almost done," she said, running a bare foot up and down his leg. "Besides, I'd quit school if there were a good job at *The Washington Tribune*. That's all she said?"

"Hey, that's a foot in the door. Don't knock it."

"I just thought that with your clout, you'd be able to set something up for me, get me a job instead of just an interview."

"I never promised you anything, Kelly," he said, uncomfortable with this turn in the conversation. "I'd better be going."

"You said you were going to stay the night," she said. "You said your wife was away and—"

"That's right, she is, but I've got some things to do at home." He went to the bedroom and started dressing.

She stood in the doorway, a hand on her hip. "Sometimes I have a fantasy," she said, "about knocking on your door some day and introducing myself to your wife as your mistress. Not that I'd ever do it, but sometimes I—"

He faced her and extended a finger. "Don't even kid about such a thing," he said, his voice low and serious. "Don't . . . ever."

"You don't have to get in a huff about it," she said. "I was just kidding around."

He finished dressing and went to the living room where he'd left his briefcase. She followed.

"Maybe you'd better go," she said. "I don't like it when you get this way."

"I'll be tied up for the next few weeks," he said. "Trips out of town and—"

"Translation: You won't be calling me."

"Not for a while."

"But you will set up the interview with the editor at Panache."

"I gave her your name and number. She'll probably call you."

"Sure. Have a nice life, Mr. Paul Morehouse."

He thought of a number of responses but said nothing; he simply left.

TWENTY-SEVEN

Edith Vargas-Swayze was in good spirits as she walked into the detectives' room at the First Precinct. She'd come from the meeting with her lawyer at which she learned that her estranged husband, Peter, had landed a new job at an even higher salary than he'd been paid at his previous one. As a result, he was dropping his insistence that he cease making alimony payments, and that she pay *him* since he was out of work.

❧

"What a guy," she'd said, to which her sober-sided attorney replied, "Your husband's lawyer is as big a jerk as he is. One request, though."

"Yes?"

"Stop going around saying you want to shoot him. I know you're kidding, but it doesn't sound good coming from a cop."

"Okay," she said. "I promise I won't—unless—"

"Get out of here," he said. "And next time pick a better guy to get involved with."

❧

"Is Wade in?" she asked Bernie Evans, her boss, as he passed through the room where detectives milled about, some just arriving after having conducted investigations, others about to launch theirs.

"He called in. His leg. You'll have to work solo today. We're short-handed. Or short-legged."

"Not a problem," she said, going to her desk and picking up a file folder from the forensic lab that had been dropped there minutes earlier. The FBI central fingerprint registry had compared prints on the first letter with known prints in its massive file. Although the few prints on the page were smeared and smudged, two partials matched samples in the database. They belonged to *Washington Tribune* employees Joe Wilcox and Paul Morehouse. No surprise. Wilcox had opened the envelope and removed the letter, and he'd handed it to Morehouse. They'd acknowledged as much when she was there.

What did grab her interest was the note on the bottom of the report. The print belonging to Joseph Wilcox appeared to have been placed on the paper prior to any words having been typed.

She sat back and contemplated what she'd read. The forensic lab had told her that its preliminary analysis indicated that one of the prints could have preceded the typing. If true, they'd agreed, it could mean that the person making that print might be the letter writer.

Joe Wilcox?

Could it be? Was it possible that he'd written a phony letter to create grist for a sensational story, and to enhance his importance?

Would prints on the second letter establish the same possibility?

The officers assigned to provide surveillance on the Wilcox home had claimed that no one had approached the mailbox aside from the mailman and Wilcox. Surely, the mailman wasn't the serial killer.

"No, no," she said aloud. "Not Joe."

If so, to say she was shocked would be a gross understatement.

She went to Evans's office. "Got a minute?" she asked.

"Sure, Edith. Pull up a chair."

She handed him the report.

He looked up over half-glasses and smiled. "Do you think your buddy Wilcox is about to join that distinguished company of journalists who get too inventive?"

"I don't know, Bernie," she said. "If I were a betting person, I'd lay my money on Joe being the last person who'd do that. He's a stand-up guy. He's never lied to me."

Evans leaned back in his chair and clasped his hands behind his head. "Maybe he's going through a midlife crisis," he said. "I recently went through mine. So did my wife. I bought a red pickup truck, and she dyed her hair red. Happens to the best of us."

Vargas-Swayze laughed.

"At least I didn't put a gun rack in the back. Have you checked on the phone taps?"

"I will when I leave here. We have one on his home now."

"Good. In the meantime, he'll write another story that will run on the front page and sell a slew of papers." He came forward in his chair. "If Wilcox has been writing these so-called letters to himself, where did he do it? Forensics says they weren't from a computer printer. Had to be a typewriter. Does he have one at home?"

"I've never seen one," she replied, "but that doesn't prove anything."

"If the second letter indicates the same result, maybe we should get a warrant."

She winced. "I'd hate to do that, Bernie. He's a friend."

"You've never had a friend break the law under your nose?" he asked.

"No."

"Look, all I can say is that if Wilcox has been writing these letters to himself, he's not only dishonoring his profession, he's committing a crime. Keep that in mind."

"I will," she said, getting up to leave. "Red pickup truck?" she said. "You have a red pickup truck?"

"Yes. A nifty little vehicle. Great for bringing home plants from the nursery, or sheetrock from the lumber yard."

"Interesting," she said to herself as she left his office and went to the communications room to check on the taps.

꩜

Roberta Wilcox's mood was not as ebullient that morning as Vargas-Swayze's had been. She and Tom Curtis had argued on the phone to start the day. He wanted her to join him that evening to meet friends from out of town who were in D.C. on a visit. She declined, claiming she needed every hour she could muster to work on a developing big story. He became angry at her constant unavailability, causing her to accuse him of insensitivity to her career needs. That was bad enough. But he ended the conversation by saying that not only was she married to her job—and he didn't want to be married to someone wedded to something else—but that her chronic lateness was a sophomoric call for attention. The conversation ended abruptly when he hung up—forcefully.

She'd fumed about the call while showering and dressing, and over a breakfast of a limp bagel and brown water called coffee in a neighborhood luncheonette. But once she reached the TV station and was ensconced in her tiny office in the newsroom, angry thoughts about Tom Curtis were replaced by images of Michael Wilcox, aka Michael LaRue, and the page from his manuscript that now sat on the desk. Next to it was a clip of her father's first article announcing that he'd received a letter from the serial killer, and in which the letter had been reproduced. She was no document expert, but her untrained, albeit critical eye, left no doubt that the manuscript page and the letter had come from the same typewriter. It was a startling, shocking conclusion. The problem was that she didn't have the slightest idea what to do with her discovery.

The options were self-evident, but none seemed palatable. The sensible step would be to report her conclusions to the police, give them the manuscript page, and let their experts compare it to the alleged killer's letter. Would not doing that constitute some sort of crime on her part, the withholding of evidence? She decided it wouldn't. All she had at this point was a theory. The police received theories every day from crackpots all over the city. She was on safe ground here.

She considered, but only for a minute, calling her father. After all, it was his brother whom she now thought had written the letter. But that option didn't seem viable. Truth was, she was sitting on a potential major development. Sharing it at this stage with another, father or no father, would cause her to lose control of it.

What to do with this story she controlled? That was the real dilemma. Having seen the typed manuscript pages at Michael's apartment, and connecting them in her mind with what she remembered the letter to have looked like, had prompted her second visit to the apartment. She hadn't liked lying to Michael about why she wanted to interview him, but it seemed the most expedient way to get him to talk—and ultimately to get him on videotape.

There were two possibilities, she reasoned.

Her uncle Michael might be still be mentally unbalanced enough to have written to his brother pretending to be the serial killer, getting some sort of warped psychic payoff from the act.

Or—and she wasn't sure how she would handle this prospect at the moment—was her uncle Michael . . . ?

Okay, she told herself as she sipped on the fresh coffee she'd carried back from Starbuck's, either way—he'd written the letter as a sick joke, or had killed Jean Kaporis and Colleen McNamara—she had a hell of a scoop within her grasp, and now wanted him on tape more than ever to help illustrate it.

She was deep in these thoughts when her producer poked his head in. "Hey, another coup for your old man," he said.

"What?"

"His story this morning in the *Trib*. The second letter he received from the nut."

"Oh, right. Yes, it's a real coup."

She hadn't even looked at the *Tribune* that morning, something she did religiously each day. She went into the main newsroom, picked up a copy from a pile on someone's desk, and carried it back to her office. The article was splashed over the front page of the Metro section. There were three photos accompanying the piece—Jean Kaporis, Colleen McNamara, and Joe Wilcox. In the center of the page was a reproduction of the letter that had been photographed from the Xerox copy Wilcox had retained at the house.

"Damn!" she said aloud. "Why didn't he tell me?"

She hadn't answered messages left on her machine by her mother the previous night. Maybe she should have.

The reproduction in the *Tribune* looked exactly like the first one, matching the page she'd taken from Michael's manuscript.

She started writing notes on a yellow legal pad: *Two women in media murdered . . . Dad proffers serial killer theory in article . . . Michael arrives in D.C. (arrived before murders) . . . 40 yrs in nut house for murdering neighbor girl . . . Dad gets first letter from "serial killer" . . . looks as if matches pages in Michael's manuscript (I discover) . . . Dad gets second letter . . . Both written by Michael (same typewriter) . . . Michael playing pranks with Dad? (Crazy thing to do) . . . OR Michael is the serial killer . . . God!!!*

She called Michael.

"Ah, Roberta," he said in what she now recognized was his expansive, somewhat theatrical style. "Am I ready for my close-up?" He laughed. "Good side only."

"Hi, Michael. As a matter of fact, I am calling about the documentary. I was wondering if I could bring a camera crew to the apartment sometime today? I thought we could get some generic, establishing footage, you playing the guitar, fussing in the kitchen, that sort of thing."

"Playing the guitar? I'm hardly ready to perform for the camera."

"That's silly," she said. "You play exquisitely, as good as—"

"Joe Pass?"

"Yes. Joe Pass. Can I?"

"Only for you, dear niece. What time?"

"Noon?"

"All right. What shall I wear?"

"Why not wear what I've seen you in before, the black slacks and T-shirt. You look terrific in it."

"As you wish. Noon it is. I'll have lunch for you and your colleagues."

"That would be wonderful. One favor, Uncle Michael."

"You need only to name it, Robbie."

"Please don't tell my dad what we're doing. I want it to be a surprise."

"My lips are sealed."

As she lowered the phone into its cradle, a thought assailed her. Why would he be so cooperative about being filmed for a documentary about himself if he was a serial killer? Was that part of his innocence—or craziness?

She dragged out the article written by her father in which he'd quoted the shrink who'd said that such people enjoy the notoriety. That's why they collect everything written about them and their crimes, and write taunting letters to the press and to the police.

She went to her producer's office. "I need a camera crew for a noon shoot," she said.

"What noon shoot?"

"I can't tell you now, but believe me, it's part of one hell of a big story."

"What big story?"

"The serial killer."

He stood behind his desk. "What have you got, Robbie, something about your father's letter?"

"No. Well, yes. Maybe. Trust me. This could be a bombshell. I want Carlos and Margo. They can keep their mouths shut."

"Okay, okay. But you will let me in on the secret at some point."

"Of course. Thanks."

Back in her office, she called her father's number at the *Trib*.

"Dad, it's Robbie."

"Hi, sweetheart."

"Dad, why did you lie to me last night? I have to read in the newspaper about the second letter being delivered to the house? Mom must be terrified."

"She's okay. I've been insanely busy as you can imagine," he said.

"But why didn't you tell me about the letter?" she insisted.

"I didn't want to concern you," he lied, and she knew he was lying. He didn't want to be scooped by her.

Until that moment, she'd considered sharing with him her conclusion about Michael and the letters. It wasn't that she thought he'd be upset to know his own brother might have written them that kept her from doing it. It wasn't because she thought he might be upset at the steps she'd taken, and the conclusions to which she'd come. She said nothing because, to be perfectly honest, it could jeopardize the exclusive she had on this emerging story, and she wasn't about to give that up. Not for anyone. No one. Two could play the same game.

"We're doing fine," he said. "Edith Vargas-Swayze has arranged for police protection at the house. Nothing to worry about. I've got some media interviews this afternoon, including your own *Cityscape* at five."

"Good," she said. "I'll pop in if I'm around."

"Great. Mom wonders when you're coming by again for dinner."

"Soon."

"How's your Mr. Curtis?"

"Tom? He's okay. Haven't seen much of him lately. Too busy. Have to run."

"Love you, Robbie."

But not enough to be honest with me, she thought, choosing to ignore her own dishonesty.

☙

Wilcox stared at the phone for what seemed a long time after his conversation with Roberta. Should he be ashamed at withholding information from her in an attempt to protect his exclusivity? The second letter would, after all, be of concern to her, if only out of fear for her mother. He decided he couldn't worry about it. There would be time later for introspection. His day was filling up fast, thanks to the article that morning. The book editor in New York had called and asked if she could come to Washington that day and meet with him, and he'd readily agreed. The news of a second letter from the serial killer had made the news there in the Big Apple, which also prompted a call from a New York literary agent, as well as from one headquartered in Washington. When informed about the editor, the New York agent told Wilcox, "Don't sign anything with her without representation. She'll try and lowball you. You're sitting on something big. Don't give it away." Wilcox promised he'd think about it.

☙

"Looks like he's about to make a score," the officer monitoring the tap on Wilcox's phone at the newspaper said to his colleague.

"Couldn't happen to a nicer guy."

"You know him?"

"Met him a few times. Not like the rest of the media whores. A standup guy, a straight shooter."

"Maybe he'll give you a plug in his book."

"Then I'll be famous, too. But I'll never forget my roots."

They both laughed and went back to reading magazines while waiting for the next call.

～

"Joseph, it's Michael."

Wilcox glanced around to make sure no one was within listening distance.

"Hello, Michael. How are you?"

"I'm fine, but you must be exhausted. I read the article in the paper this morning. Good lord, the maniac actually had the gall to personally deliver a letter to your home?"

"Yeah. Everyone's pretty uptight."

"I would certainly imagine you would be. Is there anything I can do, any way I can help relieve the tension?"

"No, but thanks for the offer."

"It's the least a brother can do for a brother, Joseph. How is Georgia faring?"

"She's fine. Look, I'm due at a meeting. I'll call later."

"Of course. I'll be here all day."

"No word on a job?"

"Not yet, but I'm not discouraged. Take care."

～

An hour later, Detective Edith Vargas-Swayze returned to the communications center to check on calls made by, or to, Wilcox.

"Nothing interesting," the officer said. "He's gonna become a millionaire. He's got book companies and agents chasing him."

"Really?"

"He got a call from his daughter at the TV station. He's gonna be on some show over there."

"He talked to his brother, too," the second officer on duty said.

"I didn't know he had a brother. Play them for me."

"All of them?"

"Uh huh."

After they'd played the recordings of Wilcox's phone conversations that morning, Vargas-Swayze said, "Play the brother's call again."

"Thanks," she said after she'd heard it for the second time. "Give me who the brother's phone number is listed under."

It took only a few minutes to trace the phone number that had automatically been displayed during the call. "Michael LaRue," the officer said, and gave her the address.

"Something wrong?" the second officer asked, taking note of her grave expression.

"What? No, nothing wrong. Thanks guys."

TWENTY-EIGHT

Michael had prepared a lunch of sautéed chicken breasts accompanied by a platter of raw carrots, string beans, and radishes, and French bread. Roberta nibbled on a carrot or two, but was less interested in food than she was in setting up the shoot. Her crew grabbed bites as they went about their chores.

"Let's start with some shots of him playing guitar," Roberta said. After much fussing with the equipment, particularly the lights, the taping started. Michael sat on a chair with a blank white wall behind him and played "Our Love Is Here to Stay," his body hunched over the guitar as though it were part of him, head moving in time with the tempo he'd established, an occasional grunt of satisfaction accompanying a difficult run. They taped the entire song. When he'd struck his final chord, Roberta and the crew applauded.

"Thank you, thank you," Michael said, bowing.

"How about some shots in the kitchen?" Roberta suggested.

"I'm afraid all the cooking is done," Michael said.

"We can fake it," Roberta said.

And so they did, Carlos maneuvering with the camera propped on his shoulder, *cinema verite* style, and Margo positioning the microphone on a boom just out of camera range as Michael pretended to apply his culinary skills.

"That's enough," Roberta directed. "Let's go back to the living room and do an interview."

She settled Michael in a chair, and pulled one up for herself so that she faced him. "Now, Uncle Michael," she said, "if I start asking anything that makes you uncomfortable, just let me know and we'll turn off the tape."

Carlos and Margo looked at each other. *Uncle Michael? He's her uncle?*

"What kind of things will you be asking me?"

"I'd like to talk about your childhood—including that unfortunate incident with your neighbor."

"Marjorie," he said flatly.

"Was that her name?" Roberta asked, aware that the camera was already running.

She and Carlos had worked together on many occasions and knew what each was thinking without words needing to be spoken. The best material from an interview often came during the setup, when the interviewee didn't think the camera was on and spoke freely.

෴

That this debatable technique had been taught by one of her college professors tended to mitigate in her mind its deceitfulness. The professor, who taught a class in television interviewing, had cited a New York radio talk show host of yesteryear, Long John Nebel, known for his acerbic on-air approach to guests, especially those for whom he had little regard. The guest would spend preshow time in the Green Room signing releases and talking with Nebel's producer. At some point, the producer would ask, "Is there anything you don't want John to get into on the show, anything you'd just as soon not make public?" The guest might cite some incident in his life that would be embarrassing to have broadcast to thousands of listeners. Unknown to the guest, there was a microphone in the Green Room, and Nebel, sitting in his office, heard every word. At an appropriate moment in the show, the guest could count on being asked about the very thing he wished to avoid.

"This may seem unfair to you," the professor had lectured, "just as running the camera before an interview without the interviewee's knowledge might strike you as, well, mendacious. But your job as a journalist is to get the story, the *real* story. Once someone agrees to sit for an interview, it isn't necessary to give him or her an official signal that you're starting. In fact, it's best not to. Grab whatever you can, however you can, and sleep well at night knowing you've gone after and gotten the truth. And always remember that the person agreeing to the interview is looking for something out of it, too. Catching them off-guard helps ensure that you'll be capturing who they *really* are, without the spin they'll put on things during the more structured interview." It was one of the most popular courses at the university until the professor was eventually fired for, as the university's provost put it, "misleading our students." By that time, Roberta had graduated and had begun her career.

◆

"Yes," Michael said. "Marjorie Jones. You want to talk about her?"

"If it's all right with you."

"It isn't easy," he said.

"I know," she said. "If you'd rather not—"

"Oh, no, no restrictions, Robbie. Complete honesty is crucial, I was told over and over. I will talk about anything and anyone you wish."

"One of the things I'd like to ask is how it feels to kill someone."

The camera continued to roll, the microphone picking up every word.

"How it feels?" He became pensive, head back, eyes fixed on the ceiling. He came forward and leaned toward her. "In my case, rage, and fear of being found out and punished by my parents preceded the act. As the act continued, the rage abated. I suppose there was some pleasure in it, but I really don't recall specifically."

Carlos and Margo were now totally immersed in what they were hearing. This guy who played beautiful guitar and was a good cook had murdered somebody named Marjorie Jones? What was Roberta onto? Her uncle? She'd sworn them to secrecy on the way over to the apartment. Now they knew why.

"Do you want to start the interview now?" he asked Roberta.

"If you're ready."

"As ready as I will ever be," he said, drawing the back of his hand across his brow in an exaggerated display.

Roberta turned to Carlos and Margo. "Ready?" she asked.

"Ready," they said in unison, the camera and Nagra tape recorder still rolling.

Roberta held up her hand. "Before we begin," she said, "I'd like to get something from you about what's happening right here in Washington, D.C. You know that a serial killer is walking the streets."

"Of course. I've read your father's articles about it."

She hesitated as though grappling with whether to ask the next question. "All right," she said, "I'll be direct. With a serial killer roaming the streets, do you ever think that because of your past, you might be considered a suspect?" She didn't allow him to reply. "Do you think that because you've killed someone yourself, you have a better understanding of the mind of someone else who kills?"

It was his turn to ponder. After a long pause, he said, "Perhaps I do, Robbie. Killing someone is anathema to those who've never done it. But once you've killed, that act no longer seems so heinous. It's like breaking through a barrier, I suppose. Kill someone? Inconceivable! But it becomes conceivable once you've broken through that barrier." He held up his hand, and a pained expression crossed his tan, chiseled face. "I am not saying, of course, that I consider myself as having crossed that barrier and would now find killing someone easier. I'm speaking conceptually, and—"

He continued with his stipulation, and Roberta allowed him to talk. She didn't care what he said at this point. She had on tape his provocative statement about crossing barriers to edit and use as she saw fit.

Sensing she might have pushed this line of discussion as far as she could, she shifted gears and got Michael to speak of his childhood, his family and friends, the impact of his parents' deep religious faith on his life, and his relationship with his brother.

"Joseph was such good boy," he said, smiling, "always eager to please Mother and Father. He looked up to me as his big brother, which is understandable. But I'm afraid I ended up not being a sterling role model."

"What happened with Marjorie Jones?"

He sighed, and squeezed his eyes tightly shut.

"Would you tell me about it, how it happened, what you were thinking, and the aftermath?"

He spoke without interruption for twenty minutes. It was a wrenching tale that focused on the act of murder itself and the subsequent trial. At one point, Roberta thought she might become ill, and considered pausing the interview, but she didn't want him to lose his train of thought and fought through her nausea.

"Whew!" he said when Roberta told Carlos and Margo that they were breaking.

"That was—it was powerful," she said. "A remarkable story."

"Not so remarkable, I'm afraid," he said. "More tragic than anything."

"I think we've done enough for today," she said. "Next time, I'd like to have you talk about your stay in the hospital, how you put that time to good use, and the way you've reinvented your life since coming to Washington. Believe me, Michael, your story, properly told, will be an inspiration to everyone."

"If you say so," he said. "I do have a concern, however," he added.

"What's that?" she replied.

"I wouldn't want this documentary to lead people to speculate that I might have had something to do with the terrible thing that happened to those two young women, the one who worked with your father, and the girl in the park."

"Of course it won't," she said, pleased that the lights were still on and that Carlos had started the camera again, and that the mike was live. "I'll make sure that it reflects the exemplary life you've led since leaving the hospital."

"I know you will," he said, getting up and leaning over to kiss her on the cheek. "More chicken?" he asked.

"We have to get back," Roberta told him. "The lunch was wonderful."

He walked them from the building to the small van with the station's call letters emblazoned on the side.

"This most recent letter to your father must have your dear mother frantic with worry," he told her as Carlos and Margo carefully packed their equipment into the rear of the van.

"She's a pretty strong person," Roberta responded. "I'm not worried about her."

He looked back at the building. "I miss my friend Rudy," he said.

"Yes, I'm so sorry about that. Any leads that you know of?"

"No. Funny. He was an irascible sort, drinking too much to alleviate the physical pain of his war wounds—and I'm sure the mental pain that accompanied it—but there was a side of him that was likable and decent. I liked him. We used to play chess, you know, and checkers. He wasn't very good, but he tried hard. What sort of world do we live in, Robbie?"

"The only world we have," she said, kissing his cheek. "Thank you so much for your honesty, and for allowing me to capture it. You're an astonishing person, Uncle Michael. I'll be in touch."

He watched them drive away before turning and walking slowly back to the building.

Edith Vargas-Swayze had watched the scene, too, from an unmarked car parked across the broad avenue. *What was Roberta Wilcox doing there with a camera crew?* she wondered as she pulled away and headed for the precinct.

TWENTY-NINE

"Here's to our star!"

Others at the National Press Club's Reliable Source bar raised their glasses in a tribute to Joe Wilcox.

"I'll drink to that," he said, holding up a glass of sparkling water garnished with a lime wedge.

"You drinking water, Joe?" someone asked.

"I've got a TV and a radio interview later on," Wilcox said, defending his choice of drink. "Wouldn't do to pass out on the set."

"This N.Y. editor is coming to D.C.?" he was asked.

"This afternoon. I'm meeting her here at the club."

"Introduce me to her," said a colleague. "I'll write a book about any damn thing she wants as long as the money's right."

They retreated to a table where the drinks kept coming along with their lunches.

"What's this break in the serial killer case your daughter hinted at on the news?" was the question.

"I don't know," Wilcox replied. "She's playing it close to the vest."

"Even with her old man?"

Wilcox laughed and finished his sandwich. "Afraid so. I taught her right. Never reveal a source."

"And these days go to jail," said one of the other women at the table.

This led to a semiserious discussion of recent court rulings in which reporters found themselves in legal hot water for not revealing their sources in criminal cases. Wilcox half listened to the conversation as he mentally ran down his commitments that afternoon.

"Keep the movie rights," someone said.

"And get a real drink, Joe. Water'll just corrode your pipes."

As Wilcox pulled out his wallet, his cell phone sounded.

"Wilcox."

"Joe, it's Edith Vargas-Swayze."

"Hello. How goes it?"

"Where are you?"

"The Press Club. About to leave."

"I have to speak with you."

"Great. I'm jammed up all afternoon and into the early evening, but—"

"Joe, I have to talk to you right away. It's important."

He left the table and went to an unoccupied corner, the phone to his ear, his hand covering the mouthpiece. He'd received many calls from Edith over the years asking to speak with him. This time, her tone was different. His stomach tightened.

"What is it?" he asked.

"I'll tell you when we meet."

"Where?"

"The Press Club. I'm five minutes from there. I'll pick you up in front."

"Edith, can't you tell me what this is about?"

"I'll be there in five," she said.

As he clicked the phone shut, he had a fleeting notion to leave the building and not wait for her, but he knew he couldn't do that. He returned to the table. "Got to run," he said.

"Another call from the coast, Joe?"

"Yeah." He tossed money on the table. "They want me to star in the movie. See ya."

He rode the elevator down to street level and went to the street where Vargas-Swayze sat behind the wheel of a bilious-green unmarked police car with a dented fender. He got in. She slipped the gearshift into drive and pulled into traffic.

"Where are we going?" he asked, checking his watch. "I've got some TV things and a meeting with—"

"Later, Joe," she said, her eyes straight ahead.

As she turned onto Connecticut Avenue NW and he realized that she was driving in the direction of Michael's apartment building, bile came up and stung his throat. He reached in his pocket for a Tums that wasn't there.

"Edith, will you please tell me what this is all about?"

She pulled to the curb in front of a fire hydrant, directly across the street from where Michael lived, turned off the ignition, drew a breath, and faced him. "Want to tell me about it, Joe?"

"Tell you about what?" The quaver in his voice said much.

She pointed at the apartment building. "There," she said. "Where your brother lives."

"Michael?"

"Michael LaRue. Michael Wilcox. Whatever he chooses to call himself. Is that where you wrote the letters?"

He became smaller in his seat, as though developing a slow leak. He couldn't face her, looked in every direction but hers. She placed a hand on his arm. "Joe, listen to me, please. I know you wrote those letters yourself. Your fingerprint is beneath the typed words. No one approached your mailbox the day the letter showed up except the mailman—and you."

He said nothing for what seemed an eternity. Finally, he looked at her, his lips tightly compressed, his eyes squeezed almost shut. "How did you learn about Michael?"

"The tap on your phone. The conversation you had with him this morning."

He'd forgotten about the tap despite knowing from years of interacting with MPD that most people soon forget their phones are tapped, the way interview subjects forget a tape recorder is running even though it's right in front of them.

"What's this all about, Joe?"

"You already seem to have all the answers, Edith."

She shook her head. "I want to hear them from you."

He sat sullenly, although it didn't represent what he was feeling. He didn't know what to say, so said nothing. But he would have to say something, attempt to explain his actions, rationalize what he'd done. He forced himself to think more clearly. All she knew was that Michael was his brother. He couldn't refute that. As for having written the letters, that was hardly her concern. It wasn't a police matter—maybe. It was between him, his conscience, and whoever he might have to answer to at the *Tribune*.

"What if I did write those letters?" he asked, not combative, a sincere question. "Why should that concern you?"

"Did you? Are you saying you did?"

"I'm not admitting anything. But if I did write those letters, it's hardly a police matter. Who's hurt?"

The words exploded from her. "Who's hurt?" she said. "Come on, you know better. Who's hurt? Let's start with you and your reputation. What about the integrity of the newspaper? What about all the young women in the city looking over their shoulders, adding locks to their doors, their worried parents, husbands, and boyfriends? *Caramba*, Joe, you can't dismiss it as nothing more than a prank that doesn't seriously impact others."

She was right, of course, and he didn't have a comeback. Had she stopped there, she'd have accomplished a lot, shaming him, making him feel like a naughty kid.But she didn't stop.

"All that's bad enough, Joe," she said, her hand now back on his arm. "But it goes beyond those things. What you did was criminal, a criminal act. Hindering an investigation. Producing false evidence. Withholding evidence. Lying to authorities. Need I go on? A prosecutor could add a dozen other charges, anything that tickles their fancy."

When he didn't respond, she squeezed his arm as hard as she could. "Joe," she said, "it's me, Edith, your friend. I'm not out to hurt you. I want to help."

"I know."

"I have to ask you a question."

"Go ahead."

"Did you write those letters in order to generate a sensational story for yourself, or—?"

"Or what?"

"Or did you write them in order to throw suspicion on someone else?"

"Why would I do that?"

"You'd do it if you were involved in the Jean Kaporis murder."

"Oh, God, Edith. That's absurd. Of course I didn't have anything to do with that. I may have made a mistake with the letters, but I'm no murderer."

"Why was Roberta at your brother's apartment today with a camera crew?"

He was jolted into an upright position. "Roberta here with a camera crew? I have no idea."

She placed her hands on the steering wheel and drummed her fingertips against it.

"Anything else?" Wilcox asked.

"A lot more, Joe. Tell me about your brother. My partner, Wade, failed to run a background check on Michael LaRue, but I initiated one today. He's been on the list of possible suspects in the Kaporis case, same with the stabbing of his neighbor in Franklin Park. That's where Colleen was killed, too."

"Michael is—"

"Michael is *what*?"

"You don't need to run a background on him, Edith. I'll give you one."

He told her about Michael's past, the murder of the neighbor girl, being judged insane, and his forty years in a mental hospital. He didn't look at her as he related these things in a flat, emotionless voice despite tears forming. When he was finished, he asked, "What do you intend to do, Edith?"

"I don't know," she replied honestly. "I have to do something. I can try to keep it within channels and away from the *Trib*. But you know as well as I do that it'll be leaked. Want my suggestion?"

"Go ahead."

"Level with Morehouse before he finds out from someone else. Maybe you can get him to run something about new evidence being uncovered pointing to different individuals having committed the murders. I don't know whether Morehouse and the *Trib* would be willing to publish something that vague, without naming you and citing the letters, but you can try."

"Yeah. I can try."

"The paper might be happy to cover it up to save face," she offered.

"Maybe."

"I have to admit, Joe, that I questioned the serial killer angle from the beginning. Two murders don't add up to serial killing. If you hadn't written the letters and just continued speculating, it wouldn't have mattered so much."

He managed a smile. "I think I'd better cancel the TV and radio appearances, Edith, and my meeting with the New York publisher."

She said nothing.

"And I want to talk with Roberta about what she was doing here today with Michael."

"Sure." She started the engine. "I'll drive you back to the *Trib*, but we'll have to talk again, more formal next time."

"I understand," he said. "No, I'm not going back to work. I think I'll head straight home. I want Georgia to hear it from me. Just drop me at my car."

"Of course. I'm sorry, Joe."

"Not nearly as sorry as I am, Edith. Thanks for breaking it to me this way, private, just the two of us. I appreciate it."

"Joe," she said as they neared the parking garage. "What about your brother? Do you think he might have had something to do with the murders?"

"I don't know."

"Did you write the letters at his place?" she asked.

His sigh was unmistakably affirmative.

To frame him? she wondered.

He was out of the car before she could ask.

THIRTY

Roberta Wilcox was at the studio screening the tape they'd recorded at Michael's apartment when Vargas-Swayze's call came in.

"Hi, Edith. What's the occasion?"

"Does there have to be an occasion for me to call?"

Roberta laughed. "No, of course not. Just surprised, that's all. We haven't spoken in a while. What's up?"

"I'm calling to ask you the same question."

Vargas-Swayze waited for Roberta's silence to end. "Just insanely busy," Roberta finally said.

"What's with your dad's brother, Michael?"

This time, the silence was broken by Roberta's audible, deep breath.

"I know you were at his place today with a camera crew," Vargas-Swayze said. "Does he have an interesting story to tell?"

"I don't know what you're talking about, Edith."

"Please, Roberta, don't insult me. If you're sitting on evidence in a murder case—make that plural—you're treading on thin ice." Roberta started to respond but Vargas-Swayze said, "And don't give me the shield law speech. I'm not impressed by it."

"Dad told you about Michael?" Roberta asked.

"In a sense. I know about your uncle's history, the murder of the young girl, the years in confinement, all of it. So let's not do this dance. What do you know about the letters?"

"What letters?"

"The ones allegedly written by the killer."

"What do I know? I know my dad received two of them, one at the office, one at home."

"Any idea who wrote them?"

Roberta guffawed, gathering courage. "Of course I don't know who wrote them," she said. "If I did, MPD would know, too. You don't think I'd hold back something like that—do you?"

"You're a reporter," Vargas-Swayze said.

"And a citizen," Roberta retorted. "And, I might add, a single young woman who happens to work in a media job. I'm not into being a victim."

Vargas-Swayze gave it a beat: "What sort of story are you doing with your uncle?"

"A—a human interest piece."

"Is he that interesting, aside from having killed someone and spending most of his adult life in a mental institution?"

"I really don't think that's any of your—"

"That depends," the detective said. "Look, Roberta, you have your job and I have mine. They don't have to be mutually exclusive. Helping us solve a couple of murders would give you a juicy inside scoop. So if there's anything you want to share with me, do it now. Once I hang up, all bets are off. We can be collaborators—or, we can butt heads. Your choice."

She could almost hear Roberta's mind working.

"I have to go, Roberta," Vargas-Swayze said.

"What?" she heard Roberta say to someone.

"Edith? I have to go, too. Can I get back to you?"

"Sure. But don't let much time pass, Roberta."

Vargas-Swayze recited her cell number and hung up.

Joe Wilcox didn't go directly home. He drove deliberately slowly, taking a long, meandering route, his mind racing, hurtling past major thoughts so fast that he couldn't linger long enough to process them. He pulled into a small parking area in Rock Creek Park and held his head in his hands, massaging his temples as though to knead clarity.

The conversation with Edith was a blur. It had happened so suddenly, so unexpectedly, that he'd been unable to formulate rational responses to her accusations. He'd acquiesced almost immediately, had admitted he'd written the letters without putting up a defense. He could have denied it, of course. He could have held firm and dismissed her charge, hung tough, challenged her to prove it, told her to put up or shut up. Bring it on!

But he hadn't. Her knowing about Michael had shocked him into inaction. She was right about the letters, although her assumption that he'd written them at Michael's apartment was nothing more than speculation. But what did it matter where he'd written them? His fingerprint was beneath the typed words, she'd said. Was that true, or was she lying? Cops lie all the time to get people to confess to something. He rubbed his temples harder. Think, damn it! It had to have been the fingerprint. Why else would she even imagine that he'd written the letters to himself? A stakeout at the house? Who was to say that the cops assigned to it hadn't fallen asleep, hadn't been distracted enough to miss someone other than the mailman and him going to the mailbox?

He'd reacted the way Michael had the morning Marjorie Jones was found dead in the berry patch. His brother hadn't denied what he'd done, aside from hiding in the closet and yelling, "I didn't do nothing!" But by the time he'd been dragged from the house, he was blubbering and saying he didn't mean to kill her and that it was a mistake and that he was very sorry and—

He envisioned facing Paul Morehouse, dreading that more than facing his wife. Georgia would be stunned by what he'd done but would stand by him, get over her shock and comfort him as she always had when things went poorly, when he was despondent and low. Morehouse wouldn't. Oh, he might feign concern and portray himself as a friend.

But there would be no real comforting from his editor and boss. The growling would get louder: "I don't have any choice but to take it upstairs, Joe," he would say, and he would—take it upstairs—where he, Joseph Carlton Wilcox, would join the ranks of other wayward journalists who'd created stories out of whole cloth, been disgraced, cited in J-schools across the country as a miscreant.

His thoughts went to the Press Club and his colleagues, whose friendship he treasured. They'd be nice to him initially, would slap him on the back, make a few jokes out of it, and then gradually and subtly avoid him as if his disgraced side might rub off on them. It didn't really matter, he knew, because he wouldn't step foot in the club again once word got out that he was a fraud, a media whore who'd sold out for self-gratification and fame—and yes, ultimately money. Maybe the esteemed club's by-laws would call for his expulsion despite being a member of long-standing. The shame . . .

Roberta!

What would he tell her? *How* would he tell her?

From the day she decided to pursue a career in journalism, he'd preached fidelity to the profession, citing examples of journalists who'd taken the high road. "You have only one thing as a journalist, Robbie," he'd said many times, "and that's your integrity and reputation. No story is worth compromising your ideals. You'll feel pressure from management, especially those on the advertising side, but you must resist it. If you're ever put in a position where you have to decide between honesty as a reporter and job security, go with honesty every time. You may suffer in the short term, but you'll be able to hold your head high, and even better opportunities will come your way."

He punched the top of his thigh so hard that it bruised him.

Do as I say, not as I do.

"Good God," he said within the confines of the car. "What have I done?" He was tempted to pray as he'd done after Michael's arrest, to ask for forgiveness and to pledge anything if the past weeks could be reversed. But the hypocrisy of that was too distasteful. He hadn't prayed, nor had he stepped into a church, for decades.

He placed his hands on the steering wheel and pushed himself back into his seat as hard as he could, forcing himself into an erect posture, and by extension stiffening his resolve. He started the car, pulled away and drove faster this time. A marked police cruiser sat in front of the house, part of the security detail Vargas-Swayze had arranged for. Wilcox waved at the officer, who returned a sloppy salute.

"Anybody home?" Wilcox called as he came through the front door. When there was no response, he said louder, "Georgia? Are you here?"

He walked into the den where she sat with her back to him. A single lamp cast the only light in the room. He came up behind her and placed his hands on her shoulders. "Hey," he said, "I'm home."

As she turned, light from the lamp caught the glistening on her cheeks. He came around the chair, fell to one knee, grabbed her hands, and asked, forgetting his own problem, "What's wrong, sweetheart? What's happened?"

"Mimi was here. She left a few minutes ago."

"Mimi Morehouse?"

"Yes."

She walked to the kitchen, her husband following. "Why was she here?" he asked. "What did she say that's got you so upset?" Mimi and Georgia had forged a friendship during Joe's tenure at the *Trib*, and it wasn't unusual for them to visit each other at their homes. But he'd never seen this sort of aftermath following a visit.

"They're getting a divorce," Georgia said, busying herself at the sink.

"That's news. Why?"

She turned, leaned back against the sink, and said, "He's been cheating on her for years."

The announcement didn't surprise Wilcox, although he had little specific knowledge of his editor's private life. Morehouse was always quick to comment when a pretty woman passed: "How would you like a weekend with that?" Or, "A romp in the sack with that would do wonders for my psyche." Lots of bravado talk but never a boast about a sexual conquest, which Wilcox admired. If Morehouse had enjoyed affairs outside his marriage, he'd always maintained a discreet silence.

"Mimi is seeking the divorce?" Joe asked.

Georgia nodded.

"Well, I'm sorry it's happening, but I have something to tell you."

"Joe," she said, as though not hearing him, "according to Mimi, Paul has had affairs with many women."

"I never had a hint of that," he said, realizing he was glad that having to deliver his sad message had been postponed by Morehouse's infidelities. "Look," he said, "I—"

"Joe," she said, urgency in her voice. "He was seeing the girl who was murdered at the paper."

"*Jean?*"

"Yes. Mimi found an e-mail address on his computer she didn't know he had. There were messages from that girl threatening to expose their affair if he didn't do certain things for her."

"What things?"

"Something to do with a job, a promotion."

He thought back to his breakfast with Jean Kaporis's father and stepmother. According to them, Jean had been seeing a man named Paul who, she'd told them, turned out to be married. Her father claimed she was devastated when she learned of his marital status, which didn't make sense. Surely she knew that Morehouse had a wife. Then again, it wasn't surprising that she would claim to her parents that she'd been duped; admitting to having knowingly slept with a married man wouldn't present an especially positive image to them.

"Joe," Georgia said, clasping and unclasping her hands, "do you think that he—?"

"Might have killed her? That's a hell of a thing to contemplate. Does Mimi intend to do anything with the information, aside from filing for divorce? Go to the police with it?"

"I don't know, Joe." She raised her eyes as though having been struck with a profound, horrible thought. "Oh, my God," she said, "if he did kill that poor girl, he could be the serial killer."

Wilcox went to her, wrapped his arms around her, and said, "Let's go in the den. I have something important to talk to you about."

"About Paul?"

"No. About me."

Her furrowed brow and tight lips mirrored her concern as they left the kitchen and sat side by side on the couch.

"I don't know where to begin," he said.

"Is something wrong?" she asked. "Are you all right. Is it about Roberta?"

"It's about me, Georgia, and something I've done."

She stared at him. Her face said, *Are you about to confess to having an affair, too?*

He spoke softly, surprised at how easily the words came, how cathartic it was to share his secret with the person closest to him in this world. She listened impassively, only the movement of her eyes reflecting her reaction. When he was done reciting the facts, he said, "This will end my career at the *Trib*, Georgia. It'll end my career in general."

"I love you," she said suddenly, touching his cheek.

It was the last thing he expected to hear from her, and it tore at him in a way that nothing else she might have said would have, no matter how angry or scornful. Tears welled up and spilled down his cheeks, tears of relief and regret, inadequacy and gratitude.

"There's more to it," he said after wiping his face with a handkerchief. "There's a legal problem, too."

He explained how having written the letters constituted a criminal act, possibly more than one.

"Edith wouldn't pursue that, would she?" Georgia asked.

"As a friend? No. But she's a cop, Georgia. Besides, it's not her decision. Once her superiors at MPD know the facts, it'll be out of her hands."

"We'll fight it, Joe. We'll get the best lawyers."

"Yeah. That's what we'll do. I'd better call Roberta and tell her before it gets out."

He headed for the phone and it rang in his hand.

"Dad? It's Roberta."

"Hi sweetheart. I was just about to call you."

"What's going on with Edith?"

"You've spoken with her?"

"Yes. She called. She said she knows about Michael, his past, everything. Why did you tell her?"

"It's a long story, honey, but I'll try to make it brief."

He gave her a condensed version of what he'd told Georgia.

"*You* wrote those letters?" she said.

"Afraid so."

"I thought—"

"You thought what?"

"Nothing. Dad, I'm going to have to—"

"Run with the story? Of course. I wouldn't expect otherwise."

"Please understand that—"

"Don't Robbie. Don't apologize. You're a journalist, a better one than I've turned out to be." He choked up. "I have to go. We'll get together and really hash this out. In the meantime, do what you must."

He heard, "I love—" as he hung up.

THIRTY-ONE

M ichael?"

"Ah, Robbie, my dear. How are you?"

"Fine. I—"

"How did I look on your tape?"

"Ah, fine. Just fine. Michael, will you be available in a couple of hours?"

"For my favorite and only niece? I'd cancel receiving my Academy Award for you."

"I need to see you, Michael."

"And so you shall. What time? Shall I make dinner?"

"No, that's not necessary."

"But you are free for dinner. I've come across a splendid bistro I just know you'd love."

"I have a few things to clean up here but I can be there in an hour. Say four?"

"I'll be awaiting your arrival, Robbie."

She went back to screening the tape. The cameraman, Carlos, poked his head into the screening room and asked, "How's it look?"

"Looks great," Roberta replied. "The kitchen stuff is a little rough, but we can cut around it."

He sat. "So, what's this all about?" he asked. "He's your uncle?"

"Yes."

"And he killed some girl?"

"Right again, Carlos. But I'm afraid I had the wrong slant on it. Look, I'll fill you in later, okay? I have to finish looking at this, and I have an appointment across town. Great job, my friend, as usual."

After speaking with her father, she'd had every intention of sharing with her boss the startling revelation that her own father, the *Trib*'s crack cops reporter, had forged the letters from the alleged serial killer and had sent them to himself. But as she considered that course of action, she decided to hold off, at least for a day. At best, the story wouldn't surface for at least twenty-four hours, and she wasn't anxious to be the one to break it. She knew the minute she'd hung up on that call that her posture as the hard-bitten investigative TV journalist would take a back seat to family. That her father had invited her to do her job, no matter how destructive it would be for him, hit her hard. Be a daughter, she told herself—at least for a day.

That same sense of humanity was behind her call to Michael.

She laughed out loud at how misguided her assumption had been. She was convinced that Michael had written the serial killer letters, which meant by extension that he was probably the killer. If that thesis had been correct, she was in the front row of a sensational story, not only the first reporter to be privy to the inside facts, but the person who'd solved the crime, heady stuff for a journalist her age. Awards galore. A book contract. A movie. A correspondent on 6o *Minutes*. Fame and fortune.

But she'd been wrong. Her father had obviously used Michael's typewriter to write the letters—which raised a question not so easily answered. *Why* had he done it?

The obvious answer was that he wanted to enhance his career, be the center of attention. It had taken her a few introspective minutes to conjure the other possibilities. Had he done it because he had evidence that Michael was indeed the serial killer, and hoped to choreograph his apprehension on his own terms, control the investigation, benefit from his involvement?

Or was he attempting to frame his brother?

That second possibility raised issues worthy of a psychology textbook. Could her father's hatred for Michael, based upon what he'd done more than forty years ago, been so pervasive that he would deliberately hand his only brother up on a sacrificial platter to society, punish him again for his youthful act? She couldn't accept that, no matter how deeply seated its origins might be. That her father had kept Michael a secret from her for all these years spoke volumes of his sense of shame. And while that might have been the wrong approach, it was understandable. He was flawed in some ways—and who wasn't?—but was not a man who would do such a thing. Impossible. No. He'd sought the sort of recognition that had eluded him over the course of his career, and had erred in how he'd pursued it. That had to be it. No other answer was possible.

She owed Michael an explanation, and an apology, and intended to deliver it to him that day.

THIRTY-TWO

Vargas-Swayze met with her boss, Bernie Evans, and laid out for him what she'd learned about the letters allegedly written by the so-called serial killer, and the background of Joe's brother, Michael Wilcox, aka Michael LaRue.

"Wilcox—Joe Wilcox—acknowledges he wrote them?" he said.

"Yes."

"What the hell was he looking for, his fifteen minutes of fame?"

She shrugged. "Either that or he was trying to frame his brother."

"Why would he do that?"

"I don't know—unless—"

He cocked his head.

"God, I have trouble even saying it—unless he was trying to shift focus from himself to someone else."

"Meaning *he* might be a murderer?"

"He had nothing to do with the McNamara murder, that's for sure. He was with me that night. But Jean Kaporis at the *Trib*? I just don't know, Bernie."

Evans rubbed his eyes and moved his mouth against the tightness in his jaw.

"Bernie," Edith said, "Joe Wilcox might have really screwed up by writing the letters, but he's no killer."

"Bring him in," Evans said.

"Is that really necessary? I mean, now?"

"Edith, you're a damn good cop. You might have broken this whole serial killer thing wide open. I know Wilcox is a friend, but good cops don't let that get in their way. If you'd prefer, I'll send someone else."

"No, no, I'll do it. You're right. I'm a good cop. Not to worry."

"Good. Now, let's talk about this brother with a past. Do you think he might have killed the two women?"

"He was at the *Trib* the night Kaporis was killed. He's killed before. They decided he was criminally insane. He's still a little odd, in a nice sort of way. There's the knifing of his neighbor in Franklin Park. That's where the McNamara girl got it, too. It's not far from where he lives. Wade had bad vibes about him. Sure, he's a suspect."

"Bring him in, too."

A crinkly smile crossed his face.

"What's funny?" she asked.

"We've got a couple of brothers, one who murders the girl from next door, the other who writes letters claiming they're from a serial killer. Maybe insanity runs in the family."

Vargas-Swayze stood. "Anything else?"

"Speaking of mental stress, how's your divorce coming?"

"Okay. Peter backed off with his stupid demands. With any luck, I'll be able to drop Swayze from my name pretty soon."

"It has a nice ring to it," he said, coming around his desk. " 'Vargas-Swayze.' Hyphenated names always sound, well, important. Nice necklace."

"Thanks," she said, fingering a large, copper pendant she'd recently bought at an Adams Morgan street fair.

She sat at her desk and ran through various approaches she might take with Wilcox.

Joe, how about coming with me to headquarters? Just a couple of questions about the letters. Nothing to worry about, but—

Joe, I hate to bother you with all that's on your mind, but I was wondering if we could have a little chat down at headquarters and—

Joe, you'll never believe this but—

She called the house. Wilcox answered on the first ring.

"Joe, it's Edith. Hate to bother you but—"

"Actually, I enjoy being bothered, Edith. It's better than talking to myself."

"I understand. Joe, I just came from a meeting with Bernie Evans."

"The Professor?"

"Yes, the Professor. He wants you to come in for questioning."

"Why am I not surprised?"

"I told him I'd arrange it with you. My suggestion is that you do it immediately."

"That's understandable."

"He wants me to bring in your brother, too."

"Michael? Why?"

"Obvious reasons. His history, proximity to the murders. We're not targeting him, but he's been on our suspect list for the Kaporis murder ever since we ran down everyone who was at the paper the night she was killed. Of course, we knew him as Michael LaRue. No idea he was your brother."

"Does he know that you know, Edith?"

"No."

"I'd like to be the one to tell him."

Her silence said she had a problem with that.

"As a favor?" he said.

"What about you, Joe? I assume you'll come in voluntarily."

He forced a laugh. "I'm not the type to go on the lam, Edith. Of course I'll show up."

"You should get a lawyer."

"I will. I still haven't told Paul Morehouse."

"What time do you want to come in?"

"Give me a few hours. What is it now, three? Six? Six thirty?"

"I'll wait for you here," she said.

"I'll ask Michael to come with me. Should be quite a show, a couple of foul-ball brothers showing up together at police headquarters."

"Joe."

"Yeah?"

"I'm putting myself on the line, letting you do it your way."

"And I appreciate it. Don't worry, we'll be there. If I have a problem with Michael, I'll let you know."

"I'm sorry, Joe."

"Hey, what's that saying? Life is what happens while you're making other plans? Sure as hell is true in my case. See you in a couple of hours. But no handcuffs or perp walk, huh?"

"No handcuffs or perp walk."

He found Georgia, who'd gone to their bedroom to rest.

"That was Edith," he said, sitting on the bed next to her. "I'm going to police headquarters to be questioned."

She bolted upright, her back pressed against the headboard. "Are they arresting you?"

"No, of course not. Just routine, I'm sure. I'm going to call Frank." Frank Moss had been their family attorney since handling the purchase of their house. "He's not a criminal attorney, but he knows plenty of them. I'm also calling Michael."

"Why?"

"They want to speak with him, too."

"About the letters?

"About the murders."

She grabbed his hand with surprising strength. "Joe, you don't think that—"

"That he killed those women? No, I don't. He's gotten drawn into this because of me. The least I can do is be there for him."

He left her and made his call to the attorney, giving him a thumbnail description of the dilemma in which he'd plopped himself. Moss said he'd meet him at First District headquarters. "Joe, say nothing. I'll handle it."

"I'm afraid I've already said too much, Frank."

"Just don't add to it."

He didn't mention that he would be bringing his brother with him. His own troubles had been difficult enough to get across in a short phone conversation.

Georgia joined him in the den as he was about to place his call to Michael.

"I'm coming with you," she said.

"No, you stay here. It'll be embarrassing enough without having my wife at my side."

"I don't care about embarrassment, Joe. I want to be there—at your side."

"Suit yourself."

Michael's answering machine picked up before he could get to the phone, and they had to wait for the outgoing message to end before speaking.

"It's Joe, Michael."

"Hello," Michael said.

"Michael, I won't get into the specifics right now, but I've done something wrong, seriously wrong, and it involves you."

"Oh, my, Joseph. You? Do something terribly wrong? I refuse to believe it."

"Believe it, Michael. I'm going to MPD headquarters in a few hours. They want you to come with me."

"Oh? About the serial killer?"

"In a sense. I wrote those letters myself."

"What letters?"

"The serial killer letters. I wrote them to myself, on your typewriter."

"Joseph!"

"Yeah, yeah, I know. Maybe I can get off with an insanity plea, too." The words tumbled out too fast to stop them. "Sorry. The point is that the police want to talk to both of us. I told them I'd bring you with me. That's better than having them show up at your door."

"I don't know what to say," Michael said. "Why did you do it? Were you trying to hurt me?"

"No, not at all. I was trying to become a big shot, an important person. That's why I did it. You've got to believe me."

"I don't see that I have any choice."

"Will you come with me? I told them six or six thirty. I'll pick you up at five thirty."

His voice broke. "I don't want any trouble, Joseph. I've had too much trouble in my life."

"There won't be any trouble, Michael. My attorney is meeting us there. If you need legal help, I'll pay for it. But I'm sure you won't. You'll come?"

"Yes, I'll come. Goodbye, Joseph."

Georgia returned from having changed clothes.

"You look great," he said. "Perfect outfit for a felon's wife."

"Stop it, Joe."

"I should dress up, too, in case the paparazzi are there."

"You look fine. Michael is coming?"

"Uh-huh. We're picking him up at five thirty."

"What about Paul?" she asked.

"I dread that call more than anything else," he replied, "but I'd better make it."

"Will you mention Mimi and what she told me?"

"No. The fact that he was having an affair with Jean Kaporis doesn't mean he killed her." His words didn't match what he was thinking. While it was unthinkable for him to cast Morehouse into the role of murderer, that possibility had been swirling in his brain ever since hearing about Mimi's allegation. But that's all it was, an allegation from a wounded wife.

He picked up the phone and dialed Morehouse's direct line.

"Paul, it's Joe."

"Where are you?" Morehouse asked, gruffly.

"At home. We have to meet."

"Yeah, that would be nice. Do you have something for the paper tomorrow? Anything new about the letters?"

Wilcox strained not to laugh. "As a matter of fact, there is something new on that front, Paul."

"Like what?"

"That's why we have to meet. I have an—ah—an appointment at six. Where will you be this evening?"

"Here until eight or nine. I have an appointment, too, later. What's up? You sound strange."

"Must be an allergy. I'll call you when I'm finished with my six o'clock and see if we can get together before your date." *Was it a date?* he wondered. Did he have a young woman's bed into which to climb later that night? A vision of Morehouse and the lovely Jean Kaporis making love came and went. It wasn't a pretty picture.

At four thirty, Joe and Georgia left the house and got into one of their matching Toyota Camrys, one gray, one burgundy.

"No matter what happens," she said, "we'll get through it together."

"Thank you," he said, starting the engine and backing into the street. "Thank you very much."

THIRTY-THREE

The buzzer sounded in Michael's apartment.

"Robbie?" he said into the intercom.

"Yes."

He was waiting in the hall as she came through the front door. He extended his arms and she readily accepted his hug.

"Come in, come in," he said, stepping aside.

Music from his stereo filled the apartment, a solo jazz guitarist playing a song in three-quarter time.

"Joe Pass?" she asked pleasantly, pleased that she now had a jazz name to offer.

"No. Martin Taylor. He's Scottish. Brilliant."

"He sounds just like you."

"I can only wish. It is such a pleasure to have you visit, Robbie," he said, turning down the volume of the CD, one of six in the multiple CD player. "You look as beautiful as ever."

"Michael," she said, ignoring the compliment, "I have something very important to tell you."

He held up his hand. "I know you do, Robbie, and I am anxious to hear it. But not here."

Her puzzled expression prompted him to continue.

"How much time do you have?" he asked.

"I have all evening. I'm off tonight. But—"

"Splendid. Come." He grabbed her hand and pulled her to the door, opened it, and led her to the building's foyer.

"What are you doing, Michael?" she asked, laughing.

His answer was to propel her down the walkway to a shiny black convertible sports car, the top down. He opened the passenger door. "Get in," he said.

"Is this yours?" she asked, sliding onto the red leather seat.

"For the moment," he replied, coming around and getting behind the wheel. "I ran out and rented it for this occasion."

"What occasion?"

A woman's voice called, "Michael?"

He turned to see Carla approaching.

"I'm just leaving," he said to her, his tone not pleasant.

"I told you I was stopping by," Carla said, looking at Robbie and the car. "Did you buy this?"

"No. Excuse me, Carla, but we must be going."

Carla glared at Roberta. "A new friend?" she said to him.

"This is my niece," he said.

"Yes, I'm sure," Carla said.

He left her standing on the sidewalk as he turned the ignition key and the engine rumbled to life. He slipped the manual transmission into gear and drove away.

"A girlfriend?" Roberta asked, looking back at the bewildered woman.

"No."

Was he angry at the question? He sounded it.

"Michael," she insisted, "you must tell me why we're doing this."

He glanced at her, smiled, and said loudly, "I have found the most charming bistro not far out of the city. It has divine food, a lovely outdoor terrace, and is surprisingly moderate in price."

"I didn't come for dinner," she said, her words slipping away in the wind and cacophony of traffic sounds, her auburn hair swirling about her face. "I wanted to tell you something—in person."

"About the letters," he shouted, his laugh loud.

"You—?"

He removed his right hand from the wheel and waved it in front of her. "Not now," he said, his voice having lost its lightheartedness. "Not now!"

She fell silent as he wove through traffic, driving fast, downshifting, accelerating, changing lanes with sudden abandon, causing other drivers to honk at him, or worse.

"Michael, please slow down," she said.

"Frightened?" he asked, sounding as though he enjoyed her discomfort.

"Slow down," she said, more firmly this time.

He did, and she said nothing else until he'd crossed the Arlington Memorial Bridge, skirted the town of Arlington, and drove down a narrow road to a break between stone walls. He went through it and followed a gravel driveway to the front of a redbrick, one-story building with white shutters flanking the door and window boxes spilling over with red roses. Michael departed the car with great flourish, opened her door, bowed, and took her hand to help her out.

"This is it?" she asked.

"Yes. This is it! Ask me how I found it."

"All right," she said. "How did you find it?"

"I met the owner at a party where I happened to play a few tunes on my guitar. He offered me a job performing on the weekends."

"You said you never play in public."

"I succumbed in this case."

"That's wonderful. Are you going to do it?"

"I'm considering it. The owner brought me here a few times and I fell in love with the place. You will, too."

They entered the restaurant where a young man with multiple earrings in one earlobe, wearing black slacks and a loose fitting white overshirt, warmly greeted them. "Michael," he said, "ready to begin your performing career?"

"No, Tony," Michael said. "This night, I am strictly a guest. May I present my lovely niece, Roberta Wilcox, of television fame."

The owner took Robbie's hand. "I see you all the time on TV," he said. "And this talented fellow is your uncle?"

"He certainly is," she said.

They were led to a terrace behind the building where six tables were set for dinner. It was a lovely late afternoon and early evening, a gentle breeze creating the perfect temperature for outdoor dining. Once seated, the host asked whether they wanted drinks before dinner, or the wine list.

"A light dry, white wine," Michael said. "Your discretion."

"Happy, my dear?" Michael asked after the host had placed menus before them.

"Michael," Roberta said, "when I said I had something to tell you, you immediately referred to the letters. What do you know about them?"

"That your father, my esteemed brother, wrote them on my type-writer and sent them to himself, claiming they were from the monster stalking young women on the streets of Washington."

"How do you know?"

"He called me earlier today. I'd say he's gotten himself in a deep pile of doo-doo, as a former president was fond of eloquently saying, or so I've read."

Their wine arrived, and Michael went through the requisite ritual of judging its worth with a sniff and a sip. "Fine," he told the waiter, who poured. Roberta raised her glass to his. "To life," he said.

"Michael," she said, "I have a confession to make."

"Oh? It sounds very serious, and I rush to assure you that I am not your friendly neighborhood priest. My confessional has been closed for years." He noted that she'd laid her cell phone on the table. "No cell phones allowed," he said. "House policy."

She turned it off and returned it to her purse.

"That's better," he said. "People's public use of cell phones is infuriatingly uncivilized, don't you agree?"

"Force of habit for me," she said.

"Of course," he said, "but I doubt there will be a terrorist attack on the White House while we dine."

She smiled, wine glass held in both hands, her focus on its shimmering contents. "I believed you wrote those letters, Michael," she said, still avoiding his eyes. "I thought you were the serial killer."

She looked at him. His face was hard, taut, small muscles working his cheeks.

"I'm sorry for having thought such a thing," she said.

"The documentary?" he said. "Was it because you intended to have captured the killer on videotape?"

"Yes. I'm ashamed to admit it, but—"

"It would have been quite a feather in your pretty cap, yes?"

She nodded.

He picked up his menu. "I highly recommend the fried shrimp," he said. "They serve it with honeyed walnuts and a delicious lemon mayonnaise. The rib-eye steak is quite good, too."

"Michael, I—"

"I did not kill that young woman at the newspaper, Robbie. I'm afraid your journalistic scoop will have to be put on hold. More wine?"

❧

"Damn it!" Joe Wilcox said after returning to the car where Georgia waited with the engine running.

He'd knocked on Michael's door. When there was no answer, he let himself in with his passkey, finding the apartment empty except for Maggie, the cat, who greeted him with a version of "meow" and a rub against his leg.

"He promised he'd be here," Wilcox told his wife as he got behind the wheel. "And I promised Edith he'd show up."

"Maybe he ran out for a few minutes," she said, checking her watch. "We're a few minutes early. Let's wait. I'm sure he'll be back."

Twenty minutes later, Wilcox muttered a string of curses as he drove away. They were almost to the First Precinct building when Georgia said, "Michael must be terrified."

"Of what?"

"Of having his history made public, and people wondering whether he might have killed again."

"Disappearing won't help him," Joe said, pulling into a driveway that ran alongside the precinct, and parking in a marked spot.

"It's reserved," Georgia said.

"What are they going to do, arrest me for illegal parking? Come on before I'm tempted to disappear, too."

Vargas-Swayze was at the front desk when they entered, and motioned for them to follow her into the precinct's recesses. "Hi, Georgia," she said, opening a door into an interrogation room. "I'm sorry for this." She asked Joe, "Where's your brother?"

"I don't know," Wilcox said, slumping in a straight-back wooden chair. "He said he'd come with me, but when we got to his apartment, he was gone."

"That's foolish of him," the detective said.

Their attorney, Frank Moss, arrived, escorted by a uniformed officer from the front desk. "Sorry I'm late," Moss said, breathing heavily. "Damn traffic this time of day."

"Anyone want some station house coffee?" Vargas-Swayze asked. There were no takers. "Excuse me," she said, and left the room.

⚘

She went to Bernie Evans's office where he was meeting with detectives Jack Millius and Ron Warrick.

"Wilcox is here?" Evans asked after she'd pulled up a chair.

"Yes," Vargas-Swayze replied. "His wife is with him, and his attorney. The brother never showed."

She recounted what Wilcox had told her about Michael's failure to appear.

"Why was it left to Wilcox to bring his brother in?" Evans asked, his displeasure not lost on her.

"I thought it was the best way," she replied defensively.

"Looks like it wasn't—the best way," Evans said.

"Do you want to talk to Joe?" she asked.

"Yes, I do. But first, I think you should hear what Jack and Ron have come up with."

"We've been talking to people at Franklin Park, Edith, about the

Grau knifing," Millius said. "We came up with a live one this afternoon."

"Good," she said.

"We have an eyewitness to the killing," Warrick said.

"Even better," she said.

"It was the neighbor, LaRue."

Her heart sunk. She forced her thoughts into a semblance of order and asked, "This eyewitness knows LaRue?"

"Right on," Millius said. "He's an old guy who hangs around the park, downs too much vino, I think, but pretty clear-headed most of the time. He was there when the McNamara girl got it, too. Saw nothing. He says he knows LaRue from when LaRue would come to the park, usually with a book to read, or wearing one of those Walkman kinds of things."

"I-Pod," Warrick corrected.

"Whatever. This witness says LaRue always had some jazz type music playing. He thinks it was a guitar, only it might have been a banjo, he says."

"And he was there the night Grau was killed?" she asked, trying to maintain calm.

Warrick nodded and continued consulting a notepad. "He says — by the way, his name is Olson, Swedish I guess — he says that he was sitting against a tree —"

"Thinking great thoughts," Millius said, laughing.

". . . sitting against a tree when LaRue and Grau come into the park. He says they were arguing, and that Grau got pretty nasty, lots of four-letter words directed at LaRue, claims he called him a fag and a pervert, a sicko, stuff like that. It got pretty heated, according to Mr. Olson. Next thing he knows, LaRue is running from the park. Olson gets up from where he's sitting and goes to the bench where he finds Grau bleeding to death."

"He called it in?" Vargas-Swayze asked.

"No. He says he left the park, too, and told somebody on the street that a guy was dying there."

"Why did he never come forward?" she asked.

"Why else? He was afraid he'd get in trouble. He's got a rap sheet, mostly nuisance stuff, public urination, panhandling."

"We worked him pretty good this afternoon," Millius said. "The guy's a vet, like Grau was. We told him it was his patriotic duty to help solve the murder of a fellow vet, strike a blow against terrorism. He puffed up his chest and agreed."

"And you don't have any doubts about his story?" Vargas-Swayze asked, glancing at Evans, who'd listened quietly, chair tilted back, hands behind his head.

"It plays," Evans said, coming forward. "You have no idea, Edith, where Mr. LaRue is at the moment?"

She shook her head.

"Put out an APB," he instructed the other detectives, "and get over and stake out his apartment. Ask around. Maybe somebody knows where he went."

After they'd left the office, Evans said to Vargas-Swayze, "I'm disappointed in you, Edith."

"For good reason. I wanted to do Joe Wilcox a favor. I guess I'm not as good a cop as you thought."

"No, Edith, you're still a good cop. I figure the hassle you've been having with your hubby has occupied your mind. Just don't let it happen again." He noticed that the office door was open. "Close that, huh?"

He slid papers across the desk. "Take a look at these."

"They're copies of e-mails with everything deleted except the messages," she said. "How did you get them?"

"Dropped off in an envelope at our front door. You know Morehouse at the *Trib*, right?"

"Not well, but—according to these, he'd been having an affair with Jean Kaporis at the paper."

"That's what it looks like. I'd say this gal was pretty mad at him, judging from what she wrote, making demands of him, threatening to tell his wife. Nasty stuff. That might have made him pretty mad, too."

"I don't know," she said.

"You don't know what?"

"After finding out that the letters that supposedly came from the serial killer were phonies, I'm questioning the authenticity of everything."

"These ring true to me. You know his wife?"

"Mimi Morehouse. I've met her a few times at Joe Wilcox's house."

"They get along, Mr. and Mrs. Morehouse?"

"Beats me."

"My guess is that the proverbial woman scorned dropped these off, which most likely means his wife. You agree?"

"Makes the most sense."

"All right," he said, standing, "we've got plenty to do. Time for a talk with your buddy Wilcox. Maybe he can give us a lead on where his brother might have gone. And then let's find Mr. Morehouse and ask a few pointed questions. This could turn out to be our lucky day, not his."

⁓

Georgia Wilcox had tried unsuccessfully for the second time to reach their daughter on her cell phone. "It's not like her to turn it off," she said, snapping closed her phone's cover as Vargas-Swayze and Bernard Evans entered the room. After Evans had been introduced to Georgia and reestablished that he and Joe had met numerous times before, the head detective said, "So, Joe, why not lay it all out for us and get it over with."

"One second, detective," attorney Moss said. "Is Mr. Wilcox being charged with a crime?"

"Not yet," Evans answered.

Moss turned to Wilcox. "My best advice, Joe, is to say nothing. You're not obligated to answer his questions."

"I'm sure that's true, Frank, and I appreciate the advice. But there's no reason for me to not tell what happened. I'd feel better doing it."

"As you wish."

Wilcox didn't attempt to mitigate what he'd done, offered no excuses except that he'd lost his ego boundaries and had tried to be something he wasn't, someone important in his profession. With his hand firmly in Georgia's grasp, he laid it all out for Evans, point by point, misguided action by misguided action. "That's about it," he said after the sad tale had been told.

"Okay," Evans said. "Next. Where's your brother, Michael?"

"I don't know," Wilcox replied, and told of Michael's failure to show up at his apartment.

"We've put out an all-points for him," Evans said. "No way you can contact him, let him know that it's in his best interest to come in voluntarily?"

"No. I really don't know much about Michael's life here in Washington, who he knows, where he goes."

"You've put out an all-points on Mr. Wilcox's brother?" the attorney said. "Is *he* charged with a crime?"

"We think he might be responsible for a knife murder in Franklin Park," Evans replied.

Joe and Georgia Wilcox looked at each other.

"Will Joe be charged with a crime for writing those letters?" Georgia asked.

Evans ignored the question as his cell phone sounded. He listened without response, thanked the caller, and motioned for Vargas-Swayze to accompany him outside.

"What's up?" she asked when they were alone.

"That was Millius," Evans said. "He and Warrick are over at the brother's apartment building. A resident there, an older woman—Warrick says she's the apartment snoop—says she saw the brother leave in a fancy black sports car. He had somebody with him."

She waited for more.

"The old lady says she recognized the woman who drove off with him from television." He nodded toward the closed door to the interrogation room. "Your friend's daughter, Roberta Wilcox."

Vargas-Swayze exhaled noisily.

"You said she'd been there with a camera crew filming a documentary."

"Right. Did the woman get a plate number?"

"No. Just said it was a shiny black convertible with the top down. Warrick says the woman was afraid Ms. Wilcox would catch a cold. I like older women. They worry about the right things. Go back in with the Wilcoxes. Take a formal statement, then let them go."

"Bernie, will Joe be charged with a crime?" she asked.

"We'll see. I'd like to think I worry about the right things, too. I'll talk with someone at the DA's office. Meantime, let's take care of Mr. LaRue and Mr. Morehouse. Check in with me later."

After taking a formal statement from Wilcox, to the attorney's chagrin, Vargas-Swayze told them they were free to go. She escorted them to the lobby where Moss told Wilcox that he'd be in touch with the name of a criminal lawyer, and left.

"There's something I have to tell you," the detective told Joe and Georgia.

"What?" Georgia asked.

"According to detectives who went to Michael's apartment building, he was seen leaving in a black convertible sports car."

"I didn't know he had a car," Joe said.

"We'll check rental agencies," Vargas-Swayze said. "There's more."

The Wilcoxes waited.

"Roberta was with him."

THIRTY-FOUR

Over the course of his career in *The Washington Tribune*'s news-room, Paul Morehouse had heard every four-letter word known to man. But what he was hearing this evening on the phone from his wife rivaled it. The slight, ordinarily demure woman let loose with a string of invective that would make any contemporary comedian proud.

She paused to breathe.

"Look," he said, "I know you're upset, but we can work this out."

" '*Work this out?*' " she screamed, and started down the list of classic forbidden words again, adding a few of her own invention.

He had no choice but to continue listening or to hang up. He chose to listen, glancing nervously into the newsroom through his window and hoping her shrill, piercing voice wasn't reaching others' ears.

He'd expected the tirade; she'd thrown in his face that morning her discovery of the e-mails, sending him from the house in search of refuge at the newspaper with a sense of dread. It was the dread that trumped other emotions at that moment as she growled, "Did you kill that woman?"

"What?" His exaggerated shock sounded exactly that, exaggerated, and false.

"Jean Kaporis! Did you kill her?"

"Oh, Jesus, Mimi, come on. Look, I made a mistake, that's all. I'm sorry. I—"

"Tell that to the police, you lying bastard!"

It sounded as though she'd destroyed the phone while hanging up.

He was pondering what steps to take next when Gene Hawthorne knocked on his door.

"Not now!" Morehouse shouted.

Hawthorne opened the door.

"I said—"

"You have to hear this, Paul," the brash, young towheaded reporter said.

"What?"

Hawthorne closed the door behind him, leaned on the desk, and said, "I just got off the phone with a source at MPD."

"Yeah?" Morehouse said, his mind elsewhere.

"A *good* source," Hawthorne said. He lowered his voice and leaned closer. "Joe Wilcox is there."

"So?"

"He's there, Paul because—" It was almost a whisper now. "Because *he wrote those letters.*"

"What letters?"

Hawthorne stepped back, a smug smile on his face.

"Those letters?" Morehouse said. "The serial killer letters?"

"That's right. Joe wrote the letters. He's a phony."

"Why the hell would he do that?" the gruff veteran editor asked aloud.

"The police are searching for his brother, too," said Hawthorne.

"What brother? Joe doesn't have a brother."

"He sure as hell does, Paul. They're looking for him in connection with the knifing in Franklin Park. Rudolph Grau, the brother's neighbor."

"Are you sure?" Morehouse asked. "About the letters?"

"It's a good source, Paul. Want me to follow up on it?"

"Yeah. No. I'll have to run this by upstairs. Jesus. You're positive?"

"Like I said—"

"Keep it to yourself, huh?" Morehouse said, getting up and taking his suit jacket from an antique clothes tree that had been a gift from Mimi. Again to Hawthorne: "You tell nobody about this until I say so. Hear me?"

"Absolutely."

Hawthorne left, and Morehouse placed a call to the executive suite where he told a secretary that it was urgent that he see the publisher immediately. She checked, came back on the line, and said, "He's in a meeting, but should be free in fifteen minutes."

"Good. Thanks."

Of the many things Morehouse admired about himself, it was his ability to remain calm and collected under fire that he treasured most. He silently reminded himself of this as he realized he was about to come unraveled. "Steady goes it," he said aloud. "Easy, easy."

A clock on the wall said it was nearly time to go upstairs. He rose from behind his desk and took steps toward the door, but the ringing of his private line stopped him. Was it Mimi again? If so, he wouldn't answer. Unsure of what to do, he again reminded himself to calm down and to think things through.

He picked up the receiver.

"Paul Morehouse?" the woman asked.

"Yeah. Who's this?"

"Detective Vargas-Swayze, MPD."

His voice wasn't as convincing as he'd hoped. "What can I do for you, detective?"

"We'd like to speak with you."

"About what?"

"If you'd rather not have us come to your office, we can agree to meet someplace else," she said.

"What's it all about?" he repeated.

"We'll get into that when we meet. Your office? Ten minutes?"

"Ten minutes? I won't be here. I'm on my way to a meeting." Vargas-Swayze, he thought. Joe Wilcox's friend. "Is this about Joe Wilcox?"

"No, sir, it's about you. We can bring you in for questioning, or we can do it at the newspaper. Your choice, but you'll have to make a choice—now."

"Look," he said, "I have this meeting. It's important. I don't have any reason to play your game, detective. If you want to speak with me, call my attorney." He rattled off the name and number.

"Okay," Vargas-Swayze said from where she stood on the sidewalk in front of the *Tribune* Building. With her were two other detectives and three uniformed officers. She cut the connection and instructed the uniformed men to cover any exits from the building other than the main one. To the detectives: "Let's go."

They entered the building and flashed their IDs at the private security guard at the desk. "What floor is Paul Morehouse on?" she asked.

He told her, adding, "I'll call his extension and let him know you're here."

"No you won't," she said, and asked one of the officers to remain at the desk. "We like surprises."

THIRTY-FIVE

". . . and what do you think will happen to your father?" Michael asked Roberta. They were the only customers on the restaurant's terrace. Darkness had begun to set in; a flickering candle on the table cast flattering light on her face.

"I don't know," she said. "If it's true—and my God, I wish it weren't—he'll be disgraced as a journalist."

He saw wetness form in her eyes and placed his hand on hers. "There, there," he said. "Even if it is true, and it seems that it is—after all, he's admitted it—I'm sure time will heal the wounds. Of course, it's in his favor that he's coming to the end of what has been a rewarding career. It would be worse if he were young and starting out."

"Maybe not," she said. "At least he could claim youthful indiscretion."

"You mustn't be hard on him, Robbie."

"Another confession," she said. "I keep worrying what impact it will have on me and my reputation."

Espressos arrived at the table along with a slice of key lime pie to share. He raised his small porcelain cup. "To an evening of confessions," he said.

She touched his cup with hers.

"May I make a suggestion?" he asked.

"Of course."

"I suggest you use your cell phone now and place a call to your TV station."

"Why?"

"To capture on videotape what I am about to say."

Her stare was blank. "I don't understand."

"Just do what I say, Robbie. Call your station and arrange for one of your crews to come here, just as you did at my apartment."

Instead of asking more questions, she pulled her phone from her purse and pressed the number coinciding with the station's programmed number. An intern answered. Roberta asked to be put through to her boss, who came on the line.

"What's up, Robbie?" he asked. "It's your night off."

"I need a crew," she said.

"What for? What have you got?"

"I'm not sure," she said, "but I have a feeling it's important."

"Where are you?"

She placed her hand over the mouthpiece and asked Michael, who sat calmly across from her, a small smile on his lips, for the address. He answered by pushing a pack of matches to her on which the restaurant's address was printed. She read it into the phone.

"I hope this is worth it," her boss said. "We're stretched thin tonight."

"Just send somebody," she said, and ended the conversation.

She said to Michael, "I wish you'd tell me what's going on."

"In due time, when your friends arrive. In the meantime, let us enjoy the evening. I believe an after-dinner drink is in order." He motioned for the waiter and ordered two of their best cognacs. As the waiter walked away, Michael stopped him with, "And please ask Tony to join us."

"Excuse me," he said to Roberta as he left the table and disappeared inside the restaurant. He returned to the terrace a minute later carrying his guitar case and amplifier, which had been in the car's small trunk.

Roberta's heart sunk. Had he asked for a camera crew to record him playing? If so, she would have a very angry boss.

He read her concern. "Not to fear, Robbie," he said. "I assure you there's more to having your colleagues here with camera and microphone than music. However—"

The restaurant's owner appeared.

"Ah, Tony, thank you."

"I thought you said you weren't playing," Tony said.

"Only a song or two for my lovely niece, and for the cameras."

"Cameras?"

"A crew from Ms. Wilcox's television station will be arriving shortly. The publicity for you and your fine establishment will be welcome, I'm sure." He looked about. "Ah, an outlet. Perfect." He plugged in the amplifier, used a patch cord to connect the guitar to the amp, adjusted the controls, and strummed a few chords.

Tony looked quizzically at Roberta, whose slight shrug of her shoulders indicated she knew as little as he did. The owner walked away, leaving Michael and Roberta alone. Their drinks were served.

"I know you're confused, dear," Michael said, cupping the snifter in his hands to impart warmth to the drink, "but soon you'll know why I asked for this moment to be recorded for posterity. Did you enjoy the ride in my flashy little car?"

"I'm not sure enjoy is a word I'd use," she said, pleasantly, her mind trying to make sense of everything that had occurred. "You drove too fast for me to have enjoyed it."

"My apologies," he said. "There were many things I yearned for during my forty years of captivity. One of them was to be behind the wheel of such a car." He laughed. "Of course, I envisioned myself racing along a winding road through some bucolic countryside, the top down, the wind stinging my face, my cares lost in the exhaust. But as things developed this day, I thought I'd better experience my dream in less pastoral surroundings. Life is so fleeting, Robbie. One has to grab the moment or lose it forever."

As though not expecting a response, he began playing. "Let's see," he said, "what song would be appropriate to the moment? I know." He launched into a melody. " 'You and the Night and the Music,' " he announced, "by Dietz and Schwartz. How appropriate."

Her cell phone on the table rang.

"Hello?"

"Roberta, it's Mom. We've been trying to reach you. Are you all right?"

"I'm fine."

"That music—where are you?"

"Mom, I'm fine. I'll call you back as soon as I'm finished."

Her father replaced Georgia on the phone. "Are you with Michael?" he demanded.

"Yes. I have to go. I'll—"

"Roberta, listen to me. Michael is wanted for murder. He killed his neighbor in Franklin Park."

"I'll call later," Roberta said, shutting off the phone.

The music had drawn diners to the terrace from inside the restaurant, joined by the owner and two waiters. By the time Michael had reached the song's bridge, the two-person television crew arrived. Roberta motioned them to come to the table. As Michael continued playing, she got up and whispered into the cameraman's ear, "Just start shooting."

The camera and microphone, which the sound tech dangled over Michael on the end of a boom, captured every note. A descending arpeggio, and a resounding chord, ended the performance. He looked up at the TV crew, smiled, and said, "I have something to say."

Roberta instructed the cameraman to come around behind her and to focus on Michael's face. With the microphone dangling above his head, just out of frame, Roberta said, "What is it you want to say, Michael? Is it about the death of your neighbor, Mr. Grau?"

His face lit up. "You know," he said, "but why should I be surprised? You're as bright as you are beautiful."

"Tell me about it," she said in her best interviewing voice, soft and comforting, her you-can-trust-me-and-tell-me-everything voice.

He started to say something but stopped, as though having been struck by an important afterthought. He looked into the camera and said, "We are sitting on the terrace of one of the loveliest restaurants in the

Washington area, owned by the erudite Tony Whitaker. You must try it some time. The food is exquisite, the service impeccable." He went on to give its address, and read the number for reservations off the matchbook cover.

Roberta couldn't help but smile, and made a mental note to try and retain the plug in the finished piece.

"You were saying something about Mr. Grau's death. He was your neighbor."

"Yes, he was, a belligerent sort, an alcoholic. I didn't mind those things. But he became so abusive. When he found out that I'd been in a mental institution for forty years, the result of my having murdered a young girl when I was a teenager, he held it over my head, threatened to tell the world, the other neighbors—everyone. I was even willing to overlook those threats. But when he made sexual advances toward me, using his threats as blackmail, I wasn't able to control my anger. I offer this not as an excuse for having killed him, but simply as an explanation for my actions."

"Why are you telling me this, Michael?" Roberta asked. "Why have you chosen to tell this on television?"

"To ask for your forgiveness, Roberta. In the interest of full disclosure, I must tell your audience that I am your uncle, and that my brother, Joseph Wilcox, is an outstanding reporter on *The Washington Tribune*. Revelations will emerge about him and certain actions he chose to take which involved me, and the serial killer alleged to be roaming the streets of Washington, D.C., preying on young women. Forgive him, as I ask to be forgiven."

The camera and tape recorder rolled as Michael continued with his confession. Roberta said little, injecting only an occasional question when the his flow of words flagged. Everyone standing in the open French doors witnessed the bizarre interview being conducted on a lovely night on the terrace of a restaurant just across the Potomac from the nation's capital, where young women had been installing extra locks on their apartment doors and windows, and every man was viewed with suspicion.

When he was finished, and the camera and tape recorder had been shut off, he said to Roberta, "Don't give me too much credit, Robbie, for having the courage to come forward like this. I would not have had I not known that the police wanted to question me again about the murder. Your father was to pick me up at my apartment and bring me to their headquarters. I would have confessed to them, I know, but decided that if my deed was to become public, the least I could do was to give my favorite and only niece the exclusive story."

His words reached one of Roberta's ears. The other was pressed to her cell phone as she called her boss at the station to tell him she had a sensational story, every bit of it caught on tape, and that she would be there with the crew as soon as possible. She was about to leave when Michael said, "What about the police, Robbie? Must I call them myself?"

"No," she said. "I will."

And she did.

THIRTY-SIX

In the Weeks that Followed

No one in Kankakee, Illinois, would have believed a half-century ago that the Wilcox family would become famous. Of course, there had been the notoriety when Michael Wilcox, older of two sons, went on trial for having killed a neighbor girl and was found not guilty by reason of insanity. But that was a regional story and was quickly forgotten once Michael was put away in a mental institution, presumably for good, and the rest of the family had dispersed or died.

But that quickly changed in 2005 when the first of many news reports reverberated around the nation. *Washington Tribune* reporter Gene Hawthorne wrote the lead story for his paper. It appeared not on the front page of the Metro section, but on page one of the paper itself. It was syndicated by the *Trib* to sister papers, and the wire services ran with it, too, as did cable news channels and network newscasts.

Hollywood quickly took notice and a bidding war erupted for the screen rights. It had, as a Hollywood columnist wrote, "All the trappings of the ultimate family saga: sex, greed, betrayal, ambition, failure, and success." All it lacked was drugs, which didn't keep some tabloids from speculating that Michael Wilcox had been high when he knifed Rudolph Grau, his neighbor, to death in a Washington, D.C., park.

The arrest of *Tribune* Metro editor Paul Morehouse for the murder of staffer Jean Kaporis was big news, too, but was nothing compared to the Wilcox chronicle. Hawthorne also wrote those stories, which had a ready and anxious readership in D.C. He duly reported that Morehouse pleaded not guilty at his arraignment, although he pointed out that the MPD had uncovered additional evidence to go with information provided by Morehouse's estranged wife, Mimi Morehouse, who had sued for divorce citing multiple adulteries.

The revelation that the letters allegedly written by Washington's serial killer had been a hoax brought a collective sigh of relief to the city. TV and radio talk shows across the nation booked media pundits and college journalism professors, who decried what Joe Wilcox had done, condemning him for further eroding the public's faith in its media. They frequently evoked the names of legendary figures in journalism as examples of integrity and independence, and portrayed sellouts like Joe Wilcox as a rare and warped aberration who gave the media an unwarranted black eye.

The Washington Tribune took a double hit. One of its top editors was a murderer, and its best cops reporter was a liar and forger. Management did everything possible to put a positive spin on things, citing the paper's long and distinguished history as a first-class newspaper whose corporate motto, Ethics First, would never be compromised by the wayward acts of a few.

While Hawthorne's stories captivated those who still got their news from the printed page, Roberta Wilcox almost instantly became the most talked about broadcaster in Washington. There it was, a murder confession on tape, told exclusively to her by this madman, who was her uncle to boot, who obviously should never have been released from custody, another example of dismal failure on the part of mental health professionals and state legislatures. Members of congress seeking an issue called for new, tougher legislation to keep "the nuts" where they belonged, off the streets and safely behind bars.

Roberta Wilcox's star became brighter and farther-reaching. She was booked on myriad talk shows where she deflected questions about her father by pointing to his notable and long career as a journalist, and tearfully saying that he was a wonderful, loving father who would always have her unyielding love and respect. Her father rarely watched his daughter on those shows. He went into seclusion at the house, seldom venturing out and taking only selected phone calls. His attorney, Frank Moss, negotiated on his behalf with the *Tribune* and managed to preserve his client's pension. Together with his vested 401K and eventual Social Security, money would not be a pressing problem for Joe and Georgia, provided they didn't decide to live the high life. Criminal charges against Wilcox were never brought, which Moss proudly pointed to as an example of his lawyering skills, not aware that the district attorney hadn't planned to file charges anyway after pressure from MPD's Bernard Evans on behalf of Detective Edith Vargas, formerly Edith Vargas-Swayze.

In the Years that Followed

Michael Wilcox's confession of having murdered Rudy Grau saved the cost of a trial. Because the District of Columbia does not have a death sentence, he was sentenced to life without parole, and seemed almost happy at the contemplation of again having nothing but time in which to practice his guitar and write his novel. Roberta Wilcox and Gene Hawthorne were at the sentencing. She declined Hawthorne's offer to go out for dinner, knowing of her father's intense dislike of the young reporter. Still, she found him appealing. But romance was the last thing on her agenda. She was about to move to New York to become a correspondent on 20/20.

A jury found Paul Morehouse guilty of the second-degree murder of Jean Kaporis and sentenced him to forty years behind bars. His attorneys successfully made the point during the trial that their client, a good family man with a solid record of service to his community, had acted out of passion, nothing premeditated about the crime. Appeals were planned.

Joe and Georgia Wilcox sold their home in Rockville and moved to New Mexico, where she landed a part-time job in a library, leaving Joe at home to work on his nonfiction book about the events leading to his professional downfall. Georgia read his pages each night and thought they were wonderful. So did his editor at a New York publishing house. The book was scheduled for publication the following year.

Edith Vargas received a promotion, and took her first vacation in a year, visiting New Mexico where she dropped in on the Wilcoxes.

"You look very happy," Edith told the couple when they'd settled on the expansive veranda after dinner, the mountains providing a stunning backdrop.

"All things considered," Joe said, "things are pretty good. I want to run my manuscript past you when it's finished to make sure I've got the police angles and nomenclature right. It's been a while since I've written about them."

"Happy to," she said.

"What ever happened with the McNamara case?" he asked.

"Unsolved," Edith replied. "In the cold file. Do you ever hear from your brother?"

"Yeah, I do as a matter of fact. He writes, and he sent us this tape of him playing the guitar. He's really good."

Vargas smiled and handed the cassette back. "And how about Roberta?"

"We speak with her often," Joe said. "It took a while for her to come to grips with what her old man did, but she has. We're closer than ever."

"She's doing fine," Georgia said. "We watch her on 20/20. I wish she'd meet some nice guy and settle down, though, give me a grandchild or two."

"Too busy, I guess," Edith said.

"How about you, Edith?" Joe asked. "Any new men in your life?"

"I've been seeing a really nice guy, a detective from the Crimes Against Property unit. Hispanic. Puerto Rican."

"And?" Joe and Georgia said in unison.

"Just dating," said the detective, standing and stretching. "This has been lovely. It's great seeing you two again."

"I'm glad you feel that way," Joe said, "after what I pulled."

She playfully punched his arm. "Hey," she said, "we all make mistakes. I dumped mine in divorce court." She took in the veranda and mountains with a sweep of her hand. "And it looks like you're doing a pretty good job of dumping yours."

Georgia walked Edith to her rental car while Joe cleared a final few things from the table.

"I know about you and Joe," Georgia said flatly as the two women stood next to Edith's rental car.

"Oh? Georgia, I—"

"It's okay, Edith. He said he wanted to clear the decks. I'm glad he did. It hurt at first, but I'm beyond that now."

Edith sighed, and nodded. "No secrets, huh? That's always the better way to go. Look, I'm sorry, Georgia. You know it was only an impetuous, one-time thing. He's suffered guilt ever since. I suppose I have, too. I'm glad it's out in the open."

"He offered to give me a divorce," Georgia said. "I told him I didn't want that. And I want you to know that I don't have any ill feelings toward you, Edith. Things happen, that's all. I'm at peace with it, and with you."

Joe joined them at the curb. He kissed Edith on the cheek and said, "Say hello to anyone you run across back in D.C. who might remember me."

"Come back and do it yourself," Edith said. "No need to keep your head buried in the sand, Joe. Some of them do the same thing you did. The only difference is they haven't gotten caught." She smiled at Georgia and said to Joe, "And treat this lady right, my friend. She's a keeper."

"*Buenos noches, amiga*," Joe said as Edith got behind the wheel and started the car.

"Yeah," she said, "*buenos noches.*"

They watched Edith drive away, her taillights disappearing over a crest in the road.

"Feel like some ice cream?" he asked as they returned to the house, his arm draped loosely over her shoulder.

"That sounds nice," she said. "Yes, some ice cream sounds very good."

ABOUT THE AUTHOR

MARGARET TRUMAN has won faithful readers with her works of biography and fiction, particularly her ongoing series of Capital Crimes mysteries. Her novels let us into the corridors of power and privilege, and poverty and pageantry, in the nation's capital. She is the author of many nonfiction books, most recently The President's House, in which she shares some of the secrets and history of the White House, where she once resided. She lives in Manhattan.

ABOUT THE TYPE

This book was set in Electra, a typeface designed for
Linotype by W. A. Dwiggins, the renowned type de-
signer (1880–1956). Electra is a fluid typeface, avoiding the contrasts of thick and thin strokes that are
prevalent in most modern typefaces.

Tru

Truman, Margaret

Murder at the
Washington Trib-
une

DUE DATE   L595   24.95
